THE DRAGONFLY

by

ANNE COX

Anne Cox   2006

Visit us online at www.authorsonline.co.uk

Anne Cox was born in North Staffordshire and educated at Manchester University, North Staffs Polytechnic and the Open University.

She worked for some years as a Supply Teacher and began her writing career with a book called 'Where Is The School, Exactly?', a guide to supply teaching published by The Geographical Association.

Several other books and articles about supply teaching followed. At the same time she began to write short stories for magazines such as The Lady, People's Friend, Ireland's Own, Woman and others. Her articles have been published in Family Tree, Writer's Forum and similar publications. She also occasionally writes poetry.

As well as writing, Anne has been painting for many years and is currently a member of Cheviot Artists, a small group of enthusiasts who meet near her home in rural North Northumberland. She has sold her work at local exhibitions and craft fairs, as well as to private buyers.

Her other interests include reading, natural history, local and family history, travel (especially to Iceland) and cultivating her large country garden.

THE DRAGONFLY

PART ONE: LAURA BENNETT'S STORY 1980

Chapter One

I shall never forget my first love. I think of him often and wonder if he still lingers beside the pool among the dragonflies, searching for his lost happiness.

It was last August, when I was seventeen. I was visiting that diverse group of ladies known collectively as 'The Aunts'. I wasn't sure whose aunts they were, if anyone's. It was the first time that I had visited them alone, but this year my mother was recovering from illness so she persuaded me to go because they had an extensive library and I needed to spend some of my holiday studying for my A-levels.

The Aunts lived in an ugly, rambling house on the edge of a Hampshire village. The five women had tried hard to make it a comfortable home and the garden, at least, was attractive. I spent a great deal of time there. The lawn sloped down to a large lily pond and beyond this a gate led to a rather overgrown path through the fields and up on to the Downs. I used to sit by this pond with my books. From there I could keep an eye on the inhabitants of the house, and they on me.

The pond was busy with dragonflies and full of wriggling tadpoles. One day, soon after I arrived, I was watching these when I sensed someone watching *me*. I looked up and saw a young man on the other side of the water, staring in my direction. I wasn't really frightened as I could hear The Aunts in the workroom off the veranda. But it was a little unnerving. I got up quickly, ready to run - but he was gone. I guessed that he was a walker who had strayed from the footpath. He could have been a potential burglar but he looked too respectable for that. He seemed quiet, serious, and a little old-fashioned. The sight of me had scared him off. For some reason I found myself wondering if he lived locally and if I'd see him again.

Which way had he gone? I gathered up my books, ran back to the house and dashed upstairs. From the windows of Auntie Janet's room I could see over the pond to the fields. I looked along the line of the path in both directions but could see no-one.

'Hello, Laura. What are you looking for?' Auntie Janet bustled in with an armful of freshly ironed clothes and began to put them away.

'There was a man by . . . walking along the path at the back.' Suddenly, I didn't want to say that he'd been in the garden. 'I just wondered where he'd gone. But I can't see him now. I thought he might be a burglar.'

Auntie Janet laughed.

'It's a public footpath. People do walk along there sometimes. Audrey hates it. She thinks it invades our privacy.'

Audrey was the second oldest Aunt and the most formidable. She disapproved of almost everything. She would have had no hesitation in tackling this intruder.

He had a lucky escape, I thought.

The next morning I was working in the library. It was a large, high room opening off the hall. I sat, surrounded by books, at a round table that filled the bay window. I had been there for about an hour, turning pages and taking notes. Something, a slight sound perhaps, or a shadow, made me look up . . . and there he was! He was standing in the middle of the room, looking as I had seen him by the pond. Engrossed in my books, I hadn't heard the door open and it was now closed again, cutting me off.

He didn't move or speak. He wore a light jacket - a sort of tweed - a white shirt and a striped tie. His hands were in the pockets of his black trousers. He looked the sort of person you might meet in a library - studious, dark-rimmed glasses, dark hair - but he had no business in this one. I tried to speak, tried to scream, but no sound came. I don't know how long we stared at one another, but then, somehow, he'd gone.

I dashed for the door, fumbling with the knob. I fully expected him to jump out of hiding and grab me, or be waiting in the hall, but it was empty. I fled down the passage to the conservatory and burst in on The Aunts, who were having their morning coffee.

'He was there! In the library . . . that man!'

'Calm down, my dear,' said Aunt Edna. 'What man are you talking about?'

'The man I saw yesterday, near the pond. He came into the library!'

'Where is he now?'

'I don't know - he disappeared.'

'A man!' exclaimed Aunt Audrey. 'Well, we'd better find him.' She grasped a stout walking stick (there were several about the house) and started off into the hall. 'Come along, Janet, grab something on the way to hit him with. Child, show us where you saw him.'

Reluctantly, I followed them back to the library. Aunt Edna, the oldest Aunt, hobbled behind. The room was empty.

'I was sitting here, with my books,' I explained. 'I looked up and he was there - right where Auntie Janet is. He stood there for a minute and then . . . went.'

'Went where?'

'I don't know. I didn't see. He just seemed to vanish.' I could sense that they didn't entirely believe me. 'He might have hidden. He could have run upstairs.'

'We'll search the house,' said Aunt Audrey, and she and Auntie Janet, who was armed with a candlestick, marched upstairs.

2

'You look pale, my dear. Come and have some coffee. If there's a man in the house, Audrey will find him. And woe betide him when she does.' Aunt Edna led me back into the conservatory and plied me with strong coffee and cheerful conversation until I felt better. Audrey and Janet returned from a fruitless search and we agreed to keep a careful lookout from then on.

After this I avoided the library and studied in the garden and conservatory or on the veranda, where there was plenty of room to escape. I pondered over where the man could have gone but there seemed no answer. Perhaps I had closed my eyes in terror and he'd slipped out of the library door as quietly as he'd entered. Next time, I was determined not to take my eyes off him.

It was two days later when I saw him again. I was reading on the veranda and Auntie Janet was ironing in the workroom that opened off it. Again, something made me look up from my book and there he was by the pool, just like before.

'Auntie Janet, come quickly! Look!'

'Look where?'

'There, by the pond - that man.'

'I can't see anyone. It's shadow, dear.'

'No, no. He's standing there, hands in pockets. You *must* see him!'

'There's nothing, Laura. You're imagining it. Come on, we'll go down and see.'

We hurried down the lawn to the spot where he'd been standing. Of course, he was gone. He just wasn't there any more. Auntie Janet never saw him. We searched the area but found nothing, not even a footprint.

'There, what did I tell you? It was the shadow of this bush,' Auntie Janet said, comfortingly.

'Auntie Janet,' I asked when we got back to the house, 'who lived here before you?' I was very curious about my mysterious visitor and beginning to have some theories.

'Nobody, for years. We bought it from a builder who'd altered it but never lived here.'

'And before that?'

'The school was here. Didn't you know?'

School! 'No. I didn't know anything about that.'

'Oh. Well, it was a boys' school. It closed about 1970. The library is the most unchanged room. It still has some of their books. There's a lot of other stuff, papers and such, up in the attic. We keep meaning to sort it all out.'

'I could do that,' I said. 'It would make a good project for next term - writing about how the school used to be. I need to do something like that.' This was partly true, but I had other motives too.

'You'd like to? Good idea!' Auntie Janet sounded relieved that I had found something useful to take my mind off my fantasies. 'We'll ask Tompkins to help us get the boxes down tomorrow.'

Later, in my room, I tried to make sense of recent events. I had seen the

3

man three times - once at close quarters. Auntie Janet had not seen him - apparently *could* not. Twice he'd been in exactly the same place. He always wore the same clothes and stood in the same way. He was pale and silent. And he vanished. Just disappeared. There was only one thing he could be. He *must* be a ghost.

I was terrified. But then another emotion suddenly took over from fear. I felt a wave of sympathy for this sad, lonely spirit who was lingering here for some reason. Who was he? Was he connected with the school? A little too old for a pupil - what about a young teacher? Yes, that fitted. The library hadn't been changed. Perhaps that was why he appeared there. Would I find some clues among those old school papers? I just couldn't forget that face.

Next day, Tompkins the gardener, Auntie Janet and I went up to the attics to collect the very dusty boxes and carry them down to the conservatory 'where the mess wouldn't matter'. The attics were on a landing at the top of the house. Auntie Janet told me that the builder had been intending to turn them into a self-contained flat but had only got as far as boarding in the banisters and putting a door at the top of the stairs. The Aunts kept this door locked and, having deposited all their unwanted possessions in the attics when they moved in, now rarely visited them.

The two rooms were small, cold, damp and spidery. Between them was a former bathroom filled with rubble, broken porcelain and blocked-off pipes. The boxes relating to the school were in the first room, at the top of the stairs. Thin, dirty curtains that didn't meet in the middle were pulled across the window.

'I expect some of the boys used to sleep up here,' Auntie Janet said. 'I don't envy them.'

'I hope they weren't very tall,' I said. The rooms were in the eaves and the ceilings sloped sharply downwards.

'Perhaps they put the small new boys up here,' Auntie suggested.

I pitied them. A long way from home and having to live in this bleak little room. It must have known a lot of tears.

Armed with a notebook and a selection of empty folders, I set about sorting the archives, hoping for some clues to 'my young man'.

I worked for a while, finding nothing of interest, then, needing a break from the dust, I wandered into the garden. Tompkins was hoeing the flowerbeds - not very vigorously.

'Mr Tompkins?'

'Yes m'dear?'

'Did you work here when it was a school?'

'Oh, no. I was a younger man then. Still working on the farm.'

'So you can't tell me anything about it?'

'I used to see the boys around. Knew some of the teachers by sight. I'd see them in the village, like.'

4

'Was it a nice school?'

'Reckon it was all right as schools go. The lads seemed happy enough, most of 'em.'

'What about the teachers?'

'Well, of course you're always hearing things in a place like this. Village gossip. But there probably wasn't much truth in it. Anyhow, I wouldn't be passing on anything like that to you, m'dear. Your aunties would soon send me packing if they thought I'd been telling you anything rude-like.'

Tompkins turned back to his flowerbed and began hoeing vigorously. He had no intention of continuing that conversation. What was he implying?

I went back to my boxes. For some reason, perhaps it was his appearance, I guessed that my 'ghost' had been at the school around the time it closed. Most of the papers belonged to an earlier time, but at last I found something a little more modern. It was a copy of a letter to parents, dated Autumn 1969. In it, the Principal, a Mr Pearson had written:

We welcome the following new staff - Miss Mary Wagstaff, Mr Michael James, Mr Anthony Dean . . .

Could Michael or Anthony be the young man I was looking for?

One or two other references to these names were jotted hopefully in my notebook, but I was nearing the end of my search before I found anything really significant. It was flat on the bottom of the last-but-one box. An envelope full of photographs!

I studied them excitedly, carefully examining each one. At last - that must be him! He was in a group photo dated May 1970. The staff was seated along the front - all except two young men, one at each end of the back row.

Michael James and Anthony Dean, I wondered? The 'new boys' relegated to the back?

Which was which? My man was on the left. Despite a faint smile he had that sad look that I knew. I gazed at him for a long time. Then I ran out into the garden again.

'Mr Tompkins?'

'Yes, m'dear?'

'I'm sorry to bother you again but . . . I found this photo. I wondered if you could remember any names. It's for my school project, you see.'

'Let me see.' He took the photo from me and peered at it. 'Yes, this one's the Headmaster. Pearson. Called himself by some fancy title . . . '

'Principal.'

'Aye, that's it. This lady's his wife.'

'The young one?'

'Yes. Second wife - much younger than him. About forty, she'd be then. Can cause trouble.' He paused, then quickly changed the subject, pointing to another teacher. 'Games master. Used to run through the village with the boys. He was always in the pub.' Another silence. 'Now, I know this one.' He indicated the young man on the right at the back. 'Young James. Used to be a boy here, then came back to teach. His father was the vicar years ago.'

'And this one?' I asked, pointing to the 'ghost'.

Tompkins stared for a while, seemed about to speak, and eventually said, 'Memory's not so good these days, you know. Can't help you no more, m'dear.' He picked up his hoe and attacked the parched soil with an energy that belied his age - and his usual method of gardening.

I thanked him and returned to the house. I knew now that my man was probably Anthony Dean and that there was something about him that Tompkins thought I shouldn't hear.

I took the photo up to my room that night. Before turning out the light I spent a long time looking at that haunting face in the back row. I thought of some of my school friends, the way they gazed at pictures of their latest boyfriends and silently mocked me for my plainness and lack of 'dates'. Now I had a photo, too, and something more. I pressed the picture to my lips and whispered, 'It's all right. I'm your friend. Whatever you've done.' Then I tucked the photo under my pillow and drifted off to sleep imagining other, happier meetings with 'my' Anthony.

In the morning I completed sorting out papers. From a collection of old exercise books I chose one or two to illustrate my project and packed the rest away. Struggling to put the latter into a folder, I noticed a piece of yellowing newsprint that had slipped out of one and was catching on the edge. I opened it - and was stung!

TRAGEDY AT FIELDHOUSE SCHOOL
Teacher drowns in school pond

'Oh, no! Please, no!' I prayed. But I guessed what was to come. Trembling, I read on.

Staff and pupils at Fieldhouse School, which closed yesterday, were shocked and saddened at the death, on the final day, of teacher Anthony Dean, aged 22. Mr Dean's body was found in a pond in the school grounds. School Principal Mr Eric Pearson said, "We are all deeply sorry. Mr Dean was in his first year as a teacher. Like many young teachers he had faced problems but would have eventually become a well-respected member of staff at another school . . ."

I was still crying when Auntie Janet came in.

'Why Laura, whatever's the matter?'

I showed her the cutting and sobbed out the story.

'I *did* see him. I really did. I kept thinking he must be a ghost - but I hoped he might be one of those ghosts that comes back to a place when they're still alive somewhere else. But he's dead!' Another storm of weeping. Then I said, 'Tompkins knows something but he won't tell me. He says you wouldn't approve. So how will I ever know the story?' I buried my face in my hankie again.

Kindly Auntie Janet took pity on this emotional, over-romantic state. Perhaps she saw, in me, the girl that she had once been.

'I'll go and speak to Tompkins,' she said. 'Perhaps he'll tell me and then *I* can decide what to tell you.'

She got up and went outside. I could see her standing beside Tompkins, who was leaning on his spade and talking more freely, it seemed, than he had to me. I controlled my tears and waited anxiously. Then she returned and poured us some coffee.

'It's a sad story, Laura. But you're a young woman now and anyway you won't rest until you've heard it. It appears that Anthony was very unhappy and lonely here at first. He had a lot of discipline problems, and trouble with the games master, who disliked him for some reason. The Principal was harsh on Anthony, too. The only person who seems to have befriended him was Mrs Pearson, Helen, her name was. She was twenty years younger than her husband. Inevitably, Anthony fell in love with her, and presumably she with him. The games master found out and spread rumours. Pearson decided to close the school. He had bought a villa in Spain for his retirement so he packed his wife off there 'to prepare it' while he wound down the school. The other staff quickly found new posts for the next term but Anthony didn't. Tompkins says that Pearson gave him bad references. Anyway, in the last week of term, Anthony found himself without his love and without a job. He must have decided that life wasn't worth living.'

I sat silent for a moment, then said, 'Why did she go off to Spain if she loved Anthony?'

'Oh, Laura, if only life was so simple! She was forty, he was twenty-two. She wouldn't have expected his attraction to her to last. He had only been working for a year so probably had no money. The school was closing so *she'd* have no job either. She'd be relying on her husband's pension. I expect she thought the best thing for Anthony was to forget her and build a future with a young woman of his own age.'

'But he didn't!' I think I sounded angry.

'No, sadly, he didn't. But it all happened ten years ago. We can't change it now,' she said, gently.

'Do you think I'm silly for caring?'

'Of course not. I hope you'll never stop caring about things, Laura. The world would be a better place if more people did.'

Two days later, I placed my suitcase in the hall and walked slowly down the lawn to the pond. In my hand I carried a posy of flowers from the garden. I had painted a little card and written:

7

To Anthony,
Be at peace. I will never forget you,
Love from your friend

Laura.

I stood at the edge of the pool and dropped the flowers gently on to the water. A breeze caught them and carried them slowly towards the far bank where I had first seen him. A large blue dragonfly, attracted by the white card, landed upon it and hung there for a moment almost as if reading the words, before flying off over the fields. Then I knew that I would never see Anthony again.

I've kept that photo and the faded cutting. I look at it sometimes and wonder why he appeared to me. Did he know that I was soft hearted and would love him? Did I remind him of Helen Pearson? Or did I, however plain and shy, represent the young woman that he *should* have met? Wherever he is now, I hope he knows that I still care.

PART TWO: FIELDHOUSE SCHOOL 1947-1969

Chapter Two

'I suppose this is what you're looking for, Eric. It might do.' Vera Pearson held out the newspaper to her husband and pointed to an advert in the property section.

Eric Pearson put down his mail with a gesture of impatience. Adjusting his gold-rimmed spectacles, he took the proffered paper and read:

SCHOOL FOR SALE
Kingswater, Hampshire
Substantial house on edge of attractive village.
Converted to a school in 1940. Now offered for
sale with all fittings . . .

'Good price . . . h'm, perhaps I ought to go and have a look. I'll make some enquiries today. If it's empty we might be able to move in quickly.'

'Yes. I suppose so.'

Eric glanced over at Vera. Even though she had pointed out the house to him, he sensed the same reluctance that she had shown ever since the scheme was first mentioned. She seemed to be struggling to conceal it - and failing. Couldn't she understand what a great opportunity this was? With his own school he could be a headmaster right away, instead of waiting his turn on the promotion ladder until a generation of others had fallen off the top. She hadn't offered any other suggestions for using the small inheritance from his uncle. But then Vera never did offer any suggestions - about anything.

I expect she just wants to stay in this flat and go on as we are, he thought. But she must know that wasn't him. His career couldn't stand still.

'We might be able to set the school up in time for the autumn term, if we're lucky,' he said.

Eric Pearson *was* lucky. After a brilliant school and university career, he was now Head of English at a well-known private school in London. Everyone, including himself, expected him to become head of such a school by the time he was forty. But Eric was ambitious. He didn't want to wait another three years. Now things had started to settle down after the war he was looking for a suitable property. Eric had a dream - to preside over a small school with an enviable reputation for academic excellence. And Eric's luck held. His Uncle George had died and left him a house, which he had sold quickly. Now he had the money to start making his dream come true.

He read the advert again. Here was somewhere that was already fitted out as a school, and at a price that his funds would cover. More good fortune!

Nice part of the country too: rural but within easy reach of London. It was important for him to keep in touch with the rest of the academic world. He would be able to continue his lecturing and writing, and attend conferences. Essential to keep his name known - his school known . . . yes, it seemed perfect.

'I'll call round to see the agent at lunch time,' he said to Vera as he left for work. He heard her say something like, 'Yes, I know you will,' as he closed the door behind him.

His meeting with the agent, Mr Barnaby, was a pleasant one. They had a lot in common: Eric desperately wanted to buy Fieldhouse and Mr Barnaby desperately wanted to sell it. There were rather a lot of large houses around the country that had been ruined during the war by military or educational establishments. One less on his books would be a great relief.

Fieldhouse School proved to be an Edwardian house on the edge of Kingswater village, with the Downs behind. The accommodation sounded just as Eric had envisaged. The grounds were large enough to build additional classrooms and a field was available for sports.

Eric arranged a visit for the following weekend. He didn't ask Vera to accompany him.

'It's just a preliminary visit,' he told her. 'If it looks suitable, we'll go down together. No point in dragging you down there unnecessarily.'

Vera said nothing. She just smiled thinly and went upstairs to pack his overnight bag.

When he returned from his visit, Eric was obviously hooked.

'It's perfect! Nice location: quite rural, with plenty of large farms around. They're bound to have sons. No other small private schools in the area; I checked. And everything's there, even the crockery and linen. All ready to move in.'

'You've decided, then?' said Vera, flatly.

'Yes . . . well, no, not exactly. You must see it first. But, of course, you'll like it. The area will be new to you but you'll soon make friends. We'll go down next weekend.'

'Are there any infant schools nearby where I could teach? Did you notice? A village school, perhaps?'

Eric was surprised.

'Oh, don't you understand that I'd need you at Fieldhouse - if I buy it, that is? I thought we'd been through all that when Uncle George died. You'll have to be one of my staff.'

'As what?'

'Teacher, matron, whatever's needed. I mean, whatever you like.'

'I don't know how to be a matron. And I'm trained to teach infants. I thought this was going to be a senior school for boys. I can't teach those subjects.'

'Not now. But you'll soon learn. There are courses you could do. And the

10

other staff can advise you. It'll just be a matter of filling in until we can afford . .
. until we can recruit the staff we need. Don't fuss. The important thing is to buy
somewhere and make a start. Let's see . . . I'll need some headed paper . . . '

'Eric!'

'What?' Why was Vera being so difficult?

'You haven't bought it yet. I haven't even seen it!'

'No, no. But I have to think ahead. I'll have to be efficient if I'm going to
compete with existing schools.'

'I'm sure you'll make a great success of it. Like you do of everything.'

Eric watched her as she left the room. She looked older than her thirty-five
years. He wasn't sure that he liked the tone of that last statement. Was it
sarcastic? She wasn't usually openly hostile - just brooded about everything.
He hoped she wasn't going to spoil his moment of triumph.

A few days later Eric and Vera turned in through the gates of Fieldhouse.

'What do you think of it?' he asked as they parked outside the door.

'It's ugly.'

'Oh, the house isn't beautiful. I never said it was. But it's a grand setting,
with the Downs behind, just across the fields. It's far enough away from the
rest of the village to be private. Helps to keep the boys in check. Nice
grounds.'

Mr Barnaby met them at the door and showed them round. Eric oozed
enthusiasm and the agent was confident of a sale. He tried to convince Vera of
the house's merits too, but got little response.

'Mrs Pearson would prefer to stay in London,' explained Eric, trying to
account for his wife's indifference. 'But I know she'll love it here when she's
settled. In any case, she knows it's a wonderful opportunity and when we're
in she'll be too busy to worry about it.'

Vera gave a slight smile. It seemed an effort for her.

'Try not to look such a misery!' Eric muttered under his breath. He had no
idea whether she, or Mr Barnaby, heard.

'The gardens are pretty. Especially the pond,' Vera said. She turned and
walked quickly down the steps from the veranda and across the lawn.

'Vera is fond of gardens,' Eric said. 'We don't have one in London. That's
why I thought it would be nice for her here.'

The two men followed her down to the large pond at the end of the garden,
which backed onto the fields. She was staring into the water. Supposedly
spring, the day was bitterly cold and ice had formed among the reeds at the
edge.

'I expect you get dragonflies here in the summer,' she said.

'What?'

'Dragonflies, Eric. You can teach nature study to the boys.'

'That's only for infants, Vera. My wife is an infant teacher,' he explained,
turning to Barnaby. 'My boys will be too busy with their Latin, and doing

proper science in the lab,' he went on, to both his listeners.

'Poor boys. Well, at least they can bring their books down here in the summer, and sit by the water,' Vera said, in a low voice.

A cold wind blew suddenly across the fields from the Downs. It rustled the dead rushes and sent a bitter chill through the three watchers by the pool.

'There's a tea-shop in the village,' said Mr Barnaby. 'What do you say to calling in there to finish our discussions?'

'Good idea, Barnaby,' Eric said.

'Thank you. I'm very cold,' said Vera.

They walked up to the house. Eric wondered why Vera kept looking over her shoulder. The only thing she seemed to like about the house was that damned pool!

Fieldhouse School opened in August 1947, in time to accept its first pupils at the beginning of the new school year. Eric had used his influence to attract a small number of boys - mostly the sons of friends and contacts in the world of education. Academically, Eric was highly regarded and the reputation of the school grew quickly. He soon had a flood of applications. He took on new staff and arranged for temporary classrooms to be sited in the grounds. Plans for permanent extensions were drawn up, to be implemented if the success of the school continued. It did. He began to achieve the results he had always hoped for. His pupils performed excellently in public examinations and most went on to university or college. The school, and Eric's reputation, flourished.

Unfortunately, the Pearson's marriage did not. Vera's dislike of the house did not diminish with time. Nor did her desire to follow her chosen career as an infant teacher. She was unhappy struggling to teach older boys in subjects she knew little about. Eric felt that she should put more effort into learning secondary school subjects. He criticised her for her failure to control her classes.

'You wouldn't have problems if your teaching was more lively,' he told her. 'You are boring them to death. You need to be more forceful.'

After all, he reasoned, he could teach without difficulty, so why couldn't she?

'I'm not a forceful person, as you know perfectly well,' she replied, becoming angry. 'But I'd probably do a whole lot better without you breathing down my neck!'

'If I didn't sit in on some of your lessons, they'd *all* be a riot,' he replied, with icy calmness.

As Eric revelled in his school's success and his own achievements, Vera continued to wither. Eventually, inevitably, she left.

Eric hardly seemed to notice. She had become something of an embarrassment.

'She never took to it,' he told his friends. 'She was more interested in getting back to her own life in London, rather than supporting me in this school.'

Mere acquaintances murmured sympathetically, but those who knew them both made no comment.

Very soon after their divorce in March 1960, Eric remarried. He was fifty. His bride, Helen, was a divorcee twenty years his junior. He had known her for some time, as she had been secretary at a school where he attended frequent meetings.

For Eric, his marriage marked the high point in the history of Fieldhouse School. He looked forward confidently to fifteen years of continuous success before he retired. He then planned to sell the school as a going concern and move to Spain. He and Helen had already been looking at villas there.

Sadly, it was indeed the high point. For the advent of the new Mrs Pearson marked the beginning of a slow decline in the school's fortunes. It was no-one's fault, although Eric heard rumours that some felt he had become complacent. The main cause was economic. The salaries of the people he relied on to send him their sons - teachers, clergymen, small tradesmen - were falling behind. They could no longer afford school fees, especially when there were good grammar schools within reach.

Pupil numbers began to fall. Eric, taking the rumours to heart, redoubled his efforts to recruit new pupils. But to no avail. By 1969 he wondered whether he would be able to keep the school going for another six years. I'll probably have to sell the school a little earlier, unless things improve, he thought.

'Another two or three years,' he told Helen as they sat in the study preparing paperwork for the new term, 'then I'll sell up and we'll go and live in the villa permanently.' Her face seemed to cloud. 'We can't do it earlier, I'm afraid, my dear,' Eric went on. 'My pension, you know.'

'Oh, it's not that.'

'What is it then? I thought you liked Spain?'

'Yes, I do. But I really don't mind . . . not living there for a while yet.' As she spoke she walked over to the window and stood looking out.

Eric studied her silhouette. She was putting on weight. Losing that slender sophistication which he had thought such an asset to a Headmaster in his position. After nine years of marriage he still didn't understand her, even less recently. She sometimes seemed as silently unhappy as Vera had been. But Vera had been much more transparent. He never really knew what Helen was thinking.

She coped quietly and very efficiently with most of the administrative and secretarial work of the school. She was highly popular with both boys and staff. Yet she seemed somehow 'apart'. In her spare time she walked, read or painted. And, like Vera, she loved the gardens. She, too, was always hanging around that dratted pond. She often took groups of boys down to look at the life there. 'Pond-dipping,' she called it. Eric had several times threatened to have the pool filled in. What if a boy was drowned? He'd be held responsible. But Helen wouldn't hear of it.

13

'They need to learn how to cope with potential danger. And anyway, they love it. They are really interested in the wildlife - and not just the quiet, artistic boys, but some of the big tough boys, too. It's good for them.'

Well, perhaps it does no harm, he thought. But he preferred them to spend their time studying for their A-Levels, or playing games.

Helen was looking in the direction of the pond now. Strange how it seemed to be visible from almost every window in the house.

'Are we going to finish these papers before tea?' he said brusquely. 'We need to start files on these new staff. Here are their papers so far - and three new folders. This one's for Mary Wagstaff - Geography. This one's Michael James - Maths. It doesn't seem like three years since he was a boy here, does it? Where's that other one?' He shuffled the papers around on his desk. 'Oh, yes, Anthony Dean - English. I should be teaching that myself, of course. Don't like to leave it to a new teacher. But I really have time for little other than Upper Sixth lessons these days.'

'I'm sure Mr Dean will be perfectly competent,' said Helen quietly, moving back to her seat. She picked up the papers relating to him and began to read them carefully.

PART THREE: ANTHONY DEAN'S STORY 1969-1970.

Chapter Three

We must be nearly there, he thought. As the car negotiated the narrow lanes, its passenger gazed out of the window, trying to recognise landmarks from his previous visit. In the first week of September, the countryside already had the tinges of autumn. These gave the essential hint of melancholy to that strange mixture of anticipation, nervousness and despondency which affects all involved in education, pupils and teachers alike, at the beginning of the academic year.

For the young man in the back of the taxi, nervousness and despondency were uppermost at present. Anthony Dean, aged twenty-one and just out of university, was about to take up his first teaching post.

As if reading his thoughts, the driver said, 'Just round the corner now, guv.'

Almost immediately Anthony saw the large white sign proclaiming:

FIELDHOUSE SCHOOL
Boys from 13-18 boarded
Principal: E F Pearson MA

Anthony recalled the agitation he had felt when he saw that sign for the first time on his interview day, and with what pleasure he had passed it again on his way out four hours later, knowing he had been successful. Now he wasn't so sure.

The taxi turned in through the heavy wooden gates and pulled up at the bottom of the steps. Anthony opened the door and got out slowly, looking up at the forbidding exterior of the house. It was an ugly building of harsh red brick from the early 1900s. Little thought seemed to have gone into the original design, and subsequent additions had not improved its appearance.

'Rum-looking old place!' said the taxi-driver, echoing Anthony's thoughts again. 'Pretty cold in winter, I'd say. If I were you . . . ' he lowered his voice, ' . . . I wouldn't stay here long. Look for something else. Plenty of jobs around for a clever young man like you.' He placed Anthony's suitcases on the bottom step and pocketed his fare. 'Best of luck, guv. Don't forget what I said!' He got into his car and drove away with a wave.

What's he trying to tell me? Anthony wondered. As he watched the taxi disappear through the gates he suddenly felt very lonely. He had already made a resolution - he must learn to drive as soon as possible.

He picked up his cases and climbed the six stone steps to the front door. The heavy oak door had an impressive brass plate engraved with the name of the school and the Principal. It crossed Anthony's mind that Mr Pearson was excessively proud of his school - and himself. While he was thinking this, the door swung open and a tall thin man of around sixty came out.

'Mr Dean. Welcome to Fieldhouse School. Do come in. Leave your cases. Jones will take them to your room. Jones!' He called out to an unseen person in the interior. 'Take Mr Dean's luggage upstairs, will you? Your trunk has arrived,' he finished, turning back to Anthony. 'Mrs Pearson has organised tea. Come into the study.'

'I'm very pleased to be here, Mr Pearson,' said Anthony, not entirely truthfully. He had been impressed, not to say terrified, by Pearson at his interview. The Principal was a distinguished-looking man of powerful intellect, brisk and efficient. His eyes were a bright, hard blue and the new teacher felt he was being rapidly sized up from behind those gold-rimmed spectacles.

He won't suffer fools gladly, thought Anthony, but he'll probably make me feel like one. You had to start your career somewhere. But that knowing warning from the taxi driver bothered him.

He followed Pearson into the study. It was a dark, heavily furnished room. His stomach turned over as he recalled the grilling he had received from Pearson and his fellow interviewers, two months ago. He had never expected to be appointed after that. The other candidates must have been *really* bad. Was the fact that he had survived a good point in his favour?

'This is my wife, Helen,' Pearson said. 'This is our new English master, Anthony Dean, my dear.'

Mrs Pearson smiled gently and held out her hand.

'It's a nerve-wracking moment, starting a new career,' she said. 'A cup of tea might help. Do sit down, Mr Dean.'

'Thank you,' was all he could manage in reply.

She poured him some tea and handed him a piece of chocolate cake. It was home-made and very good.

'I always bake cake for the new staff. It makes them feel more at home. Especially when it's their first job.' Helen Pearson's eyes were also blue, but they were warm and twinkling. She was laughing, but he didn't feel that she was laughing at him. She seemed understanding.

Pearson didn't join them at the small round table beside the window. Instead he ate and drank standing up, pacing around his enormous desk in the corner facing the door, and resting his cup carefully on the blotter. While doing this he gave out a stream of information and instructions for the beginning of term. Anthony wondered how he would ever remember it all.

Helen Pearson looked at him sympathetically. 'Don't worry, you have a few days yet to learn about everything before the boys arrive,' she said.

'There's a lot to get through before term starts,' Pearson said rather sharply.

A knock came at the door.

'Excuse me a moment.' Pearson left the room and could be heard giving instructions to someone outside.

'You'll soon get used to it,' said Mrs Pearson, pouring Anthony some more tea. Did she mean 'get used to him'? 'It's awful at first,' she went on. 'Please don't be afraid to ask if you need to know anything. I'm usually around somewhere.'

'Thank you,' Anthony mumbled again. What a fool she must think him! He found himself completely tongue-tied.

Mrs Pearson didn't appear surprised or upset by this.

I suppose she's used to shy, awkward boys, he thought ruefully, wishing he could be more sophisticated.

She stood up, smoothing her short blue skirt. A little longer than the young women his age were wearing these days, but still fashionable. She had a nice figure, he thought. Not too thin. She must be about thirty-five - much younger than Pearson. Was she his second wife? Her white blouse set off the blue beads that matched the skirt - and her eyes. Anthony felt comfortable with her, despite his complete inability to make sensible conversation.

'You'll want to go to your room and unpack,' she said. 'I'll show you upstairs. You'll need time to adjust, I'm sure. Don't worry about trying to remember everything that he . . . ' she checked herself ' . . . everything at once.'

She led the way into the hall. Pearson was still talking to a man in a brown overall, presumably Jones.

'I'm showing Mr Dean to his room now,' Mrs Pearson told her husband. 'He needs to unpack and get organised.'

'Yes, of course. Sorry I was called away. When you're ready, feel free to wander around, look at the grounds. Of course, we sent you a lot of information through the post, didn't we? I expect you'll want to study that again now you're on the spot. There's some more on the table in your room. We've arranged dinner at seven. Mr James should be here by then.'

'Mr James is the new maths master,' Mrs Pearson explained to Anthony as he followed her up two flights of stairs to a small room in the attic. He had learned at his interview that most of the staff and some older boys had accommodation in the village. Only a handful of teachers had rooms in the school. The others only 'slept in' when they were on duty. The ones who lived in, mainly the young teachers, were always on call. New teachers were expected to live in for a year.

The room into which Helen Pearson showed him was bare and chilly. Being part of the attic, it had sloping ceilings, which gave little room for cupboards and meant that Anthony could only stand upright in the central part.

'Oh, dear, you're rather tall for this room,' she laughed. 'Perhaps we should only recruit short new staff. The other room is the same, but I recall that Michael James is not as tall as you.'

Anthony anticipated banging his head frequently. He made another resolution - to look for a room or flat locally for next year.

'I'll leave you to it. I'm sure you need time to yourself. Don't forget to ask for anything you need. Mr Jones, the porter, is brilliant. He'll always help you. You'll soon settle in.'

With a last, sympathetic smile, Mrs Pearson went out and closed the door quietly.

Anthony stood for a few moments without moving. The room seemed even bleaker and colder now she'd gone. He wondered what the other new staff would be like. One was a middle-aged geography mistress, he'd been told. She'd be used to teaching. Still, she might feel out of things at first, especially if she hadn't taught in a boys' school before. Or she might be able to advise him.

The other newcomer was newly-qualified, like himself. Michael James, wasn't it? He'd feel the same way, rather lost and lonely. And he'd be in the other attic room across the landing. Anthony hoped they'd become friends. At least for the first week or so they could help each other along.

He began to unpack, listening for the sound of footsteps that would announce the arrival of his colleague. He emptied the suitcase containing the essentials for the first week - clothes, toiletries, and books. Would he have any time for reading, he wondered?

He opened his briefcase, struggling with the stiff new lock. He had a ghastly vision of himself struggling to open it in front of a class of grinning boys. How he wished he'd brought his old one. This shiny leather seemed to mark him out as a greenhorn. He drew out papers and files and added them to the pile already on the table in the centre of the room. Pearson had been right. There *was* plenty more for him to look at.

Anthony had spent the two months since his interview preparing lessons. Were they what was required? It was just his luck that the Principal was an English scholar. Pearson would be looking for excellence, even from a completely inexperienced teacher. He visualised spending many late nights sitting at this table, altering what he had already prepared and frantically writing new lesson plans for the next day.

'That looks better!' he said to himself, as he set out some books and other belongings.

The sloping ceilings caused problems. There was a narrow wardrobe on the end wall opposite the window - the only place where a tall piece of furniture could fit. All his clothes had to be squashed into it. The small cupboard, a chest of drawers and a low bookcase had to hold everything else.

He tried the lights. The centre light hung over the table. It had a yellowish parchment shade. It didn't give out much light. He peered closely at the bulb. 40 watt! Will I be allowed to replace it, he wondered?

The lamp, on a tiny table squeezed between the wardrobe and the narrow bed, also had a 40w bulb. Anthony made a third resolution - to buy some light bulbs and a good torch. He could always take out the stronger bulbs during the day and replace them with the originals. But one day he was bound to forget . . .

He heard voices in the hall below. The pleasant tones of Mrs Pearson floated up. Anthony stopped to listen. This must be Mr James arriving. As their footsteps approached he caught snatches of their conversation.

'Relegated to the attic, I'm afraid, Michael - Mr James, I suppose I must call you now. Still, it will be better than your dormitory days.'

'Yes, at least I shouldn't get my sheets sewn together, and other unmentionable horrors,' replied the deeper voice. 'I always wondered what these rooms were like up here.' The voice had a trace of the local accent.

'Mr Dean is already here. You'll meet at dinner, if not before,' Helen Pearson said as they passed Anthony's door.

From the room across the landing came the sound of laughter and cheerful banter. No doubt Mr James was commenting on the comforts of his accommodation, but Anthony could not pick up what was being said. Then he heard Mrs Pearson walking back across the landing.

'The routine hasn't changed much while you've been away. Just remember you're a master, not a pupil now,' she called brightly as she descended the stairs. "They've got to do what *you* say, not the other way round.'

Anthony felt a chill wave of loneliness spread over him. Michael James was an Old Boy! He'd know all about the school, the staff, even some of the pupils. He was new to teaching, but he wouldn't have the problems that Anthony could foresee for himself. His hopes of befriending a fellow-sufferer evaporated as Helen Pearson's footsteps died away.

In a few moments he heard music filtering from across the landing. Mr James had not only brought his radio; he had dared to put it on! Anthony had placed his on top of the cupboard, wondering whether he would ever be able to play it. Now the sound of pulsing rhythms in the other room merely emphasised his isolation.

He walked over to the small sash window and peered out. Despite the sunny late summer afternoon, a cold wind was blowing. He could feel it through the gaps in the old, ill-fitting window. It made the room, and him, even colder. These thin curtains won't keep the room warm, he thought. He tried drawing them. As he expected, they didn't quite meet. Oh well, he could always drape a blanket over the window in really bad weather, and with some heating...

Heating! When he looked around, he couldn't see any. He thought he had noticed a radiator on the landing, but there wasn't one in the room. Surely there must be something? He knelt on the hard lino and lifted the edge of the faded green bedspread. Ah! He dragged out an old electric fire. It had one bar and the flex was worn. Did it work? He looked around for a socket. There was one beside the bed where the lamp was plugged in but he couldn't find another. Heat *or* light - not both. If it was this cold up here in early September, how was he going to survive the winter?

The one thing he liked about the room was the view. It looked out over the garden towards the fields and Downs. Beyond the sweep of lawn he could see a lily pond, partly surrounded by shrubs. A hedge bounded the garden at this point and in the stubble fields on the other side pheasants were searching for grain. In one direction the roofs of the village were visible and to his right was the long ridge of hills, crowned with a group of trees. The countryside looked appealing. At least there would be good walks, if he ever had the time.

Anthony checked his watch. Another hour to go to the dreaded Dinner.

'When you're ready, wander around - look at the grounds,' Pearson had said. Was that an order? Should he be seen straight away to be learning the layout of the school? He felt like a break from unpacking, but felt a little nervous about venturing from the cold cocoon of this room.

He opened the door slowly. The beat still thumped from behind his colleague's door. Anthony left quietly, taking a quick look at the old-fashioned bathroom next door. Predictably, this was also small and cold. He wondered if there would be any hot water. Personal hygiene was obviously going to be a spartan affair. He looked back to the comparative luxury of his Hall of Residence at university with regret. There, at least, he'd had central heating and his own washbasin.

This was going to be a very long year!

Anthony saw no-one as he descended two flights of stairs and slipped into the garden through the open front door. He walked across the wide expanse of lawn feeling very conspicuous. Was Pearson watching him from somewhere? Sizing him up? What about Mrs Pearson? She seemed very friendly but did she report everything to her husband? Who's on the side of a new young teacher, he wondered? Probably no-one.

Reaching the edge of the pond, he momentarily forgot his concerns. The reeds and lilies were alive with dragonflies. He watched fascinated as they criss-crossed his reflection in the dark water. He squatted down to have a closer look. Some of them were a brilliant blue.

I must bring my camera down here, he thought.

Would he be able to capture them on film? They never seemed to settle near him, only out of reach on the water-lily leaves in the middle of the pond.

Perhaps the school had a Camera Club. He imagined himself helping enthusiastic boys to photograph these beautiful insects, and then to develop the prints. They could hold an exhibition. Mr and Mrs Pearson would be full of praise for his work. He could present her ... them ... with one of his prints.

Dreaming of glory, he walked round the pond and stopped to look over the gate, which led into the fields. He longed to open it, to walk along the footpath that ran parallel with the hedge and then make for the Downs. How tempting that clump of trees looked! But it would have to wait. It was time to go in and prepare to face his first Dinner as a master at Fieldhouse School.

A tap at the door made Anthony jump and interrupted the careful knotting of his tie.

'Come in!'

A cheerful face topped with a head of light, wavy hair, appeared round the door.

'Hello. I'm Michael James - your new neighbour. Welcome to Fieldhouse.' He stepped into the room and held out his hand. 'You must be Anthony Dean.' Anthony was relieved to see that Michael was dressed in a sports jacket, not a suit.

'Pleased to meet you. Come on in. I'm nearly ready.'

Anthony put on his jacket and gave his dark hair a final comb.

'Funny, being back. I was at school here, you know,' said Michael.

'Yes, I'd heard.' Anthony tried to get an impression of his new colleague without appearing to stare. Crinkles around Michael's eyes showed a propensity for laughter. He was smiling now.

'Rooms are a bit bleak, aren't they? Not many home-comforts here.'

'No. This one's very chilly. And not high enough for me.'

'Hard luck, being that tall,' Michael grinned. He was several inches shorter and of athletic build. Anthony was sure he'd be good at sport. In fact, he looked as though he'd be competent and confident at anything.

'You'll already know all the ropes,' Anthony said, secretly hoping that he wouldn't.

'Most of them. Still, it'll be a bit different now. You're for English, aren't you? Great reader, I see.' Michael glanced at the already-full bookcase.

'Have to be. Don't know whether there'll be much time for my own reading though.'

'Pearson will keep you busy - oh yes!' Michael said.

'What's he like?'

'Terrifying, if you're a pupil. Probably the same if you're a teacher. We're about to find out. We'd better go down.'

He led the way downstairs. Dinner was in the Pearsons' small flat, as there were only five of them. The fifth, the new geography mistress, came forward to greet them.

'Hello, I'm Mary Wagstaff. Don't look so worried.' As she said this, she looked up at Anthony. It was a long way up. Mary was short and stocky. 'You'll soon settle down. This is a good school in a lovely area. We're very lucky. One day I'll tell you about some others I've been in!'

Pearson handed out sherry. Her eyes twinkling over her glass, Mary said to the two young men, 'Here's to us in our new job. Good luck.'

Helen Pearson joined them. Anthony thought she looked very attractive in a plain green dress which suited her reddish-brown hair, and which made her eyes look green rather than blue.

'You've all met, I see. I hope you've managed to do some unpacking.' She turned to Anthony. 'Did you like our pond?'

So she *was* watching! 'Yes, very much,' he answered. 'I've never seen so many dragonflies.'

'Wonderful aren't they?' She spoke with real enthusiasm. 'I watch them whenever I can. You *must* go and look at the pond,' she went on, turning to Mary, 'it's my pride and joy.'

21

They sat down at the table, Anthony opposite Mrs Pearson. He felt her eyes on him. He knew he was gauche and unused to formal social occasions, and would rapidly become tongue-tied, as he had that afternoon. I hope I'm not blushing, he thought. Would they notice in the subdued light?

Fortunately the excellent food and a generous supply of wine made the meal less of an ordeal than any of the three new staff had expected. Michael enlivened the conversation with reminiscences of his schooldays.

'My father used to be vicar here,' he told Anthony, 'so I was expected to behave. But I didn't.'

In between Michael's amusing stories, Pearson gave out facts and figures about the school in his clipped, precise way. Then Mary started to ask about the opportunities for field trips in the locality.

'Fieldwork is so important - but if you're the only geographer you need help from other staff. You can't do it otherwise. Safety, you know,' she said.

'We always encourage staff to help each other when they have free periods,' said Pearson. 'Those staff, of course, who have less responsibilities … '

'I'd love to help - if I'm free,' Anthony broke in. He immediately wished he hadn't spoken. Pearson said nothing and Anthony felt very uncomfortable. The new English master was presumably not expected to be 'free' at any time.

Helen Pearson looked animated for the first time since they sat down. She seemed to be responding to the expression on her husband's face, as though it was a challenge. Smiling across at Anthony, she said, 'Yes, go whenever you can. The countryside is lovely. And Miss Wagstaff will need a real enthusiast.'

'Indeed I will. Nothing worse than teachers who hate what they're doing. I can't wait to explore out there. I don't know the area at all but I've done some reading.'

Anthony was grateful to them for rescuing him. He hoped that he *would* be able to help Mary with her excursions. He couldn't really imagine her striding up hills. She wasn't the right shape. He smiled to himself as he visualised her leading a group of rugby-playing sixth-formers through the countryside. They would all tower over that diminutive, plump figure. I bet she won't stand any nonsense, though, he thought.

He let the others do most of the talking for the rest of the meal, listening carefully in the hope of picking up useful information. He wished he were not the only real 'new boy'. The only other people in the school who would be feeling as bad as he did would be aged about thirteen! Why did everyone else always seem so confident?

'I expect you'll all want to go to bed early,' Mrs Pearson said as they finished their coffee. 'You must be tired and your heads are probably spinning. So we won't keep you.' She glanced at Pearson, who didn't look pleased, but said nothing. 'I'm sorry your cold little rooms aren't brilliant - but I'm sure you'll soon make them homely.' Anthony thought Pearson looked even more displeased at this comment. Any implied criticism of his school was obviously regarded as treachery.

She rose from the table, smoothing her dress with that gesture that Anthony had noticed before. She smiled at him – was it a smile of encouragement? Thank you for trying to help me, he thought. She must have known that he, in particular, would not want to prolong the evening.

Michael, on the other hand, seemed happy to sit for hours telling his funny stories, which even made Pearson laugh. But then, they were mostly about his schooldays when justice, in the form of Pearson or his staff, had eventually triumphed.

As they were leaving, Pearson said, 'I'll see you all in my study at nine o'clock in the morning. I'll give you some more information then.'

Yet more information! Mrs Pearson gave Anthony a look he couldn't quite interpret. Was it amusement? Sympathy? Resignation? Even with his lack of experience of the world he had already come to the conclusion that the Pearsons were not blissfully happy. This boded ill, he felt. What sort of headmaster was Pearson going to be when even his wife didn't like him?

Chapter Four

Anthony spent a restless night. Two thin blankets and a well-worn bedspread failed to keep out the cold of his attic. He decided that one of his first purchases, when he could get to town, would be a new tracksuit. Then he could wear his old one over his pyjamas for sleeping in. He would probably also need more sweaters as the winter drew on.

His bed was narrow, hard and too short for him. His feet hung over the end, exposed to the icy air of the room. Warm socks would also have to go on the shopping list. And blankets. And another pillow - only one thin one was provided. What about a hot water bottle? His salary wasn't going to go far at this rate!

Have I made a terrible mistake coming here, he asked himself? At the time it seemed the answer to some of his problems. The recent death of his grandmother had left him effectively without a base, except for some storage space at his great-aunt's. He had thought that a boarding school with 'all found' would provide accommodation and a 'home' where he could stay during the holidays if necessary. Now, in the middle of that long, cold night it did not seem to be providing him with anything remotely like a home. Would his salary next year be enough to find a place of his own? Would he still have a job by then? He groaned once more and pulled the inadequate bedclothes tighter round him. He tried plumping up the single pillow, folding it in half, ramming his sweater under it - all to no avail. Eventually he gave up with the pillow, pulled the sweater over his pyjamas and curled his long limbs up as tightly as he could. Although the window was closed, a draught fluttered the curtains and chilled him even more. Exhausted but wide-awake, he miserably waited for dawn.

'Try for a day school,' his friend Peter had said when they were in their final year at university. 'At least if you don't like it you can escape in the evenings.'

But Peter had a fiancée. They'd make a home together wherever they worked. Anthony hadn't worried about wanting to get away from a school, only of finding somewhere he could stay all the time. Why hadn't he considered all the pros and cons?

It was too late now. He was here. And he'd have to appear in Pearson's study in the morning looking and feeling tired and drained instead of bright, alert and ready to tackle anything.

'Another black mark to go with the ones I've acquired already,' he mumbled into the pillow.

He tossed and turned as long as he could bear it and then got up. It was five o'clock. He crept onto the landing and into the icy-cold bathroom. The plumbing was ancient and very noisy and he was afraid that he'd woken the whole house. There was no hot water. He turned on the tap, which made an awful groaning sound, and splashed his face with cold water, gasping at the shock.

When he returned to his room he gingerly put on the electric fire. He expected a loud explosion, or a sheet of flame, but it merely glowed a grudging red. The smell as the heat burnt off months of accumulated dust was appalling. At least it worked. He was able to warm his frozen fingers and felt a glow come into his cheeks as he crouched as near to that one evil-smelling bar as possible. His salary was going to have to be even more elastic. An electric fire and a kettle were added to the shopping list. He didn't choose to risk his life with this battered heater and worn flex any longer than absolutely necessary. If he'd had a kettle he could make himself coffee - bliss! At least he'd be able to take all these purchases away with him on the day when he found himself a place to live away from the school.

Trying not to think about that hot coffee, Anthony dressed quickly and pushed back the flimsy curtains. Much to his surprise, he found that he was not the only early riser. In the dawn light he saw Helen Pearson walking across the lawn.

What was she doing about so early, he wondered? He watched as she picked her way over the dew-wet grass and then stopped by the pool.

'Too early for dragonflies!' he said aloud.

She was wearing black trousers and a green anorak. She pulled the latter tightly around her as she stood there. Anthony was not the only one who was cold. She seemed very fond of the garden - she must be, to be out at this hour.

Anthony was puzzled by her. Although he'd had little experience of them, she didn't fit his idea of a headmaster's wife. She seemed almost as out of place as he himself.

She walked around the pond and gazed over the gate towards the fields and Downs, just as Anthony had done the day before. For a moment she hesitated, as if deciding whether to go out or not. Then she turned and began carefully retracing her steps over the moist lawn. In the improving light he could see that she wasn't wearing any shoes.

He longed to call out, to go down to her, to talk. Perhaps she would offer him coffee... But he didn't dare. She wouldn't expect anyone to be about yet. And she'd be angry if she thought he'd been watching her.

I don't suppose she has much time to herself, he thought. He moved away from the window slightly in case she looked up as she neared the house. She didn't . . . and somehow he wished she had.

He turned to his table, loaded with books and papers. At least his early rising would enable him to study some more of this before the meeting with Pearson after breakfast. He would never be able to remember it all. And now he was beginning to feel really tired. If he could just get back into bed in his clothes he was sure he could sleep - and of course would miss that nine o'clock meeting! With a deep sigh he pulled out the rickety chair and sat down in front of his piles of work.

Breakfast was at eight. It was a long wait for a tired, hungry, cold young man. He couldn't concentrate on the masses of paperwork - syllabuses, exam papers, tests, record sheets . . . several times he felt himself nodding over the table, but the squeaking, wobbly chair jerked him awake. Eventually the time came to go downstairs. With relief he stood up, tidied himself and left the room.

'Morning. Sleep well?' Michael James was coming out of his room. Anthony was pleased. At least he wouldn't have to go into breakfast on his own.

'No, not very well. Did you?'

'Oh, not bad, not bad. Pretty cold though. Have you found your heater?'

'Yes. Lethal thing! Does give out some heat - but not enough.'

'You have to be tough to survive here,' said Michael. 'I always wondered why the new members of staff were so miserable. I used to think it was the awful way we boys treated them. Now I know it was also the conditions they lived in.'

More bad news, thought Anthony.

They went downstairs to the dining-room.

'It's in the new block,' explained Michael. 'A bit spartan.'

He was right. A modern block of buildings had been added to the side of the original house in the school's heyday, about ten years before. Built in the modern, flat-roofed style, it did nothing to improve the appearance of the house. It consisted of a dining room, several classrooms and a gym/assembly hall. On the floor above were dormitories.

'There's a tiny room up there for the master on duty,' Michael told him, pointing up the stairs. 'You'll get to know it well!'

'Is it warm?'

'No, not if it's anything like the dorms.'

The dining room, which they entered through swing doors, was indeed spartan. It looked particularly so this morning, with one corner of a table set for three.

'Good morning to you! Sleep well?'

Mary Wagstaff was walking over from the serving hatch, where one grumpy cook was serving breakfast - and making no secret of the fact that she objected to having to come in and do so just for three. Mary put down her tin tray with a grin.

'Breakfast looks OK - if you don't expect it served with a smile.' She nodded towards the hatch where the broad white back of the cook could be seen as she grumbled into her frying pans.

'Let's go and get it! I'm starving,' said Michael. 'Morning, Mrs Higginbottom, remember me?'

Mrs Higginbottom turned round slowly. She did not expect new staff to be jolly, especially on their first morning. She pushed up her health service glasses and peered closely at Michael.

'Oh, no! It's not young James?'

'Afraid so. Only you'd better call me Mr James from now on, as I'm elevated to the status of master. I've put my old ways behind me and taken up a respectable profession.'

'What, you? Respectable? Never! You're the bane of respectable people. You and your cronies!'

'Don't worry, I haven't brought any of them with me! We're just three nervous new teachers - nothing for you to worry about at all. You've met Miss Wagstaff. This is Mr Dean. And he's starving!'

'Pleased to meet you. Yes, I am starving. And nervous. And quite harmless!'

Anthony tried to pick up Michael's jocular mood. He didn't feel he'd succeeded. But he must have struck a chord of sympathy in Mrs Higginbottom because she gave him what seemed to be an extra large helping.

'Mind the plate, it's hot. There's more if you want it . . . ' She peered closely at Anthony as she passed him the plate. 'You're too thin. You look a lot like my grandson. He's going to college in a fortnight. I dare say he'll feel the same.'

The hot breakfast and the banter of his colleagues made Anthony feel almost human again. A second helping, plenty of toast and several cups of hot coffee completed the process. Or did it? When they rose from the table, Mary said, 'All ready to face Mr Pearson, then?' and Anthony found he still had a pit in his stomach, despite that large breakfast.

'Meet you both in the hall in ten minutes,' Mary went on, 'then we can all go in together.'

'United we stand!' said Michael, banging his fist on the table.

Mrs Higginbottom gave him a look that said plainly, 'Some things never change!'

'Hard luck, having to share a classroom with Pearson,' said Michael in a low voice as they emerged from the study nearly two hours later.

'I think it's more a case of him condescending to share a small part of it with me,' Anthony replied as they climbed the stairs clutching yet more books and papers.

Mary was sympathetic.

'Look at it this way. Pearson is an English scholar and he appointed you. So he must think you're good,' she said encouragingly.

Unless he doesn't want any opposition, Anthony thought. But he said nothing.

'Come and have coffee. I brought a kettle,' Mary said. 'My room's just here. She opened the door to a small room at the end of the first floor landing, beyond the studies for senior boys.

'I suppose I'm here to keep an eye on them. I'll scream up the attic stairs if I need help.'

27

'I think we're more likely to need help from you,' Anthony said. 'Well, I am anyway.'

She laughed. 'You'll be OK after the first . . . '

' . . . ten years? Or is it twenty?' Michael broke in.

'Wait and see.'

Mary boiled her kettle and handed round mugs of coffee.

'This is what I want to get - a kettle. As soon as possible. Did you bring one, Michael?' Anthony asked.

'No, but I wish I had. I'm making a list of things to send home for. Mum will say it's worse than when I was a schoolboy.'

'I wonder if I'll get one in the village?'

'You might. Powell's sell everything.'

As soon as he had sorted out the papers from the morning's meeting, Anthony decided to take a break and go into the village. Kingswater had one long main street with a mixture of brick cottages, Georgian town houses and more modern buildings. A small, dark shop with the name 'Powell' over the door eventually caught his eye.

'Electric kettle? No, sorry. You'll have to go into town for that. I've only got these little gas kettles.'

'I haven't got anything to boil it on, in my room.'

'Are you at the school? A new teacher?'

'Yes.'

'So you'll want to make your own coffee and such, make it more like home?'

'That's it.'

'Well, I've got one of these little camping stoves. And the gas cylinders. You could heat all sorts on that . . . water, soup, beans . . . have a midnight feast of your own!'

'Brilliant idea! Hot soup sounds just what I need.'

Feeling much more cheerful, Anthony returned to school clutching his purchases. He went up to his room and fixed up his camping stove. Then he put his small kettle on to boil and found a place in his overcrowded cupboard for a lightweight saucepan and frying pan, crockery and cutlery, a tin tray and various supplies from the grocer's. He placed his hot-water bottle beneath his pillow. When the coffee was ready he raised his mug. 'Here's to me in my new job. And new home,' he said.

That night, Anthony was reminded of his old granny as he filled his hot-water bottle. How she'd laugh if she could see him now. He longed to be able to tell her, tell anyone, about his experiences at Fieldhouse so far. He still felt the pain of her loss. Nothing would replace her - unless he married one day. But he never had much luck with girls. He preferred not to think too much about the shy stutterings and clumsy attempts at conversation that resulted when he met young women to whom he was attracted. Not to speak of the time a fellow-student accused him publicly of standing her up - because they'd been waiting in different places. He was never sure whose fault it was, but he got the blame - and the ridicule.

He was too tired to worry much about it tonight, and anyway there were not many girls at Fieldhouse. In fact there were none as far as he knew. The staff list didn't promise a great social life. Mary was over thirty years his senior. There was a Miss Baines who taught Latin but he thought Pearson had said she was near retirement. The school had a matron, cooks and cleaners - and Mrs Pearson.

He hadn't seen much of her today, since early morning. She hadn't been at the first meeting and the staff had lunched in the dining room again. After lunch they had been given time to organise their classrooms. In Anthony's case this consisted of putting some of his resources into a section of cupboard in the English room. Pearson controlled the rest of the space.

He wondered if he'd be able to put anything on the walls, and enjoyed the thought of the Principal gazing at his displays for a large portion of the day. He hoped to pick up some advice from the other members of staff, due to arrive the next day.

The three new staff had taken afternoon tea with the Pearsons. As usual, Mr Pearson was restless and left to deal with other matters before the others had finished. A palpable sense of relief descended on the room. Mary told some horror stories of her previous schools and Mrs Pearson assured them, none too convincingly, that things like that never happened at Fieldhouse.

Anthony had expressed his wish to learn to drive.

'There's a man in the village who gives lessons. He's taught several new staff over the years,' said Mrs Pearson.

'When you've had a few lessons, I'll take you out in my Mini,' offered Mary.

'Thanks. You may have to cut a hole in the roof for my head though!'

'I'd be pleased to take you out too,' Mrs Pearson said. 'I know how difficult it is to get enough practice. Time will be the problem for all of us, though. A boarding school never stops.'

Anthony was beginning to see how right she was. He had been busy all day and the pupils hadn't arrived yet! The previous sleepless night had really caught up with him now. He made a cup of hot chocolate and took it to bed along with his hot-water bottle and a detective novel - something completely different from the school texts he'd been studying for hours. The camp stove seemed to have warmed the room a little. Or perhaps Anthony was feeling less strange and nervous now. Whatever the reason, he suddenly felt more relaxed than he had for some time. Perhaps eventually he would even come to like Fieldhouse School.

The ringing of his alarm woke Anthony the next morning. He was pleased to have had such a good sleep but faintly disappointed not to have been up early enough to see whether Helen Pearson walked around every morning at dawn. This time when he drew the curtains the garden was empty. But was that a trace of footsteps across the lawn? The marks did seem to lead down to the pond. If he wasn't too tired, he'd try to get up earlier tomorrow.

Today the other members of staff were due to arrive. Anthony wasn't sure whether he was looking forward to that or not. At the moment it was all still rather unreal - he almost felt he could leave if he wanted to. And he was enjoying the company of his two cheerful and amusing colleagues. He was a teacher, but not actually teaching. None of the ghastly things he'd been told about were happening to him - at the moment. All that was about to change, he feared. Before it did, he wanted to try and snatch an opportunity to walk on to the Downs. Perhaps today's schedule would provide one.

He should, he supposed, have spent the whole morning preparing lessons. He started off well enough. After breakfast (Mrs Higginbottom was just as sour, but she gave him another large helping. Two, in fact) he went into the Library.

This was destined to become his favourite part of the house. Not that it had much competition, but it *was* a pleasant room. It was off the hall, across from Pearson's study and private apartments. It was high and spacious, lined with bookshelves, of course. At one end was a round table set into a bay window. This table had a notice on it, which read,

Strictly reserved for staff use

He wondered what punishment would be meted out to any boy who dared to sit there. It almost made him afraid to sit there himself. The rest of the room was filled with plain, scuffed tables and chairs for the pupils. The centre of the long wall facing the door held a large stone fireplace. Two very well-worn armchairs stood in front of it. The grate was concealed behind a faded firescreen but two pots of bronze chrysanthemums had been placed in front of this. A smaller pot stood on the curved windowsill.

Mrs Pearson must have put the flowers there, he thought. He wondered if she had grown them herself. He'd noticed a small greenhouse round the back. There must be ground staff, of course. Apart from the large area of garden there was a playing field beside the school, which looked very well-kept. Anthony expected to become very familiar with it. Pearson had suggested that he might like to 'volunteer' to help with games. He could hardly refuse. He couldn't understand why Michael was not asked as he was obviously a sportsman. No doubt Pearson had something else in mind for him.

'Perhaps he thinks *I* need toughening up,' Anthony had said to Mary.

She just laughed. 'You'd better get into training by running up the hills every morning.'

Now the pull of those hills became too strong to resist. After a couple of hours' work he took his books up to his room and slipped quietly out of the house, fortunately meeting no-one.

He stopped for a few moments to glance at the pond where the dragonflies were beginning their dance as the sun grew warmer. Then he went through the white gate, closed it behind him and, for a while at least, was free.

He wanted to run, to dance like the dragonflies, to celebrate the beauty of the morning and nature and his release from what was beginning to seem like prison. But he dared not. He could still be seen from the house. He walked quickly beside the hedge which ran along the boundary of Fieldhouse, to where the path turned upwards to the Downs. Here walkers became hidden from watchers in the school by the rambling hedge that marked the lower part of this track. It was a delightful contrast to the clipped privet that surrounded the school grounds. At this season it was spangled with haws, rosehips and blackberries, and clad with the delicate wisps of old man's beard. Goldfinches fed on the seedheads of thistles and teasels, and a robin, finding his voice again after the moult, practised his song above Anthony's head.

Anthony didn't feel lonely here, although he was the only person for miles around, it seemed. Funny, he thought, how you never feel lonely out in the wild. He suspected that he was going to feel very lonely indeed when he had to face his first class on Monday morning. Today was Friday. His time was running out.

'Better make the best of it. I wish I were you, though,' he said to the robin, which was following him up the lane, fluttering from perch to perch and treating him to an occasional burst of song.

He didn't think he should be away from school too long, so he stopped at the point where the hedge petered out and the path curved over the open downland, a white pointer to the clump of trees on the crest. Skylarks filled the air with music somewhere above him. From here he could look down over the school to the village and the surrounding farmland. In the distance a farmer was gathering in the last of the harvest.

At his feet, one late poppy blew in the soft breeze, waving defiance at the coming winter. He had a sudden urge to pick it and give it to Helen Pearson. He resisted. She'd think him extremely silly - and what on earth would Pearson think? Better to leave it here, he said to himself. Then it will set seed and there'll be poppies here again next year.

'Ah, Mr Dean. You've been out!'
Pearson was waiting in the hall as Anthony walked through the door. He didn't sound pleased.
'Yes, I just took a breath of fresh air.'
'Well, now you're back, please come into my study. I've been waiting . . . ' he paused, '. . . waiting to give you some details of pupils in the groups you'll be teaching. There are one or two things you need to know about some of the boys. Strictly private, of course.'
Pearson must have been looking for him. He was expected to be in school, not gallivanting round the countryside. Another black mark - just when he thought that life was improving.
When he came out of the study a little later on, he felt more depressed than

ever. The enjoyment brought on by a warmer night's sleep and the glories of an early autumn day outdoors had been almost completely wiped out.

It seemed that his classes contained all the most difficult pupils in the school. Had he detected a gleam in those fierce blue eyes of Pearson's as he spoke about them?

Now he really wished that he'd trained before taking a post, instead of coming straight from university. I suppose I'll manage somehow, he thought. Everyone else does. But somehow he did not find this thought comforting. How could people like Mary and Michael be so cheerful?

'Make it up as you go along!' Mary said at lunchtime. 'That's the way most teachers get by, at least some of the time. Beginning of term especially.'

The trouble was, he didn't think he knew enough to *make* up. Back in his room he turned the books and papers over and over. But it was no good. His mind had gone completely blank.

A knock on his door in mid-afternoon provided a much-needed break. Mary's round, smiling face appeared.

'Would you like afternoon tea? I've put the kettle on. Come down when you're ready.'

'Thanks. I could do with a rest. I'll be down shortly.'

He heard her knock at Michael's door but she got no reply. Had *he* sneaked out now? Anthony finished the paragraph he was writing and put down his pen with a sigh. Pushing back the elderly chair carefully, he rose, stretched and walked over to the window. A man in overalls was gardening near the pool. As he watched he heard a woman's voice, and Helen Pearson came into view. She was carrying a flat wooden basket containing flowers. She went over to the gardener and they stood talking for a few moments. The man leaned over to the back of the border and cut the last roses from a group of bushes beside the hedge. He shook them gently, then presented them to the Principal's wife.

Anthony was reminded of the poppy. Should he mention it to her? As he walked down to the next floor, he met Mrs Pearson coming up, carrying her basket of flowers. She had a glass vase in her other hand. A pair of scissors lay in the basket on top of the roses.

'Hello, Mr Dean. Have you been hard at work?'

'Yes. I took a brief walk this morning though.'

'Oh, good. Where did you go?'

'Just to where the hedge finishes and you get to the open down.'

'Were the skylarks singing?'

'Yes, lots of them. And . . . ' he blurted out ' . . . there's one lone poppy growing there. I was tempted to pick it. For you - because I know you love flowers.' Embarrassed at his admission, he gazed at her basket, not daring to meet her eyes.

'But you didn't?' she asked in a quiet voice.

'No.' He looked up. 'I thought it would probably die before I saw you. I don't think they live long when they're picked.'

'They don't. They're ephemeral - like the dragonflies.'

'I decided to leave it to set seed for next year,' he said. 'Do they always grow there?'

'It depends what the farmer grows. They like disturbed ground. That's why you don't see them on pastureland. But the seeds last for years in the soil and flower when conditions are right.'

'That's why they're always on building sites! I hadn't thought of that.'

'I've always loved poppies,' she said. He was grateful that she hadn't shown any sign of being annoyed at his foolishness. 'Dinner's in the Library tonight. Did Mr Pearson tell you?'

'No. He didn't mention it.'

'It's because of the other staff arriving back. He must have forgotten.' She looked a little exasperated. It's a tradition on the first evening. There isn't room for you all in our flat, and the dining room's a bit bleak. It's at eight. Can you tell the others? In case he forgot to tell them, too.' She smiled, left him and went into the senior boys' study.

Even they are getting flowers, he mused. Mrs Pearson obviously believed in bringing civilisation to the philistines.

'Sorry I'm late,' he apologised to Mary. 'I was talking to Mrs Pearson. Dinner's in the Library tonight, did you know?'

'I didn't. But it sounds nicer than the dining room. That's why the flowers are there, I suppose.'

'Probably. But Mrs Pearson seems to like flowers everywhere.'

'What do you think of her?'

'Oh . . . she's very nice. I mean, she seems OK. She's very different to The Boss.'

'Yes, poor woman. Much younger than him,' she said in a lower voice. 'She told me she used to be a secretary at another school. I suspect she wishes she were still there.'

'Do you think so?' Mary's words seemed to confirm his opinion that the Pearsons were not very happy.

'Well, would *you* like to be married to Mr P.?' grinned Mary.

'Certainly not!' he laughed.

It was a pleasure to be with Mary. She was so down-to-earth and funny - and missed nothing! Just what he needed to cheer him up. She made an excellent cup of tea, too.

Chapter Five

Anthony hesitated at the top of the stairs as the babble of voices rose up to greet him. It was a complete contrast to the quiet of the last few days. Below, in the hall, Helen Pearson was handing round a tray of drinks as she greeted the staff. Michael James was already down there, joking with a man who had doubtless been his teacher three or four years ago. Now, in theory at least, they were equal. Anthony did not feel equal to any of them. How could he disguise his nervousness and lack of competence?

'This time next year, you'll be as blasé as them,' a voice behind him said.

Mary had come out of her room and along the corridor as he hesitated there. She obviously knew exactly how he felt.

'I hope so!'

'We'd better go down,' she hinted.

He was blocking the stairway. 'Yes, sorry!'

He led the way slowly down into what seemed a great crowd.

'Can I offer you a glass of sherry?' Mrs Pearson was immediately alongside them as they stepped off the bottom stair. 'I'll introduce you to some of the staff.'

The introductions which followed left Anthony in a daze. He would have to study the staff list again when he went back to his room, and try to match names and faces. He felt he would never remember them all.

They didn't seem very interested in him. They were fully occupied in relating the events of the holidays to their friends and colleagues. Mr Pearson was in a corner, deep in discussion with a man of about fifty, short and bald.

'That's John Fulford,' Helen Pearson said, pausing in her 'sherry' round to give Anthony some more information. 'He acts as deputy head, although Eric doesn't like that term so we don't use it officially. He teaches modern languages - French and German mostly.'

Dinner was announced and they moved into the Library. It was transformed. Although it was a chilly evening, no fire burned in the fireplace. But the hearth had been filled with arrangements of leaves, late flowers and berries, which complemented the bronze chrysanthemums. On the table were several tiny arrangements of the same kind. Helen Pearson had been very busy.

Two of the long tables had been pushed together in the centre of the room. Anthony looked for his place card. Each card had been hand-lettered and painted with a small flower. His was a poppy.

He picked it up and stared at it for a moment. When he looked up he saw Mrs Pearson smiling at him from the place opposite. He wanted to say something but decided against it. He just smiled back and put the card down very carefully.

He found himself sitting next to a woman with her grey hair in a rather severe bun. But her voice was friendly.

'You must be the new English teacher. I'm Edith Baines - Classics. Your first start-of-year dinner is my last. I'm retiring in July. I've been very happy here and I hope you will be.'

'I'm Anthony Dean. Pleased to meet you.'

'Aren't these little cards lovely? Are you fond of poppies?'

'Yes, very.'

'I wonder how Mrs Pearson knew?'

'I think I may have mentioned it.'

'And if you did, she'd remember. She always likes to add special little touches to everything - when she can.' Miss Baines turned her head slightly in the direction of Pearson. Anthony understood.

On his right was a man slightly older than he was.

'Art and Craft' his neighbour said, holding out his hand. He wore an open-necked shirt and needed a haircut. And a shave.

'Anthony Dean. English,' Anthony replied. Did Mr Art-and-Craft have a name? Or was he too involved in the aesthetic to bother about such things? He pushed up his glasses to try and read the artist's name card. It looked like 'David Wilson'. He could check that on his staff list too. But he had a feeling that he'd never be able to think of him as anything but 'Art-and-Craft'.

Helen Pearson was speaking, leaning forward across the table. That night she was wearing a low-necked dress of autumn colours that matched the flowers she had so carefully arranged. Her gold earrings and chain sparkled in the light of small candles that she had placed on the table, their bases surrounded by rosehips.

'You can keep the name card. I do new ones every year.'

'It's lovely. Do you always do flowers?'

'No. I've done birds, then fruits, and tiny landscapes. Books too. I think of something new and do them over the summer. It's good painting practice.'

'So you'd already done the poppy?'

'I like to meet the new staff before I do theirs. Just in case. I did animals one year and this new teacher's daughter had had a serious accident on a horse in the summer. I didn't know. So now I wait.'

So she had done it specially! He could imagine her embarrassment on that previous occasion. It would be doubly uncomfortable for someone who always seemed to be in complete control. She was controlled now, speaking a little to everyone, calmly attending to everything. Controlled - yet somehow distant from it all.

In her heart, she's out there with the poppies, he thought. He guessed she had been a lot happier gathering the floral decorations than she was sitting amongst them. Perhaps that was why she had painted the poppy for him. Had she recognised a kindred spirit?

'Hope you'll like it here. Hard luck if you don't, really. Stuck out here, miles from anywhere.'

Art-and-Craft was speaking. His tone was hardly encouraging.

'Do you like it?' asked Anthony.

'It's no worse than anywhere else - if you have to be a teacher. It's gone downhill a bit lately, though.'

'Oh, really?'

'Money's tight. Not so many pupils. We've had to lose a few staff. Still, the groups are smaller. Can't be small enough for me. I just want to be able to get on with my own painting. Wish I could afford to paint full-time.'

'What do you paint?'

'Fairly large abstracts. Not to everyone's taste, unfortunately. Sold one or two. Need to sell one every week to live, though.'

'Mr Wilson's pictures are very . . . er . . . vivid,' commented Edith Baines, searching carefully for the right word. Her look said 'awful'. 'The boys like to try their hand - it's exciting for them to see him at work.'

'We've had a few good artists in my time here. But most of the lot I've got at the moment would rather paint each other!' David Wilson said, attacking his meringue as though it was one of his offending pupils.

After coffee was served, Mr Pearson rose and made a short speech, welcoming them all back and introducing the new staff. Naturally his warmest and most witty comments concerned Michael James, the spirited schoolboy-turned-master, whose exploits were known to most of the staff. He also made much of the fact that Mary Wagstaff had left her post at a very respectable girls' school in order to spend her last few years as a geography teacher amongst a school full of unruly boys.

'She says it's a challenge,' he told them. 'From what I know of her already I'm quite sure that she'll be more than equal to that challenge and won't stand any nonsense - from any of you!' General laughter. 'And this is Mr Dean, my new English assistant. We hope he'll be happy here.'

He obviously can't think of anything clever or amusing to say about me, Anthony thought. He felt his mood of gloom returning with a vengeance. He looked across the table and noticed a strange expression on Mrs Pearson's face. She was tight-lipped and was looking in the direction of her husband with almost a frown. When she realised Anthony's eyes were on her she turned and smiled but only half-lost that look of displeasure.

'Mr Dean is very interested in our landscape and natural history,' she said, rather loudly, to Edith Baines. 'He's already explored a little and I know he can't wait to see more.'

'It's a lovely area,' Miss Baines replied. 'When I first came here I used to walk on the Downs a lot. But my health isn't so good now. And, sadly, it's not as safe as it used to be for a woman alone, even here.'

'I always carry a games whistle,' said Mrs Pearson, 'You never know, it might deter someone.'

'Very sensible.'

'What's that? Misuse of school property?' The master who shouted this was a large, muscular young man further down the table. Anthony had been introduced to him briefly before the start of dinner. His name was Peter Ferguson and he taught games - hence the comment about the whistle. Mr Ferguson's face was somewhat red and Anthony had the feeling that he had refilled his glass from the variety of bottles on the table a little too often already. What else would explain his loud and rather disrespectful manner towards Mrs Pearson?

'I've never actually *used* the whistle,' she replied, a little coldly, 'but I *do* confess to taking it off the premises!'

'Detention!' shouted the games master.

Pearson glared, his wife smiled a forced smile, everybody else laughed and Anthony stared at his plate feeling uncomfortable.

'I know you'll all be anxious to get back to your accommodation and prepare yourselves for Monday,' Mr Pearson said, obviously deciding that the time had come to bring the meal to an end. 'There'll be a staff meeting - for *all* staff - tomorrow morning at ten. I wish you all a very successful term.'

Anthony carefully placed his name card in his inside pocket. Mrs Pearson watched him. As he got up from the table he found Mary at his side.

'The phoney war's nearly over!'

Seeing his puzzlement she explained. 'These few days of teaching that have been so quiet and peaceful. No boys, no lessons, no other teachers, no timetable, no duties . . . like the early days of the war when nothing seemed to be happening.'

'Phoney war! I like that. Now it's real war, is it?'

'Wait and see!'

Anthony couldn't help wondering who the enemy actually was.

Later, in his bed warmed by that wonderful hot-water bottle, Anthony sleepily pondered over the evening's events and his fellow staff. Edith Baines was kind and competent, Art-and-Craft a bit weird but probably OK and Ferguson was a drunken loudmouth. Not a very thoughtful summing-up but the best he could manage in the circumstances. And what of Mrs Pearson? His last glimpse, as he turned out the lamp, was of the poppy card propped up on his bedside table. He thought of her sitting at a table, carefully painting it for him. He tried to visualise every stroke of the paintbrush, but she had only completed one petal when he fell asleep.

The staff meeting the next morning did not bring Anthony any surprises. The couple of days that the new staff had already had in school had provided them with most of the information which was now meted out to the rest.

He was greatly relieved not to be given any night duties in the dormitory for the first week. It was emphasised though, that living-in staff members were expected to be on call at all times.

'It's vital that you learn your way about the school and know where everything and everybody is, and where to get help. It's much more important at this stage than learning your way around the local area.' A jibe at me, thought Anthony. Pearson went on, 'That can come later. But it *is* important to find out where all the boys and staff live, and where they're likely to be if needed.'

'In the pub,' said someone in a stage whisper.

'For the benefit of new staff I must emphasise that pupils are not allowed on licensed premises under any circumstances.'

'Quite right. I get the job of checking. Frequently,' joked Peter Ferguson, as if to confirm Anthony's hastily-formed opinion of him.

Pearson gave the games master one of his icy glares but Ferguson seemed quite unconcerned.

'I'd better go and start that checking,' he said a few minutes later when the meeting broke up.

'Hang on, the boys aren't back yet!' Michael said.

'True. But I need to remind myself of the places they congregate. You heard what the boss just said.'

'We'd better all go. You can show us the trouble spots. Coming, Anthony?'

Anthony was rather reluctant but he knew from previous experience that if you start off by being out of things, you stay out of them. Anyway, a beer would go down pretty well after two hours of Mr Pearson.

'Sure. I'll just run up and get my jacket.'

The remainder of the day, and the next, were taken up with the inevitable preparations for the start of term. Boys started to arrive back on the following afternoon, Sunday. Anthony was not involved in this process, it was all dealt with by the Pearsons, senior and duty staff; Matron and Mr Jones.

It was a shock to look out of his window to see and hear small boys running round the garden, and even throwing stones into the lily pond. He didn't think Helen Pearson would allow that. They must be the new boys; their uniforms were very crisp and clean. Then he realised that Mrs Pearson was out there with them, as were a group of parents. She walked down to the pool and seemed to be explaining something to the boys. They had stopped the stone-throwing. She pointed round to the other side and then led them round there. She had quite a little group with her now, including some bigger boys. Then she seemed to be telling them to explore all round the grounds, indicating the boundaries and encouraging them to run off and investigate. She must be trying to tire them out, he thought.

'The School attends church on Sunday evenings,' Pearson had said. 'Some members of staff are, of course, required to attend to maintain discipline. However, not all staff members are needed each week so we have a rota. New, junior, staff are asked to attend every week.'

There was no church on this first day, so he still had some time to prepare for the morning.

The morning! 4B at 9.30! A brief assembly in the gym and then into the classroom. Despite the hot-water bottle, hot chocolate and detective novel, Anthony didn't sleep much that Sunday night.

Chapter Six

Anthony lay on his narrow bed, wrapped in a blanket, his hot water bottle clutched to his stomach. He was shivering, his head ached, and his throat was sore.

Was it the onset of flu or one of the many bugs that new teachers often pick up to make their lives even more stressful? But surely it wouldn't have started already? Not after one day!

He knew, really, what it was. It was the reaction to what he could only describe as a disastrous first day in the classroom. As he relived it over and over again, Anthony groaned and pressed his face into the pillow.

Eventually he raised himself on one elbow and reached for the mug of coffee on the bedside table. Thank goodness he had bought that stove! He clasped the mug in trembling fingers and felt its heat comfort him.

He must get up! He must stop this! Reluctantly he disentangled himself from the blanket and stood up. A glimpse of his crumpled, strained face in the shaving mirror shocked him. If just one day had done that, what on earth would he look like after a term? A year?

'A young teacher I knew, about as dark-haired as you, went completely grey all round the edges in his first year,' Mary had told him during one of her sessions on awful schools she had known. 'Of course, that was at an appalling school. Not like this one.'

Could anything have been more appalling than today? If so, he didn't want to experience it. Fingers still clasped round the smooth, warm mug, he went over to the window. The view might cheer him, unless, of course, any of those boys were about.

But the landscape was empty. His eyes roved over the line of the Downs, longing to be up there instead of in this unhappy, freezing garret. Then he noticed a movement by the gate near the pool. Helen Pearson pushed open the gate and walked in. She stopped beside the pool and gazed into the water.

She looks as lonely as I am, Anthony thought. She wasn't, of course. She was surrounded by people. But did she want to be with them? Didn't she prefer the open Downs to Pearson's study and their small, dark flat?

He drew back from the window as she turned and walked slowly across the garden towards the house. Her face, a pale oval, looked up towards his window. Had she seen him watching her? If she had, she gave no sign. She walked on, disappearing from his view. As soon as she was out of sight he felt desolate and ill again.

Forcing himself to sit down at the table, now piled even higher with papers, he put his head in his hands as he wondered what on earth he could do to prevent another disaster like today.

The day hadn't started too badly, despite his lack of sleep. Faced with the inevitable, he'd been resignedly cheerful at breakfast.

'Today's the day. Childhood's really over!' Michael had said as they sat down.

'Don't you wish now that you'd trained?'

'Just puts off the evil moment. Still, I might feel different if I didn't know the school.'

'You'll both be perfectly OK. Just keep telling yourself that.' Mary was eating a hearty breakfast. No first day nerves for her.

'When's your first field trip, then, Mary?' Michael asked.

'Oh, come on! I'm not venturing out there with any of this lot until I've got the measure of them. That's the first thing to do,' she went on more seriously, turning to Anthony, 'get the measure of them. A Head told me that: years ago. No use trying to teach them anything until then.'

'But that might take me ages. I don't think not teaching them anything in the meantime would go down all that well with you-know-who!'

'You have to admit Anthony's at a disadvantage - under scrutiny, shall we say?' said Michael.

There's no need to remind me, Anthony thought.

The dining room was buzzing this morning, with new boys being shepherded around by staff on duty and older ones greeting each other with varying degrees of offensiveness. Some of the pupils and staff who boarded out came in for breakfast too. The new staff watched the procedure with interest, trying to remember the 'ropes' for their own duty days.

'We'd better go and prepare for assembly - and after,' Mary said, pushing back her chair. 'Good luck, both of you. I hope we'll meet again!'

Assembly had consisted of a short service and a shortened version of Pearson's speech from the evening before. The usual notices were given out, after which the School was dismissed. Anthony swallowed hard and made his way to the English room.

It was awful, ghastly, beyond belief. It was pure hell. Nothing had prepared him for the nightmare of facing 4B in the first lesson of a new school year. His memory of the most diabolical boys of his own school days did not match up to 4B. No amount of studying, of planning, or of striding about his room delivering his lessons to thin air, had prepared him for this agony. No books on teaching, no advice from friends and colleagues, no jokes with more than a grain of truth, could help him in the face of that onslaught. The onslaught that came from Simon Biggins, Mark Wilshaw and all those others whose names he hadn't learned yet but whose faces would haunt him for the rest of his life.

It was a riot. In the middle of it, Pearson had come into the room. He was furious. And, although he vented his anger on the boys, Anthony was left in no doubt about the real cause of his fury. Otherwise, wouldn't he have punished them in other ways? His parting 'I hope we never have a repetition of this!' was directed noticeably to the front of the classroom.

But there had been a repetition. In that class and in others as the appalling day dragged onwards. Only with his group of new boys did Anthony attain anything like the control and atmosphere that he wanted. Even there, he had to constantly raise his voice (which by now was failing) to a very cheeky boy. Then he discovered the boy's name - Andrew Biggins. There seemed to be nothing Anthony could do. By lunchtime he was shattered and dreading the afternoon.

His 'Not very well,' to his colleagues' enquiries as to how his morning went, was a desperate understatement.

'They haven't settled down yet. And they're not used to you. It'll get better,' Mary said kindly, patting his arm. 'Some of mine aren't too good.'

There's nothing they can do for me now, he thought, despite their kind words. I'm on my own once I get into the classroom. They've got their own classes to worry about. The 'phoney war' really *was* over.

The afternoon was little better. He imagined that the word had been quickly passed round the school during lunch. 'The new English master's hopeless! Be as awful as you can.'

And they were.

As soon as the bell went at the end of afternoon school, his class tore out with a series of whoops. This was not allowed. Anthony knew it was not allowed, but there was nothing he could do to stop them. They totally ignored his instructions, and by this time he was too exhausted and his throat was too sore to take any action. With deep relief, tinged with fear of the consequences, he let them go.

He heard them shrieking their way out of the building - and he heard the powerful voice of a master bellowing at them. I'm for it now, he thought, sinking into his chair and gazing numbly at the exercise books on the desk in front of him.

But nothing happened. No-one came, storming along the corridor, to ask what he thought he was doing allowing the boys to behave so badly. No-one put his head round the door to see if he was all right. No-one came in to offer him any advice. There was just a terrible silence.

Anthony wasn't quite sure what he was supposed to do now and no-one had told him that either. Was he expected to work in this room? What if Pearson came in wanting to work here? Should he take his work to the library? Or to the poky smoke-filled den that had the grandiose name of Masters' Common Room? Or should he just retreat to his icy garret? He gathered up his books and papers and stepped out of the classroom. There was no-one around. His pounding head decided him. He went quickly up to his room and shut the door.

That was two hours ago. Now he'd crawled out of the bed to which he'd retreated in abject misery at the end of the afternoon. He'd even managed to do a little marking. Several cups of coffee had revived him a little. He still had dinner to face. He tried his voice to see if it would work but was only able to croak. It would be a good excuse not to be lively, anyway. He certainly did not feel lively.

As he went downstairs he saw Mrs Pearson going along to Mary's room. When she saw him she turned and walked back towards him.

'I'm just going round asking how you all got on,' she said. 'Michael seems to have enjoyed his day. How was yours?'

Anthony hoped his voice would work. He was desperate to sound normal. He made a great effort. 'Not very good. But tomorrow will be better.' He didn't believe himself but it sounded positive.

She looked concerned.

'I heard . . . I mean, did you have one or two bad moments?'

'You could say that!' he wanted to say. 'No-one warns you, or tells you what you really need to know.' Instead he went on, with a croaky laugh, 'I've already learnt a lot of things not to do.'

She smiled sympathetically. He could tell she wasn't fooled by his fake jocularity.

'It's very hard at first. They take advantage. It's hard on the voice, too. Don't despair, Mr Dean. It may take a while but you'll be fine.' She hesitated, as if she wanted to say more but felt she shouldn't. 'I'd better see Miss Wagstaff now, before dinner,' she finished. With a final gentle smile, she turned and walked away. He watched her knock on Mary's door, heard a cheery call from within, and carried on down the stairs quickly.

'How'd it go?' Michael was already collecting his food from Mrs Higginbottom as Anthony entered the noisy dining room and walked quickly to the serving hatch without looking in the direction of the boys' tables.

'Don't remind me of it!'

'Bad, was it? Cheer up, it gets better, so they say.'

It may do for you, Anthony thought. But he knew that he could not convey the sheer awfulness of being totally out of control, of being a figure of ridicule even to the most nervous of new boys. His colleagues would only think he'd had a few sharp words with a boy or two, even a whole class. But he knew that in his own schooldays he had never seen a teacher so utterly demoralised as he had been today and would be tomorrow, would be in the next few seconds as he walked through the dining room to his table with the pupils watching - and knowing.

He struggled through dinner, eating little and saying even less. It hurt to swallow, it hurt to talk. It hurt to listen to the buzz of talk and laughter and see the boys' sidelong glances in his direction. At this moment, everything hurt.

Later that evening, he struggled to enliven his planned lessons for the next day, in the hope of keeping the boys interested. It dawned on him that he had received no advice whatsoever about actually *teaching*. He had been told *what* to teach. He had more curriculum information than he had been able to study so far. He had been told the school rules and regulations, which ran into pages. He had been told who to look out for - which pupils had, or caused, problems. He had been told where to obtain stationery, books, and crackly old filmstrips of Shakespeare's plays. He was well provided with record sheets, report forms, registers and numerous other ways of recording the attendance and performance of his classes, good and bad. But there was nothing, absolutely nothing, on how to USE any of it.

He had been in the school since Wednesday afternoon. Since then, the amount of books and papers had spread from the table on to the cupboard and the floor. He had had endless meetings with Pearson and other staff - but still there was nothing on how he should set about imparting all this knowledge to the boys or using it himself. Not even a word on how this particular school expected English to be taught.

Somebody ought to write it down, he thought. I should. Now. While it's still fresh in my mind.

'What every new teacher needs to know'

That'll be the title of my book! I'll do it now. Before I forget like the rest have, and start thinking it's easy.

He took a notebook from his cupboard, made yet another coffee, and started to write. It took his mind off the horrors of tomorrow for an hour. Then the exhaustion, sore throat and shivers got the better of him and he crawled into bed. But he didn't sleep. He couldn't stop thinking about having to get up and face it all again the next day. He now knew how condemned men felt.

By the end of that week Anthony's shivers and sneezes were the real thing. He dragged himself from his bed every morning and faced the torment of lessons with the added discomfort of aching bones and streaming nose.

'Got a cold?'

'Yes.'

'Hard luck,' Michael grinned. He appeared to be totally unaffected by germs or the behaviour of his pupils. He seemed to think Anthony's misery - and his cold - were amusing. Mary was more sympathetic.

'Try these,' she said, handing him a packet of tablets. 'You always pick up bugs when you start teaching. You become immune to it after a while. Have you had measles and all those things?'

'I think so.'

'You can get some of them more than once,' said Michael.

'You are really cheering him up!' Mary scolded him. 'It's all right for you. Just wait till you get something.'

'I'll survive. It'll clear up eventually.' Anthony tried to sound unconcerned. If only simply having a cold was his main problem. He would willingly endure any amount of physical illness if his classroom troubles would evaporate.

They wouldn't. He'd tried. But he was no match for the Biggins's of this world, he knew that - and so did they.

'It gets easier when they get to know you,' Mary said, as if reading his thoughts, as she watched him push bits of hard bacon around on his plate. He had no appetite.

'How long does that take?'

She put her hand on his arm with a comforting gesture.

'You'll be much better in a week or two. If you haven't fallen down a grid by then! You must eat. You can't do this job on an empty stomach. You're thin enough as it is.'

'You're only jealous,' Michael remarked, rather ungallantly Anthony thought.

'Of course I am!' Mary didn't seem offended by the comment about her figure. She cleared her plate. 'Now I'm going back for more! You can think what you like, young man, but I can't face glaciated landscapes without a good breakfast.'

She rose from the table and marched up to the hatch, where Mrs Higginbottom piled her plate high again. Anthony looked across the table at Michael. He was desperately trying not to laugh. Michael wasn't even trying. They both exploded. Anthony realised that he hadn't laughed for several days - or was it weeks? Those long, long hours in the classroom certainly *seemed* like weeks. And it was nearly time for more of them to start.

Pearson was in the classroom when he entered. He was sitting at the desk, writing. Anthony hesitated at the door. Only ten minutes ago the Principal had given him a very disapproving look when Anthony had a fit of sneezing during assembly.

'Come in, Mr Dean,' Pearson said in his clipped manner. 'Are you ill?'

'It's just a cold. It's nothing.'

Pearson gathered up his books and rose.

'I just wondered if ill health was the reason for your poor performance so far. I trust I won't be disturbed by any of that noise today.'

Before Anthony could reply, if indeed he could think of any reply, Pearson swept past him and out of the room.

'Poor performance.' Yes, it was poor. It was awful. But he didn't like being told in that brusque, unhelpful way. He would at least like to discuss it, ask for advice, explain some of the things that had gone slightly better. But he was never given the chance. Had Pearson made his mind up about him already? And how could he improve today when he felt so lousy?

Another sneezing fit overtook him just as the class arrived. Within seconds the whole group were sneezing loudly. Surely they could be heard all over the school? He tried to shout, but no raw, sore throat could produce enough decibels to be heard above this mocking, lunatic sneezing. He banged on the desk. Nothing happened. He banged harder. Still they ignored him. He picked up a thick book and banged with that. The class picked up their English textbooks and did likewise. Bang, sneeze, bang, sneeze, sneeze, sneeze, bang . . . BANG!

The door flew open and crashed against the shelf behind it. The whole room seemed to judder. Pearson, livid, stood in the doorway. The sudden complete silence was worse than the bangs and sneezes.

'I find I have to work in here this morning after all, Mr Dean,' the Principal said when he had controlled his anger. His voice was tight. 'While I'm doing so, I can give this class some exercises to do. That will give you the opportunity to undertake some further preparation . . . Biggins! Were you smiling, Biggins?'

'No, sir.'

'Stand out here at the front!' Pearson turned from the shuffling, smirking boy and went on, 'The library is available, I believe, Mr Dean.'

He and the class watched in silence as Anthony gathered up his books and papers with trembling hands. He felt cold, but his face was burning. He fumbled with that wretched lock on his briefcase. He had known it would embarrass him one day. But he hadn't expected the total humiliation of this moment. Every eye was on him as he rammed in the last crumpled worksheets and books, making ugly bulges in the shiny new leather. With what hope he had bought that case! It marked his entry into the adult world. Now he was lower than the lowliest pupil in the school.

What was he supposed to do and say now? Speak to the class? Speak to Pearson? Or slink out with his briefcase under his arm, because his nervous, hasty packing prevented it from closing?

The problem was partly solved by Pearson. As soon as Anthony had removed the last of his work from the desk Pearson placed his own slim, neat file on it, opened it and began to address the class. He ignored Anthony - and Biggins. The latter looked at the young teacher from under thick black eyebrows, and almost seemed to wink. His look of mocking triumph was only modified by the proximity of the headmaster, who now glanced briefly in his direction before carrying on his lesson. A similar glance towards Anthony - and both recalcitrant pupil and failed teacher were effectively dismissed. Anthony left without a word.

After the end of afternoon school, Anthony dragged his aching, sneezing, unhappy body up to his room. The day that had started so badly was at last over. In fact, the 'free' period in the library had helped his cold and enabled him to face the rest of his classes with slightly less disastrous results. One or two of the more difficult pupils were also unwell and either quieter than usual, or absent. There were unexpected benefits from epidemics that he had never thought of!

But he could not, would never, erase the memory of that dreadful first lesson. He could not imagine what the consequences would be. What was Pearson going to do or say? Would he be asked to leave? In any case, how could he face 4B again?

He poured over the newspaper, then flung it aside in disgust. There was nothing in it that he could apply for. Plenty of opportunities for people qualified in economics, science, or engineering. 'Fluency in Russian desirable . . . ' Apparently the world was not queuing up for English graduates with little else to offer. But he had to find something. He couldn't stay here for long. Not after this week.

Perhaps he could go back to college and train for something. He'd once had an idea about studying librarianship. The quiet of a library seemed like paradise after his classroom experiences. The library at Fieldhouse was the only room he felt comfortable in.

He couldn't start a new course until next year, though. What was he to do in the meantime? He could take any old job. It couldn't be any worse than here. He'd rent a cheap room - he was already used to primitive conditions. Yes, that was what he'd do. He picked up the paper again and started to read through every single job advert. He could probably find something new by next weekend.

Then he remembered something that destroyed his immediate plans. He had to work notice - quite a lot of it. He groaned. The thought was almost unbearable. Those few minutes when he imagined himself sweeping the roads - anything - by next Friday had been the happiest minutes of the week. He sneezed several times and began to shiver again. Maybe he'd become so ill that he'd have to leave. Wasn't there an author who was often ill when teaching? He thought back to his university course. Yes, three authors, in fact. The Brontes. So he was in good company. Perhaps he'd turn his wretched experiences into a novel one day.

A light tap at the door interrupted his reverie. It must be Michael, although he'd been too lost in misery to notice his sprightly step on the stairs. He half-opened the door. Helen Pearson was standing outside, carrying a jug with a floral design.

'I hear you're not very well. I've brought you this.' She held out the jug. 'It's hot lemon. Really good for colds.'

'That's very kind of you Won't you come in? If you don't mind the germs. Sorry the room's a bit of a mess.'

He felt ashamed of the newspaper lying open at the 'Vacancies' page. It showed weakness, he thought.

'Can I put this on here? It's very hot.' Mrs Pearson carried the jug carefully to the cupboard and placed it on the metal tray beside the camping stove. 'You've got yourself a cooker! Very sensible.' She smiled. 'You will drink this, won't you?'

'Yes. Thank you. I will. Did Mr Pearson tell you I was ill?'

She gave him a strange look, which he couldn't quite interpret.

'No, Mary did.' She hesitated. 'We usually call the staff by their Christian names in private, unless they object. Is that all right?'

'Yes, please do.'

'Only . . . you're supposed to call us Mr and Mrs all the time.'

'I understand.'

Anthony was looking beyond her at the steaming jug. It was covered with a lacy cloth edged with coloured beads. She saw what had caught his eye.

'An old-fashioned idea, but so practical. It keeps the flies out. You don't see covers like that now.'

It's too cold up here for flies to live, Anthony thought. 'My Gran had some just like it,' he said. For an instant he was back at the breakfast table, idly counting the beads as she tried to hustle him off to school.

'Did she make them herself?'

'I don't know. She probably did. She made most things. She was very economical.'

'I made mine, too,' Helen Pearson replied.

He must have shown his surprise, for she went on, 'I make a lot of things myself, especially in the winter when I can't get out so much. I enjoy it.'

Anthony tried to visualise the Pearson fireside at the end of a school day in January - Mrs Pearson busy with her needlework, Mr Pearson in a hand-knitted sweater and slippers comfortably reading a western or thriller. He couldn't visualise it.

'I must be going,' she said, brushing down her red skirt with that gesture he'd noticed before, even though she had not been sitting.

'You've been very kind. I'm sure I'll be fine in a day or two.'

'Yes, I'm sure you will.' She walked towards the door and opened it before he had a chance to do it for her. Then she turned and said, rather awkwardly,

'If you ever feel . . . if you need any help or advice, please ask. I *did* mean it on your first day. Please don't feel alone.' She slipped out and went downstairs quickly, her heels clicking on each step.

When the sound died away, he did feel alone. Terribly. She knows everything, he thought. He poured a glass of the hot lemon. It was very comforting. She'd meant to comfort him, hadn't she? Pearson had told her about the morning, about the whole week. No doubt he'd said some pretty uncomplimentary things about his new English assistant. So Mrs Pearson had gone into her kitchen and made him some hot lemon. She had been discussing him with Mary, too. Well, it was nice to think that two people were on his side. He poured more lemon, closed his eyes and drifted back to the days when he'd been ill as a child. But instead of his mother, or Gran, it was Helen Pearson he visualised at his bedside.

Chapter Seven

'Monday again! Second week already!' said Michael in greeting as they left their respective garrets at the same moment. 'If time passes this quickly, we'll be headmasters before you can say "Eric Pearson".'

'You speak for yourself,' returned Anthony. 'I don't think I'll ever be a headmaster.'

He wondered how much longer he'd even be a mere teacher.

But, despite it's being Monday, he felt better. The weekend had been a wet one and he'd spent most of the time in his room nursing his cold and preparing his lessons yet again. He'd had plenty of rest, too. He'd slept really well on Friday night, after the hot lemon. He'd wondered if Mrs Pearson would come for her jug, but he hadn't seen her. He was certainly not going to take it down to her door. It might embarrass both of them.

'We're on duty now, don't forget,' Michael reminded him as they reached the bottom of the stairs.' Got to sit with the boys for meals and be erudite or something. Last week was the easy bit.'

Whenever I start to feel better, Anthony thought miserably, something happens to deflate me. He had enjoyed the meals at a small table - just Mary and Michael and perhaps another colleague or two. They'd been a welcome break and he'd picked up useful tips, too. Now it seemed that even that amount of peace was to be denied him. The living-in staff had to do all these extra duties to justify the expense of their high-class accommodation, he supposed!

When they entered the dining room, it was empty.

'We're rather early,' said Michael.

'What do we do, then?'

'Oh, go and sit at a table each. Then when the boys arrive they'll come and join us.'

'Who else will be doing this?'

'Mary, David Wilson and Peter Ferguson, anybody who happens to be around - and the teachers whose official duty day it is, of course.'

They collected their breakfasts from Mrs Higginbottom, who had nothing good to say about Mondays.

'He's got more than me!' complained Michael, looking at Anthony's loaded plate.

'Feed a cold,' replied the cook. 'Anyway, he's too thin. You look healthy enough to me.'

'Well, I won't be if you starve me!'

'Get away! You're a master now. Supposed to set a good example.'

'Yes, ma'am.'

They carried their trays into the still mainly empty seating area. Anthony chose a table in the farthest corner, by the window. Boys were starting to arrive now, and feeling the sharpness of Mrs Higginbottom's tongue. If only he had her control over them. The other staff had arrived, too. Mary came over and asked about his cold.

'Awful, being ill in your first week. There's enough to put up with, without that. I do hope you'll have a better week. Do ask if I can help at all.'

They all know everything, thought Anthony glumly. Of course, you couldn't have any secrets in a place like this.

The room was busier now. The younger pupils had clattered down from the dormitories accompanied by the teacher on night duty, Peter Ferguson. With a perfunctory 'Morning' and a brief nod in his direction, the games master sat at a table near Anthony and was soon surrounded by excited pupils, all giving their accounts of the weekend's sporting events at once. Anthony realised that he would have to keep up to date with both school and national sports if he were to have common topics of conversation with the boys.

More pupils arrived. The 'outdoor' boys who ate here rushed in, hungry after their walk or cycle from the village. They shouted their news to the boarders as they queued impatiently for breakfast. Mrs Higginbottom and her staff were as quick with their retorts as they were dishing out the food. They stood no nonsense.

'*You* can have a small helping. And when you can queue in a civilised fashion, you can come back for more!' was their response to any troublemaker.

And it worked. Anthony was filled with admiration. Of course *he* didn't have the sanction of withholding food, which was a pity.

The tables were filling up. But still Anthony sat in splendid isolation in his corner. Sometimes a boy would come in his direction, then turn away and squash in to a small space elsewhere. He pretended not to notice. He didn't know whether to be glad or sorry. He was not fond of communal eating at the best of times, and this was not the best of times. But he did not want to be shunned, and, worse still, to be seen being shunned. If only some nice, quiet first year pupils, still polite and missing home, would come and sit by him! But they didn't. Nobody did. And he was aware of occasional glances from the other tables, by staff and pupils. They would turn away quickly if they caught his eye.

Then he heard a commotion at the servery. Mrs Higginbottom was laying down the law in no uncertain terms. And the recipient of her wrath was Simon Biggins. He, Mark Wilshaw and their small group of followers, had arrived late and were demanding instant service. When Mrs H. had finished with them, they'd need a table . . . No! Not them. Please, not them! There was only one way of escape. Anthony gulped down the rest of his coffee, joined a group of older boys clearing their trays on to the trolley, and slipped out of the dining room. He could feel eyes boring into his back as he did so, but he didn't look round.

Outside the dining room he composed himself and strolled back to the main building in an attempt to hide his discomfiture. Pearson was in the hall. When he saw Anthony he looked at his watch.

'Good morning Mr Dean. You're rather late for breakfast,' he said in his clipped manner.

'Oh, no, I've had breakfast. I was there when it opened. I'm now going up to do some more preparation before assembly.'

'I see.' Pearson paused and then said, 'You are aware that the new members of staff have additional duties from today? You *have* received a timetable and information about these?'

'Yes, thank you. I have.'

'I see,' said Pearson again. 'I'm sure you have a great deal of work to do.'

He turned to go back into his study without another word. As he did so, Helen Pearson came out of their flat door, which was next to the study.

'Oh, Mr Dean, are you better?'

'Yes, thank you. I'm much better today.'

'I'm so glad. You *did* have a rough time last week, didn't you? This week will be better.' She glanced over at her husband without smiling. He seemed to stare right through Anthony with those hard blue eyes.

'Mr Dean is going upstairs to complete some work,' he said.

'I am. Good morning.' Anthony sprinted up the stairs two at a time to get away quickly. He couldn't help feeling that he'd blotted his copybook yet again.

He fingered the lacy cover on the jug, which still stood on his cupboard. There were ten beads around the edge, arranged in a pattern of colours. What had Gran called this work? 'Crochett' - that was it. Only he thought it was pronounced in the French manner - 'croshay'. Gran had always said that 'crochett' was good enough for her but he suspected it wouldn't be good enough for Helen Pearson. In any case he didn't think that Pearson would allow her to mispronounce anything.

He wasn't sure what to do about the jug. She would want it back, surely? As he pondered, he heard footsteps coming up the stairs, and the sound of laughter. It was Mrs Pearson talking to Michael as he returned from breakfast.

'I'm going to inquire how Mr Dean is,' he heard her say. But she had already seen him and asked. So she *must* be embarrassed about the hot lemon. He was glad he hadn't given her away. She knocked.

'Come in!'

'I've come to collect the jug. Did you drink it or tip it away? Be honest!'

'I drank every last drop and it worked wonders. I wouldn't dream of tipping it away!'

'Are you really feeling better?'

'Much better . . . but . . . '

'Yes?'

'Oh, I just hope my teaching's better too.'

'No-one can teach well when they're ill. It'll improve. It takes time. Don't worry too much about it.'

'I'll try not to.'

'You must take some breaks. Get up on the Downs. It'll raise your spirits.'

'I'll be up there as soon as I get the chance, I promise.'

'In the meantime, there are still some late dragonflies to watch.' She was smiling but looked uncertain. Anthony felt she wanted to say more, but he was too tongue-tied to encourage her. As she was leaving she said, 'I'll look out for you by the pool.' This time, as she descended the stairs, she looked back and said quietly, 'Good luck this morning.'

He would need it. But in the event he wasn't sure whether the lessons went slightly better than last week or whether he was more prepared for their awfulness. Whichever it was, the noise level didn't attract the attention of Pearson, the insolence was just bearable, and some of the new boys actually seemed to like him. He even felt that he might have taught something to some of them. By lunchtime he was feeling very slightly more like a teacher. The next problem was to face a repetition of breakfast but fortunately it was not to be. By the time he arrived in the dining room it was full and there were staff in attendance on all tables. Mary motioned him to a spare seat near her and the meal passed pleasantly enough. Mary kept the conversation going with tales of field trips in appalling conditions.

'You'll all be out there, whatever the weather!' she told the boys. 'And Mr Dean, too. He likes the Great Outdoors, don't you Mr Dean?'

Anthony was grateful to her for trying to include him in the conversation.

'Yes - but only in fine weather and with a good stock of supplies.' He knew that food was always a good topic to discuss with boys. 'Of course, Miss Wagstaff makes you take field rations and cook them yourselves. She doesn't believe in packed lunches.'

'No, quite right. Much too soft,' laughed Mary. 'You really get a feel for the land when you've been on a trip with me. You know every hill, stone and stream.'

'And of course she makes you write about it in great detail when you get back. Pages and pages of it,' Anthony went on, really getting into the swing of things now. 'Maps, diagrams, cross-sections, everything. No stone left unturned, you might say!'

The groans, quips and laughter, told Mary and Anthony that the boys were enjoying themselves. Anthony's day brightened even more. Perhaps he wouldn't dread these mealtimes in the future.

He should have known! Hadn't he thought first thing this morning that, whenever he got a boost, something always happened to drag him down?

'Ah, Mr Dean.' The Principal was working in the English room when Anthony went in for the first afternoon lesson. 'I have to finish this work on the stock so I'll be in here for your first period.'

"An Inspector Calls" thought Anthony gloomily. How could he teach with

Pearson in the room? Almost certainly the boys would behave better. So his teaching of English would be on the line this time. His content, delivery, questioning. So far, he'd been concentrating his thoughts on discipline and classroom organisation. After all, you couldn't worry about your delivery if no-one could hear it. And the content was largely irrelevant if the boys only used their books to bang on the desks and refused to read or write anything. Thank goodness he hadn't chosen to show one of those ancient filmstrips. He hadn't had an opportunity to practise with the projector yet, and this would not have been the lesson in which to do it. He must remember to try it out at the weekend.

As he feared, the lesson went badly. It would have been a dream compared to the rest of his experiences, if only Eric Pearson's gimlet eyes and sharp ears were not ever-present at the back of the class. Discipline was not a problem. No boy dared to cross Mr Pearson. Silence reigned. But it was not a silence born of concentrated learning and respect for the class teacher. And everybody knew it.

In that silence, Anthony's hesitant delivery, wooden explanations, lack of voice control and awkwardness in dealing with pupils was all too evident, not to mention the return of his croaking voice and his tendency towards fits of coughing and sneezing. His failings were exaggerated threefold in the strained atmosphere. After five minutes he began to long for the return of the noise! But with Pearson's presence, there was none. Not even the clatter of a ruler, the rustle of paper, the squeak of a chair. It was uncanny. The boys need not have worried, though. It was not they who were on trial. And Anthony had little doubt about the verdict of the jury.

With immense relief he heard the bell in the corridor. This time the pupils did not run out, but waited in silence to be dismissed. So did their teacher. But the head said nothing. He merely gathered up his papers and left the room, as though Anthony wasn't there.

For a precious hour, later that afternoon, Anthony had a free period - one of very few in the week. He knew that 'free' didn't really mean that. Preparation and marking were all supposed to be squeezed into these periods or done in what was euphemistically called 'your own time'. But the day had taken its toll. Anthony needed a real break. Surely they wouldn't begrudge him a few minutes walking round the garden?

Looking out, he could see nobody. Break was over and the school was quiet. He walked quickly down the sloping lawn, wishing that he were shorter and not so dark-haired - less conspicuous! He stopped beside the pool and looked for dragonflies, but there didn't seem to be any. Perhaps he was too late in the day, or maybe the cold weekend's rain had ended their short lives.

'You took my advice, then?'

He swung round. He hadn't heard Helen Pearson's footsteps on the damp, soft grass. Now she stood behind him, dressed for outdoors in beige trousers and a green sweater. The white collar of her blouse set off her face, which was bright and smiling. Was she really so pleased to see him?

'Yes. But I can't see any dragonflies. Have they all gone?'

'No. There's one. A brilliant blue one. Look!' She took his arm and directed his gaze to the far side of the pond. 'Let's walk round there.'

They tottered on the edge of the water, trying to get a closer look at the insect now resting among the reeds.

'Don't fall in! That won't help your cold at all,' she laughed.

'Is it deep?'

'It's quite deep in the centre, I believe. And the mud's very soft. Definitely not for swimming.'

'Has anyone tried?'

'Oh, we've had to rescue a few stupid boys over the years. There's always one, isn't there?' He could think of several. She went on, 'When we first came here, Eric wanted to fill it in. But I stopped him. I thought it was beautiful - and educational. He was afraid all his pupils would drown. But, of course, they haven't. Just got stuck in the mud occasionally. They're not allowed to wade, so stop any that you see.'

'I will,' he said. Not that they'd take any notice of him.

'I was just going to walk out into the field. Will you come?' Mrs Pearson moved towards the gate.

'I'd love to but . . . '

'What time's your next lesson?'

'Half-past four.'

'Well, that's plenty of time.'

'I'm supposed to be working.'

'It's a free period. You don't have to work twenty-four hours a day, even though it seems that way. You need breaks and fresh air. Come on!' She opened the gate.

Anthony glanced furtively over his shoulder. She laughed.

'It's all right. You're not a prisoner. Half an hour away from here will do you good.'

He followed her, fervently hoping that no-one was watching, but convinced that somebody would be.

'Now I can call you Anthony,' she said, closing the gate behind them. 'If you don't mind, that is.'

'No, of course not.'

'You can call me Helen if you like.'

'I thought you said . . .'

'That was in school. Out here's different.'

He wasn't sure whether Pearson would approve of that sort of familiarity. No, he *was* sure - the Head most certainly would not.

They walked along the path beyond the school grounds, like he had on that first exploration. It seemed a long time ago now. Helen talked about the plants

53

and trees as they walked, telling him their names and history. He felt very ignorant.

'You're lucky to know all this,' he said. 'It makes walking much more interesting. I wish I knew as much.'

'You'll learn eventually, if you're keen,' she said. 'All you need is a good reference book.'

'Or a good teacher,' he replied, shyly. He wasn't quite sure how to converse with her on this new, informal basis.

'You're the teacher, not me,' she smiled.

'A very bad one!'

She said nothing in reply but swished at the tall dry grasses by the side of the track.   Anthony was angry with himself for embarrassing her. Of course it wasn't for her to comment on his teaching, whatever she had undoubtedly heard from her husband. If she offered too much consolation or told him not to worry about it, she would appear to be condoning his poor performance and would certainly be going against Pearson's opinion. Her position was a difficult one and he was ashamed of unintentionally making it more so. He had no idea what to say next.

Suddenly she stopped and turned to look up at him with a serious expression. 'Don't let it get you down. There *are* other things in life. You're young, you don't have to do a job for ever if It doesn't suit you. Plenty of time to make changes.' Was that a hint, he wondered? Had Pearson indicated that he would never make a teacher? She went on, 'There's nothing worse than being trapped in something you don't like. You don't have to decide the rest of your life yet. Give things a try - but don't feel you can't change.'

He longed to ask whether she was trapped in something she didn't like. He wasn't sure whether Mr Pearson would approve of his wife's advice to new teachers. Was this another example of their differences?

'I'd like to give teaching a fair trial,' he replied. But wasn't he considering doing just the opposite? Had she seen that open newspaper?

'I hope you will. I . . . we . . . don't want to lose you.' So she had seen the paper. And heard all about his disasters. 'You can always come out here when it gets too much for you.' Helen glanced at her watch. 'There isn't time to go to the top today, but another time we will.'

They had just reached the spot where the hedges ended.

'This is as far as I got before,' Anthony told her.

'Where the poppy was?' she asked in a very soft voice.

'Yes. Look, the seedhead is still here.'

'It'll be dry in a week or two if we don't have too much rain.'

I'll come back and pick it when the seeds have gone, Anthony thought. Then I can give her the dried seedhead.

'We'd better go back, Anthony. I don't want to make you late.'

The time had passed so quickly. He certainly didn't want to go back to the classroom but 'mooning around won't pay the rent' as Gran had constantly admonished him.

As they turned in to the school gate, Helen asked, 'Do you feel better for that?'

'Much better. I've really enjoyed it.'

'So have I. We must do it again. I hope the rest of the day goes well. You'd better be going now.'

He took the hint. Mrs Pearson lingered by the pool as Anthony strode briskly across the lawn to the house. Just before he entered, he looked round but her back was turned and she gazed across the pool without moving. For some reason, he felt slightly deflated. Still, it had been a very enjoyable interlude and he felt more light-hearted than he had done for a fortnight. It helped him to survive the rest of the day's teaching without excessive misery.

'Hi! How's it going?'

Anthony's surreptitious scanning of vacancies in the Common Room newspapers was interrupted as Art-and-Craft's untidy head appeared round the door.

'Oh, OK,' he replied, not very convincingly, pushing the papers under his chair.

Art-and-Craft slumped into a worn armchair. Anthony wondered how he kept his beard in a perpetual state of two or three days' growth. Did he occasionally have some kind of half-shave? Or did it just not grow any longer? Perhaps it was something to do with the chemicals in paint.

'One good thing about being the only teacher in a subject - you get the whole range, good and bad. I expect you've been lumbered with all the bad eggs. Have you even been given Biggins and Co.?'

'Yes, 'fraid so.'

'Rotten luck. Old P. could have spared you that, at least. What does he do?'

'Mostly the Sixth.'

'Typical. How to put good people off teaching for life!' The art master jumped up and paced around the room, then flung himself down in the chair again. 'So you're having a rough time?'

No use pretending, thought Anthony. He knows perfectly well. 'A bit,' he replied.

'Don't let it get to you.' Art-and-Craft picked lumps of paint and clay from his tattered jumper. 'Know much about art?'

'Not enough. I'm keen to learn. Theory anyway. I don't know that I'd be much of a painter. Too uncoordinated.'

'Mrs P. paints.' Art-and-Craft looked at Anthony from under his straggly, greasy hair.

Had he seen them outside? Anthony replied, 'I know. I haven't seen any of her pictures though, except the place cards.'

'She's OK. All pretty landscape and flower stuff - the kind of thing ladies do. At least she's keen.' He looked hard at Anthony again. 'She's all right,

Mrs P. Can't understand how she puts up with Old P. What do you think of her . . . them?'

Anthony did not want to get into any kind of discussion about the Pearsons. Yet he realised that they were bound to be one of the main topics of conversation when the staff were together in private. What position would he take? They wouldn't allow him to remain neutral, he was sure.

'I'll reserve my judgement until I've been here longer,' he said.

'Well, I'd have thought you'd have got the measure of him already. He's a bastard!' Art-and-Craft exclaimed in a sort of half-whisper which Anthony felt could be heard all over the school. 'Like I say, she's all right. Pretty cool. You can't tell what she's thinking. Fergus thinks he can, mind you.'

'Oh, yes?'

'You'll find out! Well, better get back to the pots. Come round to the art room some time. I'm nearly always there - have a whirl with the wheel.'

'What?'

'The potter's wheel. Make yourself a set of coffee mugs. Great fun. Don't wear your best suit, though.'

'Brilliant. I'll have a go. Thanks.'

The art teacher stubbed out his cigarette and rose to go. He seemed about to say something else then changed his mind. He made for the door, then turned and said, 'Don't take too much notice of what Fergus tells you. He boasts.'

What is he trying to tell me, Anthony wondered? Is it about Helen . . . no, Mrs Pearson? I must remember. But 'Helen' sounded more like her - not so formal. He got the impression that she didn't care much for formality.

He folded up the papers that he had hastily tucked under his chair. They had not provided the dream job. He'd told Helen he'd give teaching a fair trial. But that had been in a happy moment, out in the fields with a pleasant, attractive companion. Back in school his resolve was not so strong. It wouldn't do any harm to keep looking.

'When's your duty night?' Michael asked as they returned from dinner. 'Mine's tonight. Should be interesting!'

'Not until Friday. You can tell me what it's like, and what to do.' Anthony replied. 'I'm rather worried about it.'

' When I was here, the master just slept in that little room - have you seen it yet?'

'No. Is it worse than our garret?'

'How could anything be? Anyway, the guy used to work in there all evening after dinner and keep checking on us. Then he'd send us all to bed. I suppose he'd go to bed himself about twelve. We'd always try to think of some reason to call him in the night but often we were too tired. We'd fall asleep and forget to go and annoy him.'

'Let's hope we're so lucky!'

'Touch wood. If there's a medical problem you have to send for Matron.

Her room's where the new blocks join the house. Did you know? Anyway, the boys will fetch her. If you need extra help, you'll probably send for Mary or me. We're always on duty, you know!'

'So I believe. Well, enjoy yourself this evening.'

'Take plenty to do - it can get pretty boring, I should think.'

'Especially if you're too nervous to go to sleep,' Anthony laughed. It wasn't really a joke. He could imagine the boys cooking up all kinds of delights for the ineffectual English master. Before that he had to face the trial of his first afternoon as Games Assistant. A treat for tomorrow!

At nine o'clock, after an evening's preparation, Anthony put some water on to boil. As he was wondering how Michael was getting on, there was a tap at the door. Probably a boy sent from the dormitories to recruit extra help. He groaned and turned off his camping stove.

'Come in!'

'I'm sorry to disturb you, Mr Dean, but I thought you might like to borrow this book.' Helen Pearson slipped quietly into his room carrying a natural history guidebook. 'Perhaps you'll be able to find a minute or two to look at it sometime.' She placed the book on top of his bookcase and looked around. 'You seem very busy!'

'I was just boiling the water for some coffee. Would you like some?'

She hesitated, then said, 'I'd love some, but I'd better be going back. Eric will wonder where I've gone and he may need me for something.' Her eyes lingered on the stove and mugs on top of the cupboard. 'I promise I'll stay on another occasion, when I've got more time.'

She opened the door and left as quietly as she had come. She must have been wearing very soft shoes, although Anthony hadn't noticed. What he did notice was her air of secrecy and the feeling that she would really have liked to sit and talk, look at the book together perhaps. He still couldn't imagine her and Pearson in an atmosphere of domestic bliss.

He lit the gas under his kettle again, but his enthusiasm for coffee had gone. So had any desire to continue working. The severe cold still lingered and now he felt tired and chilly and the room seemed very bleak. He filled his hot-water bottle, made some hot chocolate instead, and had an early night.

Chapter Eight

'A word in your ear.' Michael leaned towards Anthony and lowered his voice.

They were leaving the dining room after a quick lunch. Michael had marking to do before afternoon school and Anthony had to change for games.

'Try not to get on the wrong side of Fergus. He'll have you for dinner!'

Anthony bristled slightly at the implication that he was the sort of person who was easily gobbled up. His annoyance must have been visible.

Michael continued hastily, 'I'm not being funny. I mean it. There was a young teacher here when I was in the Fifth. Fergus made his life a misery. He didn't last long. I think even we hardened boys were uncomfortable with the way he treated poor Rigby on games afternoons.'

'Thanks for the warning.'

Anthony ascended the stairs to collect his kit with a heavy tread. It had happened again! The morning hadn't been a complete disaster, and anything less gave him hope. Now he was being told to watch out for his colleague as well as the boys. Cannons to the right, cannons to the left, he thought, despairingly.

His perusal of the newspapers hadn't yet provided him with a brilliant new career. In any case it seemed he was stuck here until Christmas. That seemed a century away. He'd have to cope until then, somehow. Only another four weeks until half term! Perhaps he could look for another job then.

Despite the mountains of papers and instructions he'd been given, he hadn't been told what equipment or clothing he'd need for games, either today or in the future - something else to note down for his book! So he'd packed just about everything except cricket whites into his sports bag. Collecting it from his room, he lugged it down to the changing rooms, which opened on to the small gym in the new block, on one side, and the playing field on the other. An economical arrangement - but extremely overcrowded when several groups were using the facilities at the same time.

So far Anthony had exchanged only a few words with Peter Ferguson. But even before Michael's comforting words of warning, he'd already formed the opinion that the games-master considered him the lowest form of life. Michael's tale suggested that this was Fergus's normal reaction to any green young teacher. Obviously things could become even more unpleasant if he took an active dislike to you. That mysterious conversation with Art-and-Craft could mean that Anthony was in line for an 'active dislike' if Fergus suspected him of being too friendly with Helen Pearson.

The changing rooms were already filling up when Anthony arrived. Peter Ferguson was busy organising the new boys, with help from two prefects. He merely nodded as Anthony emerged on to the field. Once again, Anthony wished he were shorter. There just wasn't enough material in a sports kit to hide you. Once again he wished he had brought his old, worn kit instead of this bright new one. Conspicuous wasn't the word! As he joined the group Peter Ferguson decided to acknowledge him at last.

'We've got Mr Dean to help us this term,' he announced, drawing the boys' attention to the lanky figure whose outfit was as gleaming as that of the First Years. 'At least, I *think* it's Mr Dean. It *might* be a netball post.'

The boys all laughed loudly, turning to stare at the new teacher and delighting in the mockery of the games-master. Anthony smiled thinly. This was going to set the tone of the afternoon, he feared.

It did. He seemed to be the object of more derision than even the clumsiest, least athletic boy was. Everything he did, every move, was held up as a bad example. If he wasn't doing anything wrong at that moment, then he was asked to, in order to show the pupils how not to do it. He had never been brilliant at games, and he hadn't played much at university, but he *knew* he wasn't that bad.

Having been ridiculed by the teacher in charge, he was totally unable to control the group when he was asked to lead a session of catching practice. The boys just continued mocking and laughing. His misery started to give way to anger. How dared Peter Ferguson put him in this position? Surely he should be giving advice and help to make games lessons a success, not damaging them? In the midst of the noisy shambles that was his group, he looked across to where Fergus was instructing a well-motivated group of sixth-formers. As he did so, he saw the games-master glance over towards him, then direct the attention of his group to the rumpus. There was a burst of laughter, and then they all turned quickly away when they saw Anthony watching them. Undermining my position with the senior boys, as well, thought Anthony bitterly.

It was a long, long afternoon. By the end, Anthony's sore throat had returned to the point where he could hardly speak, let alone shout as loudly as he needed to, to exercise even the slightest control. He was very cold, exhausted, unhappy and ill-tempered.

As they filed towards the gym, Peter Ferguson's only words were, 'Go round the field before you go in, will you, and check nothing's been left?'

'Shouldn't one of the prefects . . . ' Anthony began with what was left of his voice. But Fergus had already gone into the changing rooms, still joking with the older boys. The only boys left outside were a couple of quiet first-years. Anthony was tempted to ask them, but thought better of it. Something was bound to go wrong, and he'd be blamed. Better do it himself.

'Go in and get changed, you two,' he told them wearily, envying them as they scampered inside.

A very cold wind was now blowing across the playing field as one lone figure, still clad in shorts and thin top, slowly traced the perimeter. At least his efforts weren't completely wasted. He found a football tucked under the hedge. He'd have been in more trouble if it hadn't been discovered until the next day. When *he* was at school, it had been the job of the pupils to collect all the equipment - and to pay the penalty if they missed any. But it seemed the boys here were privileged in comparison with a mere teacher.

Teeth gritted, Anthony gave the football an angry swipe as he approached the buildings - and produced the kick of his life! The ball rocketed towards the gymnasium window. He stood frozen, his eyes screwed closed, waiting for the shattering sound of breaking glass. He heard the loud bang as the ball hit the window, then a series of smaller bumps as it bounced back onto the ground. Anthony slowly opened his eyes and started to breathe again. The window appeared undamaged and fortunately there was no-one in the gym to see the incident. Quickly he picked up the football, which was rolling back towards him, a pointer to his guilt. He muttered several words that were on the 'forbidden' list for use on school premises, and hurried indoors.

'How did the games go?' Mary asked, as they went down to dinner that evening.

'It was . . . OK. Something else to get used to.'

'I don't envy you. How did you find Mr Ferguson?'

'Er … busy. Lots of new boys and keen seniors to deal with.'

'Didn't bother much with you, is that right? Didn't tell you what to do, but complained when you didn't do it? Tried to make you look silly?'

Tried and succeeded. 'How did you know?' Anthony asked.

'Michael was telling me about him. He said you were out there this afternoon. We were worrying about you.'

'I'm glad somebody was,' Anthony replied, with a rueful smile. He decided not to mention the football incident, the fewer people who knew about that, the better. He just prayed that a large crack wouldn't appear in the gym window overnight. Perhaps he'd better slip in first thing in the morning and check.

Dinner was uncomfortable. Some of the boys on his table were the ones who had made such a fool of him that afternoon. He felt uneasy as he saw them exchange glances. He knew exactly what they were thinking. He was grateful for a couple of pleasant boys on either side of him who were telling him about their summer holidays. He made a great effort to keep this innocuous topic of conversation going throughout the meal.

As he left the dining room he met Helen Pearson in the hall.

'Did I see you out on the field this afternoon,' she asked.

'I'm afraid so.'

'Don't you like games?'

'I'm not a passionate enthusiast - they're OK.'

'You'd rather be out walking on the Downs?' she said with an expression that was almost like a wink. 'Preferably without a crowd of boys.'

'Yes, I think I would.'

'Perhaps we could go out there again soon. Unless you class me in the same category as the boys?'

'Certainly not! I really enjoyed walking with you. You know so much about the wildlife. I looked at your book last night. I wish I had more time to study it.'

'You'll find more time eventually. The first year is the worst. I'll try to find a little time later this week. When are you free?'

'Not until Friday. Then I have an hour after lunch.'

'I'll let you know if I can make that . . . I expect you've plenty to do upstairs, Mr Dean.' Her tone changed as Eric Pearson appeared in the hall. She turned and went into the library without another word.

Pearson muttered a brief 'Good evening,' as he walked past Anthony towards the dining hall.

'I'm making coffee for us all,' said a voice behind him. It was Mary. 'Come on, you don't need to get back to work yet. Michael will be along in a minute.'

Anthony followed her up the stairs and along the corridor to her room. Mary kept up a stream of conversation but his answers were automatic. His mind was fixed on how he could keep that Friday period free to walk with Helen Pearson.

'Signed up for England yet?' Michael joked as he rushed into the room behind them and collapsed into a chair.

'Not a hope. I wouldn't even get into a primary school team these days,' Anthony answered. He smiled as he thought of his brilliant kick. Best not to mention that! Sitting in Mary's cosy room with a hot mug of coffee in his hands and congenial companions, the awful events of the day began to fade. But they'd be back. He *must* remember to check that window in the morning.

'How was Fergus?'

'How do you think?'

'Bloody. Have you got into his bad books already?'

'Not intentionally. But he doesn't like me.'

'Don't let him bully you,' said Mary, bringing over the biscuit tin. 'Stand up to him!'

Easier said than done, Anthony thought. Especially when you don't have any weapons to fight with.

'You'd better give me some advice about duty night,' he said to Michael. This was another area where trouble was brewing.

'Mine was quiet - very dull. Perhaps you'll be as lucky.'

'Perhaps.'

But Anthony was not hopeful.

The week dragged on interminably. The boys had decided that Anthony was a soft touch and there was nothing he could do or say which seemed to change things. No shouting, detentions or written punishments had any effect. Serious and persistent offenders could be caned - by Pearson. Anthony could have sent almost all his pupils in every class. But he didn't dare send even one. He was under no delusions about Pearson's opinion of him. He felt *he* was more likely to get the cane than the boys were.

61

Pearson continued to find excuses (not that he needed any) to stay in Anthony's lessons as often as he could. He would be sorting through the stock cupboard or taking notes from a selection of books as though preparing one of his many talks or articles. But he was, of course, carefully watching Anthony. Every hesitation, and there were many, in the young teacher's delivery, would result in a cold look from those icy eyes. Every fumbled word seemed to echo around the silent classroom, while the boys looked at each other furtively and smirked. The noisy, uncontrolled lessons when Pearson was absent were almost a relief.

Anthony knew he would never take any steps towards becoming a successful teacher in the two situations that prevailed at the moment - insolent near-riot or the steely unnerving presence of Pearson. He needed at least one group of boys who were reasonably well motivated and, most of all, he needed some advice on how to deal with the others. He got neither.

His throat was perpetually sore now. His voice rasped and cracked - another source of amusement for his pupils. He focused on Friday afternoon in his efforts to get through the week. He counted the hours. Nothing must happen to spoil that one island of pleasure in a sea of misery that stretched to the horizon.

He almost lost it. Pearson had been working in the English room when Anthony's first lesson began on Friday morning and had shown no inclination to leave. In Pearson's presence the boys, although silent, showed their contempt for their new teacher in other ways. They appeared totally unable to answer any questions. Those who were the loudest on other occasions could only mumble some entirely inappropriate response, if they could be persuaded to speak at all. The boys whose pens were normally fluent in producing insulting comment on Anthony in words and pictures could now hardly write a coherent line. This lesson was no different. It became a monologue with Anthony desperately trying to find things to say to fill in the time which would normally be spent on discussion. The silence was punctuated by a series of pointed sighs and yawns.

Half way through the lesson, Pearson rose abruptly from his desk in a corner of the room and walked out, remarking in a low but clear voice to Anthony as he passed, 'Your free periods are provided for the purpose of more thorough preparation of material.'

In that silent, strained room, the comment was perfectly audible to all. Amidst the babble and chaos that broke out as soon as Pearson was deemed to be out of earshot, Anthony heard several creditable imitations of the Head's words and tone.

What free periods, he thought bitterly? He only had three and he had lost one each week so far.

'Be quiet!' he yelled in what should have been the top of his voice. A guttural croak was all that was left of that voice. The class ignored him. He struggled on and prayed for the bell. Would Pearson be watching to see how he spent his free period after lunch?

He was lucky. A group of visitors arrived at the school and Pearson was fully occupied. Then Anthony realised that Helen would probably be entertaining them too. So she wouldn't be able to get away after all. Well, he'd walk by himself. He certainly needed some fresh air and a break from the stress of the classroom. But he'd been so looking forward to her company.

As he left the dining room he was surprised to meet her, just going out, dressed in trousers and a thick sweater. She looked around quickly before saying in a low voice, 'Are you able to get away this afternoon?'

'Yes, so far.'

'I'll meet you in the lane in half an hour. I have to go now.'

With another glance around, she slipped out by the back door.

The next thirty minutes seemed like eternity as Anthony caught up with a little work in his room, praying that no-one would come looking for him. Could he, too, slip out unseen? It might be easier to amble down to the pond now, while the pupils were still milling round during their lunch break. Then he could leave by the back gate when the bell went.

He walked across the damp grass past small groups of boys who eyed him curiously and, in some cases, malevolently. As he passed he heard his own feeble attempts at discipline repeated in mockery, interspersed with imitations of the words of Pearson. He shuddered.

At the pond he stopped to talk to two of his first-year group. If only all his pupils were like them! He drew their attention to the lingering dragonflies and went on to discuss photography, in which the boys showed an interest. The clamour of the bell broke in and he hurried them off towards the school.

Leaning on the gate, he watched the last of the reluctant boys being urged on by the prefects, who had far more control over them than he had. He opened the gate quickly and passed through. Once outside the school grounds, he walked quickly along the back of the school and turned up the hill between the hedgerows. As he climbed, a robin fluttered ahead of him in the cover of the hedge, tick-ticking its annoyance at being disturbed on such an afternoon.

It *was* a glorious day. The low sun shone through the leaves, making the colours glow. Above, the open Downs were a smooth ochre-green curve with that tempting white track carved through to the summit. Would there be time to reach the top today? Anthony's spirits rose with every step up the flinty pathway. He hurried forward, wondering where Helen was.

She was waiting. She sat on a tree stump at the spot where he had seen the poppy. She stood up when she saw him.

'I'm glad you could come,' she said.

'I nearly couldn't.'

'Nor me. Did you see those visiting parents? I managed to get away before Eric caught me to entertain them.'

Anthony wondered if she would be in trouble for this. He didn't like to ask.

'If we hurry, we should be able to make it to the top and back, if you want to,' Helen went on quickly.

Before he could reply, she started up the slope, walking briskly. He had the impression that she felt awkward about her admission that she had dodged her duty. Not the sort of thing that she'd want junior staff to know, he thought. Pearson certainly wouldn't be pleased if he had heard her.

Anthony looked down at her. The breeze was blowing her red-brown hair over her eyes and she pushed it back with a careless gesture. Up here, free from the constraints of school life, she seemed much younger. He could hardly believe she wasn't a contemporary of his. And he knew he was beginning to wish that she were. She seemed so out of place as a headmaster's wife - or at least, his impression of what a headmaster's wife should be like.

She must have felt his eyes on her, for she looked up and smiled gently. She always seemed to know what he was thinking. He felt his cheeks flush as she asked: 'You wonder why I'm doing this, don't you?'

'Well . . . yes, I suppose I do.'

'I just have to get away sometimes.'

Would she go on? He knew there was more to it than that. He said, 'I'm sure you do.'

She was silent for a moment. Then she said, 'It's more than that. It's having congenial company, too. We seem to . . . have a lot in common.'

'We do. Only I'm so . . . '

'What?'

'Ignorant. About the things you like. About most things really.'

'Nonsense!' But she said it gently, with that quiet, wistful smile.

They said no more for a while. The path was becoming steeper and they began to puff - Helen in particular. Suddenly she stopped, began to laugh, and took off her thick sweater.

'It's all right for you! I have to take three steps to your one. And I'm getting on a bit.'

'Oh no, you're not!' Anthony winced as she drew attention to their difference in age.

She just gave him another wistful smile, but there was a twinkle in her eye. Had she noticed him looking admiringly at her figure as she wriggled out of the sweater? He felt his cheeks redden again. She tied the sweater around her waist by the sleeves and they went on up the hill, a little slower now.

'How's this week been?' she panted as they walked.

'Almost as bad as last week.' Anthony could see no point in concealing anything from her.

'Oh, dear. It *will* get better. I know that doesn't seem much comfort now.'

'It needs to get an awful lot better, quickly. I'm on duty tonight.'

'Then I'll be praying for a peaceful night. But you must send for extra help if you need it. Michael will help. He knows the ropes. Don't try and struggle on alone.' Helen looked up at him and must have read his expression again. 'Oh, I know you don't like to ask for help. Nobody does. But you must. I may even get the chance to pop over myself during the evening. Can't promise, though.'

'Thanks. I'm sure I'll be OK.' Anthony began to look forward to his duty night with considerably less dread.

'Here's the top at last, thank goodness!' Helen took a few deep breaths. 'Look at that wonderful view.'

'Brilliant! What a spot! I must bring my camera up here.'

'Views like this are hard to photograph, aren't they? Hard to paint, too! I've tried.'

'Will you let me see?'

'Not until I've done a good one. I haven't yet,' she laughed.

Anthony tried to visualise her sitting up here alone, with her paintbox. What did she think about? What was her husband's reaction to her lonely wandering and sketching?

'We must go down now,' she broke into his musings, 'or you'll be late and . . . ' and be in even more trouble, he thought, but said only ' . . . and miss my lesson.'

'Yes. That would never do.'

She turned and led the way down the track again.

'It's lovely up here,' he said, lingering.

'Then we must come back, for longer next time. If you want to.'

'I do.'

He wanted to say 'I hope you do' but shyness overcame him and he said nothing. Their footsteps crunched on the chalk and flint as they hurried downwards. The sound almost seemed to be saying 'you've missed your chance again'. That was what always happened to Anthony. At nearly twenty-two he saw his life as already full of regrets and missed opportunities. But Helen might come to see him this evening . . .

They arrived at the spot where the track turned at right angles to run along the back of the school grounds.

'You'd better rush ahead now. I'm in no hurry to meet those visitors. But you mustn't be late.'

She doesn't want us to be seen together, he thought as he dashed along to the gate. He composed himself to walk through without apparent haste and strode purposefully across the lawn. He had five minutes in which to prepare himself for the next lesson. Fortunately not enough time to worry about it too much, or for the elation of his walk to have left him. Biggins and Co could go to the devil. What did he care?

'You skived off somewhere after lunch?' a voice remarked enquiringly. Michael was hanging over the banister watching as Anthony plodded wearily upstairs at the end of afternoon school. Anthony looked up with a jolt. He'd been gazing at his feet as he climbed, his thoughts on another, pleasanter, uphill walk.

'Yes, I went out for a bit,' he said, shortly. What business was it of Michael's?

'Oh . . . OK.' Michael turned back towards his room.

'Hey, sorry!' Anthony certainly didn't want to lose one of his few friends. Michael was hearty but well-meaning. 'I didn't mean to snap - had a bad afternoon.'

Michael turned round again.

'The kettle's just boiled. I'll make you a coffee and fill you in for tonight.'

'Thanks. I'll just dump this stuff.' Anthony was glad that he had not, for once, missed an opportunity and allowed ill-feeling to fester. Perhaps he was beginning to learn something.

'Put your feet up.' Michael gestured towards the bed, which formed the only seat other than the hard wooden chair by the table, which he took himself.

'You still got Pearson breathing down your neck every lesson?'

'Not this afternoon, thank goodness. I believe he's got visitors.'

'Still, it's a bit rough. I mean, it's bad enough being a new teacher, without that strain. No wonder you look ragged.'

Do I, wondered Anthony? The elation of his walk had soon passed. Despite his earlier resolution to allow the Prince of Darkness to take charge of his most trying pupils, they had once again made mincemeat of him.

'I dare say I'll survive, one way or another,' he said. 'I just need to know how to get through tonight.'

'Right. You go along after dinner to the duty room. Take plenty of work, your night things and . . . '

'Is there a kettle?' interrupted Anthony, suddenly thinking of the most important resource, 'And coffee, mugs etcetera?'

'Yes, it's all there. Take something to eat though, if you've got anything. If not, you can take these biscuits. You just work in the duty room, and walk round a bit. Lights out at ten. Somebody will call you if there's any trouble.'

'Is it that easy?'

'Mine was. But I have to confess that when I was a boy here the duty master didn't always have an easy time. You know who to look out for by now?'

'Most of them. I expect there are some angels I haven't come across.'

'If you have any real trouble, send for Mary or me. That, after all, is the price we pay for having this luxurious accommodation!'

'I will.'

But Anthony desperately hoped that he wouldn't need to. Helen had been right. He didn't like asking for help. Especially as his whole performance in the school so far had been an unrelieved disaster. Perhaps he had better use some of the evening to consider his future. He must call in to the Common Room and study the vacancies in the paper before dinner.

Chapter Nine

Anthony made his way slowly over to the duty room. As he passed the dining room, cheerful late diners, staff and pupils, were still sitting in the brightly-lit room which, normally rather bleak, now seemed a haven of comfort and desirability. In his pocket jingled the key to the 'cell' where he was to spend the next twelve hours. Twelve hours! Did any criminal begin his sentence with such dread as he felt? At that moment he would gladly have exchanged his freedom for the safety of a real prison cell. The other inmates would surely be more civilised, less vindictive, than the boys of Fieldhouse School.

The duty room was upstairs in the new block, off a corridor that separated the two dormitories. Also off this hallway were shower rooms, a couple of shared study bedrooms for older boys, a quiet room and a games room. Even though pupil numbers had apparently gone down recently, and many boys lived out, the accommodation was still cramped. Michael had hinted that conditions used to be appalling, but parents were sufficiently impressed by the reputation of the school to send their sons there.

What with the hollow echoes of the corridor and the proximity of the games room and showers, Anthony did not expect a very quiet evening. One of his duties would be to ensure that the quiet room remained just that - a place for prep and reading. Fortunately he believed that a prefect would be on duty in there for at least part of the evening. No doubt he'd be far more competent than Anthony at enforcing the rules.

'If anyone's ill, you send someone for Matron,' Michael had said. 'Her room's at the end of Dorm One, where it joins the main building. She usually walks through the dorms in the evening, checking on cleanliness and so on. She'll help with any problems.'

'Matron' was Jean Benton, who had been at the school for several years. Firm but cheerful, she had the knack of enjoying the company of the boys while commanding their utmost respect. The contact Anthony had had with her suggested that she regarded new young teachers as part of her brood. This thought comforted Anthony. Perhaps her presence nearby would help keep things under control, especially if she was inclined to take pity on him.

He unlocked the door to the duty room and stepped inside. Michael had warned him that the room wasn't very swish. It was small and square, with the usual narrow, hard bed, a desk and chair, a small bedside table and a cupboard-cum-bookcase. A misshapen wire coathanger on a hook at the back of the door constituted the only 'wardrobe'. The desk had a lamp that gave out the same dim light as the one in his room. A worn flex trailed to it across the dingy brown carpet, from the direction of the bedside cabinet. Obviously you had to move the lamp between the two as required. Could he do so without being electrocuted? On top of the desk was a large rubber torch. Was this to supply the failings of the electrical system, to enable the master to sneak around in the dead of night checking on midnight feasts, or to be used as a weapon against intruders - burglars or boys? Anthony suspected all three. He picked up the heavy object and pressed the 'ON' button. Nothing happened. Well, that eliminated its usefulness for either of the first two options. He might still need it for the third, though. He walked over and placed it on the bedside table.

Also on the desk there was a small, cheap notepad and a dog-eared card of typed instructions to the duty master. It consisted of a list of points, mostly beginning with the words 'Masters must . . . ' In Point One, someone had inserted the words 'or Mistresses' after 'Masters', in large red letters, presumably in deference to the female staff. They had not bothered to continue with this correction all down the page. In view of Pearson's enthusiasm for efficiency and paperwork, Anthony was surprised that this scruffy card had not been replaced. A few minutes typing could have produced a much more acceptable set of instructions. A stub of chewed pencil lay beside the notebook. On reading down the card, Anthony discovered that this was provided for the purpose of writing down the names of miscreants. No suggestion was given as to what to do with this list afterwards. There was no telephone in the room.

The only decoration was a picture on the wall above the bed. Looking at it closely in the poor light, Anthony saw that it was a watercolour of the main building, showing the garden side. The painting had a delicate touch. The artist had paid attention to detail in painting the shrubs and pots of flowers around the house. He thought it must have been done some time ago. In one corner he could just see the faded initials of the artist. Carefully he lifted it down from the wall. A layer of dust covered the top of the frame and various cobwebs had gathered behind. Peering at it under the lamp he picked out the initials - 'H.P.'

Helen Pearson! This must be one of her paintings. Relegated to the duty room. Or had she placed it there herself to brighten the lot of the poor souls condemned to spend a night here? Had she put it there just for him? No, of course not. What a stupid idea! He didn't know much about dust but he reckoned it would take a while for all that to accumulate. A slight feeling of disappointment followed this realisation. He replaced the picture on the wall, first wiping off the dust and cobwebs with his sleeve. Then he took out his handkerchief and polished the glass. The hankie came away grubby and the picture seemed to glow more brightly. He was pleased.

He pulled the desk round slightly and positioned the lamp so that the light fell on the picture as well as the file and piles of exercise books which he had placed ready to begin work. Now he would at least have something pleasant to look at. He could gaze at it while he was having his coffee.

Coffee! Where were the means for making coffee? He opened the door of

68

the cupboard-cum-bookcase. Inside, there was an electric kettle, two chipped mugs and a bent spoon. Beside these there was a jar of cheap coffee and a honey jar half-full of lumpy sugar into which someone had frequently dipped a damp coffee spoon. There was no milk. Anthony did not much like black coffee and the idea of making it more palatable with that sugar was not appealing. Well, it would have to do. He'd know next time. Thank goodness he'd taken Michael's hint and provided himself with some food. Sweets, chocolate, crisps and biscuits should provide some comfort and compensate for the lack of coffee.

The other half of this piece of furniture was a bookcase. The master (or, of course, mistress) on duty was provided with a range of reading material - a copy of the school rules, one or two old school magazines, an atlas, a Bible and an English textbook written by Eric Pearson. Anthony pondered the significance of these. The Bible for comfort and self-improvement, the textbook to remind him who was boss, and the atlas to help plan his escape. He felt that the most useful addition might be several recent copies of the newspaper containing vacancy lists. But perhaps this was putting too much temptation in the way of lonely, unhappy teachers isolated in this drab little room for long nights, without even a novel or two to cheer them up.

Cold nights too. The bed had one thin blanket and a worn, faded bedspread identical to the one on his own bed. Michael should have told him to bring another blanket and his hot-water bottle. But this was the 'new' block and there *was* a radiator. It was off. Anthony turned the black knob at the side and heard a hopeful gurgle as the hot water began to circulate. As he turned the knob full on he felt a slight dampness around the pipe below it. A leak! Only a slight one, thank goodness. He wound his long-suffering handkerchief around the pipe several times. Hopefully that would contain it. He could always use his towel if necessary.

Right! He was ready to start his night's work. He supposed his first job, before beginning on the marking, was to patrol outside. There was already quite a lot of noise in the corridor and surrounding rooms. But he'd better lay out his work first, so as to look purposeful if anyone should come in. Then he'd go out and take a look around.

He opened his file and placed a blue and red pen on the desk beside it. Then he arranged the pile of exercise books neatly. At least with Pearson's presence in many of his lessons, his pupils had had no choice but to produce at least some written work. They also appeared to have done the prep he'd set - perhaps forced into it by the masters on duty in the last few evenings. That was another of his tasks. He had to check what prep boys had been given and whether they had done it. He must go and start on this job now, before someone checked up on *him.*

He grasped the door handle - then stopped. Just a minute! Although there was some noise around, it was only what you would expect from a large group of boys returning from their evening meal. It didn't sound like a riot.

Perhaps they didn't know who the duty master was, so they were being careful. As soon as they knew . . . Cocooned in this little room, investigating the 'facilities' and organising his work, he felt safe, even confident. But the moment he opened that door and stepped out into the corridor, all that would come to an abrupt, and probably unpleasant, end.

He stepped back to the desk and flicked over the pages of his file. Then he opened the first exercise book and laid it down for marking. The noise level from outside seemed to be rising. It was no use. He'd *have* to go out there.

He opened the door. A small knot of boys outside the games room straightened up and fell silent. Then, seeing which ogre it was who emerged from the duty room, their faces creased into insolent grins.

'Oh, it's Mr Dean! Are *you* on duty tonight, sir?'

Anthony admitted that he was.

'Oh, good. Hey, you lot, it's Mr Dean!'

With whoops of delight they disappeared into the games room, conveying the good news to their fellows.

Anthony had no wish to follow them. Instead he went to the quiet room on the opposite side and put his head round the door. Again the hasty, shuffling silence followed by an outbreak of delight as they recognised their victim.

'Is it you, Mr . . . sorry, can't remember your name.'

'It's Mr Dean. The new English Master. Aren't you, sir?'

Anthony once more reluctantly admitted that he was.

Under the eagle eye of the prefect on duty they quietened down to grins and whispers, but Anthony knew exactly what they were thinking.

'Any problems in here?' he said to the prefect.

'No, sir.'

'Well, call me if there are,' he said, irritated by the knowledge that young Grey would be wasting his time by doing so. The sixth-former had far more control than Anthony felt he would ever have.

He closed the door again. He really would have to tackle that noisy games room next. He caught sight of a figure shambling along the corridor in his direction. No mistaking the large, untidy boy and his rolling walk.

'Miller!'

'Yes, sir.'

'Where are you going?'

The boy's round, red face had a look of surprise.

'To the games room, sir.'

'Didn't you have any prep?'

'Yes, sir'

'Then why aren't you doing it?'

'I've done it, sir.'

'Where is it?'

'In my locker in the dorm, sir.'

'Well, please go back and get it. I want to see it.'

'Oh, sir! Do I have to?'

'Yes. Bring it to the duty room in five minutes.'

The boy turned with a downcast air and shuffled back down the corridor again. Watching his bulky, graceless form, Anthony felt ashamed. He'd picked on this unfortunate boy who was doing nothing wrong, simply because he was an easy target. Didn't the lad suffer enough from his school fellows as it was? Anthony knew he should really be tackling the noise in the games room. But he'd wanted to appear to be doing his duty while avoiding the real problem. Still, he consoled himself, he *was* supposed to check on prep. He just hoped that Miller had done it properly, so that he could give him some praise.

The noise from the games room had reached a crescendo. Anthony entered and slammed the door loudly behind him. In the momentary silence he glanced round and quickly took in the features of the room. It was large and rather bare. In the centre stood a shabby snooker table and behind it, on the wall, a dart-board bristling with darts. He shuddered at the sight of these - what havoc *they* might wreak. Around the perimeter was a motley collection of stained, rickety tables and chairs, some broken. One or two of these tables were strewn with cards or the remnants of board games. A shelf in the corner held a battered selection of boxes containing, he supposed, more games and jigsaws. He couldn't imagine any of these boys doing jigsaws, at least not in here. Any more than he could imagine them playing with what appeared to be the remains of a clockwork train set. A transistor radio was making a feeble attempt to relay pop music from some obscure station - and mainly failing.

In one corner, surrounded by a ring of onlookers, two boys were disentangling themselves from the fight they had been enjoying and which had been the source of most of the din.

'Get up!' ordered Anthony.

They did so amidst rising noise levels as the pupils realised that it was not, after all, the dreaded 'Old P' who had caught them. Anthony banged on the nearest table with a convenient empty soft drink bottle.

'Silence! Stand up straight, you two. What's your name?' he asked the boy nearest to him.

There was no reply. Muffled giggles from the assembled mob.

'Answer me at once!'

'I can't remember . . . sir.'

'And you?' He turned to the other offender.

'I've forgotten. Sorry, sir.'

Anthony looked around the room. There was usually somebody who would give the game away. But not tonight.

'P'raps they never had a name, sir.'

'They never remember anything, sir.'

'They've got no brains, sir.'

'Send them to Mr Pearson, sir.'

The group took up this theme as each boy vied with the others to convince the irate master of the stupidity of their classmates. He needed no such convincing.

'You two, go to the duty room. The rest of you - if you can't behave sensibly in here I'll set you some work to do. You know the rules.'

Anthony stalked out of the room behind his two captives, slamming the door again in a gesture of defiance. They *would* do as he said - eventually.

'You - stand facing that wall. And you, stand facing this one. You can stand there until you remember your names.'

He hoped they'd soon get tired of the joke and give in. He certainly didn't want them in with him all evening. He began to wonder if he'd dug himself a hole. What if Helen called in? He sat down at the desk and began his marking. The two boys, obviously experts at this, had devised ways of sending signals to each other every time his head was bent over his books, which made it impossible for him to concentrate. If only he could remember their names. One of them was in a class of his and he'd already had trouble from him. But his class lists were back in his room. Was it John? The school was full of Johns. It would be so much easier when he'd learnt all this.

He could see their shoulders beginning to shake with laughter. They were obviously only too aware of his discomfiture. Then he heard the shuffling footsteps of Miller approaching the door.

'Come in.'

The ungainly boy entered, clutching several tattered exercise books. The two detainees glanced round, then began to splutter and shake all the more.

'Quiet!' Anthony addressed them firmly. It had little effect. Peter Miller seemed very uncomfortable in their presence. Once again Anthony hoped, somewhat vainly, that his work would be good. He took the first book from the boy's large, inkstained hand and looked at the open page. As he did so, he heard a light step in the corridor outside.

Helen! He was beginning to recognise her footsteps now. He looked up expectantly from the pages of scrawled calculations that Miller had placed before him, fervently wishing she had come at a less awkward moment. The door was partly open. He listened for the steps to stop outside, for a knock, or for her face to appear in the opening. Only the first of these occurred. The steps halted, then turned and retreated down the corridor in a more hurried fashion than they had approached.

Damn! Damn! thought Anthony. Damn these boys with their infernal fights and insolence and their scrawled exercises. Don't go, Helen! Come back! But she wouldn't have interrupted him. She was much too sensitive for that.

He bent his head to the book. Miller was watching him, a puzzled expression on his face.

'I thought I heard someone coming,' Anthony offered in explanation for his distraction. 'They've gone now. Which teacher is this for?'

'It's maths, sir. For Mr James.'

The pages were creased and dirty and the writing almost unintelligible, especially to someone as unmathematical as Anthony. Despite the remarks about presentation written large in red on every page the previous work appeared to be mostly correct and had received good marks.

'Your work is very messy. But you seem to get the right answers. Well done.'

'Thank you, sir.'

'Do you always do well at maths?'

'Yes, sir, mostly.'

The boy shuffled his feet and transferred the two remaining books from hand to hand, looking down at his enormous hands as he did so. He glanced nervously from under his lank dark hair at the two miscreants who would doubtless become his tormentors as soon as they were all free. Anthony was sympathetic. But he had to go on with the interview for one and the punishment for the others. After all, they had already cost him a visit from Helen.

'Did you have other prep?'

Miller silently handed over the two books with which he had been toying. At Anthony's questioning look he said, 'This one's science for Mr Beech. And the other one's for Mr Wilson. It's a design we had to do in rough for next week.'

The science was like the maths - hopelessly messy but apparently correct. The design Anthony could not comment on but he knew it was better than anything he could do. There was obviously a lot more to this boy than the overweight scruff that met the eye. He was really sorry that the interview had taken place under such conditions. He must try and make time to speak to him again. He handed back the books with a smile.

'You're doing well. Keep it up. And try to improve that neatness. You can go now.'

'Thank you, sir!'

With an audible sigh of relief, the boy took his books and hurried out, throwing a look of triumph to the others as he left.

Now to somehow deal with these two! As he stared grimly at them, that light knock he'd been expecting earlier came on the door, then a familiar head appeared.

'Oh, you're still busy, Mr Dean. Please don't let me interrupt.'

She seemed about to depart again.

'Oh, please come in, Mrs Pearson. I'm afraid these two will be here for some time.'

'What have you done, Riley?' she asked the boy on the right in a severe tone.

Riley! Of course, John Riley. He wouldn't forget that name now.

'Fighting, miss.'

'And you, Basford?'

73

'Fighting, miss.'

'Mrs Pearson! And what else besides fighting?'

How does she know there's something else, thought Anthony?

The two boys looked down at their feet and said nothing.

'Well, perhaps Mr Dean can tell us?'

'Loss of memory. They've forgotten their names.'

'They'd better have remembered them by nine o'clock tomorrow morning when they will be having an interview with Mr Pearson,' said Helen sharply.

Anthony felt disconcerted. He'd rather Pearson had not known about this incident. And what was he to do now? Dismiss them? Helen had so much more command of the situation than he did. She came to his rescue.

'I can see that Mr Dean has work to do and he'd probably prefer to do it without your presence all evening.'

'Yes, you can go now,' Anthony said with relief, 'but you are not allowed back in the games room tonight.'

The two boys departed. Helen grimaced at their retreating backs and said, 'Those two always make trouble.'

'Thanks for your help. I'd offer you coffee only there's no milk.'

Helen looked exasperated.

'There should be. There's supposed to be fresh milk brought up here every evening, and a snack. You can't expect teachers to sit here all night with nothing to eat or drink. I'll go down and get some.'

'Oh, don't go to any trouble for me.'

'It's no trouble - and I'll make sure it doesn't happen again.'

She walked towards the door.

'I'll go on patrol round the dorms while you're gone. I haven't had time to do that yet.'

'I'll do Dorm One on my way down. Then you'll only need to do Dorm Two.'

Before he could reply, she had gone.

She shouldn't be doing my work for me, Anthony thought guiltily, but she does make things a lot easier. And he could hardly send her away. She was Pearson's wife, after all, although somehow he was finding it increasingly difficult to think of her as such.

As he left the room, he saw Helen come out of the games room, calling over her shoulder,

'No more trouble this evening - or you'll all be banned from here for a week.'

She'd been reading the Riot Act in there too! She smiled in his direction, then went off towards the dormitory. He turned and walked slowly down to Dorm Two, hoping he'd find it quiet.

It was a long room with a row of beds down each side. Between each bed was a tall, narrow metal cupboard where the boys had to keep all their belongings. They also had a tiny bedside table with shelf space underneath. At one end of the room was a stack of chairs which boys could place beside their beds during the evening if they wanted to read or work there. Tonight there were only two boys in the room. One was Miller. He was sitting on one of the hard chairs working on the design he'd showed Anthony earlier, resting his notebook on an atlas. The other boy was a first year. He was writing a letter. They both looked up as Anthony entered.

'It's very peaceful in here,' he said. 'What are you both doing?'

'I'm working on my design for Mr Wilson,' said Miller. 'I've changed it a bit now.'

He passed over the book.

'Is it a design for something in particular?'

'Yes, for the Art Room. Mr Wilson wants a mural.'

'Is it a competition?'

'Sort of.'

'Well, good luck.'

'Thank you sir.'

'I'm writing to my mother, sir,' said the other boy, who looked rather unhappy.

Anthony could guess the sort of thing that was being written. He felt sorry for any young boy in his first weeks away from home. He said quietly, 'Have you done your prep?'

'Yes, sir.'

He didn't ask to see it. He just said, 'You know where to find me if you need anything. I'm just along the corridor.'

He couldn't find any words of comfort for someone who was trapped in a place where he himself felt like a condemned man.

He made a quick check of the showers and hurried back to the duty room. Helen was boiling the kettle.

'I would have done that.'

She laughed. 'It's OK. I'm quite capable of boiling a kettle. And making the coffee too. Here's the milk - and some cakes and cheese and biscuits.'

She indicated the plates on the table. He guessed they were from her own kitchen. She took her mug of coffee and perched on the edge of the bed. Anthony wondered where Eric was. He asked, 'Have your visitors gone?'

'Yes, thank goodness. Eric's out now, speaking at a meeting about English teaching. I'm surprised he didn't ask you to go. Because of your duty night I suppose.'

There was something faintly amusing at the prospect of Eric Pearson asking him to accompany him to a meeting. He merely answered, 'Probably.'

Helen seemed to read his thoughts as usual.

'Do you get much advice and help from Eric?'

'Er . . . ' he hesitated ' . . . no.' It was nothing less than the truth.

'Never?'

'No, not really.'

'But he comes into your classroom?'

'Yes. But it's his classroom really.'

Helen stared down at her coffee.

'Eric's always very busy,' she said at last. 'I'm sure he'll find time to advise you eventually.'

Or sack me eventually, Anthony thought, unless I pre-empt him. But sitting here in this warm little room with plentiful food and excellent company, the search for another post didn't seem quite such an urgent necessity. However, it might by the morning.

'I must go,' Helen said, putting down her mug. 'I'm sure you'll be fine. I'll do the rounds again before I go - keeps them on their toes! Don't forget to send for help if you need it.'

'I'm glad you came,' Anthony said, suddenly shy.

'I don't believe in throwing people to the lions,' she said.

'I was admiring your picture,' he said, hoping she'd stay a little longer.

'Oh, that! I did it when I first came here. It used to hang in the library. Then Eric decided that there should be something better in there. Eventually I put it here to cheer the place up.'

'I really like it.'

'Then you'd better take it for your room.'

'Oh, I don't think I'd better be seen stealing pictures,' he laughed.

'It doesn't belong to the school. It's mine, to do as I like with.' Helen sounded defiant. He wondered if she had a problem, defending what she thought was hers. 'I can put another one here. There are plenty in the flat. I'll organise it.'

Anthony didn't see any point in arguing. Besides, he'd love to have one of her pictures in his room.

'Enjoy the rest of your evening,' she smiled as she left the room.

After she'd gone, the room seemed much colder. And it was not yet nine-thirty.

Anthony turned to his marking. Helen's patrol would keep things under control for a while. Engrossed in deciphering the semi-literate compositions that had been written during one of Pearson's visits to his class, he was shocked by the sudden metallic ringing of the electric bell outside his room. Was it a fire or some other disaster sent to plague him? He pushed back his chair and made for the door. Then a thought struck him. He turned back to the desk and scanned the dog-eared instruction card.

A warning bell will ring at 9.45pm precisely. Masters must ensure that all boys leave the games and quiet rooms and go to the dormitories to prepare for bed. The prefects will assist in this. At 10pm the 'Lights Out' bell will sound . . .

Anthony wasn't sure how all those boys were to wash and be in bed in fifteen minutes, given the small number of showers and washbasins. Of course, the instructions didn't actually say anything about washing. So presumably he was not expected to see that it was carried out.

The noise in the corridor told him that most of the pupils had obeyed the bell, at least as far as leaving the rooms was concerned. He heard the raised voices of two prefects telling them to be quiet and hurry. He opened the door and stood outside. As usual his presence caused sly looks and sniggers. He wondered what they had in store for him when the lights were out and the prefects had gone back to their rooms in the main block.

As he stood there feeling rather helpless he saw the head of Matron above the throng in the dormitory doorway. Joking with some boys, and administering sharp words to others, she pushed her way towards him along the corridor.

'Ah, Mr Dean, hello! How's the evening been? Sorry I haven't been along before but I've been carrying out urgent repairs to a boy's knees - and his trousers. I kept my eye on the dormitory though.'

'It's been OK. No real problems so far.'

'There won't be. The senior boys in both dormitories and the little rooms are fairly sensible. Of course there are some others . . . but I expect you know about them?'

'I've met some of them,' answered Anthony ruefully.

'We all know them!' said Matron in a tone that implied that others had problems too, not just him. 'You will call me if you need help, won't you? Don't hesitate - I'm used to it.'

'I will, thanks.'

At ten o'clock the bell sounded again. Five minutes later Anthony went on patrol and found all quiet, apart from some whispering. He went back to his room and recommenced work. Every half-hour he patrolled again. He enjoyed the break from the hard chair and the stress of reading those compositions.

Around midnight he decided to turn in himself. A hot shower warmed him - the heating had long since gone off - and after a final coffee and biscuit he climbed into the hard, narrow bed. Should he have locked the door? Yes, he should. He got up and did so, first peering down the corridor and listening. He heard nothing. He lay down again and tried to sleep. He was tired but it got colder and colder. He rose again and put on his sweater and gave another glance outside. He wrapped himself up tightly and tried to think of pleasant things, like his walk with Helen.

Trrring! Anthony jumped up, alarmed. Where was he? What was that? Then he remembered. He must have drifted off to sleep. But the room seemed lighter . . . he looked at his watch. It was seven o'clock. That was the rising bell! Good God! What had gone on in the night without him knowing? Dressing quickly, he unlocked the door and turned the handle. Or tried to. Nothing happened. He pulled again, shaking and wrenching at the door. At last he felt something give. There was a loud crash and the door swung inwards, nearly knocking him off his feet. He dashed out into the corridor - but got no further. The whole passageway was filled with furniture. Chairs, tables, bookcases, even the snooker table had been brought into service. He couldn't move in any direction. With grim amusement he noticed that a small section on the opposite side to his room had been left clear, giving access to the shower rooms - for them, not for him! Thank goodness he hadn't needed to get up in the night.

As he stood there, the first of the boys appeared at the dormitory door, in response to the bell. They were as uncertain of what to do as he was. He recovered himself.

'Get all those boys up and out here now, moving this stuff! I'll count to ten. One, two, three, four . . . ' he bellowed.

The boys in the doorway scuttled back into the Dorm. Meanwhile, a little group had gathered outside the dormitory at the other end of the blocked corridor. Anthony repeated his demands. A voice responded.

'Get this stuff moved, you lot. We'll be in dead trouble if Old P. catches us.'

It was Miller. The large boy began moving the furniture single-handed.

'Spoil-sport!' and other complaints accompanied his efforts but at last, with Anthony's frantic threats from the middle goading them, the boys eventually replaced the offending furniture where it belonged. Miller seemed delighted to show off both his superior strength and his superior behaviour. Anthony, infuriated and desperate though he was, was determined not to move a single piece himself. He stood in his trap, alternating his shouts with what he hoped were stern, determined looks of anger.

At last he was freed. But by this time, most of the perpetrators had disappeared down the stairs to breakfast. There was no-one left except a few senior boys who were carefully ensuring that the games and quiet rooms would pass any inspection during the day. Thank goodness someone was on his side! But of course they were only protecting their own skins against the wrath of Mr Pearson. They knew they would all be punished equally if the story got about.

Anthony gathered up his belongings, tidied the duty room and walked slowly across to his garret in the main building. Duty Night was over. Bar the shouting.

Chapter Ten

Anthony entered his room and flopped down on his bed. Funny how it suddenly seemed like home in here, despite its discomforts. He supposed he ought to go in to breakfast but he couldn't face all those sniggering faces. The story of his night, or rather, morning, would be all round the school by now. Anyway, he still had some of Helen's cheese and biscuits. He'd give breakfast a miss.

He lit his stove and boiled some water for coffee. While he was waiting he changed his shirt and put on a tie. He hadn't had much time to worry about his appearance so far this morning. He couldn't understand how he had slept so soundly with everything that had gone on outside his room. The absurd notion that he'd somehow been drugged or gassed occurred to him. But he felt quite normal. No, they'd just been very careful not to wake him.

There were footsteps on the landing, then a knock.

'Come in.'

Michael put his head round the door.

'How was it?'

'I survived,' Anthony replied. Michael would find out soon enough.

'Coming to breakfast?'

'No. I'll give it a miss. Just having coffee.' He was glad the cheese was hidden under a pile of papers. Perhaps Michael would think he was ill.

'Aren't you well?'

'Er . . . bit queasy. And I didn't get through all the marking I wanted to last night. I'll just finish it with this cup of coffee.'

'Oh, well, OK.' Michael looked doubtful. 'We *are* meant to be on duty . . . '

'I've been on duty all night,' said Anthony firmly.

'OK,' said Michael again. 'See you later, I expect.'

He went out and closed the door quietly. Anthony sighed. He didn't want to be unfriendly, and certainly not untruthful, but neither did he want to have to give a blow-by-blow account of his misfortunes. Not now, anyway. He'd have plenty of time to relate events to Michael over the weekend.

Lessons on Saturday morning started a little later, at nine-thirty. Dutifully, Anthony completed his marking, sustained by cheese and coffee, then went down to the English room. As he was arranging his desk, Pearson walked in. Without a word, he crossed the room briskly to the desk near the stock cupboard at the back, where he worked. Anthony was nonplussed. The Principal had neither spoken nor looked in his direction. Should he address Pearson's back? Suddenly, without turning his head, Pearson said, 'Mr Dean?'

'Yes, sir?'

'You sent two boys to me this morning?'

What boys, thought Anthony, taken aback. Then he remembered. Before he could frame his answer, Pearson half-turned and said irritably, 'Those boys, Basford and Riley. You sent them, I believe?'

What was Anthony to say? He hadn't sent them, of course. He hadn't wanted them to go. But he couldn't give Helen away. Did Pearson know she went up to the duty room and helped young teachers out? Had she ever done it before? And why had the boys said that he'd sent them? Or had the headmaster simply assumed that?

In the end he just said 'Yes.'

'I'm a very busy man, Mr Dean. Kindly remember that.'

He picked up a batch of papers and walked out as he came in, without further words and without glancing in Anthony's direction.

Anthony groaned deeply. What would Helen think if she knew that her efforts to help had misfired? Should he tell her, warn her? Could he find a diplomatic way of doing it? With a despairing sigh he prepared to face the morning's lessons.

Anthony hesitated a moment before opening the library door. He could hear no sound from within. He turned the worn brass knob as quietly as possible and stepped inside. The room was almost in darkness, although it was only three o'clock. All ideas of exploring the neighbourhood that Sunday afternoon had been abandoned because of a continuous heavy downpour. Rain was still battering the library windows, gurgling down drainpipes and over the edge of gutters.

He shivered. The library felt damp and chilly. But pulling the dusty red velvet curtains and switching on a lamp gave it a warmer feel. He was pleased that there was no-one else there. He wanted to work in peace. He took several books down from the shelves of the English section and arranged them on the table with his pens and pad of file paper.

As he gazed round the room, with its polished tables and well-used leather chairs he could imagine himself a participant in a Victorian country house mystery. All the room needed to complete the illusion was a roaring fire and someone relating the story of the resident ghost. But instead there was a cold fireplace and that dreary, yellowing parchment firescreen. The flowers that had decorated the room on his arrival had long since faded and had not been replaced. The only ornaments on the hearth were a blackened poker, a small shovel and a long-handled brush with worn bristles. He wondered how long it was since they had been used.

The only heating came from a very small radiator near the door. The warmth did not penetrate as far as Anthony's seat by the window. He shivered again, wishing he had worn a tweed jacket over his sweater. Should he go up and fetch it? No, he was bound to meet someone and be asked to do something. Free, quiet times were so precious. He wasn't exactly resting, but he *was* working at his own pace at things he enjoyed - studying books and gleaning information.

He had been there about an hour, and was becoming stiff and cold. He was hurrying to finish his work and go back upstairs when a slight sound caused him to look up. The door was opening very quietly, just as he had opened it. Helen Pearson, casually dressed in trousers and sweater, entered the room. When she saw him she smiled with what seemed genuine pleasure.

'Oh, Ant . . . Mr Dean, it's you!' She walked over to him. 'You're not working, are you?'

'Yes and no. I'm just enjoying a quiet afternoon. I like this room. Anyway it's not fit to go out.'

'No. I'd hoped we might . . . ' she checked herself. 'You should take more breaks. You mustn't work all the time. Would you like a cup of tea?'

'I'd love one, but don't go to any trouble for me.'

'It's no trouble. I want one myself.'

She went out and Anthony was suddenly aware of how cold he was. The room seemed bleaker somehow. He hoped the tea wouldn't be too long.

Helen returned with an old-fashioned wooden tray. He remembered Gran having one very similar. From this tray she took a cup of tea and a very large slice of fruit-cake on a china plate and placed it before him.

'I hope you're hungry.'

Her expression said, 'Young men are always hungry.' And she was right, he was. But her unspoken reference to his age disturbed him.

'Aren't you having any?'

'I'll have some later. I'm trying not to eat too much.' She patted her stomach. 'Eric's always complaining about my weight these days. He never puts on any weight himself. But then, he doesn't like cake much.'

Anthony wanted to make some complimentary comment about her figure but decided against it. Instead he munched his cake and said nothing.

As she sat in the chair beside him at the circular table, sipping her tea, she clasped her hands round the hot cup.

'It's very cold in here,' she said. She hesitated, as if she had something on her mind. After a short silence she went on, 'Mr D . . . Anthony, I got you into a mess about those boys, didn't I? I'm terribly sorry. I just didn't think of it rebounding on you.'

So Pearson had told her.

'It was . . . mentioned,' he replied, carefully.

'I suppose you didn't say that *I'd* been responsible, did you?'

'I don't think I said anything. I didn't really have the opportunity and anyway it was me who was on duty. It was my responsibility. I certainly wasn't going to . . . '

'Give me away? No, I know you wouldn't.' She reached over and laid her hand on his arm. 'I'm so sorry to have caused you more trouble. You're having a bad time, aren't you?'

'Yes.' There didn't seem any point in being other than truthful. Her hand squeezed his arm.

81

'And I've made things worse. I really wanted to help you.'

'I know you did. I'm really grateful for your help. Anyway I'm not sure they could get any worse,' he went on, half-jokingly.

Still pressing her fingers into his arm, she looked at him for a moment with an expression of warmth and compassion, which caused him to turn what he imagined must be a very bright scarlet. Was that why she suddenly took her hand away, seeming embarrassed?

As she lifted her drink again, she was able to cover the lower part of her face with the cup to hide her expression. Anthony also drank, hoping to conceal that burning redness. He was amazed that he could feel the pressure of her hand, as though it was still resting on his sleeve. If he had looked at his arm he was sure he would see an impression of it imprinted on his flesh.

They finished their tea in silence. Sitting there in the lamplight she looked no older than he was. He half-expected her to take out a pile of papers and work alongside him. Then she seemed to remember who and where she was. She jumped up, with that brushing gesture he'd come to know.

'I must go now. I'll be missed . . . ' She gathered up the tea things and walked towards the door. When she reached it she turned and said in a low voice, 'I told Eric I sent them. I didn't want you blamed.'

Before he could answer, she opened the door and was gone.

Anthony walked slowly along the lane towards Fieldhouse, scuffing the wet leaves with his feet in the manner of a schoolboy. His hands were deep in his anorak pockets to keep out the chill of the damp mid-October day. Another Sunday afternoon alone. Only a week or two ago his misery had been tempered by the foolish thought that most of his limited free time might be spent with Helen, walking on the Downs.

He should have known better. After the episode over the two boys she sent to Pearson, he hadn't seen much of her. She'd been around the school, of course. But she hadn't had time for much conversation, and walks had never been mentioned. He'd been stupid to think that she would be able to spend much time with him and now he was paying the price. He kicked fiercely at a large pile of leaves blown into a heap beside the hedge by the strong, cold wind. The action made him wince as he thought of that spectacular football kick which had so nearly destroyed the gym window - and him.

He was near the school gate now, but despite the cold, he didn't feel like going in. He decided to walk on a little. Just as he passed the gate he heard someone call, 'Hello, are you going out or coming in?'

It was Art-and-Craft, hurrying out of the gate with his long, straggly hair blowing across his face.

'I'm just walking on a bit. Don't feel like going in and working yet.'

'Mind if I join you?'

'Please do.' Anthony found his colleague's irreverent manner very refreshing.

'How's it going these days? Any better?'

'No, afraid not. It's tough. Don't know how long I'll stick it. Don't pass that on, will you?'

'I won't. How are you getting on with Fergus?'

'He thinks I'm a fool.'

'He thinks everybody's a fool. Don't worry, he's always the same. I should watch out for him this week though. Bear with an even sorer head.'

'Too much to drink?'

'No, that's normal. Worse than that. Got put in his place by Mrs P.'

'Oh?' Anthony tried not to sound too interested.

'The usual thing. He tries it every term. She puts him down. He sulks.'

'Tries what?'

'Oh, you know!' said Art-and-Craft, looking at him in surprise. 'Trying to get off with Mrs P. He's always doing it. He knows she can't stand Old P so he thinks he's in with a chance.'

'Oh,' said Anthony again, not quite sure what to say next. 'And is he?'

'Not bloody likely!' replied Art-and-Craft vigorously. 'Mrs P's got better taste than that. I reckon she loathes Fergus even more than her old man.' Something like a sigh of relief escaped Anthony. Art-and-Craft went on, 'I told you Fergus boasts. Tells everybody he's getting somewhere. But we usually hear the truth eventually. There's bound to be somebody around who saw her slap his face!' He laughed and kicked up the leaves like Anthony had done earlier.

'I'd better watch out on games day, then,' Anthony said. His dislike of Peter Ferguson went up another few notches. How strange that Helen's activities seemed to have the knack of getting him into trouble.

They walked along, talking now of pupils and their problems, until they reached the point where the track from the Downs came down to the road.

'Have you been up there?' asked Art-and-Craft.

'Once or twice.'

'Mrs P goes up there a lot.'

'Yes, I believe she does.'

His companion gave Anthony another puzzled look, but said no more. Had he seen them, upon the hill? Anthony pondered as to whose side Art-and-Craft might be on. He obviously didn't like Fergus, or Pearson, but he seemed to have a high regard for Helen. What about himself? Why had the art teacher seemingly gone out of his way to tell him about Helen and Fergus? This wild-looking man striding along at his side reminded him of the 'outsider' in literature who stands on the sidelines, seeing all - a sort of Rustic Chorus of one!

'Getting colder - shall we go in?'

'Suppose we'd better,' Anthony replied.

They turned and retraced their steps towards the school gates.

'Like to come up to the Art Room?' Art-and-Craft asked as they entered the hall. 'I've got a kettle up there, and coffee.'

'Yes, why not?' said Anthony. 'I'm not in a great hurry to prepare for tomorrow.'

Monday mornings were a particular horror. After the short break of the weekend, the insolent, defiant behaviour of pupils like the Biggins seemed even more horrific.

'You going to church?'

'I'd better,' Anthony answered. 'What about you?'

'No, I never go. Made that quite clear some time ago. I'm an atheist.'

'I wouldn't go if I hadn't been told to. Isn't it supposed to be part of the job?'

'Ye...es. But there are limits. Still, when you're new you can't afford to be difficult.'

That's true, Anthony thought. Especially when your record is as bad as mine.

He'd been meaning to go up to the art room since the beginning of term, but he'd always been busy, unwell or just avoiding company. He certainly hadn't had much time for leisure. Now he was determined to enjoy the last hour before supper and evensong.

The room had a distinctive smell but he couldn't decide what it was. It was liberally spattered with paint, glue and clay. Drying models stood on a side bench. The walls were adorned with artwork of all kinds; some of it appearing excellent even to Anthony's inexperienced eye. On an easel at one end stood a large abstract painting in which shades of purple predominated.

Art-and-Craft filled a clay-spotted kettle at the multi-coloured sink, and plugged it in. He rinsed two hand-thrown mugs and prepared the coffee. Anthony, preferring not to watch the rather unhygienic arrangements, wandered around the room. A still life was set up and the drawings of a group of pupils remained on their seats, half-finished. One in particular caught his eye. It was boldly drawn in a cubist style. He picked it up and read the scrawled signature - P. Miller.

'Peter Miller. I've come across him, though I don't teach him. He showed me a design he'd done. Looked pretty good.'

'Yes, he's got some talent. Good at Maths too, I believe.'

The art master brought over two steaming mugs and handed one to Anthony. He took a sip, wondering whether paint and clay were poisonous.

'Is this good? I'm no judge.' Anthony handed him the still life.

'Very, for a boy his age. Pity he's such a lump, and so untidy in work and person. Appearances *do* count.'

Anthony almost choked on the hot coffee as he tried to suppress his amusement at this statement. Art-and-Craft was hardly in a position to criticise! He must have detected Anthony's spluttering.

'Oh, I know *I* look a mess. But I'm an artist. At least that's what I want to be. Just waiting for the big break. Then I can be free of this place forever. This is one of mine.' He indicated the easel. 'I want to get enough work together for a one-man exhibition. Might have enough by the summer. If it's a success I can send in my notice!'

Lucky you, thought Anthony, to have a plan of escape. At half term he'd have to make his own decision.

'How easy is it, do you think, for a teacher to move into something else?'

'Depends what you want to move into. Really thinking of leaving, are you?'

'Oh, no. Well, possibly . . . I just wondered.'

'Got any money?'

'No.'

'Nor me. That's the problem. Need to save enough to keep yourself for a while. I'm not too good at saving, myself. Spend a lot on materials and frames. Don't make anything on sales. Help my mother a bit, too.'

Anthony could not imagine Art-and-Craft supporting an elderly mother. He didn't seem the type. He wondered what Mrs Wilson thought of her son's appearance and his paintings.

'Have you tried applying for other jobs?' he asked.

'One or two. Not lately, though. I just want to paint full-time. It's very frustrating having to teach all these ignorant boys and have Old P. breathing down my neck when all I want to do is slap paint on canvas.'

'I don't have any other talents. No, I don't have *any* talents,' Anthony said. 'So I don't know what else I could do. Anyway, it's all just a thought, nothing more. But, like I said, don't pass it on, will you? I don't want anybody to know I've even thought of it.'

'Have no fear. I don't gossip. I know what it's like for you. Come up and have a chat anytime, specially if you feel down. I'm usually up here. Always got coffee on the go. Come and make those coffee mugs!'

'I will. Better go and get ready for supper. Going down?'

'No. Got some grub in the cupboard there. Want to get on with this picture.'

'OK. Thanks for the coffee.'

Anthony hurried out in case he was asked to share any of the 'grub'. He wondered how long it had been in the cupboard. Probably it had formed the basis of a still life or two in the past fortnight . . .

Before going to his room he popped into the Common Room to scan the vacancy list yet again. His perusal on Friday had been interrupted by the unwelcome arrival of Fergus in the room. It certainly wouldn't do to let *him* discover his intentions. But his careful study produced nothing except a collection of desperate inner-city schools that Anthony knew would make Fieldhouse seem like paradise. In any case, as his ability to teach was so poor, and was not improving, what was the point of looking in here? He would be better off looking in the general vacancy columns of papers like *The Times*. This was a much more sensible plan. He left the room feeling as though he had made a fresh start already . . . and almost bumped into Helen Pearson.

'Oh, Mr Dean. I haven't seen you for a day or two!'

It was nearly a week. He'd counted. He said, 'You haven't been out on the Downs this afternoon, have you? It's very cold out.'

'No. Have you?'

'I just walked through the village. Then I met Art - I mean Mr Wilson. We walked together a bit then he showed me some of his work in the art room.'

'Hasn't he got you making coffee mugs yet?' she laughed.

'He's mentioned it. I'd like to have a go.'

'It's fun. Mine weren't fit to drink out of, though.'

Anthony felt a strange pang at the thought of Art-and-Craft showing Helen how to make pottery, up in the art room. He imagined them talking and laughing together. He had nothing like that to offer her.

'We must try to fit in another walk - if you'd like to,' she said

'Yes, I would, very much!'

'What did you think of David's paintings?' she asked, changing the subject again, rather too quickly for Anthony's liking.

'Not to my taste. But I know nothing about them. I much prefer yours though.'

She looked suddenly concerned. 'Of course! You wanted the one out of the duty room didn't you? I'm so sorry, Anthony. I completely forgot. I've been so busy recently. I'll go and get it at once.'

'Oh no, please don't go to any trouble.'

'Do you still want it?' she asked, very quietly.

'It's a lovely picture, but I don't want to bother you . . . '

'I'll bring it to your room in five minutes!' she said, turning away quickly and disappearing into her flat.

Anthony went upstairs in a state of confusion. Why did she always have this disturbing effect on him? He'd been convinced their brief friendship was over, a few minutes ago he'd decided to make a real effort to change his career, then he'd found himself stupidly jealous - yes, that was it, jealous - of her being in the art room. And now she'd dashed off to get him a picture!

He made an effort to compose himself and appear nonchalant before she returned. She was back in a few minutes.

'Here you are. I've put another up there. So the duty teachers will have something different to look at.' She held out the watercolour. 'Have you got anywhere to hang it?'

'I'll find the best place. Thank you. I really like it.'

'Don't hang it where it's in the sun all day. It'll fade.'

'I don't get much sun in here.'

'No. I don't suppose you do. Is it freezing?'

'It can be. There's this electric fire.'

'One bar! In this room! Poor Anthony! Why didn't you say? I'll send up a better one.'

'Michael's is the same.'

'Then I'll buy a new one for him, too.'

She would, out of her own purse. He wished he had never mentioned the cold.

'You've got enough to put up with,' she went on. 'How are things, by the way?'

She knows perfectly well, he thought.

'OK. The same.'

'Not OK. We must walk and have another chat. I'll see what I can fix. Are you going to supper and church?'

'Yes.'

'Let's go down, then.'

They walked down the stairs together and Anthony felt strange - almost as though he was floating.

Chapter Eleven

In the week before half term Anthony had some decisions to make. He'd planned to stay at school during most of the holidays but he really felt like a break and besides, he still had some belongings at his great-aunt's that he wanted to sort out. Staying there would give him an opportunity to decide about his future. He had to hand in his notice immediately he returned if he wanted to leave at Christmas. Otherwise he'd be forced to stay until Easter. An interminable time!

But if he went to Aunty's there'd be no opportunity to explore the Kingswater area. Helen had hinted that Pearson might be away for a day or two over the holiday so she'd have more chance to go out walking.

She'd mentioned it on a short walk they'd had soon after she had given him the picture. They had walked to that spot on the hillside where the poppy had been. They hadn't said much; there hadn't been time. But she'd seemed pleased that he was planning to spend holidays at the school. She'd talked about him 'making it his permanent home'. Well, he didn't know about that! But he was certainly tempted by the prospect of some uninterrupted walks on the Downs with her. They got on so well together. Still, she hadn't said any more about it and he'd seen little of her since then. He felt she was avoiding him. So perhaps he should go to his aunt's, at least for a couple of days.

'I'm just choosing a book for my holiday,' Helen greeted him, as he went into the library on Wednesday. He waited, wondering what was coming next. 'I'm going to Sheffield, to that conference for head teachers. I'll need something good to read while Eric's busy.'

She showed no sign that she had ever indicated anything else. With a struggle, Anthony answered, 'What about Hardy? There's the whole set here.'

'I know. I've read them all. But I might take the short stories. I can't remember many of those.'

Anthony handed her the thick book without speaking. His hands felt clammy.

Then she said, 'What about you? Are you staying here?'

There wasn't much point now. He swallowed hard and said, 'I'm thinking of going to my great-aunt's near Stafford for a day or two. She's got some stuff of mine I want to go through. I'll probably do some walking there too.'

'Oh, yes, do. Then you can tell me all about it. I don't know the area at all.'

She walked towards the door, clutching her Hardy book. Suddenly she turned and said in a different, softer voice, 'You will take care while you're away, won't you? Make sure you come back safely.'

The door closed behind her, leaving Anthony perturbed that he didn't really understand her at all. She seemed to be at least two different people. He wondered if she was going away voluntarily. Then there was that comment just as she was leaving. Did she really care about him coming back safely? He didn't quite understand himself either. But he knew that he *wanted* her to care about his safe return.

As Anthony left the library, Eric Pearson was just leaving his office. The Principal hadn't been spending quite so much time in Anthony's lessons recently. This solved some difficulties and created others. Discipline was still a very major problem.

'Mr Dean.'

'Yes?'

'Are you going away next week?'

'Just for a few days.'

'You understand that half term is an important opportunity to improve on one's preparation for the rest of the term?'

Anthony said nothing. Pearson waited for a moment, then went on, 'It also marks the time when staff consider their future employment. You do understand, don't you, that two months notice, expiring at the end of a term, is required for any changes you may wish to make?'

Was this a broad hint? But still Anthony said nothing except, 'Yes.'

'Mr Fulford will give you any information on matters of this sort that you require.'

The Head turned on the heels of his well-polished shoes and went back into his study.

If he wants to get rid of me, why doesn't he say so, Anthony thought? He would rather know the worst and save himself the problem of making up his mind. He realised, though, that Pearson had the same dilemma. It would be much better if unsatisfactory staff left of their own accord. Sacking people was unpleasant and did the school's reputation no good. It damaged the morale of the rest of the staff too. So why not make life ghastly for someone you wanted to be rid of, and drop a few hints that they might like to look elsewhere?

Anthony wondered if these hints would make his own resolve stiffen. He'd decide at the end of the holiday. The thought of returning to Biggins and friends after a break might just tip the scales. Well, he'd better go and face them now.

He saw little of Helen in the next two days. When he did, she seemed cheerful at the prospect of her half term break. She must have completely forgotten about those walks. Ridiculous of him to think she had nothing else on her mind but a few words she'd said to him in passing!

It was Friday afternoon. School was over and the pupils dispersing. From his room, where he was packing his bag for the week away, Anthony could hear the banging of car doors as parents arrive to collect their sons. He straightened up and walked over to the window.

It had been a grey, wet day and now it was rapidly getting dark. But the rain clouds had begun to clear and the sky beyond the Downs was much brighter than it had been for several days. Against this sky, the top of the Downs was silhouetted - and so was something else. A small figure was moving briskly along the ridge. Then the outline disappeared as whoever it was dropped below the crest.

Anthony stood still for a moment. Then he quickly put on his shoes, grabbed an anorak from the back of the door, and ran out. He didn't know what he was going to do or say. He just knew that the figure was Helen, out there on her own, and he wanted to be there too.

As he rushed through the hall he almost bumped into a very well dressed couple. 'Sorry, sorry!' Damn those superior, wealthy parents!

He didn't stop, but as he hurried on he saw Pearson through the open door of his study. He was bound to have seen - and chalked up another cross against Anthony's name. Damn Pearson! It couldn't be helped now.

He sped down the lawn in the gathering gloom, then checked his pace as he opened the gate. He must appear to be out for a casual stroll before the supper that was being laid on for those individuals still at school. Taking a deep breath, he walked along the path behind the school grounds, listening for the sound of approaching footsteps. But he heard nothing.

Perhaps Helen would return another way. She could carry on straight down from the hill and come out on the road at the spot where Art-and-Craft had spoken of her. If she did, she'd be back at school before he realised and could turn and catch her up. Then his rush would be wasted and he'd have disgraced himself yet again for nothing.

Now he'd reached the point where the path forked. Was she still up there? He couldn't hear a sound. What if it wasn't Helen after all? It could have been someone aiming for a place on the other side of the Downs. He couldn't be sure that the figure had dropped down on this side. It just seemed likely because there was not much beyond for several miles.

He stood at the junction, undecided. Then he thought he heard the rattle of a stone on the hillside ahead. He made up his mind, and strode up the hill between the hedges. It was quite dark in there now, but there was still that gleam of light behind the crest. As he walked up towards the spot where the hedge ended, he thought he could see something in the gloom. He wasn't sure. It could just be a patch of old man's beard draped over the hedge, catching that last fading light.

He had slowed now, partly to get his breath and partly to compose himself and account for his hurry, if he were to meet . . .

'What brings *you* out here in such a hurry, at this time of day?'

Helen stepped out of the shadows into the centre of the path. He couldn't see her face clearly but there was laughter in her voice.

Anthony stopped and looked up at her as she walked slowly down towards him. Was there any point in pretending?

'I was just . . . out for a bit of fresh air, like you,' he said, losing his nerve at the last minute.

'Do you often come up here in the dark?'

He could still detect that note of laughter.

'No, but the afternoon's been a bit . . . well, I needed a break. I was just packing.'

'Yes, I saw your light on, from up there. I saw you, too.'

She was beside him now, well wrapped against the autumn chill in a padded anorak and boots. In her hand she held a knitted hat and gloves. More evidence of her handiwork, he imagined. She'd pulled off the hat as he approached, and run her fingers through her hair. He wasn't sure why.

'Can you see into my room from the top?' he asked, wondering if she often spied on him from the Downs.

'No, not really. But you came to the window and I saw your silhouette.'

'And I saw yours on the top,' he blurted out, giving himself away.

'So you came to meet me?'

'Well, I thought a walk out here in the dusk would do me good . . . '

'I'm glad you did.' She hesitated and then went on, 'It's rather lonely after dark.' Was that the only reason she was pleased? She went on, 'You're not going to the top, I take it?'

'No, this is far enough in the dark.'

They started to walk slowly back to the school

'So you're off to Stafford?' she asked presently.

'Yes, tomorrow. Is that when you go?'

'Yes.' She was quiet for a moment, then said, 'Eric was very anxious that I should accompany him.' She didn't sound very pleased.

'Of course. I'm sure you'll enjoy a break from here.'

'I'm not sure that I will. But I've got my Hardy. Sir will be able to give me a test on it when I come back!' she laughed, suddenly more light-hearted.

'I wish I had time to study it enough myself. I think you'll be able to test me!' Anthony replied. He made a mental note to buy a copy of Hardy short stories as soon as he could get to a bookshop. Then they'd have something else in common after the holiday. The thought cheered him.

They were back at the school gate now. The outside lights had not been switched on and the garden was in total darkness.

'Holiday shut-down,' Helen explained. 'There's hardly anyone here now and Eric doesn't believe in waste.'

Anthony opened the gate and they passed through.

'Keep to the left,' Helen advised. 'You don't want to fall in the pond, do you?'

'I'll be very careful,' Anthony promised.

At the door, Helen looked up at him and said, in a low voice, 'We'd planned some walks this week, hadn't we, if I could get away? But I'm being dragged away instead.' She looked around nervously, as if she expected someone to be watching and listening. 'I had no choice. I'd much rather be up there. We'll have to save it for another time.'

'Yes, I'd rather be up there, too,' he admitted.

'We will be. Have a lovely break - and do take care!'

She put her hand on his arm and squeezed it like she had that evening in the library. It took only a second, then she was gone.

Anthony spent a pleasant enough few days with Aunt Florence ('Not "Florrie" if you please, young man.') She was not such a kind, homely woman as Gran had been but he felt that she'd mellowed towards him in his absence.

She had always had a low opinion of university students, even such quiet, inoffensive ones as Anthony had been. But the very particular old lady was much more favourably disposed towards a respectable master at a private school.

Anthony did not tell her the truth about his situation there. Instead he amused her with descriptions of his colleagues and pupils, leaving out the less salubrious aspects of their character. He told her of the school and its surroundings and the brief excursions he'd had into the countryside. He only made brief mention of 'Mrs Pearson'.

'Are there no young female teachers?' Aunt asked with the nearest thing to a twinkle in her eye that he had ever seen.

'No, I'm afraid not. Not many female teachers at all. You don't get them much in boys' schools.'

'They've got more sense!' she replied. 'Never mind. A nice young man like you is bound to meet a nice young lady one of these days - you'll see.'

Anthony had never heard her describe him as a 'nice young man' before. In fact he couldn't remember anyone describing him in such flattering terms. He began to wonder if indeed Helen thought of him as such. What did she think of him? He wished he dared ask her. He was sure she wasn't exactly what Aunt had in mind when she talked about young ladies though. He couldn't imagine that she would approve of a friendship, however innocent, between himself and a married woman twice his age. He shuddered as he watched her sipping tea from a china cup - the essence of respectability. He could hardly bear to think what she would say. His newly-acquired 'niceness' would disappear in an instant.

He spent the days sorting and re-packing his belongings and making himself useful around the house. He took several long walks and cycle rides in the surrounding area and in the evenings he prepared and marked work and read his Thomas Hardy. As he read, he imagined Helen, somewhere in Sheffield, reading the same story. He thought of them walking together on the hills, discussing what they had read. The countryside around the school would give the appropriate ambience to such a discussion.

In fact, he spent a great deal of the holiday thinking about Helen in one way or another. It began to worry him. His aunt's question about his social life, or lack of it, had disturbed him. He tried to analyse why he was more enthusiastic about the thought of walking on the Downs with Helen than he was about investigating any of the local pubs or meeting places. Since his friendship with her began, he had hardly given a thought to the prospect of meeting any of those 'nice young ladies'. Was it because her maturity masked his own lack of confidence? Or simply because they had a lot in common?

He leaned on the parapet of the canal bridge and gazed down into the water. He'd cycled over to the Shropshire Union Canal at Norbury Junction. He was hot from his exertions but the day was cold and grey. The surface of the canal mirrored the bare trees and the canalside buildings. Leaves floated slowly and sadly beneath him. There was no-one around, although smoke issuing from the chimney of a narrow boat moored further along the canal suggested a cosy occupied cabin.

But strangely, he didn't feel alone. He was mentally describing the scene to Helen, just as she had asked him to do, and he felt that she was there beside him. He could imagine her answers and comments so vividly. She'd probably be saying that the scene would be lovely to paint, especially with the soft autumn colours. He should have brought his camera. Then he could have shown her what it was really like. How stupid of him not to have thought of it before! Well, it was too late now. He had to go back tomorrow and anyway his camera was locked in his big suitcase under his bed at Fieldhouse. But he'd remember next time.

If there was a next time. The holiday was almost over and he still hadn't made up his mind what to do. He'd have some time to think about it on the train. He couldn't concentrate on it now. He went back to thinking about Helen.

The next day, Thursday, Anthony put away his bicycle in Aunt's garage alongside an old car that she no longer used. She had told him he could have it when he had learned to drive. That was something he'd vowed to do on his first day at the school but he'd had so many other problems that he hadn't been able to think about it. Besides, he had so little free time. But he must try and organise some lessons when he got back. Especially now he had the offer of this car. Being able to drive might help him to find another job if he decided to - and it would make him more flexible in choosing a location.

'Are you coming back for Christmas? You can, you know,' Aunt Florence said as he left her at the gate.

'I'll let you know,' Anthony replied. He couldn't tell her the answer to that question now. He had no idea. He had until Monday morning to decide his immediate future. He certainly hadn't seen any likely jobs in the local paper here. Anyway, Aunt wouldn't want him here permanently. Especially if he'd given up what she obviously considered a prestigious post. If only she knew!

He nearly made his decision on the train back. As the train took him ever further south he thought with horror of the English room and those rude, uncontrollable boys. Then there was Fergus and the dreaded games afternoon, which was a continuous agony of struggle and ridicule. There'd be duty nights. And there'd be Eric Pearson. What about those hints he'd dropped? No, Anthony thought, he would have to hand in his notice and take the consequences. He couldn't possible endure that misery until Easter.

Then he thought of Helen. If he left, he'd never see her again. But she was only an acquaintance, wasn't she? He hardly knew her really. He certainly couldn't allow his slight friendship with her to influence the rest of his life. He'd left friends before - leaving school, leaving university. That was life, wasn't it? You had to make your own way in the world. She certainly wouldn't let her friendship with him affect her life. Look how she'd gone away this week when she'd said they would spend half term walking together.

Damn! Now he was being silly and unreasonable. She was in a different world to him. She wouldn't have given him a thought this week, mixing with all those highbrow academics. Why should she? She *might* have said to one of her fellow delegates, 'We've got three new teachers this term. Two are fine. The other's an interesting young man but absolutely hopeless as a teacher.'

And they would all have laughed, sympathised with the harassed Principal and his wife, and gone on to talk of other things.

Anthony cursed again, and, since the train was fairly empty, kicked the seat opposite rather violently.

'Damn! I'm getting stupider!' he said out loud.

He arrived back at the school without having made any decision. Unlike his previous two arrivals, he had no deadline to meet, so took the local bus to the village and walked up to Fieldhouse carrying the bags containing his work and the articles retrieved from Aunt's spare room. When he saw the now-familiar white signboard at the gate he couldn't help thinking of those other two occasions, the first full of hope, the second with considerable apprehension. Now his feelings were mainly of despair.

He was a failure. Half a term had passed already and he hadn't made any progress towards gaining the respect of his pupils or being able to control them. Only the fear of Pearson, whether in or out of the room, caused the majority of them to make any attempt to produce written work. After Christmas there would be school exams, and mock 'O' levels for the fifth years'. Then the lack of good teaching would become only too apparent. He couldn't teach when there was a riot going on. No, he must leave as soon as possible. Things could only get worse. He'd finally made up his mind. He'd compose the appropriate letter over the next couple of days. He needed to make a completely fresh start somewhere else. If he did, perhaps one of Aunt's 'nice young ladies' would put in an appearance. This prospect made him feel quite light-hearted as he strode into school.

As Anthony walked through the hall he glanced sideways at the pigeon holes which held the mail. There was never anything for him, except the odd letter from the Inland Revenue and terse notes from Pearson. So he didn't expect the white envelope in the space he shared with Michael to be his own. But it was.

Mr A. Dean was written in neat black ink on the front. He began to rip it open, then changed his mind and took it upstairs.

His room was freezing. It was the beginning of November now and today was bright but very cold. Walking with the bags had been warm enough but that little garret chilled him to the bone. After Aunt's well furnished home it seemed even more spartan. He was very wise to have made up his mind to leave.

He dragged out his electric fire from under the bed and switched on its one bar. The promised new one hadn't materialised yet. Perhaps Helen had forgotten. Or had not dared to waste money. Then he took his kettle into the even icier bathroom next door and filled it with water for coffee. He'd remembered to bring back milk and a supply of food, which he knew he would be grateful for, even if it had made his bags even heavier. While the water was boiling on his stove, he pulled up his one chair as close to the fire as he could and opened his mystery letter.

Dear Anthony,
I hope you have enjoyed your holiday. I returned this morning.
I spent much of the time reading Hardy, for which I was very grateful.
I would love to discuss the stories with you, and to hear about your trip.
I will try to contact you when you return.

Best wishes
Helen

PS There is still time for a walk before term starts.

Anthony read this note over several times in a state of confusion. What did it mean? Why had Helen gone to so much trouble to write to him? Was she really so anxious to see him?

A hiss and splash broke his reverie. The water was boiling over and running down the side of the kettle onto the metal tray where he kept the stove. He took it off and poured his coffee, taking a gulp immediately without thinking and burning his tongue painfully.

Damn! Another bloody stupid thing I've done because of this woman!

He screwed up the note angrily and flung it into the waste-paper basket. He immediately felt guilty. He retrieved it from the bin and tried to flatten out the creases. What on earth would Helen think if she saw him? What a ridiculous state he was in!

He sat down in front of the fire again, reread the note, placed it carefully in the centre of his table, and sipped his coffee cautiously and not without considerable discomfort.

Now he was alert, listening. As he got up to unpack his bags he made every effort to do it noiselessly. Every rustle of paper angered him, as it seemed it might blot out the sound he wanted to hear: that quiet footstep on the stairs. Because of his caution, the unpacking took some time, yet neither the step nor the knock was to be heard.

He went out on to the landing and into the bathroom to wash his mug. For a while he stood by the banister, listening for any movement below. Then he thought of an excuse to wander about downstairs. He had some books to return to the library and the English room. No hurry to do them at this moment - but he thought he would.

As he passed the door to the Pearson's flat he slowed and walked very quietly. There was nothing to be seen or heard. Helen must be out, he thought. Of course, she'd have shopping and so on to do, after being away. She'd probably driven into town. Or they both had. But she'd only mentioned that she had returned. She was unlikely to have come back alone, though.

He rattled the large brass knob of the library door as he entered, and left the solid door open. As he crossed the room to the bookcase, the door swung closed with a loud bang. Startled, he turned, but the room was empty. It was only a draught, or the heavy door's momentum. There was no ghost - and no Helen. He opened the door again and looked out. The noise had not attracted any attention and the school was as silent as before.

He spent some time in there, looking at the many books which interested him but which he hadn't had time to study before. One, perhaps the only, advantage of working at a school run by a fellow English scholar, was the excellent selection of books here. The library was well-stocked in all subjects and the books were well-organised and generally in good condition. Unlike many other things around the school, he mused.

He should have done a librarianship course instead of teaching. He was convinced of that now. He was so much happier here among all these books than he was in the classroom. Perhaps that was what he should do, if he could get a place. Would they take him if he'd failed in his first career? It must be worth a try.

He spent about an hour in the library, then went along to the English room. Here he was much less happy. There were books here too, but they were kept in the stock cupboards and the bookcase beside Pearson's desk - the desk from which he surveyed every word and action of Anthony's. The room was quiet enough now, the chairs on desks to help the caretaker and the cleaners who came in from the village. But in a day or two it would once again be filled with the callous mirth and smirking insolence of Simon Biggins and the others who made Anthony's life such a misery. The neat piles of exercise books would be strewn everywhere and the waste bin would be full of ink pellets (thrown at Anthony and collected up by him after the lesson so that no-one - not even one of the cleaners - should see his ignominy). The chairs would be overturned, and the noise would be appalling. And then there'd be those awful strained silences when Pearson was in the room. He hated it in here.

He returned to his room and took out a pad of file paper. Putting more water on to boil, he cut a large slice of Aunt's fruit cake, and sat down to compose his letter of resignation. A well-stocked library was not enough inducement to carry on enduring the nightmare of that English room. Not to speak of games afternoon and duty nights, awkward meals with the boys and the disgust with which Eric Pearson obviously regarded him. This letter would mark the beginning of his freedom. Then, once he'd left, he could put it all down to experience. He might even be able to laugh about it in years to come.

Chapter Twelve

Dear Mr Pearson,
It is with regret that I feel I must tender my resignation, with effect
from 31ˢᵗ December 1969 . . .

Anthony's table and floor were littered with the screwed up remains of
aborted letters as he tried to word his resignation in a way that would assure
Pearson of his good intentions. He *had* worked hard to try and improve his
performance and his lesson content and he wanted that aspect of his teaching,
at least, to be recognised.

By choosing his words carefully he hoped the Head would write him a
reference which would encourage some other employer or college tutor to
give him a second chance. He didn't expect to teach again - not unless he took
a training course. Nor did he really want to. He wasn't sure what he wanted.
He just wanted to escape from the misery which awaited him on Monday
morning, and every morning. He somehow couldn't forget that puff of smoke
from the canal boat that he'd seen on his cycle ride. It all seemed so peaceful,
such a world away from the awfulness of Fieldhouse School. Perhaps he
could take to the roving life, become a tramp. How long would the small
amount of savings he'd have by Christmas from his term's salary last him?
How long could he wander the towpaths on £50 or so?

Tap tap!

Startled, he jumped and the pen shot across the paper, cutting through his
neatly-written words with a great blue slash. One more for the bin!

'Come in.'

'I'm not disturbing you, am I?' Helen entered, carrying the book of Hardy
stories she had borrowed from the library.

'Oh no. Please come in.'

Anthony hastily removed the papers on which he found he had been
sitting, and gratefully placed them on the table on top of his letter. He pulled
the chair nearer to the fire and indicated that she should sit on it. She did, and
he sat on the only other 'seat'- the edge of the bed.

'I'm just doing some preparation,' he said, noticing her glance at the
papers littering the floor. 'But there's no hurry.'

'Did you get my note? I'm sorry, I had to go out after I'd written it, and
I've only just got back. Did you enjoy your holiday?'

'Yes, it was a good break. I did some walking and cycling.'

'Cycling? Have you brought a bike back with you? You said you were
going to collect some stuff.'

'No. I'd rather learn to drive. It'll be more useful. And my aunt's got an
old car I can have.'

'Lucky you.'

'Do you know of a good local instructor?'

'Most people from here use Williams. You might have seen his car about the village. They say he's good. Very patient.'

'He'll need to be!'

Anthony suddenly realised that a course of driving lessons plus the cost of a test and licence would make a considerable hole in that nest-egg he was hoping to amass by the time he left.

'I wonder how many lessons I'll need,' he murmured, almost to himself.

Helen laughed.

'That depends how good you are. And how much practice you get. Perhaps I'll be able to take you out occasionally.'

'Oh, would you?' This was something that Anthony hadn't even considered. He'd expected his attempt to learn to drive to be a lonely struggle without the benefit of helpful relations and friends that made other people's path through life seem so easy. 'That would be wonderful. I wasn't expecting to get any practice in between lessons.'

'Oh, the staff usually try to help. Mary's got her Mini - but you'd need to cut a hole in the roof for your head.'

They both laughed. But Anthony felt a little deflated that her offer to take him out driving wasn't a unique one. She'd obviously done the same for others in the past. Perhaps she'd gone walking with others too. After all, over the years there must have been some people on the staff that she could relate to - men who were older and less naïve than he was. The thought made him shuffle uncomfortably on the edge of the bed. He knew he was gawky and awkward, while she was mature, calm and sophisticated. So why was she here? He didn't know.

She watched him in silence for what seemed a long time. Then she said, 'If you've time, we could go for a walk tomorrow. Eric's had to go to London.' She spoke slowly. 'An elderly aunt is ill. He probably won't be back until Saturday.'

'I'd love to.'

'We'll go in the morning if you like. People will start to trickle back in the afternoon, I expect.' She paused. 'Then I'll be wanted, as Eric's not here. Yes, morning would be best for me. Would nine-thirty be too early?'

'Not at all. Where . . . '

'On the path at the back,' she cut in before he'd finished.

She's still being cautious, he thought, even thought there's hardly anyone here.

'I must go, in case the phone rings.' She stood up and brushed down her skirt as usual. 'I won't keep you from your work any longer. I'll see you tomorrow.'

She left and closed the door quietly behind her.

He listened intently until the last step faded from his hearing. Then he picked up the discarded papers and threw them in the bin. Moving the pile of papers he'd hastily placed on the table, he tore the latest letter, with the jagged scrawl through it, off the pad and threw that away too. He did not start another.

The next morning was cold and clear. Anthony breakfasted on a piece of aunt's cake and lukewarm coffee. His mouth was still sore.

At nine twenty-five he was walking across the wet lawn to the gate. He stopped for a moment to look at his reflection in the pond. Did he resemble the 'nice young man' that Aunt had so surprisingly spoken of? Well, he was no film star, but he was passable, he supposed. He'd seen worse - a few. He would doubtless become windswept and muddy on the walk but he was starting off clean and tidy. Gran would have been pleased about that! He smoothed his hair and went out through the gate.

The path behind the school was empty. After a few minutes he glimpsed a movement in the school grounds, through the bare patches of the hedge. The figure also stopped beside the pool then opened the gate and came out.

'We can go to the top and walk along to the knoll,' Helen said, without preamble. 'If you've time.'

'Oh, yes, plenty of time.'

Helen was well equipped for walking, with strong boots and thick woollen socks.

'Haven't you got any walking boots?' she asked, looking down at his wellingtons.

'No. I haven't walked much before. Not seriously.'

'You should get boots if you do. They grip better,' she said. 'Did you get your work finished yesterday?'

'I'm not sure it's ever finished,' he replied with a smile. He wasn't going to tell her about the letter. He'd write it this evening. Or tomorrow.

'You'll probably find it's easier now,' she said, looking at him kindly. 'I know you've had a rough time. But a lot of new teachers do. It gradually gets better and they're fine.'

'I hope so. I've done all I can - I think.'

'I know you have.'

'I think Mr Pearson would rather I left,' he blurted out, his guard weakened by her obvious sympathy.

Helen stopped and turned to him. 'What makes you think that?'

Did he detect a note of sharpness in her voice?

'Oh, just something he . . . just a feeling I have,' he finished lamely, wishing fervently that he'd kept quiet.

'But you're not going to, are you?'

Was that an order? It sounded a lot like one. She didn't seem to expect a reply, but turned again and continued up the hill.

Anthony said nothing. Was she urging him to defy her husband? What was it to her? He wished he knew.

Seeming almost to read his mind, she turned to him again.

'I really enjoy these walks. And talking to you. You're interesting - not all beer and skittles. I'd be very sorry if you left.'

'Would you?'

'Yes, of course. I think we've got a lot in common. That's not always easy to find.'

She quickened her step, as she often did when she seemed to have said more than she intended. Anthony didn't know what to reply so again said nothing.

'The view's wonderful now - it's so clear!' she exclaimed when they reached the top of the Downs. 'It's even better from the knoll. Do you want to go along there? Then we can drop down beyond there and come out on the road outside the village.'

'Yes, I'd like to.'

Anthony wasn't sure how to talk to her today. He was confused. How could he balance the pleasure of a week away from that dreadful classroom, the decision to leave it for ever, the way that he had missed Helen so much during his holiday and the intense happiness he experienced from being in her company in these beautiful surroundings? Would it be possible to resolve this conflict?

Helen set off along the white ridge path leading to the group of trees. On each side the land dropped away, giving extensive views. In the far distance, a silver gleam of sea was visible. Below, some of the trees in the hedgerows and around the village glowed brilliantly in the last of the autumn colours. Others were already bare and skeletal. Anthony's eyes absorbed all this, but constantly came back to rest on the figure of Helen, sometimes in front, sometimes at his side. In the morning sun her russet-brown hair matched the trees . . .

'You're very quiet today, Anthony. Are you all right?'

'Yes, yes. I'm just enjoying the view.' He hesitated. 'And the company.'

'You enjoy my company too, then?'

'Very much!'

He was sure that the colour that he felt rise to his cheeks was as bright as the telephone box he could see on the roadside below.

Helen smiled up at him. He couldn't interpret the look on her face.

'That's all right then!' she said and led the way into the clump of trees.

She was right. The view *was* even better from there. The low, bright sun shone between the slender trunks of the pines, which formed frames for the landscape beyond. The school was hardly visible - just the highest points of the roof could be seen above the belt of trees that screened it on this side. But still Anthony felt that they were being watched. He always felt that.

'Isn't it glorious!' Helen exclaimed. 'I've walked miles over these Downs in the last ten years, but I still haven't found a spot to match this one - right on my doorstep.'

'I must bring my camera up here. I should have brought it today.' Once again he had forgotten, in his haste to meet her.

'There'll be plenty of other days,' Helen said, confidently.

But would there? There wouldn't be many lovely autumn days now. Then it would be grey, cold and sodden, and often foggy, until after Christmas. Where would he be then?

'Yes, I suppose so. But I'd have got some good photographs today.'

'Come up tomorrow morning at the same time, if it's fine. Then you should get the same light effects. I won't be able to come, though. I have to stay in school until Eric arrives.'

'Yes, I could do that,' Anthony replied. But he didn't think he would. He wanted photos taken at the actual moment - even, perhaps, one of Helen. He *must* remember his camera in future.

They walked down the hill on another path. Although further from the school, it was much more exposed than the one they had previously used, and again Anthony had the strong feeling that they were being observed. This path had no sheltering hedge half way down. It was open the whole way to the road. Helen didn't seem concerned, although she'd seemed to be cautious about where they met. I suppose she could always say that we'd met on the hill, he thought. In any case why shouldn't two colleagues take a walk together? Was it just his crazy romanticism making a story out of nothing?

'Have you enjoyed yourself? You *do* seem quiet today,' Helen asked, as they neared the school.

'Yes, I really have. I'm perfectly OK. It's been a glorious walk.' Anthony felt he was making a mess of this but he didn't know what to do about it. 'It's just . . . well I suppose it's the contrast between up there and . . . and reality,' he finished, wondering what she'd make of his state of mind.

'I know. That's why I go up there as often as I can. I try and make *that* my reality - and the rest just a dream.'

'A nightmare in my case!'

'There are a lot of different ways to be . . . unhappy,' she finished and went on quickly, 'You don't always see them. People become good at hiding things.'

They turned in at the school gate. Peter Ferguson was standing on the steps. Anthony heard Helen catch her breath, but she walked up to the door with a bright smile.

'Good morning, Mr Ferguson. You're back early. Have you enjoyed your break?'

'Yes, thanks. I got back late last night - early morning rather. What about you - and Mr Dean?'

He spoke Anthony's name with a sneering intonation which implied things Anthony could only half imagine.

'Yes, I was just telling Mr Dean, when we met outside the gate, that I had spent a few days peacefully reading while Eric attended a conference. Very restful.'

Fergus gazed them intently. Anthony thought he was observing the pale, sticky chalk mud adhering to both pairs of boots. The games-master gave them a look that said plainly 'I know where you've been.'

Apparently oblivious, Helen went on, 'My holiday's over now, but you two gentlemen still have until Sunday afternoon, so make the best of it. Cheerio, Mr Ferguson. And you, Mr Dean.'

She walked up the steps and into the school without looking back.

Anthony and Fergus were left outside.

'Have you been here all week, then?' Fergus asked, lighting a cigarette despite the fact that smoking by staff was only allowed in the Common Room or private rooms, "to avoid setting a bad example".

'No, I've been away, at a relative's. I came back yesterday afternoon.'

'Couldn't wait to get back, eh?' That sneering tone again.

'I didn't want to impose on my aunt any longer. And I had work to do.'

'Oh, yes, of course. You've got Old P. to compete with. Apart from the problems of being new and green. Hard luck. Still, I dare say there are compensations.' He gave a sidelong glance up the steps in the direction that Helen had taken.

What the hell do I say to this, thought Anthony. Eventually he said, 'If you hear of any, let me know! I've obviously missed them so far. Better go and start on the day's grind, I suppose.'

He walked up the steps and in through the door before Fergus had time to reply - or ask any more unpleasant questions. Once in the hall, he slipped off his wellingtons and carried them upstairs. He cleaned off the give-away mud in the bathroom while his water boiled, then he made coffee and sat down to work - or rather to ponder the morning's events.

Anthony was awake early on Monday morning. Or rather, he got up early. The cold and the prospect of another half a term of lessons before he could escape had caused him to toss and turn through an endless night.

As he dressed, his eyes constantly turned towards the slim brown envelope lying on his table. He had managed to write that letter at last. Should he take it down on his way to breakfast? He had until lunchtime, according to one of the reams of instructions he'd received at the beginning of term. Would Pearson be around? If not, should he leave it on the Head's desk? The instructions didn't cover these important points.

At eight o'clock he prepared to go down to breakfast. Yes, he'd take it now and be done with it. As he walked across the room he glanced out of the window. The knoll stood out against the pink sky of a cold autumn morning.

He stopped. He could trace almost the whole route that he and Helen had taken, from the faint track across the lawn to the hilltop, along the ridge and down beyond the clump of trees. He wanted to go there again. He could go alone. But he'd rather go with Helen. Next time he wouldn't be so stupidly tongue-tied. He'd pick up on the hints she dropped. He might even ask her if she really liked him - and why.

He left the letter on the table and went reluctantly downstairs.

He was not the only reluctant breakfaster this morning. There were few pupils or staff in the dining room yet. This made things a little easier. Even Mrs Higginbottom was not there to provide words of comfort and an extra large helping for 'her young man'. She was unwell and in her place was a sour-faced assistant who preferred washing-up to serving what she described as 'those disgusting boys'. She obviously classed Anthony in that category and gave him neither an ample portion nor any cheery conversation.

'There!' she said, slamming his ill-filled plate down on the servery. Her expression said 'Don't dare ask for more!' He didn't.

He sat at his usual table in the corner, and experienced his usual feelings of loneliness and embarrassment as he was avoided by boy after boy as they trickled in from the dormitories and village lodgings.

One benefit of having a small plateful was that he finished quickly. This was a relief as some of his most insolent pupils had begun to appear. Their behind-the-hand stage whispers suggested that they were surprised to see him. Perhaps they thought he'd be sacked by now. Or that he'd been a student on teaching practice. They were probably hoping for a new innocent to torture. But he felt he detected a note of glee as they realised that they had at least another six weeks in which to torment *him.*

As before, he was forced to abandon his hitherto lonely table as a crowd of the worst offenders collected their food. Their cheeky 'Good *morning* Mr Dean' was enough to make him flee the room. He *must* go up and collect that letter now. Then perhaps he could grit his teeth until Christmas.

'Good morning, Mr Dean!'

The same words, but the tone was soft and genuine. Helen stood on the first landing, almost as though she was waiting for him.

'Don't look so glum! It'll be OK,' she went on, comfortingly.

'I don't know. I'm not confident,' he replied, truthfully.

She gave him that concerned look which had the disconcerting effect of turning his legs to jelly.

'I can see you're not. But don't let it - or them - get the better of you.' She put her hand on his arm and pressed it like she had that evening in the library. 'I'll help you if I can. I really want you to make a go of it.' Pearson's voice reached them from somewhere below. She stopped, then went on, 'If it gets bad, think of the Downs. That's what I do.'

She gave his arm another squeeze, then let go hurriedly and went downstairs without looking back.

Anthony stood on the landing feeling unable to move. In a foolish gesture he put his hand over the place on his arm where she had squeezed, trying to recreate the feeling. He couldn't.

With a great effort, he managed to climb the stairs, two at a time, and hurried into his garret. When he came down ten minutes later, carrying his briefcase and a pile of exercise books, the brown envelope still lay in the middle of his table.

All through that stressful morning he thought of that envelope. At break he was going to go up and get it - but Pearson was interviewing boys in his study. Anthony couldn't go in with his letter then.

When lunchtime came, he knew his time was running out ('Resignations will **not** be accepted after the deadline . . . '). He ate hastily and once again ran upstairs as soon as he was free. The letter still lay there. Again he looked out into the grounds. It was a cold day and few boys had ventured into the garden. But someone had. Helen was standing beside the pool, gazing across it to the Downs beyond.

Did she sense him watching her? Something made her turn and look up towards his window. He drew back quickly but it was too late. She waved, then stood looking up as though she expected him to join her. He grabbed his jacket and rushed out.

'How was your morning?' she asked, as he came across the lawn. She did not seem at all surprised to see him.

'Not very good.'

'Not as good as a walk up there?' she asked rather wistfully, looking towards the summit of the hills.

'Definitely not! I wish I was there now. But instead I've a full and difficult afternoon.'

'Has Eric been in?'

'No, not today, so far.'

'You'll be OK this afternoon. He'll be at a meeting.' Anthony wasn't sure what to reply to that, so he said nothing. 'We'd better go in. I've a lot to do,' Helen went on. 'Console yourself with the thought that you'll soon be in your second term. Not "new" any more. That's the worst part, being new. Next term will seem a lot easier.'

Would there be a next term?

Anthony went to his room and gathered up his afternoon's work. He thought of Helen's grey-blue eyes looking up at him, those eyes that seemed to change colour with the weather and surroundings, promising that the future would be better He thought of the way she had almost willed him to go down and join her in the garden. He thought of the walks they'd had and the walks they might have, especially in the spring when everything would come to life again.

He thought of Simon Biggins and his rude and insolent cronies. He thought of Eric Pearson sitting silent and disapproving at the back of the English room. He thought of those dreadful games afternoons . . .

He picked up the letter from the table and put it into his pocket. Downstairs, he placed his briefcase and books on a hall chair, took out the envelope and smoothed out the creases. Then, thinking that he might be a little creased himself, he combed his hair and straightened his tie in the hall mirror. Then he squared his shoulders, took a deep breath and knocked on the study door.

There was no answer. He knocked again, not quite so confidently. Still no answer. Should he go in? Leave the envelope on the desk? Gingerly he put his hand on the large brass doorknob.

'Oh, did you want Eric?'

Anthony jumped and wheeled round, dropping the letter. He stood there with it at his feet, feeling embarrassed and stupid.

'Eric's already left for his meeting. He won't be back until this evening. Can I help?' Helen had opened the door of her flat silently. Now she came right out into the hall.

'It's all right. It's not urgent,' Anthony said hastily, bending to pick up the letter and ramming it back into his pocket. Helen watched but said nothing. 'I'll see him tomorrow. I'd better get down to the English room now.'

He picked up his possessions from the chair. Helen looked on, still silent. Then she said, 'I'd really like you to stay. I hope you will. Things will be much better next term.'

She went back inside the flat and closed the door, leaving Anthony standing in the hall with his arms full of books.

When he got to the English room he took the letter out of his pocket and looked at it for a moment. As the bell rang for the start of afternoon school, he carefully tore the envelope in half and put the pieces into his briefcase. The deadline's passed now, he thought. It's too late. I can't stand this place - but I don't want to leave her.

Chapter Thirteen

Anthony's teaching problems continued after half term, just as he feared. But perhaps things weren't quite as bad as at the beginning. He was getting to know the boys now, and they him. A few of the quiet ones even showed signs of liking him. Biggins's crowd not included, of course. Nor Fergus. Games afternoon was still a very unpleasant experience. Anthony did get the impression, though, that some of his tormentors were becoming bored. They needed someone new to torture, or some new reason to torment *him.* Anthony took great care not to give them one.

This was one factor which caused him to put off starting his driving lessons immediately. He could imagine only too well the consequences of a 'Biggins Boy' seeing his first juddering efforts to drive away from the school. He could visualise them plotting to put obstacles in his way - probably literally. The thought of what they might do turned him cold.

Helen hadn't forgotten. She reminded him on every occasion that she saw him during the first week back. And Mary proffered her precious Mini. So eventually he contacted Mr Williams and the lessons began.

At first it went fairly well. Mr Williams proved an understanding and patient teacher. And at first *he* did the driving until they were well away from the school and village. He'd taught young teachers from Fieldhouse before. Anthony had expressed dread at the thought of damaging either pupils or property. So he didn't take over the wheel until that danger was well past.

Although Anthony had never been particularly mechanically-minded, he soon picked up the basics. Beginner's luck, his colleagues said. They were probably right. At least, his rapid early progress slowed because he had no opportunity to practise in between lessons. He hoped that Helen or Mary would soon renew their offers of some extra tuition, although he appreciated that they were very busy and days were short in November.

The boys did not let this chance for further ribaldry pass without notice, of course. But as there was no evidence so far that 'Sir' had knocked down any trees or caused a major accident, interest soon began to wane, especially as they had not seen their teacher actually doing any driving.

But there was one important question that the boys asked him frequently - when was he going to take his test? Anthony realised with horror that he must give no clue as to when this still-distant event was to be. If, as was likely, he failed, they would really have something to celebrate!

'You need some practice, I'm sure,' said Helen one day after his first few lessons.

He'd met her in the library and mentioned, in answer to her inquiry, that his progress had slowed a little.

'I do. I can only afford one lesson a week. Maybe two nearer my test.'

'Well, now you're hopefully past the absolutely lethal stage, perhaps you'd like me to take you out. After school this afternoon if you like. It'll be a bit dark so we won't go far.'

The late afternoon was cold, wet and gloomy. Anthony's initial enthusiasm had waned by the time his stressful lessons finally ended. As usual, his head ached and his throat was sore. At least, he thought, he'd be spending time with Helen. The problem was that he'd be showing himself up as an even more incompetent fool than she already thought. One more thing he was hopeless at!

As the time drew near he became more and more nervous. He was so desperate to make a good impression on Helen. After all, hadn't he given up his chance to escape from the hell of teaching, just because of her? Ever since that Monday, he'd wondered if he should tell her how near he'd been to resigning. Had she guessed what was in that letter he'd so clumsily dropped? She'd immediately said something about not wanting to lose him. He'd had no opportunity for long conversations or walks with her since then. But although he kept trying to dismiss his feelings as wishful thinking, or even ridiculous youthful folly, there was no doubt about the place she had come to occupy in his life. He thought about her constantly and longed to feel that touch of her hand once again.

Now he was standing by the front door, looking out into the gloom, waiting anxiously. 'Ready to go?'

As usual, she'd caught him unawares, coming out of the door silently.

'Ye...es.'

'I'll drive until we get away from the school, if you like. We can't afford to lose any pupils,' she joked.

Anthony was grateful. He admired the way she always seemed to know what he was thinking, what his concerns were. Was it just her greater experience? Or was it, as he preferred to think, because they were very much on the same wavelength?

They walked out to the green Morris Traveller. Helen was very proud of this car and was often to be seen cleaning it and polishing the woodwork. Inside it was spotless, too. Anthony watched carefully as she started the engine, trying to memorise the position of the controls and everything that he'd been taught. He was so afraid of getting it all wrong.

'Your turn now!' she smiled after she had driven through Kingswater. She turned into a side road at the far end of the village and pulled in beside a gate.

They changed places. As Anthony walked round to the other side of the car he wiped his hands on his jacket, took a few deep breaths and tried to appear much more calm and confident than he felt.

'Don't be nervous. We'll just go down this road a little way. It's quite straight and there won't be any traffic,' Helen said.

He wondered if *she* was nervous. She didn't give any sign. How nice it must be to be so cool and controlled. He started the engine and they moved off slowly, Helen quietly giving him instructions.

'There's a place to turn further down,' she said, 'then we'll go back. If you can turn the car round, that is!'

'I haven't done that yet!'

'I'll show you. There's plenty of space.'

They reached the spot where a broad track went off to the left. Helen guided him carefully as he slowly reversed into the track.

'Stop for a minute. Then you can practise starting and moving off out of this muddy spot. That was OK wasn't it?' she asked, as he turned off the engine.

'Yes, but we're not back yet!'

'We'll get back, don't worry.'

'I'm not worried about getting back or not, just about damaging your car - or you.'

'Well, that's my problem,' she said. 'I invited you, and I think you're doing fine. We must try to find time to come out when it's light - and dry.'

The rain was hammering on top of the car now, and they could see nothing outside. Cocooned in what seemed a safe haven, a world away from Fieldhouse and its problems, Anthony took his opportunity and said, 'I was thinking of resigning at half term.' He stared down at his hands, which were still clutching the steering wheel.

'I know,' Helen said softly.

He knew she was looking at him but he couldn't turn to face her.

'But I didn't.'

'I know.' A pause. 'Do you want to tell me why not?'

'Because of you!' The words tumbled out. Now it was said! Anthony was so grateful for the darkness. He knew his face was scarlet. He still gazed at his hands, the knuckles gleaming white against the black wheel.

'Me?'

'Yes.' Anthony saw a way to diffuse his embarrassment, and possibly hers. 'Every time I was going to hand in the letter, I met you and you were kind to me. I thought you wanted me to stay. So in the end I did.'

'I do want you to stay.'

She placed her hand gently over his on the wheel and they sat in silence, both looking at those two joined hands.

Anthony could neither move nor speak. His mouth was dry. What should he say or do now? Help me, Helen, he thought desperately. Show me what I'm supposed to do next.

She must have understood. She removed her hand slowly.

'I think we'd better go back now,' she said in a very quiet voice with a slight tremor. She was looking up at him and he knew he had to turn and look at her. Her face was very pale. 'You *will* stay, won't you? I'd hate to lose you.'

'Would you?'

'Yes, of course. You're very . . . important to me. Do you want me to drive back?' she finished, hurriedly.

'No. I'm sure I'll be OK.'

He didn't feel it, but he needed something to concentrate on. He started the engine and turned on the headlights. In the improved light he turned and looked at her again. She looked younger and much more vulnerable than he'd seen her look before.

'Select first gear. And drive off very slowly, because of this mud,' she said, still softly. She smiled. 'Otherwise we might get stuck here.'

Anthony got the impression that she wouldn't be too upset about that. Neither would he. But they had to go back. He tried to pull away smoothly but in his anxiety he caused the car to judder and jolt.

'Sorry!'

'Just take it calmly,' she said.

How could he be calm after what had just passed? But perhaps it meant a lot more to him. I'm such a fool, he thought.

'Change down for this hill'

Concentrate! Forget that hand over his. Concentrate on watching the road through the rain and on what his feet were doing with those pedals . . .

When they arrived back at the village Helen, who had been silent for a while, said, 'I'll drive into the school. Without dual controls, it's safer. Eric would never forgive me if . . . '

'Yes, of course.'

They changed places again. Helen drove into the school gates and round the back to where the Pearsons had a rather rickety wooden garage. The doors were open and they drove straight in. she turned off the engine and looked at him.

'Did you enjoy that?'

'Oh, yes, very much!'

'You did well.'

She leaned over and kissed him on the cheek.

'I'll take you out again soon,' she whispered.

Then she got out quickly. Anthony did the same. At least, he supposed he must have done because he found himself standing at the side of the car.

'You'd better go in now,' she said across the car roof.

'Yes. Thanks for everything.'

He dashed over the gravel, round the corner and up the steps. When he reached the front door he tried to compose himself and hoped no-one was in the hall. He was lucky. The hall was empty. He raced upstairs, flung his jacket down on the bed and himself after it. His face, especially one small part of it, burned like fire. He pressed his knuckles into his eyes.

He was inexperienced with women, even of his own age. How could he be expected to understand a mature woman like Helen? But how much experience did he need to interpret what had just passed between them? Surely he could not mistake her words, her expression, her touch - and that kiss?

He didn't know what to do. Should he bury himself under the covers and weep? Or put on some music and dance for joy? He felt like doing both. And, during the course of that long, disturbed, sleepless, wonderful, agonising night, he did.

Anthony wasn't sure what he expected to happen over the next few days. Did he think that Helen would throw herself into his arms at every opportunity? That he would be able to shout his feelings from every rooftop and that she would do the same? No, not seriously. He really had no idea what the next step would be. Thinking about it rationally, he knew that any relationship they might possibly have would have to be conducted with the utmost discretion and secrecy. And therefore that any meeting, however brief, was likely to be followed by a period of drought, if only to throw any 'spies' off the scent. But people who are newly in love are not rational, especially if they are young, inexperienced and lacking in self-confidence. They are vulnerable to every tiny incident that suggests that their beloved has changed their mind.

What Anthony hadn't expected was to be avoided or ignored. And that was how he felt Helen treated him during the following week. The first time he met her, she hurried past with a mumbled greeting, seeming highly embarrassed. On the other occasions she behaved as though nothing had happened. Anthony's 'high' soon collapsed into a deep low.

Two additional factors added to his misery. The events with Helen had led to a total inability to concentrate, making lessons and preparation even more fraught than usual. And as the week went on and she did not contact him, his increasing misery made him even less able to cope.

In the midst of this, Pearson, having presumably cleared the administrative matters accumulated over half term, had begun sitting 'working' in Anthony's lessons again. Anthony knew that those iceberg-blue eyes, ostensibly bent over books and papers, missed nothing of his stutteringly nervous, incompetent delivery and lack of class control. And now this man was Anthony's rival in love! After all, Helen had held his hand and kissed him, hadn't she? Anthony went cold as he thought of Eric Pearson's likely reaction to the information that this hopeless young English master was involved with his wife. Human nature suggested that Anthony should experience a certain triumph at that thought, but for him this was far outweighed by sheer terror.

Pearson also made it quite plain that he had been disappointed not to receive Anthony's resignation after half term. 'As you have chosen to stay with us for another term, Mr Dean, I will expect you to show a very marked improvement in all aspects of your teaching,' - without suggesting ways that Anthony might do this - 'as all pupils have exams next term and we expect excellent results. That, after all, is what our parents pay for.'

In other words, this is your last chance and, if you won't go voluntarily, I'll get rid of you as soon as I find an excuse.

A week that had started so promisingly ended in black despair.

'Like a bit of driving practice?' Mary asked after Saturday lunch. 'I'm going out to look at some villages. D'you want to come?'

'Yes, I'd love to.' Anthony had still seen almost nothing of Helen and now their flat seemed to be shut up.

Mary brought her Mini round to the front door and picked him up.

'I know a good place where you can practise some manoeuvres. It's very quiet. Mrs Pearson took you out, didn't she?'

'Only once. She seems to be very busy this week.'

'They're recruiting for next year. That's where they are this weekend - visiting prep schools and such. It's not easy at the moment. I hope they're successful or we'll all be out in the autumn.'

I will anyway, thought Anthony. At least he now had some reason for Helen's preoccupation. No doubt she'd been dragged off by Pearson against her will. That would be it. She'd have wanted to spend time with him but she hadn't been allowed. And he supposed the school was *her* livelihood too. She had to put her time into supporting it.

'Are you insured for me to drive?' Anthony asked. 'She . . . Mrs Pearson said her car was insured for anyone so that it could be used in emergencies.'

'Just don't ask,' Mary answered with an arch look. 'And don't hit anything either!'

'Where are we going?'

'I'm going to take a look at some villages to see whether they'll be suitable for fieldwork - you know, what facilities they've got, where people work and so on.'

'Can't you do that in Kingswater?'

'Yes, I can. But I think they need to go somewhere different. Familiarity breeds contempt. It does them good to get out. And me!'

'If you need help, I'll come if I can.'

'How's your geography?'

'Not brilliant.'

'I thought not. But still you can come and keep order.'

Then, no doubt realising she'd been tactless, she changed the subject. Anthony could not fail to notice. My uselessness is common knowledge, he thought.

Mary drove to a road high up on the Downs. The view, and the road, seemed to stretch for miles.

'You can see if anything's coming on this road,' she laughed. 'So, get in.'

It took him some time to organise himself in the Mini, but eventually he pulled away. It was very enjoyable driving in such a vast open space. He began to imagine himself spinning along here in his own car. Not, of course, the elderly saloon which had been lying in Aunt's garage for several years, but a rather smart red sports car. And in the passenger seat, Helen, with her hair and scarf blowing out behind her. Then they'd find a quiet spot and stop for a picnic . . .

'Watch out!'

'Sorry. I was miles away.'

'Well, don't be,' Mary said sternly. 'Concentrate on keeping the car in a straight line - on the left-hand side of the road. It's safer that way. By the way,' she went on when order was restored, 'you don't mind me asking this, I hope, but do you have a girlfriend somewhere?'

Was this a deduction from his faraway expression and erratic driving?

'Er . . . not at the moment,' he answered, rather untruthfully he felt. 'I didn't keep in touch with anyone after I left university. I thought a fresh start was better.'

This was also not quite the truth. There hadn't been anyone to keep in touch *with*. Unlike most of his friends, he hadn't had a girlfriend for some time before he graduated. And the less said the better about those very few brief, awkward relationships that had comprised his sole experience of romance - until now.

'Well, I'm sure a nice young man like you won't be footloose for long,' she grinned at him.

Someone else calling him a nice young man!

'I don't get much opportunity to meet people,' he said. But he *had* met someone.

'No, I suppose not. We're all a bit old, aren't we? Still, perhaps there'll be some young ladies on the staff next year.'

'Somehow I can't imagine Old Pearson recruiting young ladies.'

'I don't know about that. He's obviously got an eye for the ladies himself. Look at Helen!'

'What about her?'

'Well, he had an affair with her, didn't he? Broke up his first marriage - although it was just about over anyway, so they say. Apparently he used to parade her as his glamorous young wife.'

Anthony shuddered. The thought of Helen being 'paraded' appalled him. So did the thought of her having an affair with Pearson, although logic told him that they must have got together somehow. And why did she seem so indifferent to her husband now. Had it all gone sour or had she never really cared for Pearson? Simply been impressed by him, perhaps. Or, horror of horrors, was she inclined to have affairs every so often? Surely not! It didn't seem like her. And yet - she'd avoided him all week since that kiss . . .

'Stop by this gate,' Mary ordered, breaking into his thoughts. 'Now we'll do some reversing, and a three-point turn. Are you ready?'

Anthony was so busy concentrating for the next ten minutes that all thoughts of Helen were mercifully banished from his head.

The Pearsons returned on Sunday morning. After lunch, Anthony decided to take a short walk before tackling the pile of marking which awaited him.

As he was leaving he met Helen coming out of the library.

'Oh, hello Mr Dean,' she said, 'how's the driving going? Sorry I haven't been able to take you out again. I've been terribly busy this week. We're recruiting for next year.'

She spoke quite normally, as thought nothing had ever happened between them.

'Yes, I know. Mary took me out. And I've had another lesson. I think I'm doing OK.'

He tried to sound natural but it didn't feel that way. He felt uncomfortable, unsure what his position was. Had he read far too much into the whole thing? He'd done that on other occasions - and been crushed.

'I'm sorry we can't go today either. It's a pity as it's a pleasant afternoon. Are you going out?'

'Only for half an hour. Then it's back to the marking.'

'Well, I'd better not keep you any longer.' She turned and walked across the hall into her flat. As she turned the door handle she looked back at him and continued, 'We must go out driving again next week. I'll make time somehow, I promise.'

Anthony felt much lighter of heart as he walked briskly along the village street. Michael had told him of another path at the far end of the village, which he wanted to find. The search provided a focus for this short walk and he'd then know where to go on another occasion when he had more time - and less marking - whenever that would be. He thought he might even be able to find the path, once he had pinpointed it, from the top of the ridge, and follow it down. Mary would be proud of him! Her explanations of her village study work the previous day had made him aware of things around him that he had never thought about before. He *would* help her with the field trip if he could.

On his return, he went into the library to find books for his preparation - and there was Helen, on her knees in front of the fireplace, arranging some grasses and seedheads in a vase on the hearth. Much to his surprise, Art-and-Craft, whom he had never seen in the library since that first dinner, was comfortably seated in a chair in front of what should have been the fire, talking to her.

'Oh, come and join us,' she said. He thought she looked lovely, gazing up at him with her arms full of grasses. 'Look at these,' she went on enthusiastically, 'aren't they wonderful. And they last for ages in an arrangement.'

'I'd like to paint those,' said Art-and-Craft.

'Bring your paints down, then. I might even be inspired myself,' she replied. 'Only don't get oil paint all over the tables or floor. Eric will not be pleased. You're not going to join the painting party, Anthony?'

'No talent, I'm afraid. But if you're really going to paint I'll bring my marking down and watch.'

'Yes, do. Why not? I'm going to fetch my watercolours.'

'You're on!' Art-and-Craft uncurled his lanky form from the well-worn chair and said 'I'll get my paints. And something to cover the floor.'

'You will join us, won't you?' Helen asked Anthony, as the art teacher left the room.

'Do you want me to?'

'Yes, very much. I'm going to sit here. You can sit next to me if you want to see how I work. And there's plenty of room for your marking. Then David can move that table and put his easel over there.' She indicated an area to the right of the fireplace.

'I'll go up and get my stuff.'

When he returned, Art-and-Craft had swathed that area with a paint-stained cloth and set up his sketching easel. This contraption was also liberally coated in dried paint, which in places had formed a thick crust. A layer of newspaper covered the table beside him, on which he was laying out his paints. Anthony wondered how he could tell which colour was in the tubes, as they too were encrusted with dried oil paint - several shades to a tube. But the artist seemed to pick out the ones he wanted without trouble, and squeezed blobs from each tube on to a large wooden palette.

Seeing those brilliant colours emerging from the dirty, twisted metal tubes gave Anthony a sudden understanding of the attraction of painting. He almost felt as though he could pick up a brush and have a go himself.

He took his place at the table where Helen had suggested. Presently she returned with her paints and three mugs of coffee on a tray.

'What a super way to spend a Sunday afternoon,' she said. 'Why haven't we thought of it before?'

The next hour or so passed very happily for Anthony. He spent a great deal more time watching the two artists at work than he did marking English essays.

Art-and-Craft set to work with a large brush, attacking his canvas board vigorously and plastering it with a range of colours which seemed to bear little resemblance to the beiges and browns of the arrangement or the deep green and gold of the vase.

Helen's picture was much more delicate. First she did a light pencil sketch of the vase and the fireplace and then began to add very dilute colour. While she was doing this her brush strayed towards, not her water pot, but her half-full coffee mug.

Anthony, watching her closely, clapped his hand over the mug's rim, just in time. Helen turned to him, laughing.

'Oh, you're not an artist until you've dipped your brush in your drink at least once! I'm glad I'm not an oil painter though. I see David's put his mug well out of the way.' She paused and looked down at Anthony's hand, still protecting her coffee. 'I suppose I'd better finish this drink.'

With a sidelong glance at Art-and-Craft, who appeared engrossed in his work, she picked up the hand and removed it from the top of her mug. Instead of letting go, she carried it down out of sight under the tabletop. There she held Anthony's hand tightly while she slowly drank her coffee, looking at him over the rim of the mug in a way which made him redden and squirm. Only when she had finished the drink down to the last drop and replaced the mug carefully on the table, did she let go of his hand with a final squeeze.

'You're not getting through much marking, Anthony,' she said, with a secretive smile.

His eyes said to her, 'I can't mark without my hand!'

'I'm too interested in watching the artists,' he replied, truthfully.

'Next time, you must have a go yourself. I'll help you. I'm going to paint the vase with this green now.'

She mixed several shades of green and he looked on as she flooded it on to the vase, leaving little white spaces where the gold decoration would eventually go. It all seemed very casual, but it worked.

The pile of open exercise books at Anthony's elbow grew very gradually smaller as the afternoon wore on. The two paintings also progressed towards completion. Then Helen stopped and looked at her watch.

'Hey, we'd better clear up. It's nearly time for supper and church.'

'I'd like to do some more work on this, when it's dried a bit.' Art-and-Craft stepped back from his painting and studied it, as he had done at frequent intervals throughout the afternoon.

'Take the vase up to the art room whenever you want it - as long as you bring it back,' Helen told him, as she tidied her paintbox.

Art-and-Craft threw his paint tubes back into an old box and wrapped his palette and brushes in newspaper.

'I'll come back for the easel,' he said, carefully removing his picture and carrying it out of the library paint-side out.

'Did you enjoy the afternoon?' Helen asked Anthony when the art teacher had gone.

'Brilliant. I loved watching you paint.'

'You could come out and sit with me when the weather's better. I'm always a bit nervous of sitting out alone.'

She picked up her belongings and prepared to leave. For a moment, she stood very close to Anthony, looking up at him as though deciding what to do or say next. He wondered if she was going to kiss him again, but then they heard the footsteps of Art-and-Craft hurrying back for his easel.

Disappointed, Anthony turned to the table and gathered up his books.

'I promise I will take you out this week. I know you need the practice,' she said. 'I'll let you know when.'

And she was gone.

Chapter Fourteen

Anthony found the next two weeks very long ones. Helen did manage to give him a driving lesson, but it was brief and in daylight and she seemed anxious to avoid any situation which would cause them to park in an isolated spot. Instead, she told him to drive around the village.

'You need to drive where there's more going on,' she told him.

When they got back to school there were several boys hanging around the grounds. Helen parked by the front door so there was no prospect of a kiss in a darkened garage. Just a 'Cheerio, Mr Dean,' as she hurried up the steps.

Anthony was disappointed again, and his teaching suffered. The next lesson went badly. Eric Pearson's penetrating eyes seemed to be reading his thoughts. He could almost imagine the Head thinking: 'I know you want my wife, but you can't have her. And I intend to make your life a misery.'

However, his dread of Pearson did not deter him on the last Friday of these two stressful weeks. A quick word from Helen as he passed her on the stairs changed his mood completely.

'I'll be up on the hill this afternoon, during your "free". If you can come . . . '

'I'll be there if I possibly can.'

He was there. He dashed out as soon as he could get away, hoping no-one noticed his haste. The cold air seared his lungs as he ran up the steep path. Eventually he had to slow down. I must get fitter, he thought. He was annoyed at having to waste precious time.

He saw Helen waiting. She was sitting just below the crest on the far side so he was nearly at the top before she came into sight. Was she ensuring that she could not be seen from below, from the school? She hadn't bothered before, so was this different? Anthony's flushed face and pounding heart were not solely due to the exertion of climbing the hill.

As he approached, she stood up and indicated a spot even further over to the other side of the ridge.

'There's a sheltered hollow here which is good to sit in,' she said, walking down the slope. He followed. Although it was cold, the ground was dry and they sat comfortably on the springy turf, protected from the strong wind. The world of school and people seemed to have vanished. In front of them stretched a vast area of farmland, a patchwork of browns and dull greens. The only sound was the wind in the trees on the knoll further along the ridge.

'That climb has done you good. You look well,' she smiled. 'You often look pale and strained - but now you're glowing!'

'So are you,' he said.

They were sitting very close together. Emboldened by adrenalin and the joy of the moment, he bent forward and touched her forehead lightly with his lips. To his distress, she drew back quickly.

'It'll bring sorrow,' she said in a sad, aching tone.

'I'm sorry . . . '

'There's no need to be sorry. I'm not. Perhaps I should be, but I'm not. But I do know that it'll bring sorrow,' she said again.

'Does it have to? Can't we just be happy together sometimes?'

'Little bright spots of light in the gloom?'

'Yes, why not? I thought you . . . liked me,' Anthony went on, his initial boldness rapidly waning. 'You are happy with me, aren't you?'

'Yes, very.'

'And not at other times?' He instantly wished he had not asked this. He mustn't intrude. But he had to go on with it now. He wanted to find out how she really felt about him, what she wanted him for.

'No, not at other times - can't you tell?' Almost as if to hide the pain in her expression, Helen put her hands over her face.

Anthony put his arm around her shoulder and pulled her close to him. This time she didn't draw back.

Sitting like that on the hillside, the wind blowing through the grasses all around them and grey-white clouds sending shadows scudding across the plain below, and with the school and all it contained hidden from view, Anthony was gloriously, deliriously happy. He pressed his lips against her hair over and over again.

'Have you *ever* been happy before?' he murmured at last.

'No, not like this.' She looked up at him. 'I mean it. No matter what our problems are. I've never felt so comfortable with anyone, never had so much in common. If only I could start again!' She gazed over the wide landscape. Was she seeing the last twenty years pass by? He wouldn't break the spell. He just held her and waited for her to go on. 'Yes, I am wishing that I was your age and we could start a life together,' she said at last. 'But that can never be.'

'No, but can't we have some of those bright spots of happiness?'

'Any relationship we have will have to be totally discreet,' she said, emerging from the daydream of what might have been. Did she suddenly realise the seriousness of what she was doing? 'We won't be able to meet often and there'll be long periods when we don't - if only to defeat the gossips.' Helen was back to practicalities.

'Yes, I understand that.'

'It'll be very hard. It is now. Well, I think so.'

Anthony was elated by this admission. If she found it hard, she must really want to be with him. Much more than she sometimes showed.

'I find it hard, too,' he said. 'It's awful. I've been desperate, not really knowing what you really think of me.'

'I kept on telling myself that I mustn't like you. I must leave you alone. I didn't - don't - want to hurt you. But in the end I liked you too much.'

Her face was turned up to his. She slid her arm around his neck. He tightened his embrace and kissed her for a long time.

Much against his will, he eventually forced himself to look at his watch. It had stopped!

'Oh, damn, what's the time?' he asked, anxiously.

'It's ten to three. You've got ten minutes to get back down.'

Anthony re-set his watch, reluctantly disentangled himself from Helen, and stood up. The idyll was over - for now.

'We'll meet when we can. That's all I can promise. Now go - and teach your very best,' she said.

He flew back to the school on wings - then crashed to earth as he entered the English room. Eric Pearson was standing in front of the already-assembled class, which rose as Anthony entered. A glance at the clock on the wall told him the ghastly story. Helen's watch had been slow.

'You are rather late, Mr Dean,' said Pearson icily.

'I'm sorry. My watch had stopped.'

A titter from the class was soon suppressed by a glare from the Head.

'I see. Well, now you're here, please carry on.'

Pearson walked to the back of the classroom and took his seat beside the stock cupboard, leaving Anthony breathless, red-faced and in a state of confusion for the second time that afternoon. But what a change of circumstances! Now, somehow, he had to begin a lesson.

Needless to say, it was a disaster. The euphoria of his meeting with Helen was quickly cancelled out. As he struggled through the next agonising hour he couldn't help wondering if Pearson *knew* where he had been.

'It'll bring sorrow,' Helen had said. Anthony had a feeling that she was right. But it was too late. He was committed. He longed only to be with her.

At the end of that turbulent afternoon he found an envelope tucked under his door when he returned to his attic. He tore it open.

> *Dear Anthony,*
> *I'm so sorry, my watch was slow. I hope it*
> *didn't cause you any problems.*
> > *Yours,*
> > *Helen.*

It did, Helen; if only you knew, he thought, groaning at the memory of the last dreadful hour and Pearson's disgusted expression. But it had been worth it. He pressed the letter to his lips, imagining it to be her face, then put it away carefully. Everything of Helen's was precious, even more so now. And at last he could admit it.

He spent the evening lost in thoughts and longings. It was a great effort to get through the marking but he knew he mustn't neglect it. He was in enough trouble already. He must do nothing to make anyone, least of all Pearson, suspicious. That would be letting Helen down and she'd probably be very angry. He was desperate to prove that his youth didn't mean he was immature

119

and foolish. To keep her, he would have to act *her* age, not his own.

As Helen had said, it was going to be very hard. A young man of nearly twenty-two would expect to have girlfriends who were quite free to see him as often as possible. He'd want to talk about his new love, to boast, to exaggerate, to buy her gifts, to be proudly seen in her company. *He* could do none of these things. All he could do was shiver up here while his beloved Helen sat with her ice-cold husband, talked with him, slept with him . . .

With a deep sigh he turned miserably back to his exercise books.

'There's a very fine line between joy and sorrow,' Helen had said.

As usual, she was right.

'Does anyone ever call you Tony?'

Anthony hadn't seen much of Helen for several days. At last they had a little time together and she'd been giving him a driving lesson. Now they were strolling hand-in-hand along a muddy track below the Downs - a rest from practising three-point turns.

'Hardly anyone,' he answered. 'My parents never did. If my brother did, they used to say "Please address Anthony by the name with which he was christened." Unfortunately I was christened George Anthony so he called me that all the time. It used to drive me mad.'

Helen laughed. 'I didn't know you had a brother. Did you get on well in other ways?'

'Not really. There were eight years between us. It's a big gap at that age. It wouldn't have mattered so much now.'

'Wouldn't?'

'Graham's dead. He died at school.'

'Oh, Anthony, I'm so sorry. Was he ill?'

'He fell. They were hill-walking. It was an accident, so they said.'

'Do you mean you don't think it was?'

'I'm not sure. It was twelve years ago. My parents would never talk about it. But they'd talk about Graham, all the time. He was eighteen and about to take his A-levels. They never recovered from the shock.'

They had stopped walking and were leaning on a gate looking over a stubble field. A robin was scolding them from somewhere in the hedgerow. In the distance, the alarm call of a pheasant echoed across the fields.

'Was your brother bright?' Helen asked. Her arm tightened around him as though she knew this was a difficult subject - but one that it would do him good to talk about.

'Yes, very. They idolised him. But he was . . . difficult. He made enemies at school. That's why I wondered . . . because of the secrecy and the rest.'

'Don't tell me if it's too painful,' Helen said quietly. 'I just thought it might help.'

'I want to tell you. But I don't want to bore you with it. And it's hard to talk about it very lucidly sometimes. Well, I never *do* talk about it.'

'I know. You've never mentioned your family before, so I guessed something was wrong. Did they idolise Graham at your expense?'

'I thought so at the time. After he died my mother just, well, died of a broken heart I suppose. She only lived three years and hardly came out of her room.'

'What happened to you?'

'A couple of months after she died, my father packed me off to live with my grandmother. He married a much younger woman that very week. I hardly saw him after that. His marriage didn't last very long and within two years he drank himself to death. His wife had already left by then. I never saw her.'

'Were you happy with your Gran?'

'I don't think I was ever entirely happy, because of the past. But Gran was very kind to me. She lived just long enough to see me graduate. She was so proud. She was the only person who ever appreciated me.'

Helen hugged him even tighter. 'I do,' she said. 'I knew you'd had an unhappy life. I'm glad you've told me. Where does your Auntie come in?'

'She's Great-aunt Florence, Gran's sister. Not much like her, though. When Gran died she said I could have a temporary room in her house, mainly to store things. She has a low opinion of students. But when I went at half term she seemed to think that I'd become respectable.'

'Of course you are! Come on, we'd better go back. How did we manage to get so muddy out driving?' They laughed together, lightening the mood. 'I'll have to hide my shoes when I get in.'

Helen thought of everything. He just hoped he wouldn't let her down.

A few days later he felt that he *had* let her down, or at least that she had begun to get into difficulties because of him.

He met her, as usual, in the library. He'd been supervising a group of boys there during what should have been his free period. At least he'd been able to do some marking as they'd been fairly well behaved. Being in earshot of Pearson's study, just across the hall, obviously had an effect.

The boys had left, but Anthony stayed to finish his last few essays. He was scoring his red pen through the last one when Helen entered.

She started when she saw him, almost as though she didn't want to meet him. After a slightly awkward pause she said, in a low voice, 'I'm sorry, I won't be able to take you out driving any more.'

'Oh?' Anthony felt a surge of disappointment - and dread.

'My car's going. It . . . it needs a lot of repairs and it isn't worth the expense. Eric - we - think it's silly to have two cars when we can rarely both be out at the same time - because of the school. I shall miss it, of course.'

'I'm sorry. I hope it wasn't . . . '

'Oh, no,' Helen broke in. 'It's just . . . well, economics.' She gave him a slight smile, then walked away to the far shelves and began shuffling the books around in a desultory fashion.

Anthony knew that the school was no longer thriving as it apparently had been in the past. Perhaps this *was* simply a matter of money. Maybe she'd tell him when they were alone. But being alone was going to be a lot more difficult now.

It was obvious that Helen didn't want to talk. Was she just upset about the car? He gathered up his books and prepared to leave.

'I've got to go now,' he said, rather awkwardly.

Helen turned and looked at him for a moment.

'Yes, of course.' She paused. 'I'm sorry about the driving. But you're doing fine and you'll be driving by yourself before long. Perhaps Mary . . . '

'Yes, she did offer to take me out again. I just hope I won't need to take too many tests.'

She smiled, more warmly now. 'I'm sure you won't. Then you can go and fetch your auntie's car.'

'And take *you* out,' he said, almost in a whisper.

Her lips formed the word "Yes," then she turned back to her shelves. The door opened, another group of boys came in, and Anthony departed. Once again he found himself in a state of confusion, unsure of the situation.

We'll just have to take every day as it comes, Helen had told him up on the hill. There was no possibility of him - them - planning for even the immediate future in this kind of relationship. If he wanted it to continue he'd have to grit his teeth and endure a lot of pain. And he did want it to continue.

Christmas was rapidly approaching. Anthony preferred not to think about it, but in a school that was impossible. Preparations were under way for school celebrations and staff and pupils were discussing their holiday plans.

I could have been free by then, Anthony thought. Despite his love for Helen he had frequent misgivings about his decision to stay. He was still having an appalling struggle with most of his lessons. Duty nights, although less traumatic than the first one, were very stressful, and Peter Ferguson made sure that Anthony looked a fool on, and sometimes off, the games field.

And, of course, Pearson still haunted him. His 'disappointment with your lack of improvement' was only too obvious. Anthony knew he wouldn't survive another term unless things changed drastically. He'd either resign or get the sack. Then he wouldn't see Helen again.

So his anguished thoughts went on. But he couldn't do anything about any of it now. He could only hope that in his second term the boys would consider him to be a 'proper teacher' and that their behaviour would improve enough for him to get a grip on things.

Things like exams. They would be a real test. How could he prepare pupils for exams when they wouldn't listen? He would have to make them work at the start of the spring term. If only he could believe they would!

Before that, there loomed Christmas. It would be his first Christmas completely alone in the world apart from Aunt Florence. Her apparent conversion to his cause did not really convince him. Should he stay at school? That had been the reason for choosing a boarding school. And as it was the 'boarding' part that caused a lot of his misery, he supposed he should take advantage of its few benefits.

If he stayed, would he see anything of Helen? Would he be the only person here except the Pearsons? Eric Pearson was hardly likely to relish the thought of this irritatingly incompetent teacher impinging on his privacy during the holidays. Anthony could hardly expect to be joining the Pearsons for Christmas dinner!

No, he'd be dining on soup and sandwiches in his freezing attic. What on earth would he do for three weeks? Plenty of reading and walking - but no hot meals, warm fires or company. A lonely pint in the village pub without his colleagues had no appeal.

The alternative, three weeks with Aunt Florence, didn't appeal either. Despite her last-minute invitation at the end of his half term stay, he didn't think she would want him there long. He could do some jobs for her, perhaps, and explore the countryside. But the weather might be bad. What would she think of him reading or preparing school work all the time? *And* he wouldn't see Helen.

Helen! He must buy her a present. But what? Jewellery might be too intimate. In any case he didn't have enough money to buy anything of good quality. He knew nothing about it and she didn't wear much so he wasn't sure of her tastes. He couldn't get flowers or anything large. A book? Perhaps, but she was surrounded with them. He had no idea what she had in her flat.

He'd have to get to some shops, but he had so little time. There were lessons for part of Saturday mornings, followed by sport in the afternoons. Staff, especially junior staff, were expected to turn out and watch home matches or to act as extra supervisors on the trips to away games. And as he'd been singled out to help with sport, he was given more of these duties than the others were. Bus services from the village were infrequent. He also had to fit in his driving lessons. But he'd have to make time somehow.

'What are you doing for Christmas?' asked Mary one day at breakfast. She'd arrived late and taken a seat at his sparsely populated table.

'I haven't decided. I *was* thinking of staying here, but now I'm not sure . . . '

'What, spend Christmas in that ghastly room of yours? Isn't there anywhere else you can go?'

'Yes, to an aunt. It's OK, but I'm not sure I want to spend that much time there.'

'Well, do half and half. Go away for the first week then come back after Christmas if you've had enough. You don't want to spend all your holiday in this grim place. There won't be anyone here. Except your friend Mr P. - and Helen, of course. But you won't be able to see much of her.'

Did Mary know about him and Helen? He was sure that she did.

'That's a good idea,' he said. 'Why didn't I think of it?'

'Because you haven't learnt all the strategies for survival yet,' answered Mary, devouring a large bowl of cereal. 'It takes time, but you'll get to know them eventually. "Compromise" being an important one.'

He was just going back upstairs when Helen's voice addressed him from the hall below.

'Mr Dean!' He turned and looked down at her. Was it going to be good news or bad? She looked cheerful enough. 'Are you free on Saturday afternoon?' She said this loudly so she couldn't be planning an assignation. 'I believe the match has been cancelled. I'm taking a carload into town for Christmas shopping. Can you join us?'

'I'd love too. I've been wondering how I was ever going to do any.'

Since Helen knew the state of his social life, he imagined that she'd have some idea who it was he wanted to buy a present for.

'I know it's difficult here. So I always try to help the staff at this time of year.'

It wasn't just for him then. Another pang of childish jealousy! She went back inside her flat, saying as she closed the door, 'I plan to leave immediately after lunch. I'll see you then.'

And not before? Anthony sighed. Did she know how much he longed to hold her, kiss her and even . . . No! He mustn't even think of anything more. Helen was a very respectable woman. He'd have to make do with a few snatched kisses and cuddles. Wait a minute, though! She had had an affair with Pearson, hadn't she? But that was when he was married, not her. This would be different. After all, she had her livelihood to lose now.

At least he'd be able to get her a present, he cheered himself, as he plodded up the stairs to his room. Now, how many hours was it until Saturday lunchtime?

It came at last. Anthony was out there much too early. The prospect of being with Helen, even in company, getting away from school and choosing a gift combined to make him rush through a light lunch and hurry outside.

His fellow travellers arrived at a more sedate pace. Michael had already said that he'd been asked. Another shopper was Frank Beech, the science master. Anthony saw little of him normally. He lived in the village and had an invalid wife so he spent as much time as possible at home. He was near retirement and his car had retired before him, as he put it.

Helen came out, looking very smart in a short dark coat and knee-length boots.

'Are we all here?' she asked, looking round. 'Oh no, Mr Wilson's missing. I'll go round and get the car while we're waiting.'

When she drew up to the front door in what was now the Pearson's only car, David Wilson still had not appeared.

'I'll go and look for him,' Anthony offered.

Helen looked grateful. 'Yes, please do Mr Dean. Tell him to hurry up!'

Delighted to be of service to Helen, Anthony rushed back through the school and up to the art room. The art master was putting on a shabby jacket. Had his elderly mother sewed the leather patches on the elbows, Anthony wondered? And how long ago?

'Sorry. Just coming. Had to finish a pot.'

The others were already inside the car when they returned. They were both in the back. Now Anthony faced a dilemma. Should he hastily get into the front beside Helen or would that look too obvious? Fortunately Art-and-Craft solved the problem.

'You're a bit taller than me so you'd better go in front,' he said, and folded himself into the back seat.

Anthony took his seat beside Helen - and felt on top of the world.

The drive into town was all too short.

'Back here at five. I shan't wait for stragglers,' Helen said firmly, as they left the car park. 'And it's a long, long walk!'

Alone, Anthony did not know where to start. He gazed into the windows of several jewellers, browsed in bookshops and took a sidelong glance at lacy underwear on display in shops that he would never dare to enter. Eventually he sat drinking coffee with only a magazine and a very small selection of Christmas cards to show for his first hour's shopping.

It would have to be the book, he decided, ordering another coffee. There was no point in leaving the café until he had made up his mind what to buy. He'd only waste more time and the afternoon would be over. He'd seen an old but attractive edition of Hardy short stories. He knew she didn't have that because she'd borrowed one from the school library. It wasn't cheap, but Helen was worth it. Sipping his coffee, he began to consider what he would write on the flyleaf. A quotation perhaps?

He ought to buy something for Aunt Florence too. That might prove even more difficult. What does a 'nice young man' give to an elderly great-aunt? Not frilly smalls anyway! He imagined that her opinion of his 'niceness' would deteriorate rapidly if she thought he had even looked at such things. Greatly amused by this thought he went to the counter to pay for his coffee with a broad grin on his face. The girl behind the counter obviously thought this was intended for her. She gave him a charming smile and seemed to be waiting for him to say something, but he simply picked up his change and left. He only had one woman on his mind.

He returned to the bookshop and bought the Hardy. Then he wandered back into the town centre, picking up a few more purchases on the way. He wondered where the others were and what they were buying. What about Michael? He'd been talking a lot recently about a young teacher at the village primary school. Pamela - that was it. Perhaps something would come of that. Michael would be attractive to women of course. Fair-haired, blue-eyed, athletic, amusing company and with plenty of local knowledge and contacts.

He was the life and soul of the village social events and dances, so Mary had said. That was where he had met Pamela. Anthony had never been to one. His attempts at dancing had met with such scorn in the past that he would not subject himself to ridicule again. Besides, he only wanted to meet Helen and she certainly wouldn't be there.

'Hi, Anthony! Done all your shopping?' It was Michael himself. He was standing in front of a jeweller's window. Anthony went over to him. 'Can I pick your brains?' Michael went on in a low voice, with an exaggerated glance over his shoulder. 'What do you think of that brooch for . . . um . . . a young lady? Well, Pamela actually!' He reddened slightly.

Anthony was surprised. Perhaps Michael wasn't such a man of the world as he liked people to think.

'I don't know much about jewellery,' he replied. Or young ladies, he thought. 'But it looks very nice to me. I'm sure she'd . . . ' He stopped and gazed at the back of the shop window.

'Yes?'

'Oh, sorry. Yes, I'm sure she'd like it,' Anthony finished. 'And I hope it works. Good luck!'

Before the surprised Michael could reply, Anthony had hurried on and was lost in the crowd.

Once out of sight round the corner, he stopped and drew breath. He *must* have that brooch for Helen. Not the one Michael was admiring but another, which had sparkled out at him as he looked in the direction Michael had indicated. He would go back - but not until Michael was out of the way.

Chapter Fifteen

After ten minutes or so, Anthony walked slowly back to the jewellers. He hadn't seen a price on the brooch. And he hadn't much money left. He'd need money for his train fare to Aunt's and he wanted to try and keep a little nest egg for that day when he finally walked out of Fieldhouse forever. Easter, probably.

Don't let it be too expensive, he prayed as he approached the shop. Eagerly he pressed his nose against the window, looking into that shaded corner at the back where he'd seen that eye-catching glint.

The brooch had gone!

There was just a pinhole in the velvet stand where it had been fifteen minutes ago. Cursing under his breath, Anthony entered the shop. They might have it inside for some reason - or have another.

'You had a brooch in the window, shaped like a dragonfly?'

'Sorry, sir, we've just sold it to another young gentleman. About ten minutes ago. No, sorry, we don't have anything else like it at all. Won't be coming in now till after Christmas. Can I show you anything else?'

'No, thank you.'

Anthony left the shop as quickly as he'd entered. A thought had occurred to him. He looked in the window again. Sure enough, the brooch that Michael had originally shown him was still there. He must have followed Anthony's gaze, seen the dragonfly and liked it better!

Damn, damn, it's all my fault! If I hadn't shown any response he'd never have noticed it, Anthony thought miserably. He should have encouraged Michael to buy the one he'd chosen, gone in with him and bought the dragonfly there and then. But of course, he'd been too self-conscious, too secretive. It was always his downfall.

In the time he had left, he toured all the jewellers he could find, but there was nothing even similar to that attractive brooch. Out of luck, he retraced his steps to the car park. He had to hurry. All he needed was a very long walk in the dark! But he didn't think Helen would leave without him.

On the return journey he graciously allowed the second-tallest man, David Wilson, to sit by Helen. This wasn't entirely due to his sense of fairness or concern for Art-and-Craft's lanky limbs. It wasn't even to deter the gossips, although that aspect might be a bonus. His desire to sit beside Helen was offset on this occasion by the prospect of finding out whether Michael had indeed bought the brooch.

He didn't like to ask outright. After all, he reasoned, finding an excuse for his own awkwardness, Michael wouldn't want everyone to know that he'd been buying presents for a lady. So he hoped Michael would proffer the information. But he didn't. Perhaps he was offended or puzzled by Anthony's hasty departure from the shop window. He would have to find another way.

They had been back at school about half an hour. Anthony heard Michael filling his kettle in the bathroom. He thought this might be a good time to strike. He was going to make a fool of himself, as usual, but he *had* to know. He looked out of his door.

'Just making coffee. Want some?' Michael asked when he heard the door open.

'Thanks. I . . . er . . . wanted a word, actually.'

'Oh, well come on in.' Michael plugged in his kettle and spooned coffee into the mugs. 'What can I do for you?'

'You'll think I'm crazy - but did you buy that brooch?'

Michael looked very surprised. 'Yes. Well, no, not that one. I chose another. Why?'

'Was it a dragonfly?'

'Yes!' Even more surprised.

'Can I see it?'

'What the hell!'

'Sorry. It's very important to me.'

Michael silently handed over a mug of coffee, then frowned as he began rummaging among the packets flung on the bed. Without a word, he handed Anthony a small box.

Anthony opened it slowly. He'd got himself into a very uncomfortable situation and he'd have to offer some explanation eventually. Inside the box, pinned onto dark blue velvet, the dragonfly gleamed its message to him just as it had in the shop window. It was about two inches long, with silver filigree wings and a body made of some sparkling blue-green stone set in silver. It was even more beautiful than he'd imagined. And just perfect for Helen. It would match her eyes.

'How much did you pay for this?'

Michael remained speechless and frowning for a moment. Then he said 'Would you mind telling . . . '

'Sorry,' Anthony said again. 'How much? Please!'

'Twenty pounds,' replied Michael resignedly.

Twenty pounds! Almost half of Anthony's savings. 'I'll give you twenty-five,' he said.

'What?'

'Twenty-five pounds. Thirty. If you'll sell it to me.'

Michael's expression veered between anger, amazement and concern. For a moment the concern seemed to win.

'Anthony, are you all right?'

'Yes, I'm perfectly all right. And perfectly sober. But I really want that brooch.'

'So do I. It's for Pamela.' Michael was beginning to sound angry. 'I was looking for ages. And how the hell do you expect me to get anything else, stuck out here? You had all afternoon to buy things, same as me. Why couldn't you buy it when you first saw it instead of rushing off as though the devil was behind you?'

In as few words as possible, Anthony told him what had happened at the jewellers. It didn't improve matters.

'Who do you want it for, anyway? You haven't had the decency to tell me that. I told you. I didn't know *you* had any girlfriends! That's typical of you. Always skulking around in your own miserable little world, avoiding everybody, never telling anybody anything. If you've got a girlfriend, she must be a bloody ghost!'

Michael's normal pink complexion had become very red. He picked up the box from the table beside Anthony and snapped it shut with a defiant gesture. Then he very deliberately placed it in its paper bag, wrapped it noisily and put it inside the drawer of his desk. All without speaking.

'Forty!' said Anthony, making one last valiant effort in the face of Michael's wrath.

'Don't be so bloody ridiculous. Go to hell!'

Anthony left without a word.

Another disaster! Another enemy made! He lay on his bed in the dark - cold, tired, hungry and thoroughly depressed. His head felt liked a barrel that was being re-hooped - the hot iron band growing tighter every minute. There must be a curse on him, on this place. If only he'd given in that notice. Didn't he have enough trouble without making more for himself? How stupid can you get?

He didn't know how long he lay there. He'd missed supper but he certainly couldn't have gone down to the dining room. Now he was so cold that he wasn't sure he *could* move. Then a light tap came on the door.

Helen? Quickly he sat up and put on the bedside light. Running his fingers through his tousled hair he hurried to the door, tidying his shopping out of sight as he went.

'Can I come in?' It was Michael, looking more subdued than Anthony had ever seen him. His florid colour of earlier that evening had faded to a shade paler than normal. 'Are you OK?' he asked, scanning Anthony's face anxiously.

'Yes, I'm just stupid.'

'To get yourself in this state, this must mean an awful lot to you.' Michael put his hand in his pocket and brought out that little blue box. 'Don't worry, I'm not going to ask you why. If you still want it, it's yours.' He held out the box.

Anthony stood there, hair a mess, face crumpled, unable to find words. At last he said 'No, it's yours. I was just being ridiculous.'

'Come on, you must want it very badly. You'd never have asked me for it otherwise. I know you. Please take it. I can get something else.' He pushed the box into Anthony's hand. 'I don't know if Pamela would like it anyway. I'm not even sure if she likes *me!*' he finished with a grin, trying to lighten the mood.

Anthony managed a faint smile, but all he could say was 'Thanks.'

'No hurry for the money,' Michael said, turning to leave. 'And by the way, in case you get any more silly ideas, I won't take a single ha'penny more than I paid for it. Not a ha'penny, do you hear?'

He closed the door quietly behind him and left Anthony still standing in the middle of the room, clutching that precious box.

Yes, of course Anthony would be very welcome for Christmas, the note from Aunt Florence read, although she imagined that he would only want to stay for a day or two. He would be very bored by her company and of course she was in the habit of inviting her friends round at that time of year.

Anthony had met one or two of her friends and he did not wish to meet them again. So he would have to return to school after Christmas and brave the freezing garret. He hadn't managed to have any time alone with Helen to find out what she was doing or what she wanted him to do.

Then, rather to his surprise, he met her in the village shop. He supposed she must shop somewhere but he'd never seen her there before. She seemed to keep totally aloof from the village and its activities. Anthony was renewing his supply of rations and reminding himself to buy-in a good stock for the New Year period. He needed a lot of comforting treats to make his room bearable and to ease the difficulties of his circumstances.

They walked back to the school together, heads down against the driving December rain.

'What are you doing for Christmas?' she asked.

'I can go to my great-aunt's if I want to,' he answered in a non-committal voice. He wanted to see from her reply what she would really like to happen.

'Oh, good, I'm glad you've got somewhere to go,' she said.

Anthony bit his lip. 'Well, I might just go for a few days. I suppose it would be all right for me to spend some of the holiday here? That was one of the reasons why I chose a boarding school . . . ' He trailed off, wondering whether he'd said the wrong thing. Wasn't he supposed to have chosen Fieldhouse on its merits?

'Yes, as long as you let us know beforehand. There won't be any meals, of course. You've been given a key to the front door? It's always kept locked in the holidays.'

'Yes.'

In common with the other live-in staff he'd been given a key at the beginning of term. But his life had not so far been sufficiently interesting that he'd needed to use it.

'All the rest of the buildings will be shut up. But the library will be open. I'll try to arrange an electric fire in there. There won't be any central heating on in the school.'

'Will there be anyone else here?' They were just turning in at the gate as he asked this. On this cold, wet afternoon, the school certainly did not look an appealing place in which to spend a holiday, especially alone.

'We'll be here for most of the time, I expect. Mr Jones will be around doing maintenance work sometimes. In the first few days of the holiday the cleaners will be giving the place a good scrub. That's about all.' They climbed the front steps. As she turned the large brass doorknob she went on, 'If you're going to be here I hope to see something of you.'

Nothing more. Then they were in the hall and Helen was unlocking the door of her flat.

'I *will* be here part of the time - so perhaps . . . I mean, I hope to see you,' he said.

Anthony carried his packages upstairs with that feeling of deflation that he was almost getting used to now. In the hall they had seemed like mere acquaintances. Had they really kissed so passionately up on the hill? Helen had warned him that it had to be like this. But he hadn't realised how much it would hurt.

He put on water for coffee and consoled himself with a chocolate biscuit or two. Then he wrote back to Aunt Florence telling her that he'd arrive at the end of term and stay until Christmas was over. He'd be back here for New Year. If the Pearson's held a party he could at least peer over the banisters and watch. But he didn't think they were party-givers. In fact he never saw anyone visiting them, other than on school business. Helen didn't seem to have any life outside the school, apart from her walks and paintings. And him. She hadn't mentioned any family and he hadn't asked her yet. But he would if he ever got the chance of a decent length of time alone with her.

Anthony wrapped the dragonfly brooch very carefully. He'd chosen a card for Helen showing a painting of a snow scene. It lay open on his table as he pondered over what to write in it. He didn't want to be sloppy but he did want to convey his feelings. He was worried about when he'd have the opportunity to give it to her. There were only another ten days until the end of term. He could hardly leave it around for her or present her with it in public.

Everyone in the school was busy. When he did meet Helen, she was dashing - decorating the gym for the concert, helping with rehearsals and costumes, arranging the school Christmas Dinner, these were just some of the things. Anthony realised that somehow he was not involved with any of these activities, although everyone seemed to assume that he was. But no-one had asked him to help or participate in anything. He didn't even realise that many of the staff were preparing for their own performances in the concert. Even Helen though that he must be involved. But as people became busier, Anthony became more isolated. Struggling with his discipline problems, inhibited by Pearson's threatening presence, using most of his spare time in desperate attempts to improve his teaching methods, he had little opportunity to socialise. And apparently he wasn't missed.

Anthony had two other pre-occupations - his driving lessons and Helen. The former had progressed to the stage where he had booked a test for mid-January. He had told no-one of the date, not even Helen. I expect we'll be knee-deep in snow by then, he thought.

Helen occupied his thoughts constantly, whether he was teaching, preparing, marking, eating or lying in his bed shivering and exhausted and with a constant sore throat, at the end of each day.

Even that 'luxury' was denied him tonight. It was his duty night. And he fully expected trouble. It was so near the end of term and the boys were excited. Work was out and amusement was in - and what could be more amusing than baiting the daft English master?

Adding to his misery this evening were the symptoms of yet another heavy cold. His legs would hardly propel him up the stairs of the new block to the duty room.

The first part of the evening was fairly quiet. Most boys were at rehearsals. He hoped that the sound of singing filtering up from the gym would go on for a very long time. But eventually it ended and they all came tearing back, full of beans after being cooped up for an hour or so. If only Anthony had some of their energy. The end of term is draining for even experienced teachers. Anthony felt near collapse. He was mentally counting the hours, even the minutes, until he was released from torment.

The level of noise now caused him to make frequent forays into the corridor, games room and dormitories. No chance of nursing a cold this evening. His cracked voice had little effect without the addition of banging on something to make himself heard.

He came across matron, Jean Benson, dispensing medicine and words of comfort to some similarly-affected boys.

'That's just what I need,' he croaked.

'Don't tell me you're ill, Mr Dean? You sound it. I'll get you something.'

A few minutes later she appeared in the duty room with what seemed like most of the contents of her cupboard.

'You've had a lot of this, haven't you?' she said sympathetically. 'Nothing but a succession of colds. It's like that when you start teaching. You become immune eventually.'

'I certainly hope so. It's these throats that are the worst.'

'You ought to be tucked up in bed.'

'There's nothing I'd like better. Even in the beds here! No chance though. A difficult night ahead.'

'Don't worry. Leave the dorms to me. And I'll patrol the rest on my way through from one to the other. After all, we don't want you spreading your germs all over the school. It'll only make more work for me in the end. You stay in here as much as you can.'

'Thanks. But I can't let you do my job for me.'

'Go on! I'm used to it. But I had a pretty awful time when I first started. Just like you - ill all the time. Not good for a matron. And the children wouldn't take any notice of me until they got used to me. So I know exactly what it's like. Stay in here and try not to shout.'

She went out, leaving the medicines on the desk. Thank goodness someone's on my side, Anthony thought.

Whether it was due to matron or the duty prefects, or whether Anthony was just too tired and unwell to notice, the rest of the evening passed without too much trouble. Just before the warning bell at nine forty-five there was a tap at his door. Matron with more pills, probably.

'Can I come in?' It was Helen.

'Yes, of course, please do.'

'Had a good evening?' she asked, sitting down on the edge of the bed.

'Not bad. Matron's sorted them all out and given me some cold cures.'

'Oh, poor Anthony, you're ill again! It's this school!' She said it in a tone that suggested that it was enough to make anyone ill. The bell rang.

'I'd better keep an eye on this,' he said, getting up.

'No, I'll do it. You stay here. And put the kettle on.'

Before he could protest, she'd gone out into the corridor. As he boiled the kettle and prepared two mugs he could hear her clearing everyone out of the games room. Then he heard matron's voice coming from the dormitory, urging the boys to hurry up and finish washing. Once again he envied their control. Would he ever achieve it? Helen returned and poured the coffee.

'I've left the prefects in charge of the washrooms,' she said. 'Always make use of the prefects whenever you can. They're pretty good and it's good training for them. They don't stand any nonsense!'

'How do they do it?' asked Anthony, rather miserably. It all seemed to reflect so badly on him.

'The boys know them. And they know that the prefects get Eric's backing.'

Which is more than I get, Anthony thought, even more miserably.

Helen seemed to realise that her words had upset him. She changed the subject.

'I'm glad matron's looking after you. Do you feel really awful?'

'I'm OK but I hope I get some sleep.'

'I'll go and check they're in bed. Then I'll come back,' she said, finishing her coffee.

This time, when she returned, she closed the door carefully behind her and walked over to him.

'Now,' she said, 'I can spend a few minutes with you at last.'

To his surprise and delight she put her arms around his neck and kissed him.

'I've longed to hold you,' he said.

133

'I know. So have I. But I couldn't. I can't stay long now. So make the best of it,' she smiled.

'I will!'

'We must have another private meeting before Christmas,' she murmured between kisses.

'We must. It's so awful, being without you.' He crushed her against him even harder.

'I promise I'll arrange something. Have you decided what you're doing for Christmas?'

'I thought I'd go to Auntie's for the first week then come back about the twenty-eighth.'

She didn't reply but just clung closer and kissed him again. After a while she said, 'I'll miss you. I must go now. I wish I could say longer, but . . . '

Did she glance longingly at the narrow bed? Or was he deceiving himself? She pressed her lips on his once more, then reached up and rumpled his hair.

'Goodnight. Take care. I do hope it's quiet for you, and that you feel better tomorrow.'

'So do I. If it's quiet I can think of you. I'm so glad you came.'

'And I shall think of you,' she replied. 'I'll check the dorms on my way out. You get to bed.'

She slipped out, leaving a desperate longing behind. As Anthony lay feverish and aching in that dingy little room, expecting any moment to be called from his bed to some crisis or misdeed, he could only think of the warmth and comfort that lying next to Helen would bring. How could he bear it when there seemed no prospect of such a thing, ever?

Chapter Sixteen

Anthony tucked the small parcel, wrapped in Christmas paper, deep into the pocket of his anorak. Then he pulled it out again and tried to flatten the crumpled paper. He wasn't happy with his clumsy effort at wrapping, but then he hadn't had much practice. He'd only ever bought presents for Gran and she hadn't worried about things like fancy wrappings. Now he'd creased this even more. By the time he arrived at the top of the hill, it was going to look worse still.

It had been awkward to wrap. A small square box and a larger book were not easy to enclose neatly in the same parcel. He'd put his Christmas card in there too. It had been so difficult to find the right words for it. In the end he had written,

With thanks for opening my eyes to the beauty of the countryside.
I hope we will be able to share more in 1970.

He had deliberately left it sounding a bit ambiguous. Share what? More walks? Or more of something else…? Helen could interpret it herself. It was almost entirely up to her which direction the relationship took. He certainly wasn't self-confident enough to advance things. Nor was he prepared to risk losing what he had by some inappropriate word or action.

He hadn't been sure how to sign it. You don't put 'yours sincerely' on a Christmas card, he thought. What did he usually write? Well, again, he hadn't sent many. Just Gran, Aunt Florence and one or two friends occasionally. And to a girl once, but she didn't respond. In the end he just wrote 'Anthony'. It didn't convey what he felt, but perhaps the gift would. He put the packet back into his pocket, more carefully this time, and left the school.

It was the day of the school Christmas Dinner. Everyone had the afternoon off and Helen was busy with preparations. But she'd told him that she needed some fresh air and would be up on the hill at two o'clock. He needed no second telling.

When he got to the summit she wasn't in sight so he sat down in the hollow and waited restlessly. Perhaps she wouldn't be able to get away. He was sure they wouldn't have another chance before the end of term, in two days' time. So how was he going to give her his present? It had to be in person.

Then he heard the sound of her footsteps on the flinty track. He wanted to jump up and meet her but he stopped himself. She'd made it quite obvious that she expected complete discretion.

'Sorry I'm late,' she puffed, coming over the crest and down to where he was sitting. He stood up and folded his arms around her. After a few minutes, she said 'I haven't got long. But we might not have any other time. I wanted to wish you "Happy Christmas" in private.'

Anthony fumbled in his pocket.

'I got you this. I hope you like it.' He shyly handed her the parcel, wondering what she'd think if she knew the story of it.

'Oh, how lovely! But you shouldn't spend your hard-earned money on me. Thank you, you're very kind.' She put the packet carefully in her own pocket and kissed him several times.

'There's a card inside, too,' Anthony said. He wasn't sure whether he was disappointed that she hadn't opened it. Of course, people don't open their presents until Christmas. But since they wouldn't be together and she couldn't open it with Pearson watching he had thought she might.

'I have something for you,' she was saying. 'I didn't bring it because it's a bit large for carrying up the hill. I'll . . . er . . . make sure you get it before the end of term.' She was smiling rather too brightly.

She's lying, Anthony thought. She hasn't got anything for me. I've embarrassed her. Now she'll rush out and buy something. She probably didn't think it was appropriate to exchange presents. He felt deflated. Had he made a complete fool of himself over this brooch, with Michael *and* Helen? He was beginning to wish he'd never set eyes on it.

'You look tired,' Helen said.

He forced a smile. 'I could do with a break. Couldn't you?'

'Have a good holiday and a rest,' she answered, kissing him again. 'That's what we both need.'

But not miles apart, he thought. He tightened his arms about her, feeling burning tears in his eyes. He swallowed hard. He couldn't handle this. Helen could - she was mature and sensible and knew how to hide hurt and longing. Anthony didn't.

He wanted to spend Christmas with Helen by a cosy fire. Instead she'd be with Pearson and he'd be with a very fussy old lady. The New Year seemed an eternity away.

'I'll have to go now,' Helen whispered. 'I'll see you tonight at the Dinner. The food's usually excellent.'

Oh Helen! How could she think about food when his heart was breaking? He buried his face in her hair, kissing it over and over again.

She pulled away. 'I must go. Why don't you stay up here a while? Get some fresh air. You're always so pale.' Another kiss and she was gone.

Anthony slumped down in the hollow and lay with his cheek against the rough grass. What a contrast the wind-seared ochre turf was to the bright brown hair in which his face had been buried a few minutes ago. Stay up here, she'd said. She meant, don't come down with me in case we're seen.

How could he cope with this agony? It was impossible.

The Christmas Dinner passed in a haze. Not an alcoholic one! One glass of wine was served to the staff and older boys. The food *was* excellent. Mrs Higginbottom and her team had done them proud. But Anthony hardly noticed it. All he noticed was Helen presiding over the ceremony in a calm and rather distant way. She exchanged no more words with him than she did with anyone else, or so it seemed, with the exception of Peter Ferguson, whom she carefully avoided. She looked glowing in an emerald green dress that he had admired before. Her only jewellery was a narrow gold chain and small gold earrings; no gaudy, glittering brooch. He'd never seen her wearing anything so cheap and nasty - yes, that was it, cheap and nasty - as that wretched dragonfly. It wasn't cheap to him, of course. It represented a great deal of what he had managed to save from his first term's salary - a salary which was severely pruned by the deductions for 'living in', despite the poor accommodation and the extra duties. And he had thought it was perfect for her at the time. He wondered if she had opened it when she got back to school. She'd never tell him what she really thought of it, but he might be able to deduce from her manner if she ever mentioned it.

So his mind raced as he ate silently, oblivious to the jocularity around him. He excused his quietness to his neighbours by telling them that his throat was sore, which was true. And every so often he managed to croak a few sentences to show willing. But his thoughts and his heart lay elsewhere - across the room on the Pearson's table.

When the Dinner was over and the boys had dispersed, those staff not on duty were invited into the Pearson's flat for coffee and liqueurs. For once, Anthony was not on the duty rota and he had a moment of pleasure when he saw that Fergus was - and not too pleased about it either. Well, he can't blame me for that, he thought. Or could he? Peter Ferguson would probably think that Anthony had used his influence with Helen to avoid duty himself and put Fergus on the list. It wouldn't occur to him that Helen might be solely responsible, as revenge for his unwanted attentions. Hell! I can't win, Anthony thought. He detected a definite look of malice in his direction as Fergus left the gathering.

School finished for Christmas at noon on the last day and a succession of parents arrived to collect their sons. The school was suddenly quiet. Most of the staff, too, had gone by late afternoon.

'Have a good Christmas. Don't work too hard!' Michael called through Anthony's open door as he headed down the stairs with his bags.

'Same to you. Cheerio.'

The place felt cold and empty after Michael had gone. Relations between them had been rather strained since the brooch incident but a drink together on the previous day had restored things. Michael obviously thought that stress was the cause of Anthony's strange behaviour and had given him sympathetic advice about not overworking or taking things too seriously.

Now, watching him disappear down the stairs, Anthony felt quite desolate. It was like that first day again, alone up here anxiously awaiting the arrival of his new colleague. Then there'd been the disappointment of realising that

Michael was an Old Boy. In fact, Michael's prior knowledge had proved useful on many occasions. He's a good, straightforward sort, thought Anthony, and he must think I'm a complete lunatic. He couldn't imagine Michael getting into a state about anything.

It was almost dark. Anthony finished his term's marking and tidied the room. He'd packed a few things in a travelling bag, including a gift of writing paper for Aunt Florence. She liked writing letters and didn't have much time for the telephone, which she regarded as a newfangled gadget. He was leaving early in the morning so he'd decided to relax and spend the evening reading. He wanted to try and throw off this cold before Christmas.

He ate the rest of his food, made coffee and curled up on his bed under a blanket, with a thriller. Despite the action-packed story, he found it difficult to concentrate. His sore throat, the low temperature and the empty building all combined to oppress him. He got up to make more coffee and a hot- water bottle. As he was filling his kettle in the icy bathroom he heard a step on the stairs. The silence, the thriller and his rather nervous condition caused a momentary state of terror. Burglar? Murderer? Ghost?

'Anthony?'

Never did the voice of a loved woman sound so sweet! He came out of the tiny bathroom carrying his well-used kettle, smiling broadly.

'You look more cheerful than I've seen you for ages. Amazing what the end of term can do!' she laughed.

Immediately his face clouded over. The end of term meant goodbye for them, even if it was only for a short time. He quickly put on a smile again, as she seemed to like it.

'Do you want coffee?'

'I'd love some. I'll have to be quick, though. I brought you this.' She laid the parcel she was carrying on the table and put her arms around him. 'You're cold!'

'A bit. It's this cold of mine.'

'And this horrid room. Still, you've only got to suffer one more night up here, poor thing. I'm sure you'll be more comfortable at your aunt's.'

'Yes, but . . . '

'But what?'

'But I don't want to leave you.'

'Oh Anthony! I don't want you to leave me. But there's no choice. It won't be for long.' She stroked his cheek. 'You're still very pale. I want you to come back from your holiday better. And you'll be able to tell me all about it - all the funny things about your auntie!'

She's trying to cheer me up, he thought. 'I will,' he said. 'But Aunt Florence is a bit too particular to be funny.' He handed Helen a mug of coffee.

'Well, that's funny in itself.' She drank the coffee quickly. 'I can't stay now. I may not see you before you leave. If not, have a lovely time. I *will* miss you, but I want you to have a nice rest and come back refreshed. Next term will be better. Perhaps we'll have some nice, crisp walking weather instead of all this greyness.' She put down her mug and wound her arms around his neck again. 'Happy Christmas, Anthony.'

'Happy Christmas, Helen.'

He listened until the very last slight sound of her footsteps had died away. With a hollow ache somewhere deep inside, he picked up the parcel. It was small and light. He'd been right, then. She hadn't got him anything before. She'd obviously been so busy that she'd forgotten the excuse she'd given about the parcel being heavy. He was surprised at that. It wasn't like Helen. Perhaps she wasn't so controlled as he thought. Still, she'd bought him something now. And she had seemed sad to part and genuinely concerned about his health. Was he expecting too much of her, when she was doing all she could?

He undressed and got into bed with his hot-water bottle. How much better if . . . No! Don't think of it! He couldn't have everything. He tried to think of other things, gradually became little warmer and eventually fell asleep.

Next morning he got up very early, gulped down a coffee, picked up his bag and walked quietly downstairs. Not that there was anyone to hear. As he passed Helen's door he hesitated. There was no sound. She was in there but she might as well be on another planet. The woman he longed for was in bed beside her husband and there was nothing Anthony could do to change it. His only option was to leave silently. With a deep sigh he opened the heavy front door and stepped out into the cold, dark morning.

His first term at Fieldhouse School was over.

The familiar white signboard came into view around the corner as Anthony walked slowly along the lane, stopping every now and then to change his heavy book-filled bags from one hand to the other. His footsteps crunched on the thin covering of frozen snow. It was one of those beautiful crisp days that Helen had mentioned on the last night of term. For Anthony, it marked the end of a gloomy period, personal and climatic. He could now look forward to another two weeks of freedom and the prospect of some of those delightful winter walks they had talked about.

Even Fieldhouse School had been transformed by the snowfall. With a wry smile he noticed that icicles had formed on top of the school sign and that one particularly large one pointed directly to the name of the Principal. There must be something symbolic about that!

When he reached the steps up to the front door, he placed his bags on the top one, which was clear of snow, and walked round the building to look at the garden. Helen's beloved pond was frozen. Beyond, the Downs flowed in white billows, broken here and there by clumps of dark trees, their branches picked out by a thin layer of snow. The view was magnificent. He could understand why Helen loved it and how it provided her with solace. He must get out there. Too late today: the sun was going down already and it would be very cold.

He wondered if Helen had been up the hill today, but he couldn't see any tracks across the lawn, or indeed anywhere except up to the front door. Probably the postman. Reluctantly, he picked up his bags and tried the heavy door. It was locked. He fumbled for his key, turned it in the lock, and pushed the door open. It was dark and icy cold in the hall. Helen had said that there wouldn't be any central heating on in the holidays. Except in her flat, he supposed. He hadn't thought of it affecting him very much since there was none in his room anyway. Now he realised that heat from the rest of the house must penetrate to his attic eventually and help a little. Now there was no heat and a sharp frost. His room would be bitter.

The house was silent. Even Jones was not to be seen. Anthony went to his pigeonhole but it was empty. No belated Christmas greetings, not even a bill! Not eager to rush up to the 'North Pole' he tried the library door. It swung open. The last of the day's sun was streaming in, making the room seem warm and cheerful. The view from the window across the snow-covered garden was lovely. In the fireplace was the scarlet glow of poinsettia plants put there by Helen for the Christmas celebrations. All the other decorations had disappeared, presumably removed during the cleaning blitz after term ended. If succeeding days were equally sunny he'd be able to sit in here in the afternoons and be relatively warm.

He closed the library door behind him and went upstairs. Again he hesitated as he passed the Pearson's flat - and again there was no sound from within. His room was exactly as he had left it. There had been no spring-clean in here! Wait a minute, what was this? 'This' was a large cardboard box on the floor beside the table. Attached to the top was an envelope. He ripped it away from the box and quickly tore it open.

> *Dear Anthony,*
> *We have gone to Spain as Eric felt he needed some sun.*
> *I'm not sure exactly when we plan to return.*
> *I hope the contents of this box will help you to enjoy the*
> *rest of the holiday.*
> > *Happy New Year,*
> > *Helen*

The letter dropped from his hand and fluttered to the floor, swirling in the cold draught from the open door. Anthony stood stunned. All Christmas he'd been polite to Aunt Florence and her friends sustained by the thought of being back with Helen soon. The train, the bus, the strenuous walk with his bags, had all been made enjoyable by thoughts of her, of each stage bringing him ever nearer. His return to Fieldhouse had only been made bearable by her presence. If it wasn't for her he wouldn't have been coming back at all. And now she wasn't here. She wasn't even in this country. The only certainty was that she'd be back for the beginning of term, but that was nearly two weeks away.

He turned back to the cardboard box. He had better see what she'd put in it. It was closed only by two small pieces of sticky tape across the flaps. Pulling these away he delved inside - and was amazed at her forethought. She certainly didn't intend him to go hungry. How had she managed to put all this together under Pearson's eagle eye, and probably at short notice? He was devastated by her absence but she rose yet again in his estimation. She seemed to have thought of everything. She really must care for him to go to all this trouble. He took out a large cake, chocolate biscuits, a box of chocolates, cheese and crackers, a variety of foodstuffs suitable for cooking on a camp stove, a jar of coffee, a bottle of wine - and a wine glass. At the bottom of the box was another envelope, a larger one. He pulled out a small, unframed watercolour of the Downs behind Fieldhouse - under snow, just like today. There was another note.

This is your New Year present. I wish I could be with you to enjoy the contents of this box and share the wine. As I can't, enjoy the food, and drink a toast to us.

So she wouldn't be back until after New Year. But perhaps her thoughts would be here. He propped up the painting and stood back. It looked good. He must buy a frame for it. He put away the food along with some that Aunt Florence had insisted he bring. The large jar of coffee was especially welcome. That was what he needed to warm him up and comfort himself for the absence of Helen

He took his kettle into the bathroom and turned on the tap. Nothing! Of course, the pipes would be frozen - unless Jones had turned the stopcock off to avoid such a calamity. Either way, the result was the same. He had no water. There was only one thing for it. He went downstairs with his saucepan and opened the front door. Once outside, he looked around for the cleanest-looking patch of snow he could find. Then he took it upstairs, put it on the stove and let it boil for a very long time. He'd been right about the North Pole.

It was New Year's Eve. Anthony had survived the last couple of days with less misery than he had expected. The good and useful Mr Jones had restored his water supply and the weather had in any case returned to its damp greyness. He'd had several walks and got through a lot of work, reading and studying the Highway Code. He was very lonely and longed for Helen, but at least the days were passing. Unfortunately they were also passing to the beginning of term. He *had* to make a better job of teaching this time. He'd re-written all his lessons and felt he'd done all he could in preparation. Now he just had to wait, and try to deliver it to the pupils, if they'd let him. If only Pearson would give him some breathing space, or even some help or advice. Not much chance of that, though. Several times since he'd been back he'd wondered if Pearson had taken Helen off to Spain because he knew that Anthony was coming back to school immediately after Christmas. Perhaps Helen would drop a hint when he next saw her. He hoped it wouldn't be too long.

Anthony had dressed himself smartly in a new shirt from Aunt Florence and the tie and plain gold tie-pin which had been Helen's present. The tie was also plain but of much better quality than any other that he had ever had. She had also bought him a book about the natural history of the area so he spent the evening reading this, and listening to the radio. It was pleasant enough but he felt cut off from the world, totally isolated. As the evening wore on he began to feel depressed. He was very tired but he was determined to stay up and drink that toast with Helen's wine. Just before midnight he opened the bottle and poured a glass. On the hour, the church bells began to ring out. Perhaps that's where I should have gone, he thought. But then he wouldn't have been able to drink to Helen.

'Happy New Year, Helen,' he said, raising his glass. 'Here's to us.'

He drank the wine quickly, then poured another, and another . . . The bells were still ringing. He got up, slightly unsteadily, and went to the window. A bright moon shone overhead. That same moon's looking down on Helen, he though. He wondered if she was looking at it too, and thinking of him. She'd guess he'd be drinking her health. A shaft of moonlight gleamed down on the garden. His eyes followed it to the pool, where he could see the moon itself reflected in the water. How magical it would have been if he and Helen could have take their wine outside and stood beside the pool, listening to the bells and wishing each other a happy New Year. He could almost see them there, raising their glasses and sealing their wishes with a kiss. He filled his glass again.

'Happy 1970, Helen. Let it be a year when we declare our love. Yes, I do love you. And I desperately want to tell you. Please come back to me soon. Can you hear me, wherever you are? Happy New Year, my love.'

Then the moon and the bells, the wine and the loneliness, became too much for him. He turned from the window, threw himself on his bed, and wept.

Chapter Seventeen

'I'm sorry, Mr Dean . . . '

Anthony took the piece of paper marking the painful result of his first attempt at the driving test and walked into the Test Centre, where his instructor was waiting.

'Cheer up. You only failed on a couple of minor things. Nerves, that's all. You'll be fine next time.' Mr Williams was cheerful. Anthony wondered if this was due to the prospect of his continuing custom for a while longer.

Anthony was not cheerful. All that preparation - and expense. All that study of the Highway Code when he should have been doing other things. Even wearing Helen's tie hadn't saved him. Thank goodness no-one knew it was his test today. He *had* been very nervous and he knew where he had gone wrong. I must get it right next time, he told himself.

Gloomily he drove back to the school. It was the end of the second week back and he pondered on the term so far. It wasn't going well. Exams started in February and his classes knew nothing! He had to admit that their behaviour was a little better, at least sometimes. They also were aware of the need for good marks. At the beginning of term, Pearson had been too busy to sit in on Anthony's lessons very often, but now it was becoming a more frequent occurrence. Once again his pupils' improved behaviour on those occasions was offset by the sheer agony of being constantly watched. Games afternoons were as unpleasant as ever. In this case he detected a worsening of the situation. Was it due to that Christmas Dinner incident? Could that have been another of Helen's attempts to help him that had backfired?

Helen. The only light in the darkness. The Pearsons had returned from Spain two days before the term began and Helen had come up to his room as soon as she could, thanking him profusely for the beautiful brooch. She'd been so sorry to have to go away, she said. She'd been thinking of him all the time, especially on New Year's Eve. He'd told her that he had drunk a toast to them, just as she'd asked. He even mentioned his feelings about the moon shining on them both. She seemed to understand perfectly. They'd had one walk since, full of tender, warm moments such as he had never believed possible. Had she drawn closer to him in her absence? Or was she just letting her guard down a little more as time passed.

So engrossed was he in these thoughts that he overshot the school gate.

'Don't want to go back, eh?' laughed Mr Williams. 'Well, it's not a job I'd like. All them young hooligans! And they say the Head's a bit of a tartar.'

Anthony had never heard Williams comment on the school before, although as the local instructor he knew it well.

'It's always hard when you're new,' he said guardedly. 'Whatever school you're at.'

'Yes, but some's worse than others - there's been a lot of young teachers gone in and out of here pretty quick.'

Then, sensing that he'd perhaps said too much, he got out his diary and began booking Anthony's next lesson. Anthony suddenly remembered the taxi driver on his very first day saying: 'I wouldn't stay here long . . . ' If only he'd taken that advice. But he couldn't leave Helen. Not now.

Should he tell her about this test? He had vowed not to mention it to anyone but he felt guilty about not doing so. He was sure she'd be annoyed if she found out. Even now she would complain that he hadn't given her the chance to advise him or wish him luck. Perhaps he had better tell her, but absolutely no-one else. He would book another test for the earliest possible date and hopefully be less nervous next time.

Now he had to concentrate on preparing his classes for the exams. He had two weeks. The presence of the Head would ensure silence and better attention to work in some lessons. At other times the nearness of the exams might make the pupils concentrate a little more. He was busy devising a selection of tests and mock exam papers, which he hoped would keep his classes relatively quiet and fully occupied. With all the additional prep he was doling out, he had far more marking than he could cope with, but he was prepared to go to any lengths to avoid a complete disaster in the exams. His classes had to make up for the time they had wasted last term. Passing his test would have given him a much-needed boost and relieved him of one worry for the immediate future.

Pearson certainly took exams very seriously. Anthony wondered what on earth he would be like in the summer when the public examinations took place. At the beginning of every lesson of Anthony's which the Principal sat in on, and presumably in his own lessons too, he stood up and exhorted the boys to study, study, study. At the end of each assembly he urged pupils (and staff too) to apply themselves constantly to preparation and revision. Fieldhouse School, he told them, had always had a fine reputation for academic excellence. They must all uphold it. And so on, every day.

'Eric is a little fanatic about exams!' Helen said.

'Old P.'s terrified that this school's going down the drain,' said Art-and-Craft.

'It's so that he can blame us if the results are bad,' Michael explained. 'He was the same when I was here, only not quite so bad.'

'Probably you weren't listening,' Mary suggested.

'No, he's getting worse, as the school gets worse.'

'Why doesn't the old fool just sell up and retire? I'd have to paint full-time then,' Art-and-Craft said hopefully.

'Should have quit while he was ahead, as they say.' Michael put down his coffee mug on the stained Common Room table. 'Well, come on, back to it. "It is the duty of the staff, etc." I've told you, we'll get the blame. Our job is to turn the brainless into geniuses - however impossible that may be.'

Art-and-Craft rose laconically from the sunken armchair where he had been engaged, as usual, in removing particles of paint and clay from his clothing.

'Yes, back to the grind. If any of you can't stand it a minute longer, come up to the art room and do some wedging.'

'What?'

'Wedging. With clay. You throw it around and bash it. Gets the air out. Excellent therapy. You can pretend it's Old P.'

They all laughed.

'Shh!' Mary said. 'He's bound to be listening.'

'Well, he can come and wedge if he likes. He can pretend it's you lot!'

They shambled out of the Common Room, the cheerful banter only partly disguising the stress and overwork they were all experiencing. They would all be glad when the exams actually started.

'I can't bear it any more!' said Michael, later that evening putting his head round Anthony's door.

'Going to do some - what is it, wedging?'

'No, going down to the village for a drink. Coming?'

The fresh air, the company and the beer did Anthony a lot of good. But then he had to sit up for an extra hour or so to make up for lost time. Going to bed at two a.m. is not conducive to a good day's teaching.

Helen was keeping a discreet distance. She told Anthony that she did not want to feel in any way responsible for distracting him at this difficult time. She was supporting them all behind the scenes, though. Most evenings she paid a brief visit to some of the staff, especially the new ones, distributing hot drinks, homemade cakes and chocolate. She lingered just a little longer with Anthony, gave him extra supplies and wound her arms around his neck. He begged her to stay longer, but she wouldn't.

'I want you to succeed,' she kept telling him.

So her short visits left Anthony burning with desire, and with determination not to let her down. To hell with Old P.! He was doing this for Helen.

Anthony sat at the front of a silent classroom, looking at the bent heads of a group of boys writing furiously, faces screwed up in concentration. If only this scene marked a magical change in Anthony's class control and teaching abilities. But it was simply that no pupil in the school dared misbehave during an exam, no matter *who* was invigilating. Once exams were over it would be 'business as usual'.

For this quietness alone Anthony would have quite enjoyed exam time. He thought he had done everything he could to prepare his pupils and now he could only wait. Most of the English marking would be done by Pearson - but he'd worry about that later. There were other compensations to exam weeks. The normal timetable was suspended and there were no Games. Between invigilations (of which he had more than most) he was free.

He looked at his watch. 'Stop writing please.'

Anthony recognised only too well from his own recent schooldays the look of despair on some faces as the boys put down their pens. He gathered in the papers and dismissed the pupils, who hurried out to discuss their blunders in the grounds or games room. Anthony was ready to escape, too.

Dashing upstairs, he changed into his new boots, put on an anorak and set out for the Downs. Despite the cold, the garden was full of shouting boys letting off steam, so Anthony slipped out of school through a back door and into the lane outside the front gates. His boots made rather too loud a noise on the tarmac and he was glad to reach the track up the hill. As he turned into it he caught a glimpse of Helen ahead of him, near the top. Thank goodness, she'd managed to get away! Then the hedges on either side of him hid her from view until he, too, reached the top.

There was never any hesitation about their embraces now, at least up here. He held her tightly; longing to tell her that he loved her. But he resisted. He was saving it for a special occasion in the near future - Valentine's Day. For once he was determined that this was going to be a happy day for him. Normally it was just the opposite. He still had a little time to choose a card and decide exactly what to say.

'How are the exams going?' she broke in to his reverie.

'The invigilation's marvellous. I wish all my lessons were like that. I'm worried about the results though. I'm not doing the marking so I shan't know … I've really tried.'

'Yes, you have. I'm keeping my fingers crossed for you. And for your next Test.'

Helen had been sympathetic about his failure and a little annoyed that he hadn't told her about it beforehand. But she understood the reason.

'You'll need to. I'd rather be up here than having to worry about all those things. It's wonderful!'

'It is, even on a grey, cold day like today.'

They were walking hand in hand towards the knoll, keeping just below the crest, out of sight of Fieldhouse. Anthony thought Helen looked radiant with her hair blowing in the strong wind, which had brought colour to her cheeks. She was light-hearted and laughing, making Anthony feel light-hearted too. *And* he didn't have to go back and teach Simon Biggins! That was a real bonus. He didn't even have a cold. Were things looking up at last?

'Let's run!' she said suddenly, pulling his arm.

They ran, awkwardly on the slope in their heavy boots, but joyfully. When they reached the group of trees they clasped each other in the shadows, with the wind murmuring its own words of love in the treetops above. Anthony nearly said it then. He was so happy and the moment was so beautiful. But no, he must save it. It's very special to tell someone that you love them. He was desperate to get it right.

'This is magic!' Helen said, echoing his thoughts. 'I can't believe it, after all the pain I've known.'

He waited for a moment but she said no more.

'Do you want to tell me?' he asked. Part of him wanted to hear about her previous life and part knew that he would be jealous, stupidly jealous, whatever she told him.

'As we're not in our usual rush, I *will* tell you some of it. I don't want to bore you with it, though.'

'You won't.' You might hurt me though, he thought.

She pressed her face against his shoulder.

'I married at twenty. It wasn't a great success. Edward was very career-minded. No time for things of the heart like painting and literature. Didn't want a family. Eventually I had an affair with an old friend, Jim. He was unhappily married, too.'

Anthony was glad that she couldn't see his face. He could hardly bear to think of her with other men, even if they *were* husbands. Now here was a third relationship he had known nothing about. He hoped she didn't realise how jealous he was.

'Go on,' he mumbled into her hair.

'I can feel the agony of it even now. Those brief, bittersweet meetings, those agonising partings, and the weeks of separation. It was awful.' He felt her shudder and hugged her harder against him. 'You see,' she went on, 'I *do* know what it's like for you. I was always thinking of him at home with his wife, and he was always thinking of me with my husband. That's how you feel, isn't it?'

There was no point in being anything but completely honest.

'Yes, that's exactly how I feel. Stupid, but I can't help it.'

'I know. I do know.' She looked up for the first time since she started speaking. 'Can you bear it?'

'I am bearing it - I think.'

'Do you want to go on bearing it?'

'I want to go on seeing you. So I'll have to.'

She kissed him and buried her face against his anorak again.

'That relationship with Jim ended because he wouldn't leave his children. But still I divorced. Strange as it may seem, Jim's absence caused the break-up of my marriage just as surely as his presence would eventually have done. I couldn't cope when we parted. I had to explain why I was in such a state. So - end of marriage.'

'Then you married Mr Pearson?'

'Yes, on the rebound. He flattered me. Here's a lesson in life, Anthony.' She looked up again. 'Never do anything on the rebound.' Then she shook her head with an ironic laugh. 'What am I saying? Isn't that exactly what we *are* doing?'

'I haven't got anything to rebound from,' he replied, puzzled and a little hurt.

147

'Yes, you have. Your family life, your grandmother's death, teaching here, Biggins!' Now she was really laughing.

'I don't just want you as an antidote to Biggins,' he said quietly.

'I hope not,' she said softly. 'I'm only having you on. I don't want you only as a contrast to … ' She did not finish but began kissing him tenderly. 'I want you because you make me happy. Happier than I've ever been. I just want to be up here with you. It's heaven!' She paused. 'What else do you want me to tell you?'

'Whatever you want to. And not what you don't.'

'OK. After my divorce I went to work as a secretary in one of the schools where Eric attended meetings. Fieldhouse was at its peak then. Eric's name was well known in educational circles. So I was really flattered when he started paying attention to me. He was still married to Vera then. But the marriage was in trouble. She hated it here. In the end she left and I arrived. That was ten years ago.'

'And did *you* like it?'

'I began to realise pretty quickly that Eric thought of me as a sort of prize for his success. He was always saying that he'd rescued a struggling divorcee. But I wasn't struggling by the time I met him. I'd got through all that. I had begun to value my independence. Then I threw it away. I came here and was tied to the school.'

'You feel trapped, don't you?'

'Yes, usually. I became the brilliant Eric Pearson's wife. "Helen" disappeared. What was left of her wandered about up here whenever she could - walking, thinking, painting - until she met you. Then, suddenly, I was myself again.' She raised her head, her eyes sparkling, her face animated. 'When I'm with you, I'm just me. That's what's so wonderful about it. Come on, we'd better start back.'

Arms tightly round each other, they wandered slowly back through the trees and along the ridge to the hollow where they usually met.

'A few more minutes?' asked Anthony, not wanting to let her go. Her story may have made him irrationally jealous but it had also made him feel closer to her than ever. He was flattered that she had told him all this.

'Yes, why not.' They sat down, cuddled against the cold wind. 'I have a very good friend in London, Marjorie West,' Helen went on. 'When we meet we usually talk about the good old days when we were your . . . when we were younger. Marjorie has a wonderful expression to describe the difference between now and then. She calls them "The days when I used to be a real person." I know exactly what she means. Now I *am* a real person again, thanks to you.'

The exam results of Anthony's classes were not a total disaster. However, they were certainly not good and the Principal made his opinion quite clear.

'These marks will have to improve by the summer, Mr Dean. Our parents will not accept poor 'O' and 'A' Level results. However,' he continued, very grudgingly Anthony felt, 'contrary to expectations, they are not a complete failure.'

This was the first 'encouragement' that he had ever received from Pearson. 'I made every effort.'

'Yes, quite,' the Head interrupted. 'The new staff are presumably aware that the same conditions apply at this coming half term regarding any changes they may wish to make?'

In other words, 'please leave,' thought Anthony. Well, damn him, I won't!

Valentine's Day coincided with half term. The school only had two days off in the Spring Term so Anthony decided to stay at Fieldhouse. He needed to save money. His next driving test was only two weeks away so he had arranged a couple of lessons. Mary had taken him out in the Mini and promised him more drives once the exams were over. A free afternoon during the exam period had given them the opportunity to drive into town - good practice for Anthony and the chance to buy a Valentine. He was pleased to find one with poppies on it and he'd also been extravagant and bought a pair of earrings. They were not as costly as the brooch. He could not spend that amount again, unfortunately. How wonderful it would be to be able to afford lovely things for Helen.

Anthony was breakfasting on coffee and cake. His card and gift were ready on the table for later in the day when he hoped to see Helen, if only briefly. A light tap at the door caused him to drop cake crumbs all over himself and the floor.

'Sorry I'm so early, but we're going out. I *did* want to give you this in person.' Helen stood outside his door, holding out a card and a small packet.

'Come in, come in.'

Delighted though he always was to see her, he did wish that he had had time to tidy his room, and himself, and prepare his speech. His littered room with its unmade bed and breakfast things and his own ruffled appearance, were hardly likely to provide the romantic ambience which he had envisaged for this moment. Awkwardly, he brushed the crumbs from his jumper and began to move papers from the chair.

'It's OK, I'll sit here,' Helen said, moving towards the rumpled bed.

Even more awkwardly, Anthony sat down beside her. It was funny how things felt so much more natural up on the Downs. His hands shook as he handed her the card.

'Aren't you going to open yours?' she said, laughing.

'Oh, yes. But open yours first.'

He watched her slim fingers draw out the white card and turn it over to reveal the poppies. She looked up and smiled. 'They're beautiful.'

'So are you.'

She leaned forward and kissed him.

'Open it,' he said.

She opened it and gazed for a moment at the words inside. They were very simple.

Helen, I love you.

She turned to look at him again, her face flushed, a smile on her lips.
'Anthony.'
'Helen, I love you.'
The card slid to the floor as they clasped each other in a long embrace.
After she had gone, he spent a long time just holding her card and the book of poetry bound in red leather that had accompanied it. Helen had written:

Valentines are supposed to be anonymous but my love for you is no secret.

Please be my Valentine.

All my love, Helen.

She had painted the card herself - a watercolour of the knoll, signed with her initials like the other pictures of hers he'd seen. He placed it carefully on the shelf, making a mental note to remove it before school started again. Now she was gone and he had the rest of the lonely weekend to get through. But he had, at last, declared his love.

'Hey, you had a Valentine! Let's have a look!'
Before Anthony could stop him, Michael, who had just burst in, ruddy and windswept, from his weekend away, grabbed the card from the cupboard.
Fool, fool! Why hadn't he remembered to hide it like he promised himself? Anthony stood rigid as Michael opened the card with jocular comment.
'This will be that bird that the brooch was for. Sly one, you are! Wonder who . . . ' He stopped. His cheerful expression clouded. With exaggerated carefulness he replaced the card on top of the cupboard, studying the painting on the front as he did so. 'My God!' he said, turning to Anthony. 'Is this who I think it is?'
'Yes.'
'My God! Pearson will have you hung in chains at the crossroads!' A slight smile returned as Michael thought of it. 'How did you manage that?'
'I didn't "manage" it. It just happened. We've got a lot in common.'
'I thought Mrs P. had had enough of teachers, especially English teachers. Amazing! Well - come on - tell me about it. How far have you got?'
Anthony gave him a look of disgust. The idea of his treasured relationship with Helen just being a matter of 'getting somewhere' appalled him. Michael read the expression.
'Sorry. Shouldn't have asked. Shouldn't have looked at the card in the first place. Sorry.'

150

'It's OK. I'd probably have done the same. And, if you must know, I haven't got *that* far yet. It's a very delicate situation.'

'I'll say it is. Jesus!'

Anthony wondered what Michael's father would think of all this blasphemy. Now it was his turn for a secret smile. His thoughts quickly returned to serious matters.

'You won't . . . you will keep it a secret, won't you?'

'What the hell do you think I am?'

'Sorry, but things do slip out. It's for Helen's sake.'

'If it gets round the school, it won't be due to me. But, good God, Anthony, if Old P. finds out you'll be sacked in seconds. And he'll make sure you never work in a school again - anywhere. Pearson still has influence.'

'We're very discreet.'

'You'll need to be! I promise I won't say a word. But for goodness' sake be careful. Aren't you in enough trouble already?' Michael obviously knew everything.

'More than enough!'

'Well, watch out. Especially for Fergus. He regards Mrs P. as his property - and since you've got further than he ever has . . . well, he'll have you for dinner, like I said. Lock that card away.'

'I will. Thanks.'

Michael picked up his hold-all and walked towards the door. As he put his hand on the handle he turned to look at Anthony and shook his head.

'My God! Who'd have thought it? Look at you. Talk about a dark horse!'

Anthony had to tell Helen about the card. He wanted to warn her. As usual, she blamed herself.

'I shouldn't have signed it. Valentines are supposed to be secret. I should have just bought an ordinary one from the shop instead of doing that painting and signing that too. I'm usually careful - but I made a slip this time.'

'No, it was me. I was a fool. I should have hidden it away. Now it's going to cause trouble.'

'Michael won't give us away. Don't worry.'

But Anthony did worry. Were his problems simply a matter of youth? Or was he a born fool who would be stupid like this forever?

Anthony drove despondently through the gates of the Driving Test Centre. What a disaster! Almost everything that could have gone wrong had.

The afternoon had started badly. Mr Williams was very late for that vital before-test lesson, due to an accident, which blocked the road. So the lesson was curtailed and Anthony was already flustered when he arrived at the Test Centre. Then there was that stupid woman who pushed her baby's pram out into the road before even thinking of looking! Anthony had to do a real emergency stop - successfully, thank goodness. But he felt he should have anticipated her action and stopped more

151

slowly. Now doubly flustered, he had hesitated for ages at a roundabout that today was extremely busy, although on his first test it had been empty.

After that there was the dog! That had not appeared on his first test either. The road, on a quiet estate, was chosen by examiners as suitable for manoeuvres such as reversing and three-point turns. On the first occasion the road had been deserted and the faults were entirely Anthony's. Things had seemed to be going better today.

'Pull over to the left and stop,' said the examiner, 'and when it is safe, turn the car round in the road.'

As Anthony began his turn, taking care to visibly check his mirror for approaching vehicles, something came hurtling down the previously-empty road. It was black and brown, shaped rather like a beagle and was coming in for the kill. Anthony tried to ignore it. But the loud, determined barking and jumping up at the car window were, to say the least, unnerving.

'Now drive on a little and stop beyond the next junction,' said the examiner, who seemed to be having equal difficulty in concentrating.

This was a great game! Anthony signalled and pulled out. The dog waited, tongue lolling, taking a break from its exertions. The car moved off down the road. So did the dog. Anthony accelerated. So did the dog. Barking and snarling with renewed vigour it chased along beside them, now on the right, now the left, now behind. It was obviously skilled at avoiding the wheels. As instructed, Anthony stopped beyond the turning. The dog showed its displeasure at this by keeping up a crescendo of barking. The examiner had to shout to make himself heard.

'Please reverse around this corner.'

By this time the noise had brought out a small knot of spectators. One of them, a woman in hair curlers and carpet slippers, ran forward shaking a box of dog biscuits.

'Worthington, Worthington, come here! Bad dog!'

The dog ignored her. Anthony tried to ignore the dog. He reversed shakily, expecting any moment to feel the bump of tyre on kerb, or tyre on dog. With great relief, he managed to complete the manoeuvre without feeling either. By this time the woman had made a grab for the dog's collar and was dragging him away. The onlookers burst into spontaneous applause, although whether for the woman, the dog, or himself Anthony never knew. Both he and, he suspected, the examiner, were simply glad to drive away.

The rest of the test had seemed OK. Well, anything would, after that! But as Anthony drew to a halt in front of the Centre he was feeling pretty low.

'Congratulations, Mr Dean. You've passed!'

'I passed!' he yelled to Michael as he dashed up to his room.
'Passed what?'
'My driving test. I just took it.'
'Brilliant! Well done. I'll buy you a drink later. I expect you could do with one now, though. Come on in. I've got a drop of whisky.'

Anthony did not much like whisky but it was very welcome at that moment. He told Michael the story of the dog, suitably embellished.

'I'll have to write to my aunt about the car now,' he said. 'I'll probably go up for it at Easter. Then we can all go out driving. I'll drop her a line tonight.'

Chapter Eighteen

Anthony ripped open the long brown envelope with curiosity. He did not receive many letters. This one was typewritten on thick white paper, headed by a company name and address which was vaguely familiar. But he couldn't quite place it.

Dear Mr Dean,
    As the executor of the late Mrs Florence Williamson, I am writing to request that you arrange for the removal, as soon as possible, of those personal effects that are stored on her premises.
    It is my sad duty to arrange clearance of the property and place it immediately in the hands of an estate agent.
    I do not believe we have met, but I am the great-nephew of the late Mr Joseph Williamson.
    Please telephone me on receipt of this letter to arrange a mutually convenient time for you or your agent to collect your possessions. This is necessary to enable access to the premises.
    I must stress that this is a matter of some urgency.

Yours sincerely
Cedric Simpson.

PS. Mrs Williamson is buried with her husband in the local cemetery.

Aunt Florence dead! Presumably several days ago, at least. The letter, which sat upstairs on his table, was too late. If only someone had let him know that she was ill, or about the funeral. The fact that he was the great-nephew of the late *Mrs* Williamson had not been considered. He was glad that something had made him label and address all his belongings at Christmas - perhaps a subconscious concern for just such an eventuality.

Cedric, of course, was 'poor Joseph's dear great-nephew - such an enterprising young man; started his own business. My dear Joseph gave him a *tiny* loan to help him start - but he soon paid it all back. Now he's doing really well. He didn't feel it necessary to spend three years as an idle, useless, unwashed student.'

This was the person with whom Anthony had been so unfavourably contrasted in the days before he became a schoolmaster at prestigious Fieldhouse School! As Cedric had said, they had never met. But Anthony was not sure that he quite liked the tone of his distant relative's letter. It reminded him of someone - someone he was going to have to speak to in the very near future.

How was he going to get to Stafford in the next few days? He would have to ask for time off. Otherwise he expected his pitiful belongings to be taken to a rubbish tip or a jumble sale. Most of them would not be much loss. They consisted mainly of school and university course work and textbooks and a variety of unfashionable clothes. But there was a small record collection, various books and souvenirs and some of Gran's possessions. There was his bike. And of course the car.

He braced himself to go and ask Pearson for - what was it called? - compassionate leave, although he suspected that the Principal would not regard retrieving a few boxes of junk as good grounds for absence. He'd have to try, though. No point in ringing Cedric until he'd arranged to get away.

'Yes, what is it, Mr Dean?'

Pearson laid down his pen and sat back in his chair with an irritated expression as Anthony entered his study carrying the letter. He hoped that the Head would be sufficiently impressed by the prominent letter-heading to give permission for absence.

'I've just received this letter. My great-aunt has died. She was my only relative. The executors want me to go and collect . . . to help sort out her affairs as soon as possible.'

'I see.'

'I would like permission to be absent from school this weekend. It's rather urgent.'

Pearson said nothing for a moment. Then he replied, even more irritably, 'Oh, very well, Mr Dean, if you must. We don't, of course, encourage staff to neglect their duties to the school . . . '

Before he could stop himself, Anthony burst out rather sharply, 'It won't happen again. I don't *have* any other relatives.'

If he had expected a glimmer of sympathy or even an angry response, he was disappointed. Pearson merely said, rather wearily, 'You *have* my permission, Mr Dean. Be so kind as to inform Mr Fulford so that someone else can take responsibility for your duties. Good morning.' He picked up his pen and recommenced writing.

Anthony turned on his heels and strode out, banging the door rather harder than he had intended. How he loathed Eric Pearson!

'You must be Anthony Dean.'

The man waiting in the lobby of the small bed-and-breakfast establishment looked up as Anthony came downstairs. He held out his hand, which was embellished by a large gold ring.

'Cedric Simpson?'

Anthony shook the plump, rather moist hand with some displeasure. Its owner had pale blue eyes in a cheerful, florid face and was several inches shorter than Anthony. He wore a dark overcoat and his shoes had a high polish. A bright red tie clashed rather violently with his ginger hair, cut short and already thinning. He must be about thirty.

'How was your journey - and this place?' Cedric did not wait for a reply, but turned and led the way out of the dingy hall to the gleaming car parked incongruously outside. He removed his overcoat and placed it, carefully folded, on the back seat. 'Do get in.'

As they sat in the car, a sidelong glance at his host told Anthony that prosperity and good living were taking their toll on Cedric's figure. His suit, which even to Anthony's inexperienced eyes seemed of excellent quality, was more than a little tight. Another large ring and a gold watch graced his left hand.

Anthony felt distinctly shabby. He had not thought his only suit an appropriate outfit for struggling on the train with the contents of all those boxes. His 'best' sports jacket, bought for him so proudly by Gran when he went to university, was now becoming almost as worn as his everyday one. At least he had on Helen's very tasteful tie and the gold pin.

Aunt Florence had died suddenly of a heart attack. This much Cedric had told him on the phone. Now he expanded the story.

'She was taken ill at her whist drive. They called an ambulance but she died in hospital. Never recovered consciousness. Always the best way.'

'I'm really sorry. She was my last close relative.'

Cedric looked surprised. 'Really? Oh yes, of course, you were that orphan that Flo's sister took in.'

Anthony winced, both at the 'Flo' and the 'orphan'.

'When my grandmother died, last summer, Aunt Florence kindly offered me a spare room to store things, and stay when I wanted, until I'd found a place of my own.'

'You haven't got a place yet?' Cedric looked him over in a manner that said plainly 'Not a chance!'

'New staff have to live in for a year. I'm looking for somewhere for next September,' Anthony replied, slightly untruthfully.

'You're a teacher at some school, aren't you? Like it?'

'Yes, it's fine.' Anthony wasn't going to divulge the miseries of his life to the likes of Cedric.

'Couldn't stand that, myself. Not if the boys are anything like I was. Doesn't pay, either, I suppose?' Another quick glance, taking in Anthony's appearance.

'Not in the first year or two,' Anthony admitted, again economical with the truth.

With some relief, not wishing to continue this dissection of his career, Anthony recognised the turning into his aunt's road.

'Here we are,' said Cedric, pulling up outside the house.

The windows stared at them blankly, devoid of their usual spotless nets and heavy curtains. A glimpse through the front bay as they approached the door confirmed Anthony's suspicions. The house was already empty.

'We left your stuff just where it was, when the rest went,' Cedric explained. 'Didn't know what was in it - thought it might bite! Good job you labelled it. We'd never have known whose it was. How are you going to get it all back?'

'Carry as much as I can. Send the rest. I've bought all these strong bags.'

Thanks to Helen's foresight. She'd also given him a ball of thick string, tape, labels and scissors, not to mention food and a book for the journey and the lonely night in the guest- house. She thought of everything.

'I'll wait in the car,' Cedric told him when he had unlocked the doors. 'I've got some work with me to do. Take your time, no hurry. There's nothing you can steal so I'll leave you to it!'

The joke fell flat. Anthony trudged sadly up the uncarpeted stairs. There was indeed nothing he could steal - nothing left to show for seventy-odd years of a woman's life. Not even one small item to remind him of his great-aunt and her somewhat reluctant but nonetheless welcome hospitality. Thank goodness he still had some things of Gran's. Had Aunt left a will, he wondered? If so, who were the beneficiaries? No doubt the solicitors were dealing with it.

Upstairs, his boxes stood in isolation on the bare floorboards of the room where he had so recently spent restless nights thinking of Helen. Despite Cedric's jocular comments they were not exactly as he had left them. They had been moved into the centre of the room and showed signs that someone had been very curious as to their contents. Was that why Cedric had made such a laboured point? Fortunately Anthony's treasures were buried at the bottom, under piles of English essays - enough to deter even the nosiest, whether removal men or Cedric. Cedric and English Literature did not somehow go together.

Anthony packed as much as he could into two large hold-alls, two smaller bags and a rucksack. The rest would have to be sent by rail. He wanted to carry as much as he could to ensure that it got there and to save money. This trip had already cost him far more than he could afford. He lugged it all down to the hall, then went through to the kitchen. Possibly because they were usually bustling, warm places associated with food and comfort, Anthony found empty, deserted kitchens particularly poignant. He remembered taking a last look around Gran's . . .

He opened all the cupboards. They were completely empty, except for the one beside the back door. A scrap of paper had been left inside - Aunt's last shopping list, written in her careful, precise hand. With a lump in his throat he read: Bread, butter, soap powder, indigestion tablets . . . She had no need of those things now. He put the paper quickly into his pocket, almost feeling like a criminal. He *would* have *something* to remember her by.

A door from the kitchen led to the garage. Like the rest of the house, it was empty. His car was gone! He'd known, of course. He hadn't dared think or ask about it. He had just kept hoping that aunt had put it in her will or told someone before she died that it was to be his. That was before Cedric said it was very sudden. Not like a long illness when one could perhaps organise things. The blank windows had told him the rest of the story. Yes, he'd known.

His bicycle was there, with its large, prominent label. He had wondered whether to put a label on the car, too, but he'd thought Aunt might be annoyed. If only . . . Nothing left to do now but to get this lot back to Fieldhouse somehow. He carried his bike through the silent house and out of the front door. Seeing him, Cedric got out of the car and came down the path.

'Finished?'

'Yes, but I don't know how I'm going to get this bike to the station.'

'I'd thought of that. I've brought some rope. It should tie into the boot OK.'

Cedric began this task whist Anthony fetched the rest of his belongings and closed the door on the last of his temporary homes. All he had now was his drab cold attic at Fieldhouse - and Helen.

'There was an old car in the garage at one time . . . ' he began as Cedric started off for the station.

'Yes. Hadn't been used for several years. In good condition, though. A collector bought it. Fetched a high price. Old Florrie should have sold it ages ago and used the money while she was alive instead of leaving it lying there. Still, mustn't grumble.' Cedric glanced at his watch in a way that suggested that it was part of the proceeds.

Anthony felt a strong urge to snatch it from that podgy wrist and throw it out of the window. The thought of the crash that would inevitably result deterred him. Logic told him it probably wasn't Cedric's fault about the car. He obviously didn't know. And, despite his rather chilly letter, he'd been very helpful, even struggling manfully and jokingly to fit the bicycle in the boot and tie down the lid. Still, Anthony hated him.

'The house will go up for sale now?'

'It already has. I may have a buyer. Nice house, well-kept, good area. Should get a good price. I'll be able to build an extension to my own house. Come in very useful.'

Yes, it would, thought Anthony bitterly. Very useful! So would the car. Damn you. I hope your business is a disastrous failure! But of course, it wouldn't be. People like Cedric rarely failed. If they did, they very soon bounced back. Not like poor, shy and awkward schoolmasters.

At the station he dispatched his bike and boxes and somehow, he never quite knew how, he managed to carry the rest back to Fieldhouse. Both his belongings and himself arrived more or less intact. He dragged them up to his room and stood among them with aching arms, shivering in the familiar cold. It was the end of another phase in his life.

'You're going to stick it out until July, then?' Art-and-Craft asked as he and Anthony strolled around the grounds, ostensibly 'on duty', one lunchtime a few days later.

It was a warm day for early March and the gardens were looking very attractive. Daffodils and the last crocuses filled the beds near the house and were naturalised in corners of the lawns. Anthony wondered how many of them Helen had planted. In large containers beside the doors, hyacinths were just beginning to open. Even Fieldhouse looked good at this time of year.

'Yes - not much choice. What about you?'

'Oh, give it another year. That's what I always say. When I've saved enough . . . '

'How much do you reckon you'll need?'

'Enough to live on for a year.'

'A year's salary! That'll take me twenty years to save!'

'No, you don't need that much. You don't spend every ha'penny, do you? Anyway, you have to make do. You just need enough to keep you going - a safety net in case you can't earn anything.'

They arrived at the edge of the pond and stood gazing at their reflections in the water.

'Look at us!' Art-and-Craft went on. 'You - still full of youth and hope. Me - a bit older, dissipated already. What chance is there for us?'

Anthony didn't know. Was there any? His only hope at the moment was Helen and she was unattainable. A snatched cuddle occasionally and that was it. He watched as the breeze rippled their reflections, fragmenting them. Was that significant?

'There, what did I tell you,' said Art-and-Craft, reading his thoughts. 'Reduced to barely recognisable bits, like a Picasso. The public may sneer but we artists know what life's really all about.'

'What is it about?'

'Disappointment and misery, mostly. Don't your writers and poets tell you that?'

'Yes, they do. But I'd hoped they were wrong.'

'No, lad, they're not wrong. Sorry, but you had to find out some time.' Art-and-Craft was grinning but they both knew he was deadly serious.

'Isn't there anything else? There must be!'

'Oh, yes, it's also about things like stopping those two boys from knocking each other senseless. Hey there, you two . . .' he strode off, hair flying, towards the scuffling pair.

Anthony did not follow. He turned and looked back into the water again. Helen, I love you, he said over and over again. Helen, I want to make love to you, I want you to be mine, to leave this place and come away with me. Before we disintegrate, like the reflections, as soon as a cool breeze blows. We must take our chance.

His meditations were interrupted by the bell, which rang out gratingly

159

across the flowerbeds. There is no romance in a school bell. He dragged his reluctant feet across the lawn and prepared for yet another uncomfortable afternoon.

Anthony had his chance later that day - and ruined it. At least that was how he felt as he slowly descended the stairs for dinner.

He had had a bad afternoon in the classroom. Perhaps the sun and warmth had unsettled the boys. At any rate they were in no mood for learning. He had a sore throat again and by the end of the school day he was exhausted and almost voiceless. He wondered if the noise from the English room had reached Helen's ears, for she was standing on the first landing as he lugged his pile of marking wearily up the stairs.

'Are you OK?' she asked in a soft voice.

'Yes. No. Sore throat. A bit croaky,' he answered, grabbing wildly at the exercise books, which were sliding out of his arms on to the floor.

'I'll get them.' Helen bent and picked up the books. 'Let me take these up.' She relieved him of half the pile and preceded him up the stairs. 'Now sit down. I'll make you some coffee.'

He tried to protest but his voice failed completely so he gave in, sat on the bed and allowed her to take charge. He was pleased to see that she was also making a drink for herself.

'Here.' She handed him a mug. 'You'll feel better after this. It's the spring weather, you know.'

'What is? My throat?' he rasped.

'No, the boys. Being so noisy. It's a reaction to the end of winter.'

So she *had* heard - and come to provide him with comfort. Trouble is, they've been like that all year, he thought.

'Come and sit by me,' he managed to say, stretching out a hand.

They sat close together, drinking their coffee, talking (as far as Anthony could), laughing (also painful), kissing. Here, there seemed no difference between them. They were like any other young couple, just being happy together.

Gradually, after the coffee was finished, they slid down until they were lying on the narrow bed. Anthony was in an agony of longing and desperate to get it right. Would she let him go further? She seemed so relaxed, warm, comfortable - he moved his hands gently over her . . .

'No!'

He bit his lip as she pulled away, sat up and smoothed her clothes.

'I'm sorry.'

'It's all right,' she said gently. 'It's just . . . well, I haven't got much time and . . . and . . . I haven't really decided what I should do.' She stood up.

Upset, Anthony got up too and stood beside her, but he didn't touch her. She put her arms around him.

'Don't look like that. It's not you. I have to decide the best thing to do. It's complicated.'

160

'I know. I'm sorry,' he said again, stroking her hair. 'I don't want to cause you any difficulties.'

'I must go.' She unwound his arms from around her and kissed him. 'It's not that I don't want you. I do, very much. But it's got to be right.'

She had gone, and Anthony had been left embarrassed and wretched. He had prepared for dinner with a very heavy heart and little appetite. Would he ever dare try again? He was terrified of doing anything that would drive her away.

He was very quiet during dinner, once again attributing his silence to a sore throat. He ate little.

'You won't be joining us at the pub then, later?' Michael asked. 'Beer will do your throat good.'

'No, thanks, can't face it.'

He went back to his room to nurse his cold and his bruised ego - not that, after two terms at Fieldhouse, he had much of an ego left to bruise. At about eight-thirty, Michael rapped on the door.

'Sure you won't come?'

'No, honestly. Early night. Don't make a noise when you come in!'

'Not a sound! Hope you feel better tomorrow.'

Anthony heard voices downstairs as the group gathered in the hall. Then the sounds faded and the front door banged behind them. About five minutes later there was another tap on his door. A boy needing help and most of the staff out at the pub? Reluctantly he put down his pen, pushed aside his rickety chair and stumbled, bleary-eyed, over a pile of books to the door.

'Are you busy?'

Helen stood there, looking a little ill at ease.

'Come in.' Anthony felt a chill of fear. What was she going to tell him? That it was all over?

She didn't say anything at first. She just stood and looked at him. At last she said, like she had on the stairs, 'Are you OK?'

'I'm surviving.'

'I'm sorry about this afternoon.'

'Oh, no. It's me who should be sorry.'

She stepped towards him and slid her arms around his neck. Looking up, she said very softly, 'I've made up my mind - if you still want me.'

'Oh Helen, of course I want you! But only if it's what you want. If you're sure . . . '

'I wouldn't have come if I wasn't.'

He took her hand and led her over to the bed.

'I must go now.'

That jealous pain returned with a vengeance as Anthony watched her hurriedly dressing. After an hour of perfect happiness he was to be left alone, while she went back to await the return of Pearson. Suddenly, he was embarrassed by his nakedness. Strange that he hadn't been so earlier. It had all seemed so natural, as though they had been together for years. His naivety didn't seem to matter at all. Now she was dressed and 'Mrs Pearson' again, and no longer belonged to him.

He put on his dressing gown and sat watching her comb her hair. There were so many things that he'd wanted to say. In particular he wanted to ask her to go away with him, to leave Pearson and the school. But perhaps that would have spoiled things. There would be another time. Plenty of other times, he hoped.

'We won't be able to do this very often,' she said, coming over and taking his hand. How did she always know what he was thinking?

'No. I know.'

'I won't get the chance, and anyway we mustn't give anyone the slightest idea . . . '

'I told Michael we hadn't.'

'We hadn't. Now we have. Are you glad?'

'Very, very glad.' He pulled her to him and began kissing her longingly again.

'So am I. I don't want to, but I must go or I'll meet them all on the stairs. And perhaps Eric will be . . . '

'Yes, you must go.'

A last, lingering kiss, and he was alone again. But for a while, his cold, bleak garret had been transformed into paradise.

Chapter Nineteen

'How are you feeling today?' Michael asked as they collected as much breakfast as Mrs Higginbottom would allow them. 'You seem to have got your appetite back.'

'A lot better. I spent most of the evening in bed,' replied Anthony truthfully.

'You'll be fit for Games this afternoon, then. I shan't have to stand in for you?'

'I should be so lucky! You're very welcome to, if you like.'

'No thanks. I'll leave that pleasure to you. You were obviously chosen for that job for a purpose - your restraint under fire, perhaps.'

Anthony's restraint nearly broke that afternoon. For some reason that he couldn't at first fathom, Fergus dismissed the boys but stayed with Anthony to check all the equipment. This had never happened before. It was usually either Anthony alone or with the help of a couple of first years. The games master was normally the first into the changing rooms. Anthony would have preferred to do the job himself. The company of Peter Ferguson was not a pleasure. And he soon discovered the reason for Fergus's change of habit.

'You getting on any better these days?' was the opening gambit, delivered in a tone Anthony was not keen on. What business was it of his?

'I'm coping,' Anthony replied, guardedly. No thanks to you, he thought.

'Like I said, there *are* compensations, aren't there?'

'Are there?'

'Oh, come on. Drop the wide-eyed innocence. I know what you're up to, even if nobody else does. Though goodness knows what she sees in a half-baked goal-post like you!'

'Are you implying something unpleasant?'

'Oh, no. I'm sure it's very pleasant. Very pleasant indeed.'

'What is?'

'Do you want me to spell it out in words of four letters?'

'Don't bother! If you are accusing me of something, come out and say it. If not, shut up!' Anthony said angrily, throwing the last handful of bats into a corner with a loud clatter.

'It's not for me to accuse you. Far from it! And it's not for you to tell me to shut up. You are very junior, remember. I'm simply wishing you luck, like a good colleague. But if . . . when . . . she gets bored, just remind her of where she can get a better time.'

Peter Ferguson locked the equipment shed and strolled towards the changing rooms, hands in pockets, whistling. Anthony couldn't decide at that moment which he hated most: Fergus, Pearson or Cedric. He just knew he would like to apply a cricket bat to all their heads.

'Fergus knows!' he whispered to Helen later, when he found her sorting books in the library.

'He knows nothing. He's just a loud-mouthed idiot.'

'He *must* know something. He all but accused me . . . us . . . '

'Ignore him. He's always doing it. He wouldn't dare spread a false rumour about me. He'd be out.'

'But it isn't false, it's true!'

Helen's eyes twinkled with mirth. 'He doesn't know that. How could he? Unless he was hiding under your bed.'

A sudden memory of some unpleasant things that had happened to people in Halls of Residence in his student days returned to turn Anthony cold. He resolved to check under his bed every time he had been out of the room. Fortunately his cupboards were too small to hide anyone, especially someone as well built as Fergus.

'He wants to keep his job,' Helen went on. 'So don't take any notice. But don't give him any ammunition either.'

'I promise I won't.'

He watched her pick up a pile of books and turn to leave, wondering longingly when he would be able to run his hands up and down her naked back again. With a deep sigh he forced himself to return to his lesson-planning.

'What are you doing for Easter?' asked Mary as they sat drinking coffee in the Common Room.

'Not much choice but to stay here. This is my "home" now, such as it is.'

'Look, you don't have to. My sister would put you up. She's a widow with a big house. That's where I go. Plenty of room. You'd be very welcome. She might raise an eyebrow at me turning up with such a charming young gentleman, though!' Mary laughed. 'Pity I'm not a few years younger.'

Anthony smiled. 'I really wouldn't want to impose on anyone.'

'You wouldn't be. She'd love it. You wouldn't have to spend your time with the old fogies. You can get to central London easily from there. Nice walking, too. Think about it. You could just come for a few days. I'll be there all holiday.'

'Thanks. I haven't really made any plans yet, but I'll keep it in mind.'

He hadn't liked to think about it too much. He imagined the Pearsons would be going to Spain. Even if they didn't, Helen wouldn't be free for much of the time. He knew now that that was how it would be. He had plenty of work to do, of course, with summer exams looming after Easter. But he did not relish the prospect of spending three weeks alone at Fieldhouse, even if it was warmer than at Christmas. Now, if he had had that car . . .

'Eric's going away for the first week of the holidays,' Helen told him on his next duty night. 'Are you staying here?'

'Yes. If you are.'

'Good. We'll be able to do some walking,' she replied with an expression which said 'and other things'.

'What about Spain?'

'We may go later. I hope not. But I don't have a lot of choice.'

Anthony managed to stop himself from saying, 'Come away with me, leave it all.' He *would* ask her - but the master's room on Duty Night was not the time or place.

If she said yes, they would have to make careful plans for their future. If she said no - then what would he do? He had no idea. She *mustn't* say no! He had nothing to offer her except himself. As Fergus had implied, he wasn't much of a bargain. But she seemed very happy with him, although he still couldn't understand why. All he knew was that he wanted to be with her, always. Surely they could make a life together, couldn't they?

With immense relief, Anthony dismissed his class - or rather, they dismissed themselves. The Easter holiday at last. Somehow he had struggled through a second term and had committed himself to stay for a third. He was becoming quite an 'old hand' now.

He pushed his way through groups of excited boys discussing their holiday plans in the corridor, and climbed the stairs to his room. Strange how, although no-one had left yet, there was already an air of emptiness up here. He made himself a mug of coffee, pulled his chair over to the window and sat looking over the landscape that had come to mean so much.

It was time to take stock. What had he achieved since September and what was he going to do next? He was not a success as a teacher. He had to admit that only the frequent presence of Pearson, unpleasant thought that was, had enabled him to teach anything at all. Yet at the same time, the Head's constant scrutiny had prevented him from developing and improving his teaching skills, or gaining in confidence. The only group with which he had established anything like a rapport was his first year class, who had started as green and nervous as himself. He thought he might be able to relate well to the sixth form, but Pearson had not given him that opportunity. Still, he'd survived this long without being summarily dismissed. He was still teaching, still earning. He supposed he could, if necessary, continue to do so if he could not find anything else when he and Helen . . .

That was the problem. 'You'll never teach anywhere again,' Michael had said. He would need references to apply to another school and he could hardly go to Pearson and say, 'I'm running away with your wife. Will you please give me a good reference so that I can support her.'

Michael was right. Pearson had influence, and in these circumstances he would not teach again, at least in an independent or good grammar school. But what about all those schools in city slums or on overspill estates? He doubted whether the Principal's baleful influence would reach as far as those. He couldn't imagine that the precise, clipped tones of Eric Pearson at the other end of a phone would cut much ice with an overburdened Head struggling to maintain staffing levels in a school like that. There might well be openings there.

Did that solve the problem? A girl his own age might be prepared to put up with anything for the first few years - most young people had to. But he didn't think that Helen would be happy to 'escape' to a run-down industrial town or a failing estate. There would be no hills, dragonflies or poppies there. She would no doubt think she had got through that stage of life long ago. So what could he offer her? He would have to have some plan if he was going to persuade her to give up her comfortable, if oppressive, life here and take her chance with him.

However long he thought about it, he could not come up with an idea that seemed feasible. It was no use. He would have to go to Helen without a plan and see what she thought. The answer was to plan together. She wouldn't want him organising her anyway. And being far more experienced than him, she would have a much better idea of what to do. He must find time to discuss it with her in the coming week.

The first week of the holidays was absolute heaven. Left alone, he and Helen made their own piece of paradise. They walked, talked, made love. She took him into her flat and showed him her books and paintings and all her treasures. She would not make love there, though. It wouldn't be right, she said. Anthony was slightly disappointed. Was it a wicked idea of his to get some revenge on Pearson? He suspected that it was and was glad that she had taken a more noble attitude. He didn't say anything about going away at first. It would be better to wait until the end of the week when they'd had all that time together and she would be so happy she wouldn't be able to refuse him.

On the last day of their idyll, they lay entwined in their hollow on the Downs, basking in the unseasonably warm sunshine.

'Helen, Helen, my darling, this week has been glorious. We can't go on living without each other. Please, please come away with me.'

'What! What's that you're saying?'

'Come with me. We'll leave this place. I mean in the summer. Now, if you like. We'll find somewhere to live and I'll find a job and . . . '

'Anthony,' Helen sat up, looking very serious, 'do you mean this?'

'Yes, of course I mean it. I've been trying to work out a plan but I need your advice. You know so much more than I do. You'll know the best place for us to go, where to live, where to work.'

'Anthony . . . '

Her voice and expression stopped his outpourings. 'Yes?'

'If only I could. It's a wonderful idea. If only I could.'

'You can, Helen, you can. What's to stop you? It's not as though you've got children or anything. We'll manage somehow, work something out. This is too good to waste. I know I'm young but I'm not as stupid as everybody thinks. I'll work day and night if I have to. We could . . . '

'Anthony, my love . . . '

'Yes?' he said again. He knew that this was all going wrong.

'It's too premature. You'll change your mind about me. Wait a little. It's not that I don't love you. Of course I do. And I don't want you to do things you might regret. Think about it. Then ask me again in a few weeks' time.'

Thanks for throwing me that lifeline, he thought. 'We'll have to decide by half term. You know why,' he said, deflated.

'Yes. Ask me again then. Listen, you old softie, you can ask me any time you want. I don't mind you asking. I'm very flattered that you want me that much. But you must understand my difficulties. It's not that easy. It may look it, but it's not. Anyway, as long as we're here in the school together . . . '

'But that's what I'm trying to say. After July we probably won't be.'

She patted his cheek. 'Half term. Things might be clearer then. I shan't forget. And I *do* love you.'

The next two weeks dragged interminably for Anthony. Pearson returned and he could not see much of Helen. Then they went to Spain for a week. At least he had plenty of time to do some more thinking. His rush of enthusiasm for running away had not impressed Helen. Probably it had merely served to prove to her how immature he was. She hadn't been angry. In fact, she had been very tender and sympathetic. He would almost rather that she *had* been angry. Her gentle treatment seemed to him to emphasise the difference in their age and position. Would she have been as understanding with a contemporary who had proposed such a crazy scheme? He thought not.

He would have to come up with something more definite. Not only think it out, but also carry it out. The only option he could see at the moment was to leave and establish himself elsewhere, then send for Helen. This idea depressed him. Once he was away from here, she'd forget him. Out of close contact, she would carry on with her life and he would have very little part in it. There would be other new teachers next year. He would be replaced, Edith Baines was retiring, and others might leave. Helen would perhaps have more hapless new recruits to take pity on. There might even be someone she really liked, someone closer to her own age. . . No, that was a bad plan for him, except that it gave him the opportunity to prove himself. He felt, though, that it was the only idea that Helen would approve, unless he could persuade her that leaving together was a viable option. He would have to scour the papers for a suitable job without delay. He'd wasted too much time already. He had exams to prepare for, too.

By the end of the holiday he had not achieved either goal.

'You don't seem very pleased to be back,' Anthony said, surprised by

Michael's obvious bad mood. He was usually so cheerful.

'I dare say you'll be pleased to know you don't have a prerogative on misery!' Michael threw his bags on to the bed and slumped down beside them.

'What's up?'

'Seems I'm footloose and fancy-free again, as they say. Damned woman!'

'Pamela?'

Yes. Waited until I got home then wrote and told me she'd met an old friend. Well, actually she met him at Christmas but she couldn't make up her mind. Now she has .She could have told me before the Vac.'

'I'm sorry. She seemed very nice.'

'She was the first girl I've really related to. I thought this was the big one!'

'Perhaps she'll change her mind again.'

'She's engaged!'

'I'd offer you a drink if I had anything in my room,' Anthony said sympathetically.

Michael opened one of his bags and brought out a bottle of whisky.

'Pour a couple out of this. The glasses are in that cupboard.'

Pleased to be able to comfort someone else in their misery, however inadequately, Anthony found the glasses and poured two drinks - a large one for Michael and a much smaller one for himself. He wasn't sure if he would ever acquire a taste for whisky. He raised his glass.

'Here's to better times for both of us.'

'I thought you were fixed up for the time being?'

'It's a very difficult situation. It brings as much sorrow as happiness.'

'You really serious, then?'

'Yes, very.'

'That's tough.'

'To tell you the truth, I don't know what to do.'

Michael's subdued unhappiness struck many chords in Anthony. Another whisky and some strong coffee, and Michael knew the whole story.

'You haven't got much choice but to leave - whichever way it goes,' he said as Anthony finished his confessions. 'Sorry about that.'

'What about you?'

'Oh, I'll stay on here for a year or two, I expect.'

'Even though you'll keep running into . . . '

'You can't keep moving home and job every time you split up with a girl. It's lousy but you have to grit your teeth. Different for you, of course.'

'I just don't want to get Helen into any trouble - unless she chooses to be in it herself. Ferguson worries me, though.'

'He's a bastard!'

'Helen thinks he won't dare spread rumours about her in case Pearson kicks him out. I'm not sure. He drinks a lot.'

'He does.' Michael looked rather sheepishly at what little remained of the whisky. 'And he's not pleasant when he's drunk.'

'He's not pleasant when he's sober.'

'When he gets into one of the pubs or to a dance - well, he's pretty loud and vulgar. I've seen him. And heard him.'

'Have you heard him say anything about Helen and me?'

'No. I've heard him say things about both of you individually, but not in connection with one another.'

'I don't think I want to hear them.'

'I don't intend to repeat them. But he's like that about everybody. Mary heard something he said about her. I believe she wiped the floor with him.'

'Good for her!'

'As has Mrs P. Frequently.'

'Doesn't Pearson know about all this?'

'I suppose he must do. But as long as the school teams keep winning matches - Fergus does seem to bring out the best in them.'

'By encouraging them to mock junior staff.'

'H'm . . . Doubt if Pearson knows about that.'

'Or cares.'

'We might as well finish this bottle,' said Michael a little thickly, pouring the last measures with an unsteady hand.

'It hasn't solved our problems.'

'No, but we're beginning to feel oblivious to them!' Michael said with a broad grin. His face had lost its earlier unnatural pallor and become rather red. 'Pity I haven't got another bottle.'

'Thank goodness you haven't,' replied Anthony, wondering how he was going to cross the landing to his own room without falling over the banisters.

'How was Spain?'

'Er . . . OK.'

'Someone else who didn't enjoy their holiday?'

'What do you mean?'

'Oh, Michael's miserable. Pamela's ditched him. Don't mention it, though.'

'Of course I won't. No, Spain was a bit difficult. Eric was talking about when to sell up and retire. Recruitment isn't good.'

'I thought you said three or four years?'

'Yes, but it could be sooner. He expects me to advise him. But I can't.'

'Why?'

'Because . . . because I'm only happy with you. Retirement with Eric doesn't have much - any - appeal.'

Anthony had not heard Helen be quite so blunt about her marriage before.

'Well, then, do as I say. Come away with me. Or what about this idea: I'll go and settle somewhere, then send for you. I'll leave in July, get fixed up with a job, then in a month or two I'll have looked around, found somewhere decent to live. You could join me, say, in October half term.'

'You've got it all planned out now, then?' Was she laughing at him? He couldn't quite tell.

'I've had a fortnight to think about it. You *did* say I could keep asking you. But I decided I had to come up with a proper plan. I've been looking for jobs but I haven't seen anything yet. I don't think I want to go on teaching, although I will if necessary. But I'll need references.'

Helen interrupted him. 'Have you got any money, Anthony?'

'A little. Not very much.' He longed to say 'What about you?' but he didn't like to.

'I haven't got much either,' she answered for him.

'Well, two small sums will make one larger one. You *will* join me, won't you? I'll have saved more by then.'

'I'll tell you at half term, not before. But listen, Anthony . . . '

'Yes?'

'You *must* make your plans to suit *you*. You've got forty working years ahead of you. You must find something you enjoy, that uses your talents, and get established in it.'

'What about you?'

'I'm fairly adaptable,' was all she would say.

Anthony could not make out whether that was hopeful or not. He preferred to think that it was.

Chapter Twenty

A whole afternoon! It was revision-time before the school and public exams began and much of the timetable was suspended. Anthony found himself 'free' or at least he had made himself free, taking a break from planning yet more revision exercises. Fortunately Helen was able to take time off too.

'If we start right after lunch, we can go further than usual,' she said. 'I'll meet you on the top.'

It was a glorious day. Spring was merging into summer among the clouds of May blossom in the hedgerows. Poppies were beginning to spangle the downland paths. Above, almost invisible skylarks flooded the air with music.

When they were far enough from the school, Anthony and Helen walked up on to the ridge, admiring the extensive views on either side. Flowers dotted the close-cropped turf beneath their feet, from where their footsteps disturbed bees and tiny blue butterflies.

Anthony found himself almost speechless. He was in heaven. He looked down from the distant purplish haze to the glints of sunlight on Helen's red-brown hair, from the bright chalk path to the dazzling white cotton of her blouse. He felt the soft warmth of her body pressed to his side and the heat of the sun on his arm around her waist. He pressed his cheek against her sun-warmed hair and tightened his grip.

'If only all life was like this,' she said.

'Can't it be?'

'No - but it could be better than it is.'

He wanted to ask her, for the umpteenth time, to go away with him, but he knew what her answer would be.

'In what way?' he asked.

'Let's walk over to the dewpond,' she said, changing the subject. But of course they both knew the answer.

'The what?'

'The pond in the hollow over there. They're relics from the days when the Downs were full of sheep. This one's a little overgrown now.'

They walked towards the shallow depression, half-filled with reeds and water plants.

'Did you say "dewpond"?'

'Yes. People thought they were simply formed by the dew condensing. But the farmers made them specially and lined them with clay from the lowlands so that the water wouldn't drain away through the chalk. Kipling mentioned them in a poem about Sussex.'

'I'll look it up.'

They had reached the pool's marshy edge.

'Look, dragonflies!' Helen breathed, pointing to a dart of brilliant blue.

'They're everywhere. All kinds. And what are those?'

'Pond-skaters. Look how they skim the surface. Shall we go and sit over there on the bank?'

They found a spot on the far slope, away from the boggy margins of the pond. The grass grew longer here than on the exposed tops. Anthony lay back and looked up at the cloudless sky through a frame of waving grasses. Helen sat upright for a little longer, gazing across the pool at the dragonflies. The chorus of skylarks still accompanied them and other upland birds joined in the celebration from fence posts and stunted bushes.

Anthony watched Helen as she sat, her blouse billowing out in the wind. What was she thinking? Was she deciding what to do about him? He reached up and stroked her hair, willing her to turn and say yes, she would go with him. She did turn, with an expression of great tenderness in her eyes that turned him into jelly. Slowly, she leaned forward, bent her head and kissed him. He folded his arms around her and drew her down to him.

'Helen, we mustn't let this go,' he said after a while. 'It's too wonderful.'

'It's magic,' she whispered. 'It's unlike anything I've ever known before.'

'Is it? Truly?'

'Yes. Completely.'

'Well, don't let it slip away. Come with me. Then we can spend *all* our free time like this. We could be so happy!'

'I can't give you an answer yet,' she replied, very softly.

'Why not? What difference will a few weeks make? Wouldn't this be the perfect day for deciding? Here, among all the glories of nature?'

'Anthony, I can't promise now, but . . . '

She's weakening, he thought. She really wants to say yes. I need to do something to make the moment extra special.

If only he had something to give her. This was the time when he should produce a diamond ring. . . He reached up and plucked a blade of the long grass swaying in the breeze above his head. Without speaking, he took her left hand in his and wound the grass around her ring finger. As well as he could, he tied it, then raised her hand and pressed his lips to the symbolic knot.

'Helen,' he managed to say in a shaky voice, 'if you were free, would . . . would you marry me?'

She looked up at him, down at his 'ring', then into his eyes again. For a moment she hesitated, then she said, 'Yes. Yes, I would.'

'I wish I had a proper ring to give you. But of course, you couldn't wear it - yet.'

'I'll treasure this for ever.' She pressed her own lips to the ring of green then kissed Anthony. 'I've never felt like this before, never felt for anyone like I do you, never had such magical, wonderful moments surrounded by such beauty and without anything to spoil them.'

'A perfect place to seal our love,' he answered.

Did a shadow pass over her face when he said that? As if to reassure him she took his hand and led him back to the water's edge. There they stood for a while watching the dragonflies.

'It must be wonderful to be free, like them,' he said.

'Their lives are very short.'

'But happy.'

'Happiness is fleeting, like this beautiful day.'

'Then let's make it last.'

He wanted to say 'we've made our promise now' but he was afraid of spoiling things. He wasn't absolutely certain that she saw it as a promise. Still, she hadn't protested…

She seemed, as always, to read his thoughts. She looked down at her finger and again he saw that fleeting shadow on her face. She appeared to swallow hard before speaking.

'If only we could. But we should start back now.'

That wasn't what he had meant by 'making it last'. And he wasn't deluded. She had known exactly what he meant.

She looked so lovely, standing against that wide sweep of land, looking up at him with her eyes shining. But was some of that shine caused by tears? He clasped her against him with an overwhelming mixture of love, joy and fear.

'Let's stay together, Helen,' he murmured into her hair. 'Won't you?'

'I promise I'll give you my answer at half term. In the meantime you'd better get on with planning the future,' she said, smiling now.

'I will. Oh, yes, I will!' Our future, he said to himself. That's what she really means.

He grasped her grass-embellished hand and they walked slowly back along the flinty track that curved across the top of the Downs. As they did so, a warm breeze from the distant coast blew across the adjoining fields of unripe corn, rippling them like a green sea, wave after wave.

'Look at that, oh look at that! Isn't it wonderful?' Helen said.

They watched entranced until the last breath of wind died away. It was the perfect end to an afternoon of pure romance.

'See you tonight?'

'Sorry?'

'Tonight.' Michael looked rather exasperated. 'You know, Fergus's birthday treat. Drinks all round.'

'Didn't know anything about it,' Anthony replied.

'Oh. Well, he's invited us all to the pub to help him celebrate - and brace ourselves for the exams. Didn't you get a note?'

'No. I told you, he doesn't like me.'

'He's invited everybody, not just his drinking partners. I'm sure he didn't mean to leave you out. Come along anyway.'

'No thanks. There's something I must do. Don't worry. He won't miss me.'

Anthony wasn't pleased about the deliberate snub but there *was* something he wanted to do, something much more important than spending the evening with Peter Ferguson, even if it was at the latter's expense. The 'something' was a poem. He wanted to write a poem for Helen to commemorate their lovely afternoon. He'd got the first line, now he had to think of the rest. It was years since he had written any poetry and he was anxious to at least try to convey what he felt about the day, even if the results were not quite Shakespeare, or even Kipling.

Helen had said, 'If we had devised a day for ourselves, chosen all its parts, it would have been like this. It couldn't have been more magical.' Now he wanted to put that idea, that magic, into verse. This had given him his first idea for the beginning.

'We plucked a day from heaven'

It was a start, at least.

He heard the merrymakers leave for the pub. Again he felt a twinge of jealousy but he had no real wish to join them. The cold lino of his floor soon became covered with discarded paper as he struggled for the right words. It looked so easy when, say, Hardy did it, finding the perfect words and phrases to convey feeling and emotion. So apparently effortless to commemorate or commiserate - and so successful.

If only he had appreciative classes! How well he could teach the meaning of poetry now! Before, it had merely been part of the curriculum, something to be got through and probably hated by teachers and pupils alike. He remembered the dread of being asked to read aloud or comment on some 'sloppy' poem when he was at school. His attempts to teach the subject at Fieldhouse had, of course, failed miserably. But in this case he had actually sympathised with his defiant pupils - until tonight. If he continued to teach he would specialise in the teaching of romantic poetry, lecture on it, write on it, become a renowned expert... Now he understood everything - except how to write it.

We plucked a day from Heaven,
Stretched up our arms . . .

Well, maybe.

He was still struggling when the first of the revellers returned. When he heard them in the hall he quickly gathered up the crumpled paper and stuffed it into the wastepaper bin, in case Michael came in to regale him with tales of the evening. He did not want to be interrupted in the full flow of creation, so he switched off the dim main light and took his current draft over to the bedside table. Here he crouched beside the even dimmer lamp, which he shaded further with a book. Hopefully Michael would think he was asleep.

He was getting somewhere with the poem now. He didn't think it was too bad.

As he was trying to make the last verse scan, he heard Michael return. His colleague's footsteps seemed to hesitate on the landing outside Anthony's door, then they moved on across to Michael's room and Anthony breathed again. Shortly afterwards, a chorus from the very ancient and noisy plumbing in the bathroom next door told him that Michael was preparing for bed, then the silence of night descended on the attics.

Anthony got up, stretched and moved quietly over to the window. The moon was shining on the waters of the pond, just as it had been on New Year's Eve, when it had moved him so much. Now he thought of that other water, high up on the Downs. That, too, would be bathed in moonlight. There would be no trace of the two lovers who had embraced in the warm sun just a few hours ago, or of the dragonflies that had enlivened its surface. No trace - except in one tiny spot where a blade of grass had been broken off. Helen had promised to preserve it carefully. It meant so much to her, she said. So did she really think of it as an engagement ring?

He sat down at the table, took a sheet of paper and a decent pen, and began to write a final copy.

> ON THE HEIGHTS
> *We claimed a day from Heaven,*
> *Reached up our arms*
> *And drew it down to earth,*
> *Then lived it, gloriously*
>
> *We jewelled our path with poppies,*
> *Sprinkled the reed*
> *Beside the pool with dragonflies*
> *And watched them, joyfully*
>
> *We chose a warm sea -wind*
> *Billowing the corn,*
> *Waving the grass above our heads*
> *Where we lay blissfully*
>
> *I plucked a strand of green*
> *And on your finger*
> *Wound it as a lover's ring,*
> *Claimed you eternally*
>
> *Our day of joy was fragile,*
> *Only a brief, bright glow*
> *Like poppies and the dragonflies,*
> *We clasped it, and each other, on the heights,*
> *And then we let it go*

He wasn't entirely happy about the last verse. Did the extra line give it impact? Or not? Oh well, Helen would not expect perfection. It was just a response to a very special day, written at a time when he was supposed to be devising ways of helping his pupils to revise for their exams.

The next morning he slipped downstairs early, hoping to catch a glimpse of Helen before breakfast. He was lucky. She was sorting the mail beside the pigeonholes and he was able to give her the envelope containing the poem.

'I wrote this,' he said, suddenly feeling hopelessly shy. 'It's about yesterday.' He knew his cheeks were bright red.

Helen smiled and took it with a squeeze of his fingers. She lifted the rib of her sweater and tucked the envelope into the waistband of her skirt.

'It'll be safe there. I'll read it later, when I'm alone,' she whispered. In a louder voice she said, 'Here's your mail, Mr Dean.'

Anthony was flicking through his small selection of bills and circulars as he walked towards the dining room. He didn't hear anyone behind him until Michael's voice said, 'Anthony - a word before breakfast. It's about last night.'

'Yes?' Instinct told Anthony that the day that had begun on such a tender, romantic note, was about to deteriorate.

'Ferguson. He had a few too many. Many too many. He was spreading rumours.' Michael looked round to make sure no-one else was within earshot.

'About me?' Anthony didn't really need to ask.

'Yes. I just wanted to warn you.'

'Did he mention . . . another name?'

'Yes, frequently.'

'Who heard?'

'Everyone in the village, I should think.'

'My God!'

'Nobody takes much notice of him, but . . . '

'Thanks for the warning.'

They were in the dining room now. Changing the subject, they put on cheerful smiles and went up to collect their breakfasts. But despite Mrs Higginbottom's generosity with the bacon and eggs, Anthony had suddenly lost his appetite.

'Helen!'

She turned in obvious surprise at being addressed by her Christian name just outside the front door as she watered her beloved flower tubs.

'Sorry - Mrs Pearson.' Anthony was flustered now. He looked around but there was no-one near them. 'Listen,' he said quickly, in a whisper, 'they're talking about us.'

'Who is?'

'The whole village. Fergus shouted it from the rooftops last night!'

A dark shadow crossed Helen's face, much darker than the ones he had seen before, but she recovered quickly and gave a cheerful smile.

'Take no notice. I've told you, people are used to his loud mouth.' Her voice softened. 'Thanks for the poem, it's beautiful. It captures the day so well. I love it.' Then, after a quick glance round, 'And you.' She turned to go back indoors. 'I'd better go in now. Don't worry, it'll be OK.'

She walked briskly up the steps into the house with a cheery, 'Lovely afternoon Mr Dean,' but Anthony was not convinced by her performance. She was worried this time, he could tell. As he climbed slowly back up to his room, his stomach felt like an icy pit.

'Smile please!'

Anthony attempted to obey the photographer but his effort was a feeble one. Only the ghost of a smile flickered on his lips as the shutter clicked.

'That's fine. Keep perfectly still. Another one, please!'

Anthony shuffled his feet slightly. He seemed to have been here for hours. He and Michael had been relegated to stand at each end of the back row of boys, while the rest of the staff sat on chairs in the front. But this was not the only reason for his discomfiture.

The previous evening he had heard an unfamiliar footstep on his stair. He opened the door to a sharp rap, and to his surprise found Art-and-Craft on the landing.

'Are you busy?'

'No. Come in. Coffee?'

'Sorry to bother you,' said Art-and-Craft, flinging himself on to the bed among the scattered books and papers. 'Mind if I smoke?'

'Go ahead.'

The art master took out a paint-spattered old tin containing tobacco and rolled a very thin cigarette.

Anthony placed a mug of coffee on the bedside table and watched with some concern as his colleague flicked ash into the paper-filled waste bin. Was there enough water in the kettle to douse a fire? He must remember not to go to sleep without checking that bin!

'I just wanted a word,' his visitor said, getting out the tobacco tin once again. His cigarettes did not last long. 'None of my business really, but there are rumours going around.'

'About?'

'About you and Mrs P,' he said, licking the edge of the cigarette paper and sticking it down carefully. 'I just wanted to warn you. That bastard Ferguson was shouting about it at his birthday booze-up. You weren't there to defend yourself.'

'I wasn't invited. Would it have made any difference if I had been?'

'It might have. At least in the early part of the evening. Later, perhaps not.'

Hell! If only he hadn't been so anxious to write that poem . . .

'Look, I don't give a damn whether it's true or not,' Art-and-Craft went on, peering at Anthony quizzically from under that untidy mat of hair.

He knows it is, Anthony thought. He said, 'Michael did mention it. There's not much I can do. What do you advise?'

'Don't respond, keep quiet, do your job, look at the vacancy list. Oh. And don't been seen with Mrs P. in public!'

Art-and-Craft was grinning now but Anthony saw sympathy in his expression. David Wilson was a bit of a loner. He had never been up to Anthony's room before. He wouldn't have taken the trouble to come and warn him unless he genuinely wanted to help. What was *his* history? Anthony wondered if he had had some doomed love affair that he kept hidden under that eccentric exterior. Was that why he seemed to understand?

'One more! All smile. Say "Mr Pearson".'

The photographer's jocular use of the Head's name broke sharply through Anthony's reverie. They did smile, all except Anthony - and Eric Pearson. Anthony suspected that there were more reasons than the present levity to account for the Principal's tight-lipped expression.

'Resignations have to be in at half term, Mr Dean,' he had said on entering the classroom where Anthony was supervising a revision session that morning. Anthony was rather annoyed that Pearson had made such a remark in a quiet classroom for every boy to hear. Perhaps feeling that he had been a little indiscreet, Pearson continued, 'I would be grateful if you would remind all the new staff of this rule.'

Anthony was not fooled. He was being told to resign. There was no doubt that Pearson had become even more hostile. He must have heard the rumours. Helen insisted that he never listened to such talk, but what if they concerned his infuriatingly hopeless new English master? He'd probably listen then. Even if he didn't believe what he heard, it would be a wonderful excuse to rid himself of a nuisance before his school's reputation for excellent teaching took a blow from which, in today's economic climate, it might not recover. After all, the world of education in which he moved would not be impressed to hear that the famous Eric Pearson, English scholar and school Principal *par excellence* had appointed a totally useless English assistant, even if Fieldhouse School *was* past its best. It must really gall him to have chosen me out of all those possible candidates, Anthony thought. He almost felt a glow of triumph! But any such thoughts were quickly dissipated by the realisation that Pearson held all the cards. Anthony wouldn't get a second chance at Fieldhouse, or probably anywhere else. He was glad that he would never actually have to read any references that the Head might write for him.

Helen was sitting on the front row beside Pearson, but she didn't give the impression of being the proud wife of a successful headmaster. On the contrary, she was also tight-lipped, looking bored and a little anxious. Anthony noticed that she did not look in Pearson's direction and there was an obvious gap between their chairs. Was he imagining things or was Helen leaning *away* from her husband?

'How can you persuade boys to do revision when all they want to do is play cricket?' Anthony complained. It was his duty night and Helen was paying him her usual visit. 'I'm praying for rain for the next few weeks.'

'How's *your* cricket?'

'It's one of my better sports - but I'm not doing it. Michael has been asked.'

'Oh?' Helen raised her eyebrows.

'I can't understand why he wasn't asked to do the winter games since he's so much better than me.'

'Except at cricket?'

'Well, yes, apparently.'

'But it's got you off the hook?'

'Oh no, I still have to do other games. But Michael's doing swimming as well, thank goodness.'

'Aren't you a swimmer?'

'Not really. To be honest I don't like getting my head under water. Sort of claustrophobia.'

'Funny, I'm like that too. We'd better be careful not to go near water together,' she laughed. 'We won't be able to rescue each other!'

'I'd put my head under water for you,' Anthony said, kissing her.

'So you're still stuck with Fergus. What's he said?'

'Nothing. Oh, he's always getting at me. But he hasn't said anything about us. Perhaps he realises he went too far - or he can't remember anything about it!'

'Oh yes, he can. I . . . er . . . had a word with him,' Helen confessed.

'What happened?'

'I accused him of spreading malicious rumours about me. I threatened him.'

'What did he say?'

'Not much. Sort of apologised.'

'I bet he's heart-broken! What can we do?'

'Nothing. Ignore it.' She changed the subject. 'You'll be here at half term, won't you?'

'Nowhere else to go, even if I wanted to.'

'I don't want you to go anywhere else,' she said gently, stroking his cheek. 'I'm sure we can make some time together.'

'You promised me an answer,' he reminded her.

'You'll get it. I promise.'

'I'm waiting - anxiously.'

He was desperately trying to tell from her look what that answer would be, but he couldn't. She was gentle, warm, loving, sought out his company, made love to him with pleasure and passion on the few opportunities they had . . . but did she love him enough to take that drastic step?

'Don't look so pained,' she went on. 'It won't be long now.'

On that note of hope, she left him.

'Staff are expected,' announced Eric Pearson, removing his gold-rimmed glasses to give the assembled teachers the full benefit of his ice-blue gaze, 'to use the coming half-term to prepare any necessary extra revision material for pupils still to take school examinations, and especially for those taking 'O' and 'A' Levels. Also,' he continued, striding across the front of the library fireplace, thumbs in the waistcoat pocket of his immaculate three-piece suit, 'remember that you must be properly prepared for the education of pupils when their exams are over. You must be able to give introductions to next year's work for those staying on, and appropriate and purposeful tasks for those who are leaving. And finally,' the Principal stopped, replaced his spectacles and stared straight at Anthony, 'those of you who will not be remaining with us next year are asked to hand in your resignations by noon on the Monday following half term. One last point,' again glaring at Anthony. 'Recruitment to this school depends on excellent academic results. Times are difficult and staff who do not achieve these results are letting down not only their pupils but the entire school. As you are all aware, reduction in pupil numbers will inevitably mean staff losses. Competent teaching and motivation are the key to success. Thank you. Mr Fulford will deal with any other business.'

Eric Pearson strode out of the library, giving Anthony what he felt was a look of utter loathing. That's right, blame me for all the school's ills, he thought bitterly. A little assistance with 'competent teaching and motivation' would have gone a long way! He wondered how many of the other people in the room knew what that diatribe was really about? He was glad that Helen hadn't been there to hear it.

Chapter Twenty-One

'All quiet today, Mr Jones?' Anthony strolled downstairs very late on the first Sunday morning of half term. It had been a delightful luxury to have a long lie-in. His room was relatively warm, the light filtered through the thin curtains and streamed into the gap between them, the birds were singing outside. He had allowed himself the treat of making coffee and taking it back to bed. There he had lain, relaxed and comfortable, thinking of Helen. She would say yes, wouldn't she? Couldn't he tell from the tone of her voice when he mentioned it? She knew he was going to resign; that he had no choice, and she wouldn't want to lose him. He imagined her lying there beside him. Perhaps some time this week they'd be doing just that. If only they could do it every day, even if they were just lying and talking. It wouldn't matter. He just wanted to be with her, whatever they were doing.

Eventually he got up, made some more coffee, ate a slice of bread and jam and decided to go for a walk around the garden. Helen might be out there. As he descended the stairs, Jones was polishing the brass handle and nameplate on the front door.

'Just you and me today, sir. Nice bit of peace, eh?'

'What about the Pearsons?' Anthony asked, feeling a slight chill. There was no sound from their flat. Perhaps they were out for the day.

'Gone to Spain, sir. Last night. I didn't know as they were going till Mr P sent for me about seven o'clock to give me my instructions. Arranged at the last minute, he said.'

'Till when?' Anthony asked, with a knotted stomach.

'Next weekend, I suppose. Be back Friday or Saturday, I dare say.'

'Yes, of course.'

Anthony walked past the caretaker and slowly down the front steps. The bright, hopeful spring morning had turned a bleak grey to him. Now the birdsong just seemed to mock him. Gone! A whole week alone! And no word of warning! What had happened? His stomach took another sickening lurch as he thought about it. Pearson's taken her away, he thought. He doesn't want her to stay where I am. He's heard the whispers and believes them. There's not even a message in my pigeonhole.

There was nothing he could do but wait.

He would have to use the week fruitfully. He'd plan schoolwork for after the holiday, as Pearson had demanded. He'd buy a paper every day and look for a job. He'd re-write his resignation letter. What else? He could count his money - *that* wouldn't take long. A few walks and cycle rides would help pass the time. And he could pray that a week with Pearson would make Helen all the more anxious to leave.

'The Pearsons didn't leave any messages for me, since I'm the only one here all week?' he asked Jones when he went back into the school.

'No. Only Mrs Pearson said, as she was rushing out, that I wasn't to forget you were here.'

'Was that all?'

'Oh yes, and I was to make sure you got all you wanted.'

There's only one thing I want, Anthony thought.

'Mr P. was in a hurry, very impatient,' Jones went on. 'She didn't have time to say any more. If she had, I'd have remembered and made sure I told you. Course, I didn't know as *you* didn't know they'd gone.'

Jones's tone and expression gave Anthony's over-stressed stomach yet another wrench as he realised that the caretaker had heard the rumours too. In fact, he'd probably known before anyone else. He had, after all, been at the school a long time.

She was dragged away against her will, Anthony thought miserably as he plodded upstairs again. But she'd tried to send him a message. That gave him a little hope.

Tuesday morning. A letter in his pigeonhole! But it wasn't the longed-for message from Helen. It was postmarked in the Midlands and the writing looked familiar. Anthony pulled out the stiff white paper and realised where he'd seen a similar letter before.

Dear Anthony,

I have been meaning to write to you for some time but I have been extremely busy with my company and the extension to my house.

Aunt Florence's affairs are now settled. I must thank you for collecting your belongings so promptly.

I believe that I owe you something of an apology. In conversation with one of Flo's friends, I was given to understand that the old banger in the garage was meant to be yours. I don't know what arrangements you had come to with Auntie regarding the purchasing of it, but as far as I know there was never anything in writing and of course I knew nothing of it. You were obviously far too much the polite schoolmaster to mention it when you came over. In any case, as you know, the car had already gone.

I would like to discuss this matter with you in person and as I believe it is half term this week, perhaps you will be able to tear yourself away from the classroom and come over to see me. You are very welcome to stay with me as I now have a new guest suite.

Yours,
Cedric Simpson.

Anthony was not sure whether to be pleased or angry. The 'valuable car' had now become an 'old banger'. And of course there had never been any question of him 'purchasing' it. What had Cedric got in mind? Would it be worth spending some of his precious savings on the train fare? At least it would help the week pass more quickly. And while he was up there he could buy local papers and see what jobs and accommodation there were in that area. Yes, he'd go.

On the phone, Cedric invited him to stay for two or three nights. Anthony thought two would be enough. Staff were expected to be back by Saturday night, so he travelled north on Thursday. Hopefully, when he returned, Helen would be back. He had spent the time before departing putting the finishing touches to his revision lessons, cycling in the rain (the earlier good weather had broken and was now entirely appropriate to his mood) and writing that letter to Pearson. There it lay, where the other one had, in the middle of his table. This time there could be no hesitating, though. It had to be delivered. Otherwise he would be getting one from Pearson, and that would be much more unpleasant.

He also composed another poem for Helen. She had been really enthusiastic about 'On the Heights' so he'd written one about the school pool. While he was away he planned to buy her a present and find a card large enough to write out the poem. These thoughts of what he could do for Helen helped him through the week. And when she returned, well, he would insist on an answer. He wished he had better things to offer her, had found a job, and had saved more. Perhaps Cedric would employ him? No, that wasn't a good idea. He suspected that Cedric might be even worse than Pearson, in his way. He'd just have to hope that the present and poem would persuade her to decide in his favour.

As the train ground slowly northwards, Anthony once again scanned the papers. But there didn't seem to be anything he could sensibly apply for. Perhaps it would have to be teaching in a city slum. Still, he wouldn't have to live there. He could become a commuter. Expensive - but worth it if it was the only way he could set up home with Helen. Would she have come up with some ideas by the end of the week?

'Well, now,' said Cedric as they settled into the deep armchairs after dinner. 'Like a cigar?'

'No thanks, just coffee.' Anthony did not think that this was the appropriate moment to experiment with cigars. He'd experimented with cigarettes once . . .

The meal had been cooking in the oven when they arrived from the station. Anthony wondered what had happened to Mrs Cedric. He was sure there was one - or had been. But he didn't like to ask. Cedric had served an excellent casserole and a fruit pie, washed down with a quantity of strong red wine, which had made the journey from dining room to lounge rather perilous for Anthony. He hoped his conversation wasn't as incoherent as his legs were wobbly.

'About this car,' Cedric continued when the cigar was lit and the coffee poured. 'I didn't know, you see. No idea you'd planned to buy it.' Anthony said nothing. 'So I sold it. Had to get it out of the garage. Hadn't been used for years. Wouldn't start, of course. Had to be towed away. Dare say it would have cost you a fair bit to put it on the road. Like a liqueur? Whisky?'

'Not for me, thanks.' Anthony could not bear to think of the effect that more alcohol might have. 'Yes, I expect it might have cost more than I'd planned for.'

Still, the car itself would have been free, he thought, with what he knew was unreasonable anger. His host was, after all, being quite honest. Except for the 'old banger' bit.

'I felt a bit rotten when I heard the story about it. Sure I can't tempt you?' Cedric poured himself what seemed to Anthony's rather blurred vision almost as much whisky as he'd had wine. 'Old mother Harvey told me. Did you know her?'

'I met her once, last Christmas.'

'She said Flo had told her "that teacher fellow" wanted the car.' Cedric told him.

Anthony was not too flattered to be called "that teacher fellow". He could not imagine his late great-aunt speaking of anyone in that way, even if she did have a low opinion of him at one time. He guessed this was an embellishment of Cedric's.

Cedric continued, 'The estate went to me, of course.' Of course! 'But I thought it only fair that you should have something to help you get another car. One in a better state perhaps. So I hope this will come in useful.' He handed Anthony a cheque for one hundred pounds.

Anthony stared down at it, not knowing what to say. He was grateful for anything, and this would boost his savings towards the point where he could put a deposit on a *very* small house. That would be something to offer Helen. But he didn't care to be given 'the crumbs from the rich man's table' and he knew that Cedric had probably received a great deal more for the 'old banger' than that. He'd had everything else too. If it hadn't been for Helen and his own precarious position, he might have refused the money. But Aunt Florence *had* wanted him to have the car. And Cedric had been under no obligation to give him anything.

In the end he just said, 'Decent of you. Thanks,' and put the cheque safely in his wallet.

The next day Cedric took him around his company, then to lunch with a group of business colleagues. Anthony felt at a complete loss and extremely foolish. They were so worldly, so confident. He had nothing in common with them. There was something missing and at first he couldn't think what it was. Then he realised. They didn't seem to have any souls. He simply longed to escape and dream of Helen. Helen had a soul. And it was very like his own.

In the evening he was taken to an expensive restaurant, where he felt equally lost. He couldn't understand the menu, was totally incapable of choosing wine, didn't know what to do with all the various items of cutlery and glass around his plate, and just wanted to get back to his cold little attic. There he could enjoy a cup of hot chocolate and a slice of (often dry) bread. He was obviously not cut out for the high life.

Declining an invitation to accompany Cedric on the golf course on Saturday morning - he had no intention of making a fool of himself again - Anthony returned to Fieldhouse via London and stopped off to buy a bracelet for Helen. Perhaps his next purchase of jewellery for her would be a ring. He'd have to save some more money for that. He also bought a large card showing a field of poppies on which he intended to write his poem. Then it was time to get back to school. With any luck, Helen would be there waiting for him.

'The school's closing!'

Anthony stopped half way up the attic stairs and gazed in disbelief at Michael, who was hanging over the banisters.

'What did you say?' He hurried up the remaining stairs and put down his bag.

'The school's closing at the end of term. We've got letters!'

'You're joking!'

'Wish I were. But it's true. Here's your letter.'

Michael passed Anthony the long brown envelope that he had collected along with his own from the pigeonholes ten minutes before. He looked as though he wanted to say more but didn't. Anthony's expression must have deterred him.

'I'll leave you to go and read it. There's a meeting in the library before dinner. Give me a knock if you want a chat when you've unpacked.'

Michael went back into his room and left Anthony standing alone on the landing, staring down at the envelope in his hand. Dazed, he fumbled for his key in his jacket pocket, let himself into his icy room and opened the letter. It was typewritten, with his name added in Eric Pearson's handwriting.

Dear Mr Dean,

It is with regret that I have to inform you that Fieldhouse School will close at the end of this term.

As you may know, I have been considering retirement for some time and expected to sell the school within the next five years. However, circumstances now dictate that I should bring my retirement forward to the end of this academic year.

The parents and pupils were informed yesterday and naturally the school will make every effort to assist them in finding alternative educational establishments for their sons. Likewise we will do everything possible to enable the staff to obtain posts elsewhere for September.

I must apologise for your having such short notice and would like to take this opportunity to thank you for all your work at the school.

A staff meeting to discuss the closure will be held in the library at six o'clock this evening.

Eric Pearson
Principal

Anthony sat with his head in his hands. What were the 'circumstances'? Did he dare guess? Or was it mere coincidence? If only Helen would come up and tell him what had happened. But perhaps she was being watched. He was even more desperate to see her now.

When he had pulled himself together and put his belongings away, he crossed the landing to talk to Michael. Perhaps he could throw some light on the matter.

'Well, fame at last! Who'd have thought it?' exclaimed Michael, looking Anthony up and down.

'What do you mean?' He had a pretty good idea.

'The man that brought down the famous Eric Pearson, and Fieldhouse School into the bargain! I always said you were a dark horse! What was it they used to advise young ladies - watch the quiet ones, wasn't it? Certainly true in your case! Who'd have thought it,' he said again.

'Oh, come on!'

'Any other explanation? I haven't. Sit down.'

Anthony sat on the edge of the bed, pale and shaken. 'What do you know?'

'No more than you. I got back just before you. Brought your letter up because I thought you'd be here. Read mine. And drew my conclusions.'

'So you think it's all my fault?'

'It looks a bit that way. Mind you, I think Old P. was looking for an excuse. He didn't want the school to go any further downhill. First he talks about selling it, then he just says it's closing. Who'd buy this? It wants thousands spending on it - and a lot more pupils - to be viable.'

'Have you seen Helen?'

'I haven't seen anyone. Don't look so worried. I thought you were leaving anyway?'

'I was. But what about you? And the rest?'

'Old P. says he'll help us to find something. He's got plenty of contacts. I'm not bothered, nothing to keep me here now. Wait and see what he's got to say.'

The hours until six o'clock were long ones for Anthony. He sat in his room trying to work, but could not concentrate. The school was silent. Even Michael was not playing his radio. Once or twice Anthony went out on to the landing and peered over the banisters but he saw and heard nothing except the occasional ringing of a telephone. Who was answering it? Was it Helen? She'd have an awful lot of work to do in the next few weeks. What was her reaction to it all going to be? Her bracelet lay wrapped on his table alongside his letter of resignation, which he would no longer need. He was anxious to transcribe the poem on to the card but he knew that if he did it now he'd make far too many mistakes. It would have to wait until after this meeting, at least.

At ten minutes to six Michael came over and they walked down together. Mary was just coming along her corridor.

'Well, what about this, then?' she said, in an unusually subdued voice.

With an awful twinge, Anthony realised what a blow it must be to her, with only four years to go until her retirement. Oh God! Surely all this couldn't be his fault?

Many of the staff were already in the library, talking in low voices. As Anthony entered they all seemed to turn and stare him. In particular, Peter Ferguson gave him a look that made him shudder - a mixture of triumph, malice and mockery. Anthony turned his head away.

Promptly at six, Pearson entered. As usual he was smartly dressed and totally controlled, but he seemed to have aged ten years. There was no sign of Helen.

'I must apologise,' he began, 'for the short notice of the announcement. I realise that it has come as a great shock to you. It would not be appropriate for me to discuss with you the reasons for my change of plan, but I can assure you that it has not been made without a great deal of thought and discussion.'

With Helen, of course! Where was she? Anthony had so hoped she would be at this meeting.

'The decision once made,' Pearson continued, 'I put plans into action to inform all the parents at once, and yourselves immediately on your return. My wife,' he hesitated. Anthony held his breath. 'My wife is in full agreement with this decision. You may know that we have long planned to retire to Spain, where we own a villa. Mrs Pearson,' again he stopped and looked piercingly at Anthony, 'has therefore remained at the villa for the moment to prepare it for continuous occupation.'

He went on speaking but Anthony was not listening. He felt sick, dizzy, frantic. He just wanted to get out of that room. Helen still in Spain! Helen gone! Until when? The room started to go round. His hands clutched the hard wooden seat of the library chair. He must control himself. He couldn't faint or run out now. He couldn't! Whatever he did, he must not let Helen down. He tried taking deep breaths, hoping that no-one saw or heard. He started counting; one, two, three . . . He wasn't sure whether his face was bright red or deathly pale.

' . . . we will do all we can to find places for you elsewhere.' Pearson's voice came through a little more clearly. 'I've prepared some forms on which you may like to write your requirements. Mr Fulford and I will attempt to match them to schools where we have contacts. I will be speaking to you again, but for now I'll allow you to go to dinner and recover a little from the shock. Do please remember that we have half a term ahead of us, in which there are important public examinations, and your preparation and support of pupils at this time must take precedence over other concerns. If anyone wishes to speak to me urgently on any important matter, I will be in my study after dinner.'

Pearson took a last look at the assembled staff, his gaze lingering for a second or two on his distraught English assistant, then he strode out of the room.

With immense relief Anthony took another very deep breath and rose from his seat rather shakily. Mary was at his side.

'Are you all right?'

'Yes, I think so.'

'Something to eat will help. Come on!' She took his arm and he allowed himself to be led out of the library and down the hall.

There was a buzz of conversation in the dining room, but it wasn't lively. Anthony would have done anything to avoid that meal, but again it would have been letting Helen down; and Mary was right, he did feel better for some hot food.

There was a lot of speculation about the cause of the sudden closure and a lot of knowing looks in Anthony's direction. He had the feeling that they wanted him out of the way so that they could say what they really thought. But he couldn't be the first to leave the table - it would be too obvious. Art-and-Craft rescued him.

'We can talk all night but we won't know any more. I'm going to fill this form in - not that I want another teaching job - then get on as though nothing had happened. For now, anyway. I've got 'A' level students to prepare.'

The art master rose, picked up the form which they'd all been given, and left.

'He's right,' Edith Baines said. 'Nothing we can do at the moment. Concentrate on the boys. It'll be a shock for them, too. It doesn't affect me, but I hope you all get fixed up. I'm sure you will.'

She, too, pushed back her chair and left the room, followed by most of the others. Anthony hurried up to his room and threw himself on the bed.

'Oh, Helen, Helen, what have we done!' he choked into the pillow.

Chapter Twenty-Two

The next two weeks were extremely difficult for Anthony. Everyone was unsettled, yet they had to settle: especially those boys who were taking exams. And it was Anthony's job to make sure that they did. A daunting task for the person who was probably the most unsettled of all. Desperate to see, or at least hear from, Helen he struggled through the first days after the holiday with an enormous hollow where his stomach used to be. He was acutely aware that people were avoiding him, or talking with false cheerfulness about other things in his presence.

Helen's name was never mentioned; and had not been mentioned by Pearson himself since that initial meeting. As the parents' meeting had been attended by only senior staff Anthony did not know what had been said then. On Sunday evening an assembly for the boys had given Pearson the opportunity to reassure them that their future was being taken care of, and almost as an afterthought the Principal told them that 'Mrs Pearson is at present in Spain, organising our retirement home.'

Anthony felt that this was added merely to prevent questions and gossip among the boys. Since then there had been nothing. The woman who used to come in part-time to help Helen with secretarial duties was now working full-time and additional typing sent out to a local girl who was at secretarial college and doubtless grateful for the practice, and the money. Surely this was all Helen's job! With her years of experience and knowledge of the school, wasn't she the one to be organising all this extra administrative work?

Anthony searched his pigeonhole every day, but there was nothing. Of course, she wouldn't dare write from Spain! Not with Pearson sorting the mail, as he had been seen to do. Or perhaps she *had* written but the Head had confiscated the letter. No, Helen would be more careful than that. She must be planning to come back soon, maybe at the end of the week.

The weekend passed without any sign of her. Deeply troubled, Anthony dragged himself down for another Monday morning. There were a few consolations in his misery. Firstly, the boys had begun to settle down and were either doing exams or revising. Even the worst of them had been at Fieldhouse long enough to know that, at exam time, Pearson was particularly harsh on miscreants. Also, they had doubtless picked up the fact that the Principal's current mood was one of extreme irritation. Secondly, Pearson's other problems were keeping him out of the English room during Anthony's lessons. Or possibly there was another reason for his absence - his much-increased distaste for his English assistant. Whatever the reason, it was a relief to Anthony. A third crumb of comfort was that many of the boys seemed genuinely sorry that he wouldn't be teaching them any more. Perhaps he hadn't been so bad after all.

Many of the staff were now becoming philosophical about the school closure. Some who were very near retirement had decided that a couple of extra years of relaxation were probably worth the loss of income.

'I would have liked another two years at least,' Mary told him. 'But I don't really mind. I can go to my sister's. Perhaps I'll finally be able to persuade her to sell up and buy a cottage with me, somewhere nice.'

Art-and-Craft was delighted that the decision to become a full-time artist had been taken out of his hands. Oh, he'd filled in the Employment Requirements form provided by Pearson. But he had put down such stringent conditions, such as 'will teach for only a few hours a week' that he had few expectations of even the influential Eric Pearson being able to place him.

'I'm saving every ha'penny from now on,' he said. And I've told my mother to start getting the spare room ready for a bedroom-cum-studio: old furniture, no carpet: and just a bed in the corner. I can't wait to get started. I'll send you all an invitation to my first exhibition.'

Michael too, for all his earlier bravado, appeared relieved to have an excuse to leave the village over which the bells would ring out next spring for Pamela's wedding.

'Something will turn up. I've got faith in Old P. for that, at least. Maths teachers are always in demand. In any case I can always go home for a while and dig the garden.'

They all seemed to have somewhere else to go. Anthony too had filled in the form. He had to explore every avenue, otherwise Helen would think him a wastrel. And since some of the boys now seemed to like him, well, why not give teaching another chance, unless something else turned up?

It was on the Friday of the second week back that Anthony found a letter in his pigeonhole. Not from Spain, nor from Cedric. It was posted in London and he did not recognise the handwriting. With great anxiety he rushed up to his room and opened it with trembling fingers.

Inside was a brief note and another sealed envelope. The note read,

Dear Mr Dean,
My good friend Helen Pearson has sent this letter from Spain and asked me to forward it to you.

Yours
Marjorie West

Anthony's hands shook visibly as he tore open the enclosed envelope. Would it contain a declaration of love, the answer to his persistent question, news of her return - or something too agonisingly painful to think of?

My Dearest Anthony,

I am sending this via my dear friend Marjorie who will pass it on to you and ask no questions.

I was terribly distressed at having to leave so suddenly without being able to communicate with you in any way, except for a 'hint' to Jones, which I hope he passed on. I can hardly bear to imagine what your feelings must have been and must be now.

As you will have guessed, Eric heard rumours from an anonymous member of staff about our supposed activities (many of them untrue) and believed at least some of what he heard.

He does not know everything and I have tried to convince him that it was 'just a close friendship' in the hope that this will help you.

He whisked me off to Spain and then announced his plan to close the school. I was to stay here for the beginning of term, until the dust has settled a little, in the guise of 'preparing the house'.

I was, of course, planning to be back by now as there is a lot of work to be done and I am very anxious to see you. However, when Eric left, he inadvertently took my passport so I am unable to return until he sends it back to me.

I know that this is a terrible time for you but you must be brave. If you become desperate, go down to the pond and watch the dragonflies for me, or go up to the knoll and look at the view. Even, take a longer walk to the dewpond.

Wherever our bodies may be our hearts and minds will be united in these beautiful places, always.

Dear Anthony, let the love we have known give you courage in these next few difficult weeks and keep your fingers firmly crossed for a happier future.

Your ever-loving
Helen

Anthony sat looking down at the letter, which was a white blur on the table in front of him. What was he to make of it? Was she saying goodbye? No, Helen was good with words. If she had intended to say goodbye she would have done so, gently, tenderly, poetically. Here she was talking about 'planning to be back' and presumably would be when that bastard Pearson gave her back her passport. Anthony was in no doubt that he'd taken it deliberately. He couldn't keep her a prisoner in a foreign country though, surely? Eventually she'd have to see the British consul, accuse her husband of theft, or something. She'd also told him to keep his fingers crossed for a better future. She knew what he would want that to be. So no, it couldn't be goodbye.

But there was one thing - she hadn't put her address on the letter. She did not want him writing to her there, that was obvious. Why? Was it in case

191

Pearson paid her a flying visit, took the passport back himself, perhaps? She would not want a letter from him to arrive while her husband was there. Or was she afraid he'd give up what was left of his job and go out to join her?

Fortunately, Mrs West had put her own address on the note, so he could write back to Helen through her. He would tell her about his efforts to get a job and about the money from Cedric. He would tell her that now the decision to leave Fieldhouse had been made for him, she should take her chance with him. Otherwise she would be exiled in Spain and be stuck with Pearson forever. She had said that she liked Spain for holidays but she loved the English countryside so much that she did not want to be away from it for too long. That evening he wrote her a long letter. It made him feel so much better to be in communication with his soulmate again.

One day the following week, during a free period, Anthony went into the village stores, which had recently been rearranged as a rather cramped self-service shop. In order to fit everything into a small space the central shelves were very tall and even Anthony was hidden from the till as he examined the chocolate biscuits. His momentary pleasure at choosing these was utterly destroyed by the conversation that now began out of his sight, between the shop proprietor and two female customers.

They started by passing on village gossip about family and friends but the talk soon turned to the closure of Fieldhouse School.

'It'll be a bad day for us,' the shopkeeper said. 'Boys are always in here. Teachers too. Though I think the pubs will suffer more there.'

'She should have known better,' said Voice One in a tone of disgust.

'What's that? Have I missed something?' enquired Voice Two.

'Didn't you know? It's all because of that Mrs Pearson.'

'The Head's wife,' added the shopkeeper helpfully.

Anthony bent low over the bottom shelves although he had no interest in purchasing dried peas or rice.

'Yes, silly girl,' Voice One continued. 'Made a fool of herself with some young teacher.'

'Really? A woman in her position?'

'You'd be surprised what's gone on up there over the years. Anyway, the boss found out and she's been banished to Spain while he closes the school down.'

'They say it would have closed pretty soon anyway,' the shopkeeper's voice said. 'He's getting on a bit and it isn't the school it used to be - not half so many boys or staff. Place was getting a bit run down, so they say.'

'What's happened to the young man?' asked Voice Two.

'If he's still there he'll be out of a job like the rest, stupid young devil. The woman was twice his age!' the man's voice went on.

'Hey! There's hope for us yet, Ethel!' laughed Voice Two.

'I wouldn't lower myself,' replied Voice One haughtily.

'You're only jealous!'

'Rubbish! You wouldn't catch me throwing myself away on a silly young pup like that. Never brings any happiness. Stick to your own age, I always say.'

'Unless he's rich.'

'Young teachers are never rich. Stupid! Serves them all right.'

'Wonder what'll happen to the old place now?'

The two were still discussing this as they left the shop. Anthony straightened up. He knew his face was blazing. He wondered whether the shopkeeper had remembered he was there. Could he walk out quickly without buying anything? He might be accused of shoplifting if he acted suspiciously. That would be all he needed! Luckily, two more customers came into the shop. Anthony hastily paid for his biscuits and hurried out while the proprietor was in conversation with them and hardly gave him a glance.

Anthony walked slowly back to the school, hoping his burning cheeks would have regained their normal pallor before he arrived. He was distressed beyond words to hear his precious, beautiful relationship trivialised by village gossip and Helen branded as a silly woman old enough to know better. When she came back, she'd have to face all that.

'Pearson's got me a job!' Michael announced a week later. 'It's at a good school too, up in Norfolk. Nice area. Haven't even got to go for an interview. Just spoke to the Headmaster on the phone.'

'Well done!' Anthony was pleased for Michael but not a little envious.

Several of the staff had already benefited from Pearson's efforts on their behalf. Others were applying for advertised posts, with one or two interviews looming.

Anthony had also been applying. Two English posts had seemed hopeful, and a job in a library. He had also written for information about courses and a post-graduate diploma in education, although having taught for a year now, he wasn't sure about the latter. If he was going to struggle on with teaching he might as well find a post and get paid for his suffering. So far there had been no developments in any of these.

No developments regarding Helen either. Pearson had not been away for more than an hour or two so could not have paid any flying visits to Spain. Helen should have received his two letters by now, so he pinned his hopes on her reply. If only she had sent her address it would have made the whole process so much quicker.

Mary offered him tea and sympathy. She obviously knew everything so he did not attempt to conceal anything from her.

'I don't know what to do,' he told her.

'There's nothing much you can do, except soldier on until the end of term,' she replied.

The end of term! It seemed like an eternity away. It was already four weeks since he had seen Helen: four agonising weeks! How would he get though another four? And what would happen then?

Reading his thoughts, Mary asked, 'If you haven't got fixed up by then, where will you go?'

'I haven't a clue.'

'If you're stuck you must stay with me. For heaven's sake don't be homeless! You've got enough to worry about as it is.'

Anthony was very grateful. 'Thanks. I may have to do just that.'

'I'm so sorry for you, and Helen,' she went on. 'It's dreadful to love in a situation fraught with difficulties. I know. I've done it.' Anthony must have looked surprised, for she went on, 'I loved a married man once, a teacher at one of my schools. It still hurts. So you see, I do understand.'

'What happened - if you want to tell me?'

'It ended bitterly. He didn't want to rock the boat. Or perhaps he didn't think me worth rocking the boat for. I'm not exactly Julie Christie.'

'I'm not God's gift to women, either,' Anthony said.

'There's nothing wrong with you. But anyway, it's about finding the right person. Then looks shouldn't matter. Some of the plainest people I know are very happily married. Some of the most attractive are not.'

'Like Helen?'

'Yes, I suppose so. I just hope things work out for both of you. You're such lovely people and deserve something good. Everyone has one great love in their life, they say. If this is yours and Helen's, I'm keeping my fingers crossed for you.'

Bless you, Mary, he thought.

'Ferguson's got a job now!'

'The bastard!' Anthony grimaced at the mention of that offensive name.

'Thought I'd warn you,' Michael went on, 'before you heard it in Assembly.'

'Assembly?'

'Yes, Pearson's very proud of the fact that he's found his talented games-master a post at a prestigious school. He's going to announce it in Assembly. So that we can all clap!'

'Like hell!'

Michael was right. The Principal was 'delighted to announce that Peter Ferguson, whose skill has brought so much credit to Fieldhouse . . .' Brought it down, you mean, thought Anthony. ' . . . has been offered a post at one of the country's leading schools.'

Michael had been right about something else, too. When Pearson had finished his announcement, everybody clapped. Except Anthony. As he was sitting at the back he didn't think anyone would notice but when the applause died down he saw the Principal's eyes fixed on him.

Pearson gave him a look of utter disgust. At that moment Anthony finally realised that he had no hope at all of emulating the success of the games master. There would be no new teaching post for him. Pearson would move heaven and earth to prevent it.

'You fool! He saw you!' hissed Michael, as they left the gym. 'What good did it do you? Talk about a masochist!'

'I'm past being done good to!' Anthony muttered.

'You don't help yourself. For God's sake - you can't afford to be proud.'

'When you've lost everything you can do as you like,' was Anthony's response.

That night he stood gazing out of his window as he had done so many times before, in particular on that memorable eve of this year when he'd been full of hope for his new-found love and in distress at her absence. He was in distress at her absence now, but he had little hope. The moon, glinting coldly back from the surface of the pond, offered no comfort this time. Helen might be seeing it too, but it wouldn't bring her back. Pearson would not let her come back. Why didn't she defy him? Had she given in, defeated? She had told Anthony to be brave and keep his fingers crossed and he was trying. But she hadn't replied to his letters and he was beginning to fail.

At the age of twenty-two Anthony felt that the greatest moment in his life was already over. Mary had said that everybody has one great love. He was positive that he had met, loved and almost certainly lost, his. There would never be another Helen and if he ever did have another relationship it would be judged against this and found wanting. He knew she was the right woman for him. He may be young, inexperienced, and foolish - but he was absolutely positive about that. And as he watched the reflection of a dark cloud slowly blot out the moon from the water's surface, he also knew with a sickening certainty that she was gone.

.

Chapter Twenty-Three

'Oh, Lord!' Anthony looked with horror at the 'O' Level English paper that his pupils were sitting somewhere in the school that morning. The revision group he was supervising at the time looked up from their history exercise with surprise at his involuntary groan. But he could not suppress it. This was appalling!

His 'O' Level group had been very badly behaved until the last couple of weeks, when they had finally seemed to realise the proximity of their exams. Anthony didn't have time to retrace the whole year's work again so he had endeavoured to pick out the sections of the course which he thought most likely to be examined, both in Language and Literature. He had concentrated their revision work on those areas. But the exam paper had been set by someone whose ideas did not match his own. His pupils would not be able to answer anything! It was a disaster. Not so much for the boys, perhaps. They could blame their failure on the anxieties caused by the school closure, and no doubt most of them would be able to re-sit the exam at their new schools. For him it would be the absolutely final blow to any chance of ever teaching again. Eric Pearson would slaughter him - in words, in references. The results of the exams would not be out until after the school closed, but the likelihood was that he'd still be looking for a job by then, in competition with twenty or so other English masters with brilliant 'O' and 'A' Level results behind them. Not a hope! There would be newly qualified teachers applying too, of course. No-one would know what they could do, but the Heads would know exactly what Anthony could do. And they would not be impressed.

In any case, Pearson would not need to wait until the results came out. As soon as the exams were finished, the whole school would know that Anthony's classes had not been able to cope with them, had been taught, if they had been taught anything, all the wrong things. The boys would run out of the examination room waving their papers and shouting to the world about their difficulties. Even now, Pearson was probably looking at the paper, just as Anthony was, and realising, having seen much of Anthony's teaching, that it would not enable any but the very brightest to succeed. He would be able to add a few extra lines to Anthony's references long before August - today, in fact!

Later that evening he wrote to Helen once more. He had no idea whether his letters were reaching her. He wondered if Mrs West had been told not to send them on. He would try again, but for how long should he keep on trying?

My Dearest Helen,
I have not received anything from you so I don't know whether or not you have had my other letters. I did send Mrs West some money to

cover the postage.

I am in despair at not hearing from you. I don't even know if you are still alive. Please try and communicate with me in some way. The others are all asking about you too. Everyone in the school wonders what has happened to you.

Most of the staff who want one seem to have found a post now, or have interviews lined up. I have nothing. After today I know that I won't teach again. The 'O' Level papers were a disaster. Everything that I had taught was left out. The results will be appalling.

I will continue to look for some other job, of course. It would help me a lot if I knew what your plans are. I'm still waiting for an answer to my question. You did promise. I can't believe that you would treat me this way by choice. We were so happy and I had so hoped that we would be starting a new life together after this summer.

You said you would give me an answer at half term and that has long passed. Is your silence that answer?

The letter went on for several more pages, the last written through blinding tears. It chronicled all Anthony's misery, his love and longing, his hopes and dreams, his fears… When it was finished he made himself some coffee and sat down to read it through, again in tears. Then he slowly tore it into several pieces and threw it in the bin.

He took a clean sheet of paper and wrote,

My Beloved Helen,
I have heard nothing from you and I am desperate. Please, please write to me. I love you more than anything in the world.
        Your heartbroken
        Anthony

This brief, agonised note was the one that he sent to Mrs West with a plea that *she* should tell him some news of Helen. Once again, he could only wait.

'Have you heard anything from Helen?' Mary asked. Once again she had taken pity on Anthony's increasingly pale, drained face and low spirits. She had, of course, heard all about the English exams.

'No, nothing since that first note. I've written three times. But I don't know if my letters are reaching her.'

Mary was silent for a moment, busily making tea in the corner of her room. Eventually she turned, brought him over a mug, and said, 'You won't mind me saying this?'

'Say anything, please.'

'Well, is it possible that she's not answering because she thinks it's best?'

Anthony's legs turned to jelly. They seemed to have spent much of the last year, certainly the last few weeks, in that shaky state. Mary had put into words his worst fears, those which he was trying at all costs to keep at bay. He was trying to convince himself of all sorts of reasons why Helen was not replying, why she had not returned.

'Go on,' he managed to say.

'Look at it this way,' she continued, sitting down beside him on the edge of the bed. 'Helen was very fond of you. I could tell that. And I know she hadn't been happy in the past, isn't happy now. But there's a huge difference in your age and circumstances. She'd guess that any relationship might not last long. I don't know for certain, but it may be that she thinks the kindest, most loving thing to do is to set you free.'

'I don't want to be free.'

'I know you don't now. She knows that too, and I'm sure she would hate to hurt you. But human beings are very resilient. I don't know what would have happened if the school had carried on. But as it is she perhaps sees this as a way of . . . er . . . letting you out into the world to find a new career and eventually a young lady of your own age. I might be wrong of course, but . . . '

Anthony stared down at his shoes. The pattern on the carpet seemed to be moving, as though his feet were standing in water.

'She wouldn't just not reply,' he said, trying to keep his voice steady, and failing. 'She wouldn't just abandon me, she . . . ' The words were drowned in a sob he couldn't control.

'Sometimes it's the best way,' Mary said gently, putting her hand on his shaking shoulder. 'In the long run it's probably easier this way than some tragic, agonising goodbye, although it seems very terrible to you now. In the future, you'll thank her for it. I'm sure she does it for love. She wants you to make a new life.'

'I don't want a new life, any sort of life, without Helen!'

He was sobbing uncontrollably now, the carpet swirling up around his knees. Mary got up and handed him a box of tissues.

'Here. I'll be back in a minute.'

She patted him on the shoulder again and went resolutely in the direction of the bathroom.

When she returned he had composed himself and was looking out of her window, very shame-faced.

'I'm sorry,' he said as she came in.

'There's nothing to be sorry for. There's nothing wrong with caring deeply about something. What are you going to do now?'

'Nothing much.'

'Then we'll go for a walk.'

She put on a pair of outdoor shoes and bustled him through the door. Still dazed and shaken, he was willing to be organised by anybody who would be nice to him.

They walked along the lane in front of the school and out into the countryside. Mary tried to make cheerful conversation and Anthony tried to answer cheerfully. Both were struggling. But the afternoon was fine and it did Anthony a lot of good to be out among the beauties of nature, except that everything reminded him of Helen. He almost went to pieces again when he saw a line of poppies edging a cornfield. He stopped. Mary looked up and saw the expression in his watering eyes.

'Helen loved poppies.'

'She still does. So do you - and you will always.'

Mary was right. Helen had opened his eyes to so many wonderful things that he had never really noticed before. They would stay with him all his life. How wise these women were! If only he could be like them.

When they arrived back at school, Mary turned to him with a determined look.

'Anthony, if you ever need a roof over your head, or any kind of help whatsoever, contact me. At once. Any time. Whether I'm at my sister's or wherever. I'll keep in touch with you. If you need a bed, a meal, money or just a friend, don't hesitate. And that's not an offer,' she finished, 'it's an order!'

Anthony's eyes filled up again. Impulsively, he bent forwards and kissed her on the forehead, then dashed upstairs before he disgraced himself in front of her again.

The end of term was looming. Despite the absence of Helen, and Anthony's misery, the time had passed much more quickly than he'd expected. Was that because he didn't really want the term to end? The longer it went on the more chance there was of Helen returning or at least of him hearing something of, or from, her.

In any case, he still had no job and nowhere to live. The latter worried him a good deal but he could do nothing about it until he had sorted out the former. All he had was that offer from Mary, although Art-and-Craft had told him to come and share his studio any time and Michael had offered to put him up once he was settled into his new job. All the staff seemed to be fixed up now, either to retire to their potting sheds, take up new posts or, of course, become famous artists. They couldn't praise Eric Pearson highly enough for his efforts on their behalf.

He had certainly done them proud. He had personally arranged jobs for all but two, who had applied on their own behalf. For these, he had presumably provided such glowing references that they were both appointed despite having very well qualified opposition. All fixed up, then - except Anthony.

Conversation about posts faltered when he was within earshot. Colleagues had stopped asking him whether he had found anything yet. They knew perfectly well that he hadn't - and why. Most of them felt desperately sorry for him but there was nothing they could do except promise to let him know if they heard of anything suitable. Those closest to him offered sympathy, the rest avoided the subject, or him.

Pearson had hardly spoken to him except to give instructions or express displeasure. That was nothing new, but now it contrasted sharply with the Head's uncharacteristically helpful attitude towards his other displaced staff. Since the dreadful 'O' Levels Pearson had been, if possible, even more icy. Anthony's future had never been mentioned. He had had none of the discussions, offers of help, information about vacancies or application progress reports that seemed to be an almost daily occurrence for the rest of the staff. It was quite obvious that if Pearson heard of any jobs for English teachers he was not going to pass that information on to Anthony.

Likewise, somewhere along the line, Anthony's own applications were failing. He had been quickly rejected for several teaching posts and for the librarianship course. So far he'd failed to get an interview to do a diploma in education (not that he really wanted to). Neither had he had any luck with applications to local government or industry. He had hoped to at least get an interview or two, but there was nothing. He knew exactly what the problem was. It was that part of the application form that said, *"Referees: Please give the name of your current employer."* One did not cross Eric Pearson.

If I am partly responsible for bringing down Fieldhouse School and its Principal, like Michael said, it was certainly not intended, but I'm going down with it, he thought. He couldn't help likening his punishment to that of the Captain of the Titanic. In order to pass the lonely evenings and take his mind off Helen for a while, he'd been reading all that the library had to offer. One book that had fascinated him was about the ill-fated liner. He felt a great deal of sympathy for Captain Smith. Whatever degree of responsibility that august gentleman had had for the catastrophe, he certainly did not cause it deliberately, and he had, of course, paid the ultimate price and gone down with his ship. Anthony visualised him standing, alone with his feelings, on the bridge as the water came rushing up to meet him: an unimaginably terrible moment.

Anthony had not been involved in the deaths of fifteen hundred people but he *had* caused immense disruption to the lives of a large number of staff, their families and friends, the pupils, their parents and families, domestic and ground staff, village tradespeople, and landladies. Even the local church was affected (the boys and staff all contributed to the collection and some took part in church activities, youth groups and the choir), as well as suppliers, taxi drivers, Mr Williams, the bus company . . . The more he thought about it, the more appalled he became.

'Don't worry about all that!' Michael said when Anthony expressed his concern. 'The school would have closed soon anyway.'

'But Pearson was originally intending to sell it as a going concern. Then there wouldn't have been all this disruption.'

'Nobody would buy it as a school. Times are changing. Forget it,' Michael said firmly. 'These things happen all the time. We'll all go and live, work and spend our money in other places, so somebody else will benefit instead. That's life!'

Anthony was not consoled. What would happen to Helen's beloved pool? Some builder would fill it full of rubble from the house and destroy it.

Helen, my love, he agonised, you must come back and see it once more!

Ten days before the end of term. A white envelope was in his pigeonhole, postmarked London and in the same handwriting as before. Anthony's heart leapt up to the ceiling then plummeted into the floor as he felt its thinness. It could not contain another envelope. With palpitating fear he drew out the one folded sheet.

> *Dear Mr Dean,*
>
> *I have two apologies to make. One is for not replying sooner and the other is for the delay in sending your recent letters to Spain until a few days ago.*
>
> *I sent off your first one (thank you for the money for postage) but since then a family bereavement has kept me away from home for most of the last few weeks.*
>
> *Unfortunately I am unable to give you any news of Helen as I have heard nothing myself other than a brief note of thanks she sent on receipt of my letter containing yours. That was several weeks ago. I have no doubt that she is extremely busy organising her new life.*
>
> *If I do receive anything from her I will let you know if you send me your new address.*
>
> *I wish you every success in whatever you plan to do after Fieldhouse closes.*
>
> > *Yours sincerely,*
> > *Marjorie West*

Hope. Despair. Which should he be feeling? Helen hadn't been receiving his letters! But she'd had the first one. He tried to remember what he'd written. He thought he'd been fairly positive, especially as she had talked of returning very soon. He had expressed hopes of finding a new job and somewhere to live, where she could join him. She hadn't had the later ones that told of his growing misery, his failures, his fears that their relationship was over. She probably thought he was very busy preparing to start *his* new life and that she would have the option of sharing it with him.

But that mention of the 'brief note' shattered his foolish efforts at hope. Helen had had the first letter and hadn't replied, even to her best friend, and she hadn't attempted to write again.

He took out the only photograph he had of her, except for that strained school photo. He'd taken it up on the Downs one day, just before half term.

She was laughing and happy, her hair blowing in the wind, the fabric of her skirt swirling around her legs. She looked so young, so lovely, so desirable, so loving. Mary was right, of course she was. Helen was setting him free because she loved him dearly. That love showed in her face.

But he wasn't free. He would never be free. He was in chains, forever.

Chapter Twenty-Four

The last day of the school year, July 1970. Anthony took his watch from the bedside table and strapped it on his wrist. It was six o'clock. He got up, washed, dressed and made his bed.

All his belongings were packed neatly in the corner. The room was now almost exactly as he had entered it nearly a year before. But he was very different. Then, he had been hopeful of bright prospects for his future. Now . . .

He stood in front of the mirror carefully knotting the tie Helen had given him last Christmas. He recalled wearing it on New Year's Eve when he drank that emotional toast to them both - to her return, to their growing love, to the possibility of a future together. Now, there was nothing to drink to.

He fixed the gold tie-pin, put on his best jacket and combed his hair. Then he picked up an envelope from his table. It was a message for Michael. Should he push it under his colleague's door? He decided not to. It might wake him. Anthony replaced the letter on the table where so many other letters had lain during the year, one significant one especially. If he had delivered that letter to Pearson at the first half term and left at Christmas - but by then he already loved Helen too much to leave her.

A look around the room, then he slipped out quietly and descended the stairs. There was Helen's door, only she was no longer behind it. How many times had he felt miserable at the thought of her being there with Pearson? What he would give if only she could be in there now! The library door was closed but he knew there were no flowers in the hearth, no artists busily and happily painting them, no enraptured onlooker. Nor was there a woman with red-brown hair, sorting books.

Anthony opened the heavy front door and walked out into a glorious morning. Birds were singing and searching for food along the hedge. He walked across the dew-damp lawn, his well-polished shoes leaving a dark trail. His eyes were as moist as the grass as he glanced back towards the house and noticed his track. He'd seen just such a trail in his first week at Fieldhouse and realised that Helen was out early. Was that when it began, when he discovered that she wandered around alone in the early morning? Or had it already started, on that first afternoon when she plied him with cake and sympathy? He couldn't pinpoint the moment. All he could be sure of was that it had been heaven and it was over. For ever.

Tears prevented him from seeing much of the Downs beyond the pond. But he didn't need to see them. He knew exactly how they looked, could imagine the hedge opening onto the white track at the place where the poppy had been, the track that led up on to the ridge. He could visualise the hollow where they had sat and embraced out of sight of the school, the knoll to which they had run so joyfully to clasp each other in its shadows, and way beyond that, the dewpond with its one missing blade of grass.

He stopped at the edge of the pool. It was too early yet for the dragonflies, but they would be here later, flitting over the surface, packing as much activity as they could into their brief lives.

From his pocket he took out a piece of folded paper. He opened it carefully. Inside was a field poppy, crumpled but still blood red against the white. He had picked it yesterday from beside their path. It may even have grown from a seed of that one he had found in his first week and had wanted to give to Helen. That was how she found out he loved poppies and painted the poppy placecard for the first dinner. It was in his top pocket now. He drew it out and gazed at it, taking off his glasses and brushing his hand roughly across his eyes.

Mr Anthony Dean, and beside his name, the delicately painted flower. He could visualise her, head bent over her paintbox, painting it especially for him, even though she hardly knew him then. He replaced the card in his pocket, lifted the pressed poppy from the paper and cast it on to the water. As he did so, the first dragonfly skimmed low over the pond.

'Poppies and dragonflies! They are like our love, Helen,' he said aloud, in a quiet, choked voice, 'fragile and short-lived. But beautiful. So, so beautiful.'

A cool wind blew from the Downs, wafting the poppy away from him across the surface of the pool, which rippled and fragmented Anthony's reflection like a shattered mirror.

He brushed his hand across his eyes again, straightened his tie and his back, and walked slowly but steadily into the water.

PART FOUR: LAURA MARSHALL'S STORY 2005-6

Chapter Twenty-Five

The gravel crunched beneath my wheels as the car turned into the drive of Fieldhouse. I felt very much the same as that shy, seventeen-year-old who had had such a strange experience here twenty-five years before. The main difference seemed to be that this time I was driving myself. But there was another difference too - now Fieldhouse was mine. I had come to take up my inheritance.

The Aunts who had held eccentric sway over the house and garden for so long were all gone, except Auntie Janet, who was eighty and frail. She and Aunt Eva, who had recently died, had come to an arrangement with me. I was to have Fieldhouse immediately, on condition that I looked after Auntie Janet for the rest of her life.

This agreement suited me perfectly. I needed to get some order into my life after a quarter of a century of difficulties: a far from brilliant university record, a marriage to the wrong person, and the loss of two babies followed by a hysterectomy. There had followed two or three unspectacular attempts to revive my career, the inevitable divorce and a return to live with my parents. Now I intended to settle permanently at Fieldhouse.

From the exterior the house did not seem to have changed. The grounds looked much the same, although not so well-tended as when all the Aunts were in full swing. There was a glint of sunlight in the far corner - reflections in the pond. So that was still here too. But was *he* still here, I wondered?

Fieldhouse was haunted. At least it had seemed so to the impressionable, dreamy girl that I had been all those years ago. On one memorable visit I had seen a 'ghost' - and fallen in love for the first time.

Most of my romantic notions had been destroyed since then. My adult life had not lived up to my dreams. No-one else had seen my ghost and I don't think they had believed me. Still, I couldn't help wondering if there had been any truth in my imaginings. One thing struck me as odd. At that time I had been just a few years younger than my ghost, now I was almost twice his age. If he were still around he probably wouldn't bother appearing to a mature woman fast approaching middle-age!

Mrs Adams answered my ring. She had been caring for Auntie Janet for several months. Now the arrangement was that she would come one day a week and any other time that I needed to be absent. This gave me some freedom and seemed an excellent plan.

'Here you are at last, my dear,' Auntie Janet greeted me. 'Welcome home. I'm sure we'll manage very well together.'

I kissed her. 'I'm sure we will,' I said.

'You must do whatever you like with the house. It's yours. You might even open up those horrible attics.'

'I might, but not yet. I'll need to live here for a while first and see how I feel about everything. I don't suppose I'll change very much.'

After tea and cakes I went up to my room to unpack. All that I had so far was what I had been able to fit into my car. I'd hired a 'man and van' to bring the rest of my belongings from my parents' retirement home in Eastbourne where I had been living for the last year. I had spent a great deal of time in the last twenty-five years lugging my stuff around the country. It would be nice to have somewhere that I could feel was more permanent.

In the car I had packed necessities and some of my treasures. From the centre of a suitcase I lifted a flat object wrapped carefully in a thick towel. From the folds I took a framed photograph. A school photograph. It was a conventional enough school photo. The staff sat on chairs in a stiff line. In front of them were two rows of smaller boys sitting on the grass. Behind the teachers, the older boys were arranged in height order. At each end of the back row was a young male teacher, one dark, one fair. The photo was dated 'Fieldhouse School May 1970.'

'There,' I said aloud, 'you're back at Fieldhouse, Anthony! I don't suppose you expected to come back here, did you? But here we both are. I hope we'll be very happy.'

I pressed my lips to the glass, beneath which the dark-haired young teacher looked out with a faint, sad smile. Then I removed a china plate from a hook on the wall and hung the photograph in its stead, above the fireplace. It was the first of my possessions for which I found a place.

That evening, Auntie Janet and I sat in her room, which was next to mine. At least, I sat. Auntie reclined in bed. She told me that her legs were not too good and she usually went to bed early with a hot drink, a book and some needlework.

'Now we can talk comfortably,' she said.

I had always got on well with Auntie Janet and I was very happy to oblige. I took a tray containing hot chocolate and biscuits upstairs and sat in her bedside armchair, knitting and catching up with all her news. Auntie Janet was also busy. Her age and arthritis did not prevent her making articles for local fund-raisers.

When she had filled me in on all the village gossip and news of other relatives, I ventured to say, 'Did anyone ever . . . well, you remember what happened when I was here before?'

'The "ghost" you mean? I wasn't going to mention it until you did.'

'Did anyone ever see him again?' I asked. I wasn't sure what answer I wanted to hear.

'No, never. At least, they never said. I certainly didn't. I couldn't even see him when you said he was there, remember?'

206

'I remember.'

Auntie Janet laughed. 'You were so insistent, Laura, and I could see nothing. That's what comes of me not being a sensitive young lady, I suppose,' she finished tactfully. She still didn't believe me.

'You don't believe I really saw him, do you? Nobody does.'

'It's not what people do or don't see, it's what *you* believe,' said the old lady, sipping her chocolate.

That was what was so comforting about Auntie Janet, she never put you down.

'Yes, I understand that, but if it was all in my mind, how did I recognise him when I saw that photo?'

'You were a sensitive young lady, like I said. There are things that just can't be explained. Some people have a talent for them. Nothing like that's happened to you since?'

'No, nothing at all. But I've never forgotten. Never.' I didn't tell her about hanging up the photograph in my room. She would see it eventually.

'And you haven't come to any conclusion about it over the years?' Auntie Janet asked.

'No, but I've thought about it, about him, a lot. Especially when I've been beside water, watching dragonflies. I see they're still here.'

'Oh, yes, we still get them every summer. Not so many though. Their habitats have gone.'

Auntie Janet, like me, had always been an ardent conservationist. I suspect that the pond would have disappeared years ago if it wasn't for her. One or two of the other Aunts had considered it smelly and dangerous and when they learned of Anthony's death they had been very keen to get rid of it. Janet wouldn't hear of it.

'We need more wetlands, not less,' she had said, as proud of her pond as if it were some massive drainage system.

That night, before getting into bed, I pulled back my curtains and looked out of the window. My room was at the back of the house, overlooking the garden and the Downs beyond. Tonight the moon gleamed on the still surface of the pond. That was where I had first seen him and where I later learned he had taken his life. Tomorrow the water would again be alive with dragonflies, just as it was when I looked up and saw him there, just as it was when he taught here. We come and go but nature goes on, I thought. If we care for it, as Auntie Janet would say. I also had to go on. I couldn't live in the past, couldn't afford to. I had to find ways of supplementing the small inheritance that went with the house and which would soon be used up in maintenance and repairs.

'I've had a few ideas,' I told Auntie Janet at breakfast next morning. 'While I'm getting the house and garden sorted out . . .'

'Yes, I'm afraid it's been rather neglected in the last few years. We couldn't manage it, you see.'

'I know. But I'll sort it out somehow. While I'm doing it I thought I'd write. I might earn a bit. And I'd like to research the history of the house from when it was built. I could incorporate local history too, and sell the booklet in the village.'

'That sounds interesting.'

'Then I might work on a booklet of local walks. I could illustrate it. Then after that - well, I think I'll turn the house into a luxury hotel!' I laughed.

The next four weeks were very full. I started by giving the house a thorough clean. The attics would have to wait, though. I couldn't face thirty years' accumulation of spiders' webs just yet. I had plans for the garden too, but I decided to leave them until the following year. It certainly needed some attention. The Aunts had had a succession of retired men earning an extra few pounds by helping in the garden. None of them had been employed for enough hours to do anything other than keep the place tidy. The first one had been Mr Tompkins, who had, with some persuasion from Auntie Janet, eventually told all he, and presumably the rest of the village, knew about Anthony's story. He and Mrs Tompkins now lay in the churchyard and when I took flowers to my Aunts' graves I took some for them too. He had been very fond of the Fieldhouse garden and he would certainly feature in my 'History', for which I was busy collecting information.

I had started this project right away as it gave me a purpose. It would get me back into writing, something I had not done for a while. Eventually I hoped to write something more commercial, short stories for example. I wanted to illustrate my book about the house so I had also started to draw it from different angles. This made me feel that I was doing something useful towards my future income and at the same time I could think up plots for my stories.

So I already had plenty to do, even before Auntie Janet made another suggestion.

'Have you ever thought about tracing our ancestors?'

Auntie Janet was actually my father's cousin and the daughter of Aunt Edna, who had been the oldest of the group of ladies living here. The others had been related by marriage to each other but less directly related to me.

'You mean the Bennetts?'

'Yes. Your grandfather, William, was my father Charles's brother.'

'Great-grandfather was also William, I think.'

'Complications right away! He was my grandfather, of course. Could be interesting. I wish I'd done it years ago. Mother could have told me so much. Find out all you can now, while you are still young enough. Ask your father what he knows.'

A week or two later I was shopping in Winchester. It was a trip I had begun to like very much. The drive over the Downs gave me a superb view for miles around. I loved the wide-open spaces and the feeling of freedom. There was a lay-by at the highest point where I stopped to admire the scenery and think.

'Too much thinking's bad for you, Laura,' Auntie Janet was always saying to me.

She laughed about it but I knew that she understood me, probably better than my own parents. She had also had a lot of unhappiness in her life. Her first boyfriend had been killed in 1945, in the last few months of war. He was nineteen. Later she had married but it hadn't lasted long. Like me, she had no children and had eventually gone back to live with her parents. When her father, Charles, died in the early 1970s she and her mother, Aunt Edna, teamed up with Edna's cousin Audrey and two sisters, Elsie and Eva, who were relations of Audrey's. Together they had bought Fieldhouse from a builder who had begun to renovate it. He had demolished the modern classroom blocks and gym and removed all the school fittings from the old part of the house, knocking some smaller rooms into one in the process. Then he had run out of money, despite selling the playing field back to a neighbouring farmer to help pay for the work.

The Aunts had bought the house cheaply and had spent many years and much effort trying to 'make a silk purse out of a sow's ear' as Auntie Janet put it. Fortunately the library had been left more or less as it was, and the attics had not been touched since the ill-fated builder went bankrupt just as his men had started on clearing them. The Aunts had them boarded up and today they remained in exactly the same condition as when I had first seen them - with a quarter of a century's more dust. I had great plans to turn them into studios one day, but not enough money to do it.

That was one of the things I was thinking of as I sat on the top of the Downs. Another plan had suggested itself to me. The fact that Fieldhouse had once been a school and was situated in an attractive part of the country made me toy with the idea of opening one of those adult activity holiday centres - painting, walking, botany, that kind of thing. If that scheme didn't look like working, I could at least open a guest-house. Not the luxury hotel I'd joked about, but a comfortable country holiday home. When the time came that I was left alone there, I would need an income, company and a use for all that space.

My head was full of exciting schemes but there was still room in it for Anthony. I was probably being extremely foolish but I couldn't help thinking of it as his home too. Auntie Janet was right about the thinking - it *was* bad for me. The point was that I knew nothing about him, his real home, his parents, where he came from. For me he existed only at Fieldhouse. If I knew more about him would it end his haunting of me?

'Family Tracer.' That looked as though it might be the sort of thing that Auntie Janet had talked about. My morning's shopping and exhibition visiting

had left me ready for lunch. All I needed was something to read. I browsed in the newsagent's, pushing my way past all those men, young and old, who seem to have nothing better to do than stand looking through magazines for half the day. I managed to squeeze my arm between two stout young lads and take a copy of the genealogy magazine down from the shelves. Previously I had thought of ancestry tracing as something done by visiting Americans and the aristocracy. But a quick flick through this magazine opened up a whole new world to me. This was going to be an interesting lunch.

I was lucky to find a table by the window in the small vegetarian restaurant that I had discovered on a previous visit. I ordered a mushroom and nut bake and settled down to look through my latest purchase. It seemed to contain everything I needed to get me started. There were articles on a great variety of subjects from using parish records to searching for pioneer ancestors in Australia. I obviously had a lot to learn. There was advice on using computers and the Internet and plenty of interesting adverts too, even lists of people who would do your research for you.

Eventually I came to the most immediately useful part of the magazine for me - lists of names which people were researching. As my lunch got cold, I ran my finger down the list. Baker ... Barber ... Bennett - several Bennetts in fact. None of them were from the area of the Shropshire border where my father's family originated. Still, I could check every month. I could visit something called the Family Record Centre. And, best of all, I could advertise for the very names, dates and places I wanted.

Between now-cold mouthfuls I continued to look down the list, seeking other family names. Carter . . . Dawson . . . Dean - Dean! There were two adverts for nineteenth-century Deans. Not much use to me, but . . . I could advertise for Anthony too, couldn't I? I didn't want to cause any distress to his family but it was thirty-five years ago now. His parents would be quite elderly, if they were still alive. I felt I had a good excuse anyway. As the owner of Fieldhouse and the prospective author of a book about it, I needed to trace all its history, of which Anthony was a part - a significant part if all that I knew was true. His love affair had caused the school to close and he had died tragically there, perhaps the only person in the house's history to do so.

When I showed 'Family Tracer' to Auntie Janet she was full of enthusiasm and spent most of the evening looking through it. She suggested that I start by advertising for information on my great-great-grandfather.

'I was thinking of advertising for information about Anthony, too,' I told her.

She looked at me over her glasses. 'You'll never rest until you've got to the bottom of that story, will you Laura?'

'No, I don't think I will. Anyway, I want him in my 'History of Fieldhouse,' I said firmly.

'Oh yes, he should be in that,' she conceded. 'Just be careful you don't open a can of worms.'

'I'll be very discreet,' I promised.

Chapter Twenty-six

I waited eagerly for a reply to my first advertisements in *'Family Tracer'*, one for my great-great-grandfather and one which read *'DEAN Anthony: Fieldhouse School 1969/70'*. I was also anxious to complete the refurbishment of the room next to mine as a study and fix up a computer in there. Then I'd be able to do all those exciting things that I'd read about in the magazine.

I made little progress with either of these schemes. My redecoration proceeded slowly and I awaited the arrival of the postman every day without any luck. I re-advertised the following month. Still nothing came. I began to lose my initial enthusiasm. Perhaps this wasn't the way. After all, it was totally dependent on someone with a connection seeing the advert.

My other project was some work around the pool. Although I had decided to leave the bulk of the garden until next year, this area had become very overgrown and it was no longer possible to walk right round the water. The pond itself wanted clearing out but I couldn't tackle that. I'd have to try and afford to pay someone to do it. I could tackle the path clearing, though, and tidy up the pond edge.

Working down there on a succession of dove-grey autumn days was pleasant enough, but as I stood in the ooze at the pond's edge, cutting down reeds and water weed I could not help thinking about Anthony. How could he bring himself to walk into that dark water, over the soft, thick mud at the bottom, until he got to the deep part in the middle (no-one seemed to know *how* deep) and then drown himself? What state of utter hopelessness must a clever young man on the threshold of life have been in to do such a thing? And what amazing courage! I had been in despair on many occasions but I am sure I couldn't have done that. I'm just not brave enough. I hate water over my head, and the feeling of choking, even in a shower.

The white wooden gate that had led out into the fields on my earlier visits had been replaced by a tall wrought iron one with a padlock. It was still the gateway to the Downs though, and I was always anxious to finish my work and go up there, but Auntie Janet advised against it.

'It's not safe to be wandering about there on your own these days. Better wait until you've got someone to go with.'

'I don't suppose you and Auntie Audrey would be so keen to go searching for intruders in the house these days!' I said, reminding Auntie Janet of the time when I had told them that I thought Anthony was a burglar who had probably run upstairs. 'You had a candlestick to hit him with, and Audrey had a stout walking stick.'

'She would have used it, too,' laughed Auntie Janet. 'Audrey was completely fearless, even in her old age.'

'Lucky for Anthony that he wasn't really there,' I said, rather illogically.

A few days later I was sitting in my favourite spot at the round table in the library window, which caught the sun for most of the day. I was always careful, even now, to leave the heavy library door wide open when I was in there alone. I did not wish to be cornered again by any ghosts, however harmless they may be. I propped the door open with an old flat-iron that had belonged to Aunt Edna's grandmother.

The autumn sun was providing a succession of warm spots for Cola, Auntie Janet's cat, to rest in. He was so called because Auntie had been drinking that beverage when he appeared in the garden one day a few years ago. He had rubbed himself, purring, against her legs. She had carried on drinking, he had carried on purring, and by the evening he had a place to sleep, food and water, and a name. No-one ever claimed him, so here he was, a very comfortable addition to the household. He moved his ears slightly at the tapping of Auntie Janet's stick on the glazed tiles in the hall and as she hobbled through the doorway he uncurled, stretched and jumped down to wind around her feet and attempt to trip her up - or so she believed.

'Here's a letter for you,' she said, holding out a cream envelope.

The writing was unfamiliar and the postmark was London, which wasn't much of a clue. Was this an answer to one of my adverts at last?

Dear Mrs Marshall,

I was interested in your advertisement in 'Family Tracer' as I am also researching the whereabouts of an Anthony Dean.

I am afraid I know little except that he was living with his grandmother in Bedford around 1961/3 when he was thirteen or so. I'm sorry this is so vague.

If you think there may be a connection with your research, please contact me.

Yours sincerely
Simon Taylor

'News of the Bennetts?' asked Auntie Janet, after waiting politely for some time for me to speak first.

'No, it's from some man who's researching an Anthony Dean,' I replied, trying not to sound too enthusiastic. Auntie Janet had always been very understanding but I guessed that she found my obsession with Anthony rather puzzling.

'Is it the same one?' she asked after a pause that seemed to say, 'Here we go again!'

'This man's Anthony would be about the same age,' I answered, working it out.

'It's not an uncommon name. Anthony was very popular for boys at one time. Where's he from?'

'Mr Taylor's from London. His Anthony lived in Bedford as a boy,' I replied, not being sure which 'he' she had meant.

'Is he a relation?'

'He doesn't say.'

'Are you going to reply?' Silly question!

'I might as well send him what I know if only to eliminate him. His letter suggests he's looking for someone who is still alive.'

I waited a few more days but had no further replies. Then I sat down and wrote to Simon Taylor.

Dear Mr Taylor,

In reply to your letter, I am researching the history of my home, which was formerly Fieldhouse School.

In 1969/70 there was an English master here called Anthony Dean.

He was 21/22 and in his first post. This corresponds to the age of your Anthony.

Unfortunately he seems to have been very unhappy. He had teaching problems and a relationship with a much older woman, which ended when the school closed in July 1970. Sadly, he drowned himself in the school pond on the last day of term.

This is all I know about him but I would like to learn more. Please contact me again if I can be of any further help.

Yours sincerely
Laura Marshall

I'm doing my best for you, I said to Anthony's photo as I sealed up the letter.

The next day was grey and wet, with a biting easterly wind which cut through my coat as I walked along the village street to the post-box with the letter. Kingswater was deserted. There was not even a vehicle moving. The icy wind was blowing the last leaves from the trees and swirling them around until obstacles prevented them from continuing their journey. There they gathered in sodden brown heaps, soaked by the driving rain. One such obstacle was the post-box, which had a pile of them around its base.

I stood in front of the box, my boots squelching among those leaves, hesitant about posting that letter. Was it because, curious as I was, I was also worried about what I might discover? Was I afraid of him being taken from me? I did not want my illusions about Anthony to be shattered. For the last twenty-five years I had looked on him and what I knew of his story as 'mine'. But he must 'belong' somewhere else as well; was I prepared for what I might find out?

I had only ever told the true story of what happened that summer to my parents and the Aunts. To my school friends, who were so sneering about my

213

lack of boyfriends, I had woven a web of lies about how I had met this young teacher during the holidays and we had fallen in love but I didn't know whether I'd see him again. The latter, at least, was true. I had never mentioned the story to my ex-husband Martin. He wouldn't have understood at all. There was no romance, in any sense, about Martin.

If I posted this letter, I would begin the process of giving my story away - to a complete stranger. Had Auntie Janet been right about the can of worms? But if I didn't post it I might never have another chance, and I knew that I would regret it for the rest of my life.

It was done. The letter fell into the box, not with a soft thud but with a doleful metallic clang which echoed the totally desolate mood of its contents, the weather and my own feelings. It had obviously been too cold and wet for the residents of Kingswater, many of whom were elderly, to venture out with their letters today. I visualised mine lying alone on the floor of the box.

'Well, you can't hurt him now,' Auntie Janet had said.

No. I couldn't. But as I turned and faced into the piercing rain to walk back to Fieldhouse I knew that I could very easily hurt myself.

'Mrs Marshall?'

'Yes?'

My life was not sufficiently interesting (as yet!) that I received many phone calls from men. None, in fact, unless they were tradesmen wanting to charge the earth for some minor repair to the house.

'I'm Simon Taylor. You wrote to me about Anthony Dean.'

'Oh yes, of course.' That letter!

'If you're busy, I can phone some other time.' He spoke with a quiet, pleasant, educated voice.

'No, it's quite all right. Is it the same Anthony?'

'I can't tell. The age is OK, as you said. I have no idea whether my Anthony is still alive. I think they were a bright family so he could have become a teacher. It's certainly worth investigating.'

'I'd like to. I'd really love to know his story.'

'I wonder . . . do you ever come to London?'

'I haven't been for a while but there's no reason why I can't.'

'I thought I might go to the Family Record Centre,' he said. 'Perhaps you would care to meet me and we could compare notes before I go on with the research.'

'Yes, I'd like to, very much.'

'Good. I know a place for lunch nearby. We could start there.'

He gave me directions to the café and we arranged to meet the following week.

'A man has invited me to lunch,' I told Auntie Janet. 'Mr Taylor, who wrote to me about Anthony.'

'Lucky you! You will be careful, though, won't you?'

'I'm meeting him in a very public place. He sounds very pleasant.'

'How old?'

'I've no idea. Somewhere in the middle I imagine. Can't tell.'

'They all sound pleasant when they want something. Just make sure you stay in public - and don't, whatever you do, get into his car!'

'I promise I won't.' And though we were both laughing we knew she was deadly serious - and right.

For the next few days I pondered over my forthcoming trip. What would he be like? Many people took up genealogy on retirement. Perhaps Simon Taylor was one of those. He had not indicated what his connection to his Anthony was. Could I be going to meet a member of Anthony's family?

Once again I was torn between my desire to know the whole story and my fear of finding out things I would rather not have known. I also shared Auntie Janet's concerns (although I didn't tell her) about meeting a complete stranger. It almost felt like one of those dating agency adverts - and some very unpleasant things had happened recently to people who had answered those. The vulnerability of a frail old lady and me living alone in a large, rather isolated, house gave cause for anxiety. But you can't spend your whole life worrying that everyone you meet is a criminal, I told myself. You have to take a chance sometimes.

I suppose I was looking either for an older man or, more likely, for someone resembling my idea of Anthony. At any rate I was unprepared for the fair-haired young man who approached me as I waited outside the French café. By 'young' I mean about my own age - forty-something! He held out his hand.

'Laura Marshall? I'm Simon Taylor.'

His light hair was slightly wavy, thinning a little, and there were one or two grey hairs around the temples. Many less than I had. He was of medium height and build and there were creases of laughter around his blue eyes. He bore absolutely no resemblance to that tall, dark, thin, serious young teacher whose sad life and death had brought me here. Stupid of me to expect he would. I didn't even know if there was any connection, which made it even sillier of me to be slightly disappointed with my new acquaintance.

'Well,' he said, as we took our seats at one of the small tables, 'even if we don't share the same Anthony, I hope you won't feel your journey has been wasted.'

'Oh no,' I replied, not quite truthfully. 'It's a good excuse to come up to London. And this is a very nice place.'

'You don't come up very often?'

'No. I've only recently moved to Fieldhouse and there's a lot to be done. And I have an elderly relative to care for.' I did not tell him that we lived alone.

'Oh, I imagined you'd lived there for years, the way you spoke on the phone.'

'I've known it for years. It's been in the family since 1975,' I told him.

'So that's how you heard about your Anthony's story. Would you like a glass of wine with your meal?'

I had to admit that Simon was an attentive host - and he had an attractive smile. Still, I wasn't going to let that affect me. I knew nothing about him.

'An old gardener told me something of Anthony's story when I was visiting Fieldhouse as a teenager. Then I found a cutting about his death in some old school papers.' Since Simon had not yet proffered any information, I continued, with some trepidation, 'What's your connection to an Anthony Dean?'

'Oh yes, of course, sorry. I haven't told you. He's my half-brother.'

Half-brother! As close as that! What if it *was* my Anthony? This man had a far greater claim on him than I did. I looked at Simon with renewed interest but I could see no similarities. He seemed an easy-going sort of chap too. Not the sort to walk into a muddy pool, whatever his troubles.

'But you don't know anything to connect him with mine?' I asked.

'I'll tell you all I know, as briefly as I can. Just to prove I haven't dragged you up here for nothing.'

'Please do.' I took a long drink of my wine. I had a feeling I might need it.

'My father died last year. He was seventy-four,' Simon began. 'I had a happy, normal childhood and upbringing. He was a good, kind man and we always got on really well.' Simon also took a gulp of wine. Perhaps this was going to be painful and he needed sustenance too. 'You can imagine that it was a bit of a shock when my mother told me, after he died, that there was something she thought I should know.' This time Simon drank deeply of his wine and refilled both our glasses from the carafe. I could see that he was troubled. 'Mum isn't in good health and she wanted to make sure and tell me herself. Apparently Dad, John Taylor, wasn't my father at all. My mother had been married briefly, before she met him, to a George Dean.'

'George Dean!'

'Yes. Now you see where this is leading? Do you want to hear the rest?'

'Oh yes, please go on. As long as you're happy to tell me.'

'I'm very happy to tell you. Although I haven't told anyone else.'

Not even his wife or girlfriend? 'No-one at all?'

'No. It's actually quite difficult for me, as perhaps you can tell. I understand now what Mum felt when she told me. It was hell for her - but she was determined that I should know. And she wanted it out in the open after forty years.'

'Well, if I can help by listening . . . '

'You are helping, thanks. George Dean was in his late forties then and Mum was about twenty-four. His first wife had only been dead about three months when they married. He'd already been seeing Mum for quite a while. That caused a bit of a scandal and I think Mum feels ashamed about it. But she was young and he was very persuasive. The marriage didn't last, though.

George always drank heavily. Mum left him after a couple of years and he died the year after, from drink. When she left she was pregnant with me but she never told him. She didn't want her child associated with him, she said. Eventually she married Dad and I was brought up as his. I was only about two then so I knew nothing of it.'

'And Anthony?'

'George's son by his first wife. There were two sons. Graham was the oldest. He was idolised by his parents, his mother in particular. He died in an accident at school when he was about eighteen. That was what killed his mother. She never got over it.

Anthony was seven or eight years younger than Graham. When George married Mum he was sent off to live with his maternal grandmother in Bedford. He'd be about thirteen then. Mum never met him. George didn't have much time for him. Mum blamed herself at first for some of that but apparently it was nothing new. So with an indifferent father and a mother dead of a broken heart for his brother, nobody cared much for poor Anthony.'

Oh Anthony, my love! Could this really be your tragic story? Misery on misery! However many Anthony Deans there were in the world I couldn't help feeling that this was mine. That sad, haunting face . . .

'What about his grandmother?' I asked, hoping this would not be another tale of agony.

'Mum thinks he was OK there, much to her relief. George had told her that he was happy enough, so I hope it was true.'

'I hope so. My Anthony was certainly very, very sad when he was at Fieldhouse. How can we find out if they're the same one?'

'I'm not sure. We've got nothing at all to go on except that the dates fit. But, you know, I have a feeling about it.'

'Funny, so do I.'

'Then let's drink to it.' Simon emptied the rest of the wine into our glasses. 'Here's to our research. If we're proved right, we'll celebrate with champagne.'

'It's a deal!'

'Now let's finish lunch by talking about happier topics,' Simon suggested. There was a silence. Then we both laughed. We couldn't think of any!

After lunch we went along to the Centre. There was nothing we could do there to connect the two Anthonys but Simon searched the records and ordered a birth certificate for his Anthony and a marriage certificate for Anthony's parents. It was a start.

Then we went back to the café and had coffee before I returned to Fieldhouse. Simon told me a little about himself. He worked for a computer company, based in London. He had a flat in Ealing. I gathered he lived alone but he didn't talk about anything too personal, nor did he ask me any personal questions. I told him about my inheritance and my care of Auntie Janet but not about my divorce.

Despite our caginess, we got on really well. Simon was interesting company, easy to talk to and also a good listener. He had a sense of humour, too. As he escorted me back to the station I realised that I had completely forgotten about my initial disappointment on meeting him. I wanted the research to go on for that vital connection - and it wasn't just because I wanted to find out about Anthony.

Simon must have read my thoughts. As we were walking across the station concourse, he said, 'I hope we'll meet again. I've really enjoyed today. When I get those certificates would you like me to ring you with the results?'

'Oh yes, please do.'

'When I've got the names and dates from them I'll need to come here again. Perhaps you'll join me?'

'I'd like to very much. I've really enjoyed today, too. Do keep in touch - if you find anything new,' I said, feeling that I must be blushing stupidly.

'I certainly will. When is it OK to phone?'

'Oh, any time. There's only my auntie . . . ' I stopped. I'd given myself away.

Simon smiled. Did he realise?

'I'll give you a ring then. Have a safe journey.'

I passed through the barrier and as I reached the train door I stopped and looked round. He was still standing where I had left him. When he saw me turn, he waved. I waved back. Perhaps embarrassed that I'd seen him still there, he walked away, with a quick glance over his shoulder.

I stepped into the train and sat down. Suddenly, I felt very lonely.

Chapter Twenty-Seven

It was ten days before I heard from Simon again. I had to admit that I was slightly disappointed not to hear earlier and I kept telling myself that I was foolish. I knew almost nothing about him or he about me. He had been a very friendly and interesting companion for a few hours, and that was all. Somehow I couldn't even begin to think of him as possibly Anthony's half-brother. They were so different. In any case, he hadn't been brought up in Anthony's family, and he didn't even know any of them. They didn't seem to be the sort of people one would want to know.

'It sounds as though your life was wretched even before you came here - if that *is* you,' I said to the face on my wall.

I had told Auntie Janet the whole story of course and I thought I detected that what had been a kindly forbearance for my sake was changing into a genuine interest on her own behalf in tying up the loose ends of Anthony's story. Or was it because I had obviously found Simon such an agreeable companion? She *had* asked me once or twice in the last few days whether I had heard from him.

When the phone rang one evening and I jumped up, spilling a disgusted Cola from his sleep on my lap, Auntie had an amused look on her face.

'Laura? It's Simon.'

'How are you?'

'I'm fine. Are you by any chance free on Friday morning?'

'Yes, I think so. Why?'

'I'm working in Southampton for a day or two. I have to be there on Thursday, then Friday morning is free but I've got a meeting in the afternoon. I wondered if you'd like to meet me. I'll bring those certificates.'

'I'd love to. Where?'

'H'm . . . what about . . . I know. When I was here once before my colleagues took me to a nice little place not far away - a yachting centre. I just can't think of the name. Stupid, I should have thought about it before I phoned. Did it begin with an H?'

'Do you mean Hamble?'

'Yes, that's it, Hamble. Do you know it?'

'I went there years ago. Not recently, but I know how to get there. I pass the signs quite often.'

'Could you get there by ten? I recall there's a café there.'

This man thinks of nothing but food, I thought with an indulgent smile.

Simon was waiting when I arrived. He seemed genuinely pleased to see me.

'Don't go anywhere lonely. You don't know him well enough yet!'

219

Auntie Janet warned me.

That was true. But I did feel very comfortable with him, even when we spoke on the phone. Anyway, it wasn't exactly lonely here, although the busy holiday centre that I remembered from a previous visit had now put on its calm winter face. The day was cold and grey, but somehow I hadn't really noticed.

'The café's open. I checked!' Simon grinned. 'Shall we start with a coffee?'

I suddenly found myself tongue-tied, almost as though I had reverted to the adolescent whose social life consisted of dreaming of characters in books, and later of a young man who had died years before. Mature adulthood is obviously a very thin veneer. My life seemed to have come full circle.

'Are you all right?'

'Oh, yes, sorry!' I said, embarrassed. Dreaming had a habit of getting me into trouble. 'I was just thinking about . . . ' I quickly changed the subject. 'What else have you found out?' I had not said anything to Simon about my 'ghost' and I wouldn't unless it became appropriate and if he seemed to be the sort of person who would understand.

'I got these certificates,' he said, politely ignoring my air of distraction. He unfolded them. 'They tell us that George's wife was called Jean and her maiden name was Johnson. So the grandmother was Mrs Johnson of Bedford. Something to go on.'

He passed over the two documents. I stared down at Anthony's birth certificate in a sort of daze. It seemed so uncanny to be looking at - but no, this was Simon's Anthony. There was nothing to connect him with mine. Still . . . I pulled myself together and took in the details.

George Anthony Dean, born 18 November 1948, Bedford

'So he was born in Bedford too?'

'Yes. It was his mother's home-town. The family lived there for a while. But by the time Mum met George they were living near Cambridge. My mother still lives there. Shall we go for a walk? I could do with some fresh air before this meeting.'

We finished our coffee and walked down to the waterfront where most of the boats were laid up for the winter. A fresh breeze was making the water choppy and a shaft of autumn sunshine filtered through the cloud to give a sudden sparkle to the water.

'I wish I'd brought my camera,' I said.

'Lovely, isn't it? Do you sail?'

'No, I'm the world's worst sailor,' I replied. 'What about you?'

'I've been out with friends a few times, in my youth. Now I'd rather just read about it.'

We talked about books for a while. Simon's interests were wide-ranging and many of them were similar to mine: literature, travel and wildlife in particular. Then we talked about the attractive houses that we passed, and their sheltered gardens, still with flowers blooming in late autumn.

Suddenly Simon said, 'You said you lived with an . . . an aunt?' He sounded unsure of himself. He must have guessed that I'd been trying to hide it but had eventually given myself away.

'Yes. Actually she's my father's cousin. I've been looking after her and the house since the summer, like I said. I've got lots of plans for it but they'll take time.'

'But you are *Mrs* Marshall?' he asked gently.

'I'm divorced, as you probably gathered.'

'Oh, I don't want to pry. But I don't want to put my foot in it either, by saying the wrong thing. I thought I'd better check.'

'That's OK. What . . .?'

'About me? I was married. My wife died very young, in a road accident; it's eighteen years ago now. I was in another relationship for a long time but it didn't work out. Mainly because she was married to someone else.'

Was this why he was so anxious to know my situation? 'I'm so sorry,' I said, inadequately.

'We both know what it's all about, obviously,' he said quietly. 'And, dare I say it, what we would perhaps like it to be about, but it isn't.' He gave me a wistful half-smile.

Simon knew what it was to suffer, despite his normally easy-going, comfortable manner. I was glad that he knew.

We did not say any more for a while, as we slowly walked back to the car park.

'I'll have to leave at twelve-thirty,' Simon said as we approached our starting point again, 'but there's time for a quick early lunch.'

I smiled. Food again! Sad thoughts banished.

'Yes, why not?'

'Are you driving back to London tonight?' I asked as we left the café.

'No. There's a dinner organised this evening. A working meal I suspect. So I'm staying until tomorrow morning.'

'Then driving back?' I persisted. I didn't want to seem pushy, but . . .

'Yes.' He seemed surprised by my rather out-of-character questioning. 'Unless . . . '

'I wondered if you . . . '

We were both talking at the same time now.

'Go on,' he encouraged me.

Emboldened, I said, 'I just wondered if you would like to see Fieldhouse on your way back - as you're so near and in case your Anthony turns out to be mine,' I justified myself.

'I'd like that very much. How do I get there?'

'There's a map in the car. I'll show you.'

221

'I'll see you in the morning. Can't be sure what time. I'll give you a ring if there's a problem.' Simon called through his car window as he left. A last wave and he was gone.

I stood alone in what had suddenly become a very cold, dreary car park. I felt desolate as I got into my car and slowly drove away. I was afraid to admit to myself how much I was looking forward to showing Simon Fieldhouse - and how much I would dread the phone ringing tomorrow morning, in case he couldn't make it.

The phone did not ring. Half way through Saturday morning I heard the crunch of tyres on the gravel drive and dashed out with what Auntie Janet obviously considered unseemly haste.

'You found it then?' I asked, rather pointlessly.

'Yes, easily. I've been looking forward to it.'

'Come on in.'

We had lit a log fire in the library. I took Simon in and introduced him to Auntie Janet and Cola. Then I left them talking while I went to make coffee. When I returned Cola was back in his usual position in front of the hearth, from which he had been disturbed by Simon's arrival, and Simon and Auntie Janet were chatting away as though they had known each other for years. This all seemed a good omen.

'Will you stay for lunch?' I asked.

'Oh, I don't want to put you to any trouble.'

'It's no trouble. I can't drag you all the way here without feeding you.' Would this be persuasive?

'Well, in that case,' he laughed.

'Auntie Janet makes excellent soup,' I said. 'She can't stand for long now so I have to do some of the stirring - that's the most important part, of course!'

I showed Simon round the garden first, during a break in the heavy rain we had had all morning. After a tour of the area around the house we squelched across the lawn to the pond.

'This is where my Anthony drowned,' I said. 'But I still love it. It looks sombre now but in summer it's alive with dragonflies and other pond life.'

We stood quietly beside the pool, our reflections rippling on the surface.

'He must have been very, very distressed,' said Simon at last. 'I couldn't do that, and I've been in some awful states over the years.'

'So have I, but I wouldn't be brave enough to do it,' I replied. 'But if you've had a rotten time *all* your life . . . '

' . . . it doesn't take much to unhinge you. My Anthony did have a lousy childhood . . . '

' . . . and mine found life just too unbearable - right here.' Once more we gazed across the water in silence. 'Let's go and have some lunch,' I said at last.

'Yes. Life must go on.'

'Especially if there's food involved,' I said, and we both laughed.

Auntie Janet solved one problem for me.

'So you're going to help Laura track down her ghost?' she asked Simon, as we sat down to steaming bowls of thick vegetable soup, accompanied by crusty bread, cheese and pate, with a fruit pie to follow.

'I beg your pardon?'

'I haven't told Simon about the ghost yet, Auntie,' I explained, smiling at him. 'I didn't think he'd believe me. After all, nobody else does.'

'Well, you'll have to tell me now,' he said.

When I had finished my story he sat silently for a moment. 'I don't know what to say,' he said at last. 'I had wondered why you were so keen on the story. Now I understand.'

'I hope you two can sort it all out once and for all,' Auntie Janet said.

'Auntie Janet would be pleased to hear the last of it, I'm sure,' I said. 'She thinks I'm mad!'

When we were having coffee after lunch, I went upstairs and fetched the photo, and the cuttings and school magazines that referred to Anthony.

'You see,' I explained to Simon, 'when I saw this photo, I recognised Anthony straight away. Then old Mr Tompkins confirmed that this was Anthony - so I must have seen something.'

'Yes, I suppose you must. You hear of these things, but - '

'But you never expect it to happen to you, or anyone you know,' Auntie Janet said. '*I* couldn't see him at all, yet Laura was adamant. Of course, some people are susceptible to such things. Especially sensitive young ladies.'

Simon spent some time looking at the photo. Was he seeing his half-brother for the first time? He placed the photo frame carefully on the table beside him, propping it up against a vase.

'Laura, I think you ought to talk to my mother,' he said.

'I thought you said she never saw him?'

'She didn't. But she *did* live with his father for a couple of years. Who knows what she might have learned - what sort of boy he was, what his interests were, what subjects he liked at school. I never asked about any of that. I was too shocked to find out that instead of a really decent man, my father had been a heartless drunkard. And of course Mum found it very hard to tell me the truth. So it was just facts, really. If I arrange it, will you come?'

I glanced over at Auntie Janet. She was smiling broadly.

'Yes, I will, as long as it's not a problem.'

'Next weekend?'

'Yes, whenever's convenient.'

'I usually get the train up to Cambridge. Mum now lives in a flat near the centre and there's nowhere to park. Shall I meet you in London next Friday? I'll get away early.'

'That sounds better than driving in this weather.'

'Right. I'll fix it and ring you in the week. As long as you're sure you want to come?'

'I'd like to, but I don't want to be a nuisance to your mother.'

'She'll enjoy having you. Her health prevents her from going out much. She's been very lonely since Dad died. My sister - half-sister - Susan, lives in Scotland. You can have the spare room and I'll put my sleeping bag on the settee. We can return to London on Sunday morning so you won't be late back here.' He turned to Auntie Janet. 'You don't mind me taking Laura away for a couple of days?'

'No, she needs to get away sometimes. Mrs Adams will come in. I shall be perfectly all right and I'm sure your mother will be pleased to see you.'

Auntie Janet sounded quite genuine. She had obviously taken to Simon.

'I'd better be going. I'd like to do at least some of the journey while it's still light - partly light anyway.'

Simon looked out of the library window at the rain and darkness of the afternoon. Although it was only two-thirty, it was so gloomy that we needed all the lights on to look at the books and papers I was showing him. Auntie Janet had gone for a nap and Cola was firmly fixed on the hearthrug. Just as Simon spoke, there was an extra-strong gust of wind which rattled the windows and was followed by a torrential downpour, turning the sky as black as night.

'Are you sure you want to set off in this? You're very welcome to stay.'

'It might be worse later, and, as I said, it'll be dark.'

'No, stay until tomorrow I mean. We've no shortage of rooms!'

He looked out into the rain-swept darkness again and then at the glowing, flickering fire where Cola toasted comfortably.

'Tempting,' he said, 'very tempting!'

Then he looked at me. Did he think I was tempting? No, of course not. I mustn't think so stupidly. But I knew I was willing him to say yes. I hadn't had such an agreeable companion for . . . well, I couldn't remember ever having one.

'I'd like to stay. There's nothing particular to rush back for tonight. I just wanted to get the driving over in this awful weather.'

I smiled, wondering if the pleasure I felt showed on my face. Did it show too much? I didn't want to frighten him off.

'Good,' I said. 'I wouldn't like to think of you leaving in this rain. Now you're staying, I'll go and make us a cup of tea and take one to Auntie. She doesn't like to be left to sleep too long otherwise she can't sleep at night.'

'That sounds a much better idea than driving to London. I'll talk to Cola while you're gone.'

He settled himself by the fire with an air of domesticity that had a very strange effect on me.

Before Simon left the next morning we walked around the garden again. The storm had passed over and it was bright, cold and clear. Despite the season, the pond had lost its sombre look of the day before and the surface gleamed with reflections from the blue sky and dotted clouds.

'Now it looks more appealing,' I said. The dried rushes at the edge rustled in the breeze and a robin hopped around in the hedge. 'There used to be a small white gate here. Not such a need for heavy locks in those days. You could just open it and stroll out.' I turned the key in the padlock and swung the gate open. 'I'm sure Anthony used to walk out here - with Helen probably. I'll show you the track I think they would have taken.'

We walked along the path outside the hedge, the chalky clay sticking to our shoes.

'This must be lovely in summer,' Simon said, admiringly.

'It is in all seasons really, except yesterday afternoon perhaps. Look, this is where the path turns up onto the Downs. It goes up between this hedge, then it opens out. In the other direction it goes down to the road. There's another path up to the top, further over, and one at the other end of the village. This field here,' I said, pointing to the right of the school, 'used to be the school playing field. Now it belongs to the farm over there.'

It was too muddy to go any further and Simon had to leave. I really would have liked to take him up on the Downs, to show him the knoll and the walk along the ridge to where there was a reed-grown dewpond. Most of all, I wanted to put off the moment of parting.

'I'll phone in the week,' he said, putting his bag in the car. 'Thanks for the weekend, it's been great.'

'It was your idea in the first place,' I reminded him.

'A very good one, I think. I hope you do?'

'I think it was a wonderful idea.'

'I'll see you next weekend, hopefully. I'm looking forward to it. Bye, Laura.' He clasped both my hands and kissed me on the cheek, hesitated, then repeated his kiss on the lips. 'See you soon,' he said in a not too steady voice.

I watched and waved as he drove out of the gate and I stood outside until the sound of his car had completely died away. Then, feeling a strange mixture of elation and depression, I slowly walked up the steps and indoors.

Chapter Twenty-Eight

The week took forever to pass, but eventually I found myself at Kings Cross, with butterflies in my stomach, waiting for Simon. Was my foolish imagination producing a dream man who was nothing like the reality? This had happened to me before - a period of absence, however short, at the beginning of a relationship, leading to a deep disappointment when the object of my desires actually arrived. I had thought I was well past all that, but apparently not!

'Laura!'

He called before he reached me, hurrying across the concourse, late, flushed, but seemingly pleased to see me again. He kissed me and would probably have clasped me in his arms had they not been burdened with a briefcase, a large file of papers and an overnight bag. At least, that was what I chose to think he would have done.

'Sorry I'm late. I tried to leave early but the boss cornered me. I could hardly tell him I had to meet a lady to talk about a ghost, could I?'

'He might have thought that he'd been overworking you!' I laughed.

'Yes, there's that, of course. But he might have chosen to relieve me of those duties. There are rather a lot of bright young blokes just below me - and they never talk about ghosts!'

Any tension at meeting was quickly diffused by these light-hearted exchanges. He *was* just as I remembered him. I could only hope that *I* didn't disappoint *him*.

'I don't think we should show Mum the photo right away,' he said when we were on the train. 'Just let her talk and see what comes. We don't want to suggest things to her that she really can't remember.'

'What have you told her so far?'

'Just that I met you through a magazine advert and you're researching an Anthony Dean.'

'She *is* happy about me going?'

'Oh yes, no problem at all. She's looking forward to it.'

Sylvia Taylor greeted us at the door of her flat, giving every impression of being delighted by our visit. She was in her late sixties but looked older: tall, thin and gaunt. She was smartly dressed and still showed traces of the attractive, blonde young woman who had captured the heart, for a while anyway, of George Dean.

'Come in, come in. I've put a casserole in the oven. It won't be long,' she said, leading the way into her comfortable living room.

'Smells good,' said Simon. 'It's ages since I ate!'

'Starving as usual,' his mother smiled.

'I've been really busy all day. My 'working lunch' consisted of two sausage rolls.'

'Very unhealthy,' Sylvia said disapprovingly. 'Well, by the time you're ready . . . '

I was almost expecting her to tell him to go and wash his hands. From the wink he gave me behind her back, I think he was too. But she turned to me and said, 'Come this way, Laura, I'll show you your room. I bet you don't live on sausage rolls!'

Sylvia showed me into the small, rather bare but spotlessly clean spare room.

'I moved into this flat after John, my husband, died,' she explained. 'I had to get rid of a lot of furniture and other things. It hurt at the time but now I'm glad. You don't need all that stuff and it just makes work.' She opened the wardrobe door. 'Simon keeps some of his things in here still, and I've got bits and pieces for when my grandchildren come, but I've pushed them aside so you can hang your clothes, and I've cleared a shelf for you.'

I unpacked my things to the sound of cheerful banter between Simon and his mother. They obviously had a good relationship, something I had guessed from the way he spoke of her. 'You can always judge a man by the way he treats his mother, sisters, aunts,' my grandmother used to say. I knew now that she was right. I wished I had heeded her warning in the past. Next time - if there was a next time - I would.

The casserole was excellent and Simon in particular did full justice to it. It wasn't until we sat down in the easy chairs with our coffee that we began talking about the purpose of our visit: what Sylvia remembered about George Dean and his family. I had taken my cue from Simon and talked of other things during the meal.

'I was a silly young woman then,' she began slowly. Simon had already indicated that she was ashamed of her disastrous first marriage. 'Not that young - twenty-four - but very naïve. I worked in the same office and he started talking to me, telling me about his ailing wife, you know, the old story.'

'But in his case, it was true,' said Simon quietly.

'It was, and I fell for it and for him. He told me all about his brilliant son who'd died at school, climbing or something. Graham, his name was. Said his wife, she was called Jean, was just pining away. She'd kind of given up.'

'Was he drinking then?'

'Oh yes. But I didn't know about that at first. When I found out, I just put it down to his troubles. I was besotted with him by then and thought I could change him. We women always think that.' She turned to me. 'Never think that, dear. Never think you'll change them when you're married. It doesn't work.'

Simon looked embarrassed.

I said, 'I know. I thought that once. I was married - unsuccessfully.'

'Then you know all about it!'

'Did George ever mention his other son?' Simon encouraged his mother. Was he trying to divert the conversation from marriage and male failings?

'I don't remember him doing so until around the time Jean died. Then he said he didn't think it would make any difference to Anthony because she'd been in her room for so long. The boy was pretty self-sufficient, he said.'

'Were you surprised to hear about Anthony?'

'Shocked, I think. Firstly for selfish reasons. I'd been expecting to marry a widower and start my own family. Then I found he had a teenage son. I didn't want that. Perhaps that was one reason why George had been careful not to mention him. But then I started to feel sorry for the lad.'

'Did his father tell you much about him?'

'Not a lot. Self-sufficient, like I said. A bit of a loner, not that he had much choice, poor boy. Always moping about, nose in a book or watching cricket on TV. Apparently he didn't say much. He was nothing like his wonderful brother had been.'

'Was he clever, though?' I asked.

'He was at the grammar school, I remember that. So he must have been cleverer than I was! And he was always reading. That's about all George said. It was all Graham. Graham had been bright, good-looking, out-going, and athletic. Arrogant too, I should think. Full of himself. Only George never saw it like that. It was all praise.'

'In the end, Anthony didn't live with you and George?' Simon prompted.

'Oh no. I don't think George ever had any intention that he should. Just before we married he took him to his maternal grandmother in Bedford. That's where his wife had come from and they had all lived there for a while.'

'Yes, we found that from Anthony's birth certificate,' Simon told her.

'Well, George said he was fond of his Gran and he'd better off there. I was very relieved, as I had no idea how to bring up a teenage boy. But I did feel a bit sad and guilty. I never met the lad. George went over a few times, mainly to take money for his keep. He used to say that the boy was all right. That was all.'

'Did he always call him "the boy"?' I asked her.

'Yes. Almost always,' said Sylvia, pouring us all more coffee from an elegant white china pot.

'So then you got married? 1961, wasn't it?' Simon said.

'Yes, and you know the rest, but I'll tell it for completeness and for Laura's benefit. George's attraction to me died with the sound of the wedding bells - not that there were any. I should have known it would. I had enough warnings. He began to drink more and more and became violent. When I discovered I was pregnant, I left. I didn't want my baby brought up in that household. He never knew about Simon and he died of drink a year or so later. I met John Taylor and he restored my faith in men.' Her voice faltered as she recalled the husband she had so recently lost.

'He was a good man,' said Simon.

'You were both lucky,' I said.

'We were. Very.' Simon got up and walked into the spare room, returning with a carrier bag. I want you to take a look at this picture, Mum. Just have a look. No hurry. Got your reading glasses?' He handed her my school photo.

Sylvia took it and peered at the sea of faces, scanning them quickly at first, then more intently. Then she looked up at us both.

'Him,' she said, putting her finger on Anthony. 'This one here. He looks just like George!'

I felt my eyes fill up with tears. I couldn't speak. I had brought Anthony home - or as near to home as he would ever be.

Simon came to my rescue. Speaking very quietly, he said, 'Just like George, you say?'

'Yes, so like him. Of course George was in his mid-forties when I knew him. But there's that look, the way his hair falls over his forehead, the mouth. If anybody had asked me, I would have said that was George as a young man.' Sylvia looked up from the photo and at my almost-tearful face. 'Is this your Anthony?' she asked.

'Yes.'

'Then he *must* be George's son.'

We sat in silence for a moment. I fought the urge to weep, wondering if I was dreaming. Here we were, three comparative strangers, sitting in an old-peoples' flat in Cambridge; all, I suspected, with tears in our eyes for a young man who had died thirty-five years ago. Sylvia had been married to his father but never met Anthony, Simon was his half-brother but had never met him, I lived where he had lived and died but had only seen his ghost.

Once again Simon rescued us. 'I think we need a drink!' he said. 'I thought we might so I brought some. Mum doesn't keep alcohol in the house,' he said to me. His tone said, because of George.

He produced a bottle of red wine and some nibbles and we began to feel better. There was one more ordeal to come though, for Sylvia.

'You don't have any more photos?' she asked me.

' No, only a few mentions in school papers and a cutting about his death. Simon did tell you that my Anthony had died?'

'He mentioned it. Now that we're fortified, perhaps you can fill in the details for me. No point in leaving the story half-told.'

I did, and she was obviously moved, especially by the account of Anthony's suicide.

'He was doomed from the start,' was her comment.

Next morning I awoke to the sound of voices and a great deal of shuffling and scrabbling. When I was dressed, I went out and discovered Simon and his mother gradually removing the contents of a large, deep store-cupboard in the hall.

'Mum's remembered something she may still have. But she hasn't seen it for years. If it's anywhere, it'll be in a box at the back of this cupboard. The very back!' said a rueful, dusty voice.

'I'm sorry to cause all this bother,' Sylvia said, emerging from the kitchen, 'but when I was in bed, with all that going round in my head, I thought about a little photograph that used to be around. I've no idea if I've still got it. I told you I'd thrown a lot of stuff away when I moved, and at times in the past, too. But if it's anywhere, it'll be in one of those boxes of photographs.' She peered through the cupboard door and indicated some boxes to Simon. 'Pass them out and I'll go through them.'

Simon handed her a box and I took one. We carried them into the living room and placed them on the settee.

'I'll go through them while you have your breakfast,' she said. 'It's all ready.'

When we had finished eating I washed up while Simon put everything back in the cupboard. When we rejoined Sylvia she was still going through the boxes.

'No sign of it in the first box,' she said. 'Wait a minute, what's this?'

She picked out a very small black and white photograph with a white border. 'Yes, here it is. We're in luck! For some reason it survived all my purges. I suppose I couldn't bring myself to consign these two unhappy boys to the dustbin.'

She handed us the photo. Simon and I stood very close together looking down at the image. It showed a good-looking boy of about sixteen or seventeen with fair, wavy hair and a confident smile. He was wearing well-fitting tennis whites and carried a racquet. I thought he could equally well have been wearing khaki and a pith helmet - he had that slightly arrogant look about him.

Next to him, almost behind him, was a much younger boy, thin and with those hideous round Health Service glasses that children used to be forced to wear. He wore what appeared to be a khaki shirt and shorts that had presumably belonged to his older brother and he hadn't yet grown into them. His dark hair fell over his eyes and in place of a self-confident smile his face had a look of solemn nervousness. I stared at it for a moment then I looked up and said, 'It's Anthony!'

'Yes, it's Anthony and Graham,' Sylvia confirmed. 'I hadn't seen it for years but I thought I might have kept it because I felt so sorry - for both of them in different ways. And of course they were Simon's half-brothers and I always imagined that he'd know one day.'

Simon was peering hard at the photo now. He seemed unable to speak. I picked up my school photo from the table and we put the two together. That sad little boy and that sad young man were so alike it was almost impossible to believe now that they were anything other than the same person.

Simon, as on the previous night, despite his obvious emotion, broke the tension. He seemed to be good at that and I admired him for it. I am hopeless in such situations.

'I think we should celebrate,' he said with a faint tremor in his voice. 'I'll see if I can book the Millpond Hotel for dinner tonight.'

He went out into the hall. Sylvia watched him, then turned to me and said, 'He's a good son. He's nothing like George, as you can see, even in looks. He takes after me. And, funnily enough, he looks a lot like John.'

I looked at the photos again. 'It seems Anthony looked like his father. But I don't think he was much like him in other ways,' I said.

'That's just what George used to say. Only he didn't put it so politely. He, of course, thought it was a bad thing. He used to say something to the effect that "that scrawny little bastard has inherited all my worst features and he's hopeless into the bargain. I should never have given him my name. Now, Graham looked like his mother but he had all my spirit." George had a high opinion of himself, as you can imagine.'

All I could say was, 'Poor Anthony.'

'Done!' said Simon, coming in from the hall. 'Dinner at eight o'clock. We need something to cheer us up after all this sadness - and to celebrate what we've discovered.'

'That sounds wonderful,' I said.

'Here's to Anthony - for bringing us all here together!' Simon raised his glass and looked searchingly at me as he proposed the toast.

'For bringing us all together,' I echoed, with what I hoped was a look he could interpret.

We had a lovely evening in a delightful restaurant, with good food and cheerful conversation. By now I felt as though I had known Simon and Sylvia for years. But with a catch in my throat I realised that by this time tomorrow I'd be miles away from both of them.

'I want to see you again, Laura,' Simon said as we walked slowly across the station concourse, past happy couples who were travelling together, and wretched ones who were not. 'Not because of Anthony. Because of me.'

'And I want to see you again - because of me.' I told him.

He bent and kissed me lightly, and clasped my hands in his. 'I'd like to see you before Christmas. I might be able to persuade my boss that I need to go to Southampton again. If not, I'll arrange something else - if you don't object.'

'No, I don't object. This has been a very special weekend, in all sorts of ways.'

'I've never had a weekend like it before.'

'Neither have I.'

The tannoy broke through. announcing my train.

'You'd better go. I don't like it, but . . . ' He flung his arms round me and held me tight. 'Do take care. We *will* meet again soon.'

231

One last kiss and I passed through the barrier. As I reached the train door I looked back, as I had before. Simon was still there, waving. As the train pulled away, he remained waving until the train took me out of sight. Then I slumped miserably in the corned of my seat and endured one of the worst journeys of my life.

Chapter Twenty-nine

We *did* meet before Christmas – in Southampton on a dark, drizzly afternoon. We wandered hand-in-hand among the bustling Christmas shoppers. It should have been a cheerful scene despite the weather, but I, at least, had a dull ache inside. Christmas is supposed to be a time of togetherness but I wasn't going to be together with the person who was becoming so very important to me. And although he was keeping up a light-hearted conversation, Simon's blue eyes had a hint of sadness about them.

Simon would be at a family gathering, too - Sylvia and his sister Susan and her husband and two children. It was strange to think of them as Anthony's family, or near enough.

Just before we parted in a wind-and-rain-swept car park, he handed me a small parcel.

'I hope you like these. I thought they were appropriate,' he said. 'Can I phone you at Christmas? I know you'll have your parents there, but . . . '

'Yes, please. I shall miss you.'

We held each other tight, oblivious of the rain.

Christmas came and went. My parents enjoyed their stay and Mum was delighted not to have to cook Christmas dinner for once.

'It's the first time for years I haven't spent all Christmas in the kitchen,' she said.

'I hope the gentleman who bought you the dragonflies is less ephemeral than they are,' said Dad, raising his glass.

'He seems a very nice young man,' Auntie Janet told them approvingly.

'I'll tell him about the 'young'. He'll be pleased,' I laughed. When I moved my head, I could feel the earrings dangling against my neck. They were Simon's present: a pair of silver dragonflies with filigree wings and bodies made of a delicate green stone. They had been the first present I opened. Inside the card, he had written,

'I thought you would like these because of the Fieldhouse pond.
Perhaps we will watch them together this summer.'

Yes, I hope we will too, I thought. But in the dark of winter, the summer can seem very far away. My tentative new relationship, carried on from a distance, could be even more short-lived than the dragonflies. Others had been - hence my father's comment.

There were times in the next few weeks when I thought it was all over before it had really begun. The winter was very bad, with some snow and a great deal of rain, leading to severe flooding. Kingswater was completely cut off on a couple of occasions. People were warned not to travel, and, being responsible for Auntie Janet, I did not want to risk being stranded somewhere.

Simon's work did not bring him to Southampton (or did he fail to arrange that it should?). Instead, it took him all over the country, everywhere except the south. We did manage one meeting in London but it was not very satisfactory. The rain was torrential, our time was short and Simon was worried about Sylvia, who was unwell. The following week he decided to go and stay with her and commute, which took him even further away from me. His letters and phone calls kept on coming but they were full of events and complications rather than outpourings of affection.

Was I having yet another of my foolish illusions shattered? I should have known better than fall for the first man I met at the start of my new life at Fieldhouse. It had been just too easy. He probably felt the same. Another meeting in London went better - until Simon told me he had to go to the States for a month. He seemed very excited at the prospect, but I was downcast.

'I'll really miss you,' he said as we parted at the station. 'But when I come back, we'll celebrate.'

Would we? I had another miserable train journey south but this time it was a different sort of misery. When I arrived back at Fieldhouse I went up to my room and gazed at the photograph on my wall.

'It was much easier loving you,' I said to Anthony. 'You never hurt me. Perhaps I should stick to you in future.'

It was a long month. Simon wrote and phoned, full of what he had done and seen, and the people he had met. He didn't say much about me - almost nothing about *us*. Was he just a friend, after all?

Then he was coming back.

'I'm back in London. Going up to Cambridge now, but can I see you next weekend? I've missed you a lot.'

'Come down, if you can,' I said.

The weekend started brilliantly. Simon arrived on Friday evening, laden with presents for Auntie Janet and me. He held me close and told me how lonely he'd been, despite always being surrounded by people.

On Saturday we walked up on the Downs, taking the track which I was sure Anthony and Helen had trod many times - along the back of the house, up between the hedges and out on to the open downland. We sat up on the knoll looking down on the roofs of Fieldhouse. How Anthony must have dreaded going back down, if he was as unhappy at the school as it seemed he had been. Simon appeared keen to go on with his family history again now and we talked about how we could fill in some of the gaps in Anthony's story.

'We could find out when his grandmother died, and her address in Bedford,' he suggested.

'Presumably he continued to live with her while he was at school. Then what?'

'He must have been a graduate to teach here, I should think, so he'd have gone to university somewhere. It would be a very long job to find out where, but I dare say it's possible.'

'There must be people still alive who knew him,' I said. 'That other young teacher, for example. Michael James.'

'He'd be fifty-seven or so now,' Simon calculated.

'Some of the boys - but we don't know many names.'

'Helen Pearson?' Simon said slowly. 'She could still be alive, you know. She was about forty then so she'd be seventy-five now. Could be very hale and hearty.'

I was unable to speak for a moment. Helen Pearson hale and hearty! I had never really considered carefully the idea that she might still be alive. I hadn't wanted to.

'We could look for her if you like,' Simon went on, as I hadn't spoken.

'No, no!' I said, regaining my voice. 'We mustn't do that. Who knows what might have happened to her since then? It was just an episode in her past. We don't even know what it meant to her at the time. If she *is* still alive, she wouldn't thank us for raking it up!' I finished breathlessly.

Simon seemed surprised at my vehemence. I suppose he thought I'd be keen to try to open what would be a real door to the past. Perhaps he was keen himself and I had disappointed him. But I couldn't even consider contacting Helen Pearson. Helen had been Anthony's lover. She had *actually* been what I had wanted so desperately to be at the age of seventeen; a feeling I had never really been able to shake off since. How often had I daydreamed about being born in 1948 instead of 1963 so that I could have been a young teacher starting at Fieldhouse when Anthony did! Then he would have loved *me*. There are more ways than one of being haunted. The truth was that for twenty-five years I had been insanely jealous of Helen Pearson. And whatever the future held for me, I suspected that I always would be.

That evening, Simon was restless. He frequently seemed about to say something, then didn't. He shuffled in his chair, fiddled with his tie, kept taking the top off his pen. The conversation was stilted. Auntie Janet certainly noticed something was wrong. She decided to retire to bed, leaving us to sort out what she presumably imagined was some kind of argument. But there hadn't been any. Apart from my reaction to the prospect of finding Helen, we had had a perfectly amicable and apparently happy day, if somewhat lacking in passion. After Auntie left the room, I had even more of a struggle to keep the conversation going.

I guessed what was wrong and became very anxious and depressed myself: the relationship had died in America and Simon was trying to pluck up the courage to tell me. Oh yes, he'd been cheerful at first, probably hoping that it would be all right after all, but a day in my company had convinced him that we were not meant for each other. The sad thing was that a day in *his* company had convinced me that we were.

In my efforts to keep the evening alive, I was making things worse. I knew it, but nerves prevented me from talking about anything other than the subject that had brought us together.

Suddenly Simon pushed back his chair and flung down his long-suffering pen.

'I can't stand it any longer. This is just my luck. Why did I have to fall deeply in love with a woman who is only capable of loving a man who's dead, who died ten years before she had even heard of him!'

He turned and strode towards the door.

'Simon,' I managed to say. He stopped, but he didn't turn around. 'What did you say?'

He turned his head slowly. 'I said you love a man who died years ago.'

'No, not that bit. Before that.'

'I said . . .' he hesitated. 'I said I love you more than I ever loved anyone before.'

He wasn't angry now. He just stood by the door, looking helpless.

I stood up. 'If you come back,' I said, 'I'll be able to show you how capable of loving someone I am.'

We both took a step forward, stretched out our arms and clung together, pouring out our love and longing.

'I only bored you with all that because you wouldn't talk,' I said. 'You were so restless.'

'I was restless because I wanted to tell you how much I love you but I didn't know how.'

'Don't we ever learn?'

'Telling someone you love her is very special. You have to get it right. Only I didn't.'

'We don't seem to be doing too badly,' I said.

Simon and I were gloriously happy in our new-found love, although we could not spend as much time together as we would have liked. Much of our relationship was conducted by phone and we both enjoyed letter-writing - putting down our thoughts on paper.

There was still something that I longed to do, something that I felt I now *could* do, with my knowledge of his history. We had no idea where Anthony was buried. Perhaps some distant relation we knew nothing of yet had taken responsibility. He certainly wasn't in Kingswater churchyard. So I planned to place some kind of memorial to Anthony at Fieldhouse.

The idea of a birdbath had been in my mind for some time. The small birds found the edges of the pond too deep and I had placed some stones in the shallowest part for them to perch on. In particular, a robin that frequented that part of the garden was often seen attempting to bathe, then giving up and flying away.

I wanted something very special, a fitting memorial to Anthony's short, sad life and his brief moment of happiness. A magazine article gave me an idea. I drove some distance to visit the company concerned, which made garden ornaments of all types.

'I would like a birdbath,' I told the proprietor, 'with a dragonfly perched on the edge. A really nice one, similar to the one you have there with a squirrel on it. I've brought a sketch. Can you do it?'

The man looked at my drawing for a moment. 'Yes, we can do that. It will be more expensive though. More delicate, you see.'

'That's OK.' It was important enough for me to be prepared to spend some of my limited funds on the project. 'I'd like the outside of the rim to be smooth so that I can have some lettering. Can you do that too?'

'Oh, yes, we can do anything here.'

We arranged the details and I drove home feeling that at last I was perhaps coming to the end of a quarter of a century's obsession. I rang Simon and told him what I had done. He seemed pleased.

Six weeks later, when the colours of autumn were beginning to show in the hedgerows, Simon and I carried the heavy birdbath down to the place beside the pool where we had prepared a base. Auntie Janet had chosen to watch the process from the upstairs window. Always discreet, I think she preferred not to intrude.

We carefully eased the bath into place almost exactly at the spot where I had first seen Anthony. We stood back. I was delighted. It looked just as I had hoped. Beautifully crafted, it was worth every penny of its cost. It was moulded in a cream-coloured stone with a smooth bulbous pedestal and a plain circular top. The exquisitely sculptured dragonfly, perched on the rim, had just enough detail without being fussy.

Around the outside of the rim, in attractive lettering, was carved,

In loving memory of Anthony Dean, 1948-1970

Simple, but enough. I had kept my promise. He was not forgotten.

I had brought a pretty floral jug from the house. The Aunts had found it in the attics, miraculously unbroken. They had removed it from the rubble and placed it in the library. It had been beside me on the table that day when I had looked up from my studies and found Anthony there, watching me. Perhaps it had been in the house when he had taught here. I dipped it into the pond and carefully filled the birdbath. At once, the dragonfly on the rim came to life, seeming to sip the water. Above us, in the hedge, the robin burst into song.

We stood silently for a moment, deep in thought, listening to the music of nature. Then Simon took my hand and we walked slowly across the lawn to the veranda, still in silence. When we reached the steps, we looked back. The robin, ending his song, flew down and perched on the bath, drank and flew away over the hedge.

Simon clasped both my hands in his. 'Is this the end of Anthony's story, Laura?' he asked in a very quiet, unsteady voice. 'Can you let him go now?'

I held his hands against my heart. My eyes filled with tears and I just let them flow.

'Yes,' I said in a whisper, 'I'll never forget him. But now I can let him go.'

'Then will you marry me?'

POSTSCRIPT 2010

Chapter Thirty

It was about four years later when I noticed workmen preparing the base for a seat in the churchyard. When the seat was in place, I strolled over to look at it. It was in an unusual position - in the north-east corner below the tower and facing outwards, towards Fieldhouse and the knoll on the Downs. I started to read the inscription on the brass plate attached to the back of the seat - and froze.

> *This seat has been provided from the legacy of Helen Pearson,*
> *late of Fieldhouse School, who died February 21 AD2010.*
> *'She was once very happy here.'*

Helen! She *had* still been alive, like Simon had said, and she had not forgotten! I stood gazing at that inscription. Was it a message to the world, which wouldn't understand anyway, or just to me? If only she'd known that Anthony had a memorial nearby. For the first time, I wished I had tried to contact her. But now it was too late. Perhaps it was better this way.

'Ah, Mrs Taylor! You've pre-empted me. I was going to let you know about this seat and its Fieldhouse connection.' The vicar was coming along the path towards me. 'This lady, Mrs Pearson, visited the church about a year ago.'

I gave a start. 'Alone?' I asked. She had actually been here!

'No, with another elderly lady, a Mrs West. I came across them standing just here. They didn't say who they were. The one that I now know to have been Mrs Pearson said she wanted to leave a legacy to the church, from some of which we were to provide a seat.'

'Was that all?'

'I think she said something about an old friend. It was only when the instructions about the seat arrived, after she died, that I knew her name and that she had been at the school.'

'She didn't mention that at the time, then?'

'No. She just said she had been living in Spain and had come back to England because of her health. I seem to remember that they had been for a walk along the field path towards the Downs. Oh, yes, and they'd been looking through your gate, admiring the birdbath . . . '

I was no longer listening. I remembered! Simon and I had been in the upstairs study. He was working and I was curled up in the easy chair, reading. I had flu. Suddenly, Simon looked out of the window and said, 'There are two

239

old dames looking through the gate at the birdbath. Seem to be very interested in it.'

Reluctantly, I had dragged myself out of the chair and gone to the window. I recalled a short, plump woman wearing a brightly-coloured outfit: blue, I think. The other, who was looking the most intently at the bath, was taller, thin and dressed in what seemed like unrelieved black. She leaned heavily against the gate and gazed through the ironwork, across the pond. She was outside the gate, of course, but from my viewpoint she appeared to be almost at the spot where I had first 'seen' Anthony. As I moved to the window she had looked up. Her white face under the black hat reminded me of *his* paleness beneath his dark hair, as he had seemed to me all those years ago.

I waved to the two, to show that I didn't mind them looking. The dark lady raised her hand in greeting. I thought perhaps I should go down and speak to them, despite my flu, but they turned away and walked back towards the village. The lady in blue walked briskly, chatting, the dark one moved slowly and falteringly, constantly turning to look back, until she was out of sight.

Helen had come back to Fieldhouse. After forty years of exile this was one place she'd wanted to visit again before she died. Our eyes, at least, had met . . .

'Did you tell them anything about the birdbath?' I asked Mr Hardy. He had only been vicar here for three years so knew little of the place's history.

'I think I just said it was in memory of a young teacher who had died in tragic circumstances. I didn't know, then, that she'd been at the school. And she never said, so perhaps she knew nothing about it. I told her that the owner of Fieldhouse took an interest in the story and had wanted some kind of memorial at the house.'

'She must have died soon after?'

'Yes. A few months later Mrs West came down from London again with the details of the will. Mrs Pearson had been very specific about the positioning of the seat. The wording's a bit odd, too. Mrs West said that she was most insistent about the AD in the date. Can't imagine why she wanted that in.'

I knew *exactly* why! Helen had wanted herself and Anthony to be commemorated together, somehow.

'I expect she had a good reason,' I said.

'She was very particular about something else, too,' Mr Hardy went on. 'She insisted on having a crumbling blade of grass in her coffin, one she'd kept for years, so Mrs West said. She brought Mrs Pearson's ashes from London and scattered them up there on the knoll. That was another thing Mrs Pearson was insistent about. She didn't want to be buried in Spain although I believe her husband had been. They'd been out there for years, apparently.' Mr Hardy glanced up at the Downs. 'It was quite a climb for Mrs West, but she insisted on going alone. She said that an old friend of Mrs Pearson's was scattered up there, presumably the one she mentioned to me.'

240

So that was where Anthony was! And now Helen was there, too.

As soon as I could, I climbed up to the knoll and stood there for a long time. On the way down, I gathered a bunch of flowers, leaves and grasses from the track they must have walked so often. I placed half on Helen's seat and the rest on Anthony's birdbath. As I did so I thought of the love and brief happiness they had found here together - and the love their story had found for me.

In summer, dragonflies flit around both memorials and in autumn the robin sings his plaintive song nearby.

I often make a pilgrimage to the knoll to collect flowers for the two of them. It's very peaceful up there - a wonderful place to be forever.

END

Printed in the United Kingdom
by Lightning Source UK Ltd.
104696UKS00001B/43-81